Shame the Devil

Shame the Devil

A Novel

Debra Brenegan

excelsior editions

State University of New York Press
Albany, New York

FIC
413

Published by State University of New York Press, Albany

© 2011 State University of New York Press

Excelsior Editions is an imprint of State University of New York Press

For information, contact State University of New York Press, Albany, NY
www.sunypress.edu

Production by Diane Ganeles
Marketing by Fran Keneston

Library of Congress Cataloging-in-Publication Data

Brenegan, Debra.
    Shame the devil : a novel / Debra Brenegan.
        p. cm.
    ISBN 978-1-4384-3587-9 (alk. paper)
    1. Fern, Fanny, 1811-1872—Fiction.   2. Women novelists—Fiction.
3. Women journalists—Fiction.   I. Title.

    PS3602.R4486S53 2011
    813'.6—dc22   2011003865

10 9 8 7 6 5 4 3 2 1

Contents

Acknowledgments

Special thanks go to James Sappenfield for introducing me to Fanny Fern in graduate school. He was exactly right when he told me, "I have someone you need to read that you'll really like." Thanks, too, to Kristie Hamilton and Genevieve McBride for nurturing my studies of Fern. My gratitude extends to Gwynne Kennedy, George Clark, Liam Callanan, Jane Nardin, John Goulet, and all of my professors who helped support my writing and critiqued drafts of this book. I appreciate receiving a Graduate School Fellowship from the University of Wisconsin-Milwaukee and a Summer Research Stipend from Westminster College—both of which aided my research and revision.

Many thanks go to Rose Marie Kinder, Trudy Lewis, and Phong Nguyen, members of my Missouri writing group, who read every word of this novel and gave unfailing support. Other wonderfully helpful writing friends include: Rochelle Melander, Monica Rausch, and Lynn Wiese Sneyd. I've also been lucky to have the friendship of Karen Geschke, Maureen Schinner, and Betsy Stern, who have always stood by me.

I am grateful for the generous presence of everyone at Westminster College including Dave Collins, Wayne Zade, Maureen Tuthill, Theresa Adams, Heidi Levine, Carolyn Perry, Barney Forsythe, and my students, especially Sarah Blackmon, who designed the Willis family tree.

Special thanks to James Peltz, my editor, who took a chance on this book.

Thanks, too, to my brothers, Jim, Tom, Ken, and Ron, and to my stepdad, Dean, who "knew I could do it." To all my extended family and great circle of friends—thank you for your support and love.

Thanks and love go to my mom, Mary DeMille Ludvigsen, who never tired of listening to me talk about Fanny; and to Sara and Joel Rozansky, who happily shared the excitement of this project with me. Much love and special thanks to Jordan and Chelsea Brenegan for losing bits and pieces of their mother to research and writing days. We always did make it to violin lessons!

I am thankful for the loving presence of Callie, my twenty-year-old cat, who warmed my lap through many a long computer session.

And, finally, I am enormously grateful to Steve Rozansky, my wonderful husband, who is my deepest love, my best friend, and my staunchest ally. I can't imagine a better life partner.

A Note about Sources

While Fanny Fern, Walt Whitman, Harriet Beecher Stowe, Catharine Beecher, N. P. Willis, Harriet Jacobs, and other people who really lived appear in this book as fictional characters, I've tried to render their lives and times as accurately as possible. I also sought to preserve Fanny Fern's unique writing style and to present her work exactly as it first appeared in print, including intended or unintended irregularities in spelling, grammar, punctuation, and usage. I read widely about Fern and her contemporaries and am grateful to Joyce Warren, for her thoroughly researched and well-written biography, *Fanny Fern: An Independent Woman*. I also found Nancy A. Walker's book, *Fanny Fern*, very helpful. I am grateful for access to the Sophia Smith Collection at Smith College and to those who helped me wade through the Fern archives. Thanks, also, to Josephine Kuo and her husband, Hon-Ming Eng, for allowing me access to their house, formerly Fanny Fern's dwelling in New York. In addition, I gained wonderful insight from visiting the Merchant's House Museum in New York and appreciate the information they provided about life in nineteenth-century New York.

I give credit to early Fern scholars, Elaine Gellis Breslaw and Florence Bannard Adams, and read their respective texts *Popular Pundit: Fanny Fern and the Emergence of the American Newspaper Columnist*, and *Fanny Fern, or a Pair of Flaming Shoes*, with great interest. Biographic works by James Parton and Ethel Parton were also enormously helpful, as was scholarly work by a host of authors, especially Nina Baym, Mary Kelley, Nicole Tonkovich, Jane Tompkins, and Ann Wood. I even managed to get through "Moulton's" unauthorized biography, *The Life and Beauties of Fanny Fern*.

My bottomless thanks to these people and to all of those who documented, researched, and wrote about Fanny Fern before me. Their efforts made mine possible.

Hannah Parker — m. 1803 — Nathaniel Willis, Jr.

- **Lucy Douglas** 1804–
  m. 1823 Josiah Bumstead

- **Nathaniel Parker (N.P.)** 1806–
  m. 1836 Mary Stace → Imogen
  m. 1846 Cornelia Grinnell

- **Louisa Harris** 1807–1849
  m. 1824 Louis Dwight

- **Julia Dean** 1809– unm.

- **Sarah Payson** 1811–1872
  m. 1837 Charles Eldredge
  m. 1849 Samuel Farrington (div. 1853)
  m. 1856 James Parton
  - Mary Stace 1838–1845
  - Grace Harrington 1841–1862
  - Ellen Willis 1844–

- **Mary Perry** 1813–
  m. 1831 Joseph Jenkins

- **Edward Payson** 1816–1853 unm.

- **Richard Storrs** 1819–
  m. 1852 Jessie Cairns

- **Ellen Holmes** 1821–1844
  m. 1843 Charles Dennett

Grace Harrington — m. 1861 Mortimer Thomson → Grace Ethel (Effie)

Chapter One

Sarah Payson Willis, Outskirts of Boston, Saturday, June 29th, 1816

Who but God can comfort like a mother?

—Fanny Fern, *A New Story Book for Children*, 1864

Sarah would soon be five years old. Old enough, her father said, to start doing a few more chores and to learn that the world wasn't all whimsy and fun; it was work and effort and had to be taken seriously. It was a warm, sunny day. A few wispy clouds floated high in the bluebird sky and the yellow ball of sun warmed Sarah's back as she crouched among the waist-high plants in her mother's garden behind the house. Sarah's bonnet slipped down the back of her head, as it often did, and she knew she should take a moment to readjust it, yet she didn't. She broke off the tops of some daisies in the garden. There were so many daisies; surely a few wouldn't be missed. She looked around, and seeing that Louisa and Julia occupied little Mary, and Nat grubbed for fishing worms at the other end of the yard and seemed to pay her no attention, Sarah pinched the blooms off a few soft pink roses and one glorious blue hydrangea. She was making a little church, a church where all the good ants and crickets could come and worship. She stuck the hydrangea elegantly into a small puddle of mud. It would serve as the focal point—a lovely, soft statue surrounded by a shimmering moat. Sarah arranged the daisies in a circle around the hydrangea and imagined them to be cushions the insect worshippers could recline upon.

She sprinkled a few bread crumbs from her pocket near the daisy lounge—to serve as both communion and lunch, she supposed. Sarah smelled each rose, then stuck the fragrant beauties at spaced intervals to provide shade for the more delicate bugs, or for the ones who might have forgotten their bonnets or hats.

A shadow fell upon her church scene, and looking up, Sarah saw the very pregnant form of her mother silhouetted against the dazzling sun. Sarah grinned broadly at the smile she knew would be on her mother's face, even though it took her several blinks in the new light to make it out.

"I see you're making good use of the flowers," Hannah Willis said.

"Yes, Mother. It's a church," Sarah said and proceeded to explain her composition.

Hannah wiped her forehead with a small lacy handkerchief. "It's certainly nothing like Park Street Church, is it?"

"No, Mother. And the Sexton won't find us here, either." The Sexton had an eye out for Sarah, she knew. He and every other pastor that came near the family. Sarah's father adored pastors. He had spoken with all of them about his worries for her, about her wickedness. Sarah wiggled during prayers, interrupted conversations, asked too many questions for a girl growing so big. What could be done to inject modesty, humility, and piety into her—quickly, before her bad habits took root? Most of the pastors (except for Reverend Payson) eyed Sarah gravely and whispered gruff advice to her father, advice for punishment or deprivation sure to smooth her rough edges. Despite all the fuss, Sarah didn't *feel* wicked, and, so, avoided clergymen, and their lectures, as much as possible, running from the table as soon as dinner was over, if they were visiting, looking sheepishly at her shoes if Father stopped the family to talk to a minister after a sermon.

Hannah set the basket she was carrying (it smelled full of blueberry muffins) on the ground beside the flower church and gently straightened Sarah's bonnet. "How would you like to come with me this afternoon, my pet, and see a grown-up lady's flower church?"

With five siblings (the eldest, Lucy, was in the parlor learning sewing), Sarah never missed a chance to be alone with her mother, and so, the two walked for what seemed an eternity beneath a great many trees along a grassy path. They were mostly quiet as they walked, enjoying the dappling sunshine, listening to bird twitter, and watching the bushes as they passed to see if a rabbit might run out. Just as Sarah's legs grew tired, they came to a little wooden house almost engulfed by lilac bushes. The bushes weren't blooming, but in front of them, in great profusion, were hundreds of opened posies of every color and scent. Sarah wanted to pull the flower fragrance deep inside, and so she inhaled slowly and smiled up at her mother. But her mother wasn't looking at her. She was calling a greeting into the open door of the dwelling. "Hello, Fanny Miller," Hannah said, absentmindedly touching the wild fern leaf she'd placed, as was her habit, in the bodice of her dress.

"Hello, dear Hannah," came a voice in reply as Hannah and Sarah entered the little house through a low doorway, climbed two immaculate wooden steps, and found themselves in a tall, cool room where a half dozen women were arranging a variety of chairs in a circle near the gaping mouth of an enormous blackened fireplace.

"I've brought my little Sarah," Hannah said. "She'll be good and will sit quietly near me, won't you, Sweetheart?"

Sarah nodded at her mother and at the brown, wrinkled face of the person she thought might be Fanny Miller.

"The darling is certainly welcome," the old woman said and gave Sarah a brown-toothed smile.

The other women Sarah knew from the neighborhood and from church—all friends of her parents and good members of Park Street Church. They had removed their bonnets and hung them on nails near the door, then sat on the chairs, arranging their skirts to allow for a little air circulation. Hannah removed Sarah's bonnet, brushed back her damp, golden curls with her fingers, and indicated that Sarah should sit on a little stool that Fanny Miller placed near Hannah's feet. Fanny took both Sarah's and Hannah's bonnets and hung them on nails near the fireplace and Sarah thought them quite decorative against the quaint paper with so many pink shepherdesses and green dogs.

Fanny then presented each seated woman in turn with the same tin cup, which she kept filling with water from a heavy blue pitcher. After all had had a drink, even Sarah, Fanny took the basket of muffins and placed them in the center of the circle. She put the blue pitcher and the tin cup next to the basket. She lit a gnarly-looking mud-colored candle that was stuck into another tin cup and placed it in front of the empty fireplace. Buckets of asparagus branches, clustered with little red berries, stood to the left and right of the candle. Fanny sat in a chair next to the fireplace, opened a worn-looking Bible on her lap, and read.

Sarah leaned against her mother's knee. She liked Fanny's voice. It was like a song. The Bible sounded completely different coming from Fanny Miller than it ever had coming from any of the pastors Sarah had heard. It certainly was different from the way Father made it sound. Fanny made the Bible feel warm and welcoming and she didn't read any parts about hell and damnation. Sarah looked up at her mother. Hannah's eyes were closed as she listened. Sarah looked at the other women. Some of their eyes were closed, too. She noticed the cabin had only one window—wide open, though, and serving as the entry of many a lazily buzzing bee. Sarah's thoughts soon drifted like the bees around the room. She thought the house very old-fashioned with its rough ceiling trestles, hung with bunches of drying herbs, and with the high-post bedstead in the corner, the bright patchwork quilt covering it, the little washing stand, the few dishes and pans stacked on a wooden shelf, the green china parrot taking the place of honor on the mantle, the abundance of flowers gathered in jars and mugs and arranged around the room. Yet, she liked it here, in this circle of women slowly fanning themselves and listening to Fanny Miller's intoxicating voice. Birds chirped. The bees buzzed a fuzzy undertone. A fragrant breeze swept regularly through the window and door and stirred the tendrils on the feminine foreheads. Sarah couldn't think of a better place to be than here in this flower church, listening to love come from the throat of brown and wrinkled Fanny Miller and leaning against the solid strength of her mother.

After what seemed like a long, delicious interval, Fanny softly closed the book and asked Hannah to pray. Sarah's mother prayed without opening her eyes. She spoke in a low and sweet voice asking God to care for them, for their families and friends, for all the world. She sounded like she was talking with a good friend, Sarah thought. Her mother's prayer was nothing like the kingly prayers Sarah and her mother normally recited with the family under her father's direction. Flashes of those moments appeared in Sarah's thoughts—whole agonizing Sundays practically tied to a hard stool, listening to her father or one of his minister friends reading about hell and sin, yelling fear into their hearts, nearly always picking out Sarah and her fidgeting as evidence of the devil. Sarah tried to keep still Sundays, in order to be respectful of her elders, as her mother had explained, but she never believed she was the sinner they professed her to be. She felt good and happy and loved. She couldn't help laughing when things seemed funny and couldn't, as Reverend Payson had said, "turn off the twinkle" in her eye. And that was fine with her. She'd taken Mother's suggestion about looking at the fireplace tiles and making up her own stories to go along with the blue and white pictures of Elijah, Daniel, and old Nebuchadnezzar.

Hannah Willis finished her prayer and heaved her pregnant body out of the chair to kneel on the clean-swept wooden floor. Sarah and the other women joined Hannah on their knees and they all prayed silently for a few minutes, their hearts filling with the fragrance of Fanny Miller's flowers and with the buzz of the circling bees and the distant chirping of the birds. Fanny Miller finally stood and broke Hannah's blueberry muffins in half, then passed the basket for each to take a piece. They ate the muffins, then took another sip from the tin cup Fanny passed to her left. Slowly, each woman stood in time, reclaimed her bonnet from its nail, and walked outside. Sarah's mother was the last to stand and Sarah was glad Fanny Miller helped her mother to her feet and presented them with their bonnets.

"Sarah," Fanny Miller said, tying Sarah's bonnet under her chin for her. "What a pretty name for a pretty girl. Did you enjoy our prayer meeting?"

Sarah nodded. "It seemed just like church," she said, "only nicer."

Fanny and Hannah laughed.

"Nicer," Fanny repeated as they walked out the door to Fanny Miller's garden.

Outside, some of the other women lingered among the flowers—red, pink, yellow, white, and a striking spiky deep purple blossom the group kept naming as blue, much to Sarah's confusion. She knew blue. It was the color of Mother's eyes, the color of the sky. This blossom mirrored the royal ribbon Father used to mark his place in his prayer book. It was purple if it was anything. The women grinned at Sarah's assertion and tutted to Hannah over her head. Hannah smiled warmly at Sarah. "You are not to be deceived, my darling," she said and brushed a knuckle over Sarah's cheek.

Talk soon turned to Hannah's pregnancy and the naming of the soon-to-arrive baby. When Hannah told them how her husband wished to name this new one, like Sarah, after the Reverend Edward Payson, some of the women shook their heads. Deacon Willis was a firm Calvinist and his sober preoccupation with everlasting salvation cast a pall on both Sunday services and the rest of the week. How sweet Hannah remained so cheerful was anybody's guess.

"It didn't harm this one any," Fanny said, patting Sarah on the back.

"No, indeed," Hannah said. "Sarah has her own ideas."

"I like *her* name. Fanny," Sarah suddenly said.

"See?" Hannah said.

The group of women laughed.

"She's just right," Fanny said and gave Sarah a wink.

The women talked above Sarah's head for another little while and Sarah held her mother's soft, strong hand. Before long, Sarah and her mother walked home along the grassy path under the trees. They spoke about a kind and loving God, about how God's creations—the flowers, bees, birds, trees, and people—all exist to support one another, and about how they liked old Fanny Miller.

Chapter Two

Catharine Beecher, Sara Payson Willis, and Harriet Beecher (Stowe), Hartford, Hartford Female Seminary, Sunday, October 3rd, 1830

You also I remember with your head of light crepe curls with your bonnet always tipped on one side and you, with a most insidious leaning towards that broad sound of laughing & conjuration which is the horror of well regulated school ma'ams, & the many scrapes which occasioned for you secret confabulations with sister Katy up in her room. She had always a warm side toward you.

—Harriet Beecher Stowe in a letter to Fanny Fern, 1868

Schoolmistress Catharine Beecher sat at her cramped walnut desk making stacks of like papers. Yellow-pink light streamed from the mullioned window behind her and reflected off the papered walls, festooned in sprigs of pastel florals, and collected in a bright patch on her chin. Morning calls and replies of birds punctuated the whoosh of breeze that blew coolly against the shutters, shaking them in a steady rap rap rap that echoed Catharine's tapping toes. She had an enormous amount of paperwork to get through before releasing the girls tomorrow for their month off. She was calculating bills, writing letters of assessment, ordering supplies, and solidifying a curriculum she hoped compared to that followed at many men's colleges. Eager to alleviate the slight headache throbbing at her temples, probably from the lateness of last night's levee, Catharine had had her younger sister and teacher-helper, Harriet, bring up a pot of coffee before leaving for the early service at seven o'clock. It was the Sabbath, and Catharine fully intended on attending the ten o'clock service. But she also knew her school was her gift back to God and his creations and that surely *He* would understand how her time, at least this once, would be better occupied arranging the school's accounts than sitting through a whole day's worth of worship. Truthfully, Catharine was grateful. Grateful she had the opportunity of running her own female school, however it exhausted her. Grateful nobody seriously questioned her because of her father, Reverend Lyman Beecher, and his impeccable moral reputation. If Lyman Beecher's daughter wanted to start a school, especially a female seminary, then it must be the will of God.

Catharine was surprised to hear the little knock on the door and more surprised when none other than Sara Willis, with her well-known yellow curls and her enormous blue eyes, peered into the room. Catharine sighed. She was usually the one to summon Sara. That Sara was here, on her own, could either be very good or very bad.

Sara held out a little white cup she'd apparently procured from the kitchen. "I've come for a splash of coffee. They won't give me any downstairs."

"As they shouldn't," Catharine said. "Coffee is not on the menu for young ladies."

"But after such a late night!"

Catharine didn't have the energy to quarrel with Sara, not with the pile of paperwork screaming for completion and a headache that had suddenly settled heavy just behind her eyes. She sighed and poured Sara's cup half-full. "Have a little then, but don't tell your parents I spoil you. They'll never pay your bills if they think I encourage your willfulness."

"Thank you, Miss Beecher," Sara said. She took a sip of coffee and sighed in rapture. "What bills *now*?"

Catharine closed her eyes and drew a breath. "Sara Willis. I simply don't know when you have the time to visit the confectionery so often."

Sara offered a dimpled smile. "Sweets for the sweet."

Catharine wrinkled her aching forehead. Sara was and always had been Catharine's most challenging student. Her students usually arrived cloaked in appropriate modesty and humility, having been educated to age sixteen or seventeen in some or another of the region's religious boarding schools. Sara had gone to Adams with her sisters, but had failed to become "a professing Christian," and so her father sent her to Catharine with implicit directions for the salvaging of her reckless soul. Other students bowed their heads and fairly quaked in their buttoned shoes for at least a year whenever Catharine swished into the room and took her position in front of the podium. But not Sara. From the moment the carriage delivered her two and a half years ago (the driver beating a hasty retreat), sobbing her eyes out, insisting she *hated* boarding schools, especially religious ones, and swearing she'd *never* stop missing home and all the fun that was happening there and would never never never be converted so Catharine had better not try, Sara Willis had been a handful.

After warning Catharine against possible conversion efforts, Sara next announced between hiccups on that first day that since she intended to officially change the spelling of her name someday, she might as well start at this new school, nevermind what her parents might say, nevermind anything—she was *Sara*, not Sarah with an *h*, in this place she hadn't chosen but would order to her liking. Sara's father wrote long, dense letters bent on discovering not *if* but *when* his daughter's religious conversion would be complete—letters Catharine dutifully and tediously answered, the father taking as much tending as the daughter.

Catharine couldn't help but feel guilty for her epistolary omissions. She didn't detail half the trouble Sara caused, certainly didn't mention how Sara held almost weekly appointments with the local newspaper editor. The editor would sit at Sara's elbow during her lunch break, scribbling madly as she rattled off some raw and piercing wit for his publication. Apparently, Sara had been writing for her father's paper for some time, without a thought of consequence from either of them. Catharine knew it was a talent, Sara's fast and sure communication ability, even if Sara didn't. But Sara needn't be given any more praise than could be helped. Sara was clever, but Sara was also frighteningly untamed.

Catharine sipped her coffee. "You and your sweets."

"Remember the time I stole the pie from the cook's pantry?"

Catharine pressed her lips together.

"Oh, you still haven't forgiven me. We were hungry that night and the restriction against eating after hours was killing us!" Sara said. "And I daresay we'd have gotten away with it if I hadn't been a fool and thrown the pie plate out the window just as the matron's husband was walking by."

Catharine sat back in her chair. "Clucked him square on the head, as I remember."

"You had to punish me good that time," Sara said, widening her eyes. "I believe I had to sit and keep you company evenings for a week."

Catharine shook her head. Catharine kept close watch on Sara, true, and constantly tried to steer her behavior toward the appropriate, but time after time Sara's will won out and she'd throw her sewing into her basket and would burst from the circle by the fire insisting she couldn't take another dull moment with her needle and the same beige thread but needed a little romp through the yard or to help the cooks knead the bread in order to keep her sanity, to keep her thoughts from going around and around. The other students bristled then, and Catherine, too, would wince, but instinct told her not to try to snuff this flame and Sara knew it. Most of Catharine's students reacted to her guidance like a flower to the sun, gently opening, gently broadening both intellectually and spiritually. But Sara was a wild rose bush—aggressive, smothering, and loaded with both blossoms and thorns.

Catharine tapped her pen on her account book. "Not to mention the new gloves, bonnet, lace ribbons, and shoes."

"It was only one pair of shoes and because my others had gotten a hole in the toe," Sara said. "Which reminds me . . ."

"Reminds you of what? I'm afraid to ask."

"I don't suppose you spoke to the doctor after he saw me Friday?" Sara asked.

Catharine remembered now. Sara had complained early in the day that she'd not been feeling well. Catharine had sent her to her bed to rest, but, also called the doctor as a precaution. If strong Sara was sick, Catharine had better know all about it. If Sara wasn't sick, Catharine had better know all about that, too. The doctor had examined Sara and reported to Catharine that he'd given her a pill and expected her to be better in a day or so, and, thus, that was the last Catharine had thought of the matter. Of course, Sara had been at the levee last night, and had so charmingly entertained the shy, young clergyman Catharine had directed her to take under her wing. She'd actually had him laughing out loud and doubtless he'd fallen in love with her already, as most of the young men did, not that Sara cared. "The doctor said he gave you some medicine and that you'd be better within a day. Are you feeling ill again?" Catharine asked.

"Not exactly in body. More in conscience," Sara said, wiggling in her seat.

Catharine leveled her eyes at Sara. "What a welcome illness. Do tell."

"Well," Sara began, rolling her eyes in exaggeration. "I wasn't really sick, of course. You knew that, which is why you made me in charge of Humpty Dumpty all night."

"Sara! I will not have you be disrespectful of so fine a clergyman!"

Sara hung her head. "But I'm *not* being disrespectful of the clergyman in the comparison, dear Miss Beecher. If anything, I'm being disrespectful of poor Humpty Dumpty."

Catharine clamped her lips together.

Sara shook her curls. "Anyway, I believe the dull, I mean, *fine* clergyman's company was ample punishment for my transgressions, so I decided I'd best come clean about it all so I won't be made to suffer through the next levee."

"Sara! It was an honor to be chosen to entertain him."

"One I'm really not deserving of, Ma'am."

"Apparently not!"

"Next time, I think I'd better deserve his irreverent young cousin, the one with the gorgeous brown eyes," Sara said. "To place the likes of me, so careless and brazen, with one so fine as the young, dull clergyman . . ."

"Point taken," Catharine said. "Although you appeared to be having a good time."

"I always have a good time," Sara said with a dimpled smile. "The point is I want to have a better time."

"We'll see about that," Catharine said. "Now tell me what you did to make me punish you."

"It was the 'Snipping Fever,'" Sara said and took a sip of coffee.

"The what?"

"That's exactly how the doctor reacted when I first told him what ailed me," Sara said. "But once I showed him the rows of ruffles I had yet to scallop, pink, and sew onto my dress in time for the levee, he agreed that it looked like at least a day's work and gave me a little bread pill and a wink."

Catharine remembered Sara's dress. It had a cascade of cut-out ruffles that was the envy of the party.

"I think it was fitting for me to contain such fashion to the sober young clergyman as punishment. *Once*, I mean," Sara said. "I hope to circulate my creation among a broader mix next time, especially now that I've confessed all my wickedness before you even got wind of anything."

Sara held out her empty coffee cup.

Catharine sighed and poured another tablespoon of coffee into it. "Take that as punishment," she said. "And don't let me hear of you feigning illness again."

"Oh, you won't ever *hear* of it," Sara said. "*That* I can promise."

"All the promise I want from you, Sara Willis, is to display good manners before your parents so my school's reputation isn't soiled."

"And so they allow me to call on you and Harriet and your father."

Catharine shut her eyes, then finally nodded. "Yes, when Harriet and I visit Father in Boston, you'd be welcome to call."

"Thank you, Ma'am," Sara said, standing and smoothing her skirt. "I look forward to that with pleasure."

Catharine dismissed Sara. One more term to survive her. One more term to enjoy her. This time next year, life at the school would be very different without Sara Willis.

Sara left Catharine's office feeling as if she'd thrown off a wet, heavy blanket. She sprung round the corner to the stairs, thinking about visiting her schoolmistress again this holiday, as she had last May. She wanted to see more of this *other* clergyman's family. How different Reverend Beecher was from her own deacon father. He reminded her of her beloved namesake, Reverend Edward Payson, the only pastor she'd known who smiled, who patted her head warmly and instead of calling her a little devil, said out loud (once) that she was one of *His* lambs. Yes, Reverend Beecher was like that, too. Though pontificating against sensual pleasures, he played the fiddle in his shirtsleeves and munched apples and nuts all day long. The Beecher table was forever set abundantly, as if it were always Sunday, and the pantry perpetually held pies and puddings for desserts and snacks. Sara thought of her own father with a shiver. He loved her, she knew. That he coveted the religious life so fiercely for her was evidence of that. But the dour tone he set, the serious fear he conjured bounced off Sara like a dandelion puff. She simply couldn't take it in. What's more, she wouldn't.

Sara bounded down the stairs, nearly flattening Miss Harriet coming up to see her sister between services. "Pardon me, Miss Harriet," Sara said with a slight bow. Harriet was Sara's age, but since she was a pupil-teacher, Sara gave her the respect due her station.

"Sara Willis," Harriet said. "Have you been to see sister Katy so early?"

"There and gone," Sara said with a grin. "And I'm late, again, for breakfast."

"Don't forget service at ten," Harriet said.

"Me? Never," Sara said and bounced down the remaining stairs.

Harriet Beecher looked after Sara Willis as she traipsed away. Why didn't sister Katy expel her? She broke every rule and never seemed repentant. Furthermore, Sara didn't seem to *know* when she should feel remorse (which, in Harriet's opinion, was often). Sara would dash into a room and despite hearts intent on hardening against her, she'd soon have her way. Harriet didn't know how Sara managed it. It was more than her bouncing blonde curls and rosy cheeks. Even as Harriet shuddered at Sara's social gaffes, she marveled at how easily Sara's gaffes were forgiven, even strangely cherished.

Harriet bit her lip. *She* was that clever, too, though her brilliance nestled deep down, under her modesty, under her shyness. Sometimes, Harriet longed to step out of her role as teacher and poke at this Sara Willis, to see what magic boiled at her center, to gauge the magic's threat or potency. Like everyone else, she guessed, she was drawn to Sara's light even as she was horrified by her heat. Last holiday, Sara had called on Catharine and had spent a few evenings with their family. But, Harriet had sat, quietly sewing, during those visits, content to listen to Sara's lively conversation, afraid to interject a word. Still, sister Katy seemed to believe in Sara Willis, so perhaps Harriet could chance herself with Sara, too. If Sara visits again, Harriet vowed she would draw up her courage and speak to her, not as a teacher, not as sister Katy's helper, but as a peer, as Sara's equal—come what may.

Chapter Three

Nathaniel Willis, Boston, Wednesday, April 12th, 1837

I'm sure I could tell you of a hundred girls wilder than ever I was. Besides I'd like to know if my papa's mantle of gravity was expected to be capacious enough to cover us . . . when he accepted the office of deacon. Does goodness come by inheritance? tell me that! . . . Not a bit of it; the consequence is, I was born an untameable romp—and a romp I remained, and nobody would have thought of noticing it, either, if Deacon hadn't been prefixed to my papa's name.

—Fanny Fern, *Olive Branch*, August 9th, 1851

Deacon Nathaniel Willis had nine children, six of whom were daughters. He only really worried about two of those daughters, though—Julia and Sara—Julia because she was so homely and meek, and Sara because she was the direct opposite. With a shiver, he thought of Julia, her lank brown hair, her pink eyelids from too much reading, her ungraceful twanging upon the harp. She was already nearly twenty-eight and without a beau in sight. Soon, there'd be no hope for her. He'd spoken with Mr. Simon Petudalbore after services again last Sunday, hoping the fifty-eight-year-old widower would consider a third marriage. The deacon knew how Simon had doted on Jane, his second wife, a spry and lovely twenty-year-old who'd died giving him his third son in as many years, after he'd already raised a family with Elizabeth, his first wife, who died just five years before of fever. How would a man of his age manage three little boys? Julia could be the answer to his prayers and could probably have her own children soon enough. Luckily for Julia, Simon's eyes were going and, hopefully, he'd appreciate child-rearing help more than he'd mind a blemished face and dour expression.

To ease the idea along, the deacon had given Sara carte blanche with her sister, instructing her to render Julia as presentable as possible each Sunday. That Sara tried was evident. That Julia's nature resisted all correction was also evident. Julia emerged each Sunday morning from her sister's dressing room with her poker-straight hair bent at odd angles, her hunched shoulders adorned in some borrowed lacey shawl, her big feet clumping along in too-small shoes. All of this made her frown more than usual until the deacon would finally allow her to wear her hideous flat brown boots, if only to facilitate the most graceful walk someone like Julia could muster.

Sara, in her own way, was as bothersome. Whenever another living creature was nearby, she lit up like a chandelier and dispensed puns, anecdotes, and always a thousand questions upon whomever would listen. The constant conversation exhausted the deacon and he'd placed Sara in boarding schools until she was twenty, sure that he'd only have to endure a year, maybe two, of her before marrying her off. Lucy went at nineteen. Louisa, and Mary, each were seventeen. Even little Ellen already showed promise at only sixteen. Thankfully, Sara, now twenty-six, was finally engaged. It wasn't for Sara's lack of beaux. It was because of her constant rejection of them. Half the town had paraded through the deacon's parlor and sat at his table. How many evenings had he sat yawning and winding his watch, staring down some young man who couldn't bear to leave Sara's side. She was certainly pretty. But try as he would, the deacon couldn't instill the proper amount of womanly humility and subservience into Sara. She laughed as loud as the fishmongers, marched around town without a thought to propriety and safety, kissed anyone she wanted, sometimes in public. He'd rallied all of his minister friends to the cause of saving her soul, but obstinate Sara, though she'd kneel in pious prayer, refused to "submit," as she put it, to the will of God. Such vanity made the deacon shake his head.

Thank goodness she'd finally accepted respectable Charles Eldredge. In less than a month—no, a little more than a month—she'd be off his hands and into Charles' and the good deacon could concentrate on Julia's future. And then on Ellen's, and Edward's and Richard's, of course, not to mention always and still worrying about Nat, even though he was married, or so he said, despite still playing the foppish bachelor more often than the deacon thought proper.

Deacon Nathaniel Willis felt the familiar headache inching up the base of his neck and wrapping itself around his crown. He put down the rack of letters he was arranging into the *Youth's Companion*'s main story with a groan. The copy wouldn't fill the page again, and the four o'clock deadline was racing toward him. He'd dispatch the new apprentice, Luke, to fetch them some lunch from home and to bring back Julia or Sara to write some filler. He just couldn't think straight enough today to write anything more. His mind felt like a squeezed-out wash rag, hanging stiff on a peg.

The deacon summoned Luke, gave him strict instructions, then went back to setting type. He'd racked together a few more lines, at most, when Nat flew in, eyes wide, and slammed the door behind him.

"Must you break everything?" Nathaniel Willis said to his oldest son.

Nat placed one hand over his heaving chest and with the other, wiped his damp forehead with one of his garishly embroidered linens. "Shhh," Nat whispered. "Mary mustn't know I'm here. Not just yet anyway."

"Oh, Heaven's sake," the deacon said with a grimace. "What have you done now? I'm surprised she consented to marry you in the first place."

Chapter Four

Julia Willis, Sara Payson Willis, and Charles Eldredge, Boston, Wednesday, April 12th, 1837

Mrs. Chrissholm says:—"The best time to choose a wife is early in the morning. If a young lady is at all inclined to sulks and slattern-ness, it is just before breakfast. As a general thing, a woman don't get on her temper, till after 10 A.M."

Men never look slovenly before breakfast—no indeed! Never run round vestless in their stocking-feet, with dressing-gown inside out; soiled hand-kerchief hanging by one corner out of the pocket; minus dickey; minus neck-tie; pantaloon straps flying at their heels; suspenders streaming from their waistband; chin shaved on one side, lathered on the other; last night's coat and pants on the floor, just where they hopped out of them; face snarled up in forty wrinkles, because the chamber fire won't burn; and because it snows; and because the office-boy hasn't been for the keys; and because the newspaper hasn't come; and because they smoked too many cigars *by one dozen*, the night before; and because they lost *that* bet; and can't pat the *Scot-t*; and because there's an omelet instead of a chicken-leg for breakfast; and because they are out of sorts and shaving-soap; and out of cigars and credit; and can't *any how* "get their temper on," till they get some money and a mint julep!

Any time "before 10 o'clock," is the time to "choose" a husband—*perhaps!*

—Fanny Fern, *True Flag*, January 1st, 1853

17

"Sara, Father's short a piece or two," Julia Willis said to her younger sister, as she clumped from the kitchen to the front parlor to help with the daily sewing. "And you know how long it takes me, lately, to write anything he'll be pleased with."

Sara looked up from the trousers she was sewing for her brother, Richard, now eighteen and growing out of everything. "You finish these for me and I'll dash something off," Sara said, tossing the charcoal material onto the arm of the chair.

Miss Patty, the hired seamstress, snapped her sharp chin up from the lace she was fitting into the folds of Sara's wedding dress. "No no no!" she said. "Julia will have to write today because Sara hasn't yet worked an entire pair of trousers."

"And I won't either," Sara said. "I hate trousers. They're so particular."

"But you've got to learn how to fit a seat or your little boys will run around bare," Miss Patty said.

"Well, then," Sara said as she quickly tied her bonnet and headed toward the door, "I won't have any boys. I'll only have girls!"

"Thank you, Sara!" Julia called after her sister who was already dashing out the door to the *Youth's Companion* newspaper office while Miss Patty shook her head over the nearly finished wedding gown and muttered about that Sara and imagine wishing for only girls and all this wedding work for something so spoiled.

Sara decided to stop by the bank to see her "handsome Charly" for a few minutes before reporting to her father. Charly was not only the most scrumptious man Sara had ever seen—just over six feet tall and full of muscle with smoky blue-gray eyes and a head full of thick dark curls—but he was also the most fun. Their tête-à-têtes weren't like other people's—stuffy talks between ahems and indeeds on straight-backed parlor chairs or sitting glancing sideways at one another in a plodding carriage. They were laughing romps on ice skates over a bumpy pond or what they called "storytelling" in front of the fire, where they'd pop corn and blow on their too-eager burnt fingers while trying to out-tell the tallest tale of the other. Sara was crazy about Charly and she knew he was crazy about her, too. She'd had so many beaux these past six years (and fun enough); she'd gotten good at telling exactly when some young man was getting too seriously interested in her and her future, and would gently and playfully ease him from her attentions, while encouraging someone new.

But it was all different with Charles Eldredge, the wonderful bank cashier. The day she first locked eyes with Charles', she felt a strange stupor settle over her. Charles was different from any man she'd ever met. When they snuggled on hay rides, her body ached with craving. Sara looked very much forward to their upcoming wedding and to receiving, as Charles whispered, as much rapture as they both deserved.

As soon as Sara walked into Merchant's Bank, Charles escaped from behind his cashier's window and swooped upon his fiancée. He pulled her into the bank's back entryway and pressed her close.

Sara's lips lingered over his. "Oh, Charly, I can't wait a month more."

Charles took a shaky breath. "My darling, after this torturous time, we'll be able to love each other every moment we're together."

"Forever, Charly?"

"Forever. I promise. We're going to have a marriage that is the envy of every romantic everywhere."

Sara knew he was right. They'd talked frankly and often about their marital expectations. Instead of trying to curb Sara's spirit, Charly assured her it was what he loved most about her. He'd never try to confine her, a promise Sara clung to even as her father lectured Charly about his husbandly duty to correct his wife, to manage her as if she were a new horse or a parcel of land. Sara didn't need managing and would oppose anyone who thought otherwise. Her father knew it and so did Charly. The difference was that Charly didn't care. He knew Sara would be the sort of woman who went to the theater, ordered beefsteak and ale, and would be an eager participant in the bedroom.

Sara kissed Charles again, slowly and tenderly. "I have to go," she finally said. "Father needs some copy."

"Oh," Charles said, pulling her closer. "You're such a quick writer. Maybe you could stay just a little longer."

"Really, I do have to go," Sara said, then allowed one more kiss, then another.

Charles suddenly gasped. "I just remembered . . . ," he said.

Sara tucked a stray curl into her bonnet. "You'll not get me to stay longer with one of your stories," Sara said. "Though I'd love to hear it later, by the fire."

"No, this is too true," Charles said. "I promised Mother I'd help her wind yarn tonight."

Charles was the only surviving child of five. His mother counted on him more and more fiercely after each sibling's death. Winding yarn was the least of his domestic duties, though one he never really minded.

"Again?" Sara said. "I've never seen a more devoted son. Why doesn't she hire a girl to help her with the yarn?"

"She needs someone to talk with. You know Father. She gets lonely."

"She'll be a lot lonelier next month when you're all mine."

"Well," Charles stammered. "That's the trouble. The house I wanted to buy won't be for sale for a little while and so she and Father suggested we live with them until we're able to get settled for ourselves."

Sara smiled slowly, considering her reply. It wouldn't do to protest. Charly would separate from his mother in due time. "I guess your mother and I will have to get to know one another then," she finally said, raising her eyebrows. "And it looks like I'm going to get good at winding yarn."

Chapter Five

Sara Payson Willis, Nathaniel Willis, and N. P. Willis, Boston, Wednesday, April 12th, 1837

For one, I can never pass such a "fallen angel" with a "stand aside" feeling. A neglected youth, an early orphanage, poverty, beauty, coarse fare, the weary day of toil lengthened into night,—a mere pittance to reward. Youth, health, young blood, and the practiced wile of the ready tempter! Oh, where's the marvel?

Think of all this, when you poise that hardly earned dollar, on your business finger. What if it were your own delicate sister? Let a LITTLE heart creep into that shrewd bargain. 'Twill be an investment in the Bank of Heaven, that shall return to you four-fold.

—Fanny Fern, *True Flag*, January 29th, 1853

Sara Willis hurried to the *Youth's Companion* office, squinting against the alarmingly bright sun, thinking of possible story ideas as she went. She would try to add some spunk to the piece so readers could get the point without falling asleep. Why everyone always thought morals had to come wrapped in plain brown paper, Sara didn't understand. And everyone knew father's paper needed a boost. Even though it had decent subscriptions, many people ordered it for children who would as soon dive into its grim lessons on a bright spring day as sit through Sundays twice. Sara had tried explaining as much to her father, but he insisted that the Lord's work was serious work, and it was blasphemous to trivialize matters of life and death importance. When he was desperate for filler, though, he'd often take whatever she wrote, without an argument. So, today, she hoped, she could write with a dash of freedom.

As she approached the newspaper office, she stopped herself from bursting through the door. Voices bellowed through the closed window, the voice of her father and the voice of someone else—Nat! He must be in town visiting. As much as Sara longed to rush upon her brother and hear all about married life to rich, British, Mary Stace, she remained stationary on the step, in the twiggy shade of a chestnut tree, listening to her father berate her oldest brother.

Married men didn't have affairs with other women. They just didn't. But he was an artist, Nat bantered. He needed muses, stimulation. One woman would never be enough for him. Even pastries, eaten every day, would get wearisome. Muses, indeed, Nat needed a thrashing. Didn't vows mean anything? And thus, began Father's Park Street Church rant. Sara nodded along. When Nat was excommunicated, Father thought he'd die of shame. But this was worse! Running around town with a different woman every night. Dressing like a fool. Troubling a fine wife. Embarrassing his family.

What Father didn't know was that instead of causing chagrin, his lecture always emboldened Nat. When Father would detail Nat's sins, Nat beamed, considering himself a winning escapee from Park Street Church prison. Sara imagined his barely suppressed delight as he straightened his dickey, smoothed his hair, and murmured that he was hardly *young*, Father, despite his fashionable appearance and stamina, and he was accustomed to drinking—it simply didn't affect him. Father was shouting. It affects the mind, good judgment, one's soul. *His* soul was safe, Nat assured. So Father raised his squall. He rattled on without a breath for five minutes, six. Did Nat think he could proclaim to follow Christ once and that was it for the rest of his life? He might *feel* safe but feeling wasn't the basis of truth. Feeling wasn't—"

"Why isn't it?" Nat said and by the clipped tone, Sara knew his amusement had run its course. A breeze rustled the chestnut's budding branches. Sara sighed. Now this conversation would become a war. "You never get upset when *Sara* acts wild."

Sara narrowed her eyes. Nat was drawing her into this logic? She'd been called wild her whole life, but for smiling a bit too often or gobbling her dessert—things she never could equate with sinfulness, no matter how she stretched her brain.

"Don't bring your sister into this. She's set to be married in a month and that will settle that," her father said.

"Do you think so, Father? Do you think she'll settle down and be like Lucy or Louisa simply because she's married?"

"Charles will manage her. God willing."

Sara felt her cheeks redden, her jaw tighten.

"Nobody will be able to manage her! You've tried since she was a tot. She's headstrong and sensual."

"Sensual? What are you saying? Tell me!"

"I'm saying that anyone who stops by Merchant Bank at certain times of certain days will see Charles and Sara embracing, and more, in the bank's back hall. All the employees spy on them and tell everyone they know."

Sara's jaw unhinged. How could Nat equate her trivial indiscretions with his flouting of his marriage vows? She would never think of such a thing, let alone act upon it.

There was a long pause before Deacon Willis said, "I've known for some time that your sister is no stranger to a kiss. But I believe she's pure, still, and getting more pious."

Nat laughed. "More pious? She's no more pious than I am."

"She's still a church member! There's hope! And there's no reason to bring her into this conversation about you and your sins."

"No reason? You've got to keep her from Charles until after the wedding. Believe me, I know."

Sara's cheeks burned. She heard something bang inside, like maybe her father's hand had come down hard on a table, or his boot had kicked a chair leg.

"I know, too," Deacon Willis said. "And he's assured me of his solid intentions."

"I don't trust him," Nat said. "He's just a little too pretty."

Sara couldn't tolerate another instant of being talked about. She stamped her feet on the step, as if just arriving, raising a swirl of winter dust, and flung open the door.

"Sara!" both Nat and her father exclaimed.

Her father eyed the table. "I hope you've come in response to Luke's message."

"I have," Sara said, giving him a tight kiss on the cheek.

"We were just talking about you, my pet," Nat said, holding his arms out to embrace his sister.

Sara had thought she could ignore what she'd just heard, but viewing her brother's hypocrisy straight on ignited a blaze inside of her. She slipped out of the path of Nat's oncoming arms. "I know," she said. "I heard every word."

Her father knit his brows and raised his head. "Then you'd be wise, young lady, to cease those visits to the bank's chambers," he said.

"I don't see what's wrong with occasionally kissing my fiancée, especially knowing what Nat's done, and is doing—"

"Your brother's conduct is nobody's business but his," Deacon Willis said.

"And yet mine, however innocent, is the business of my father, my brother, and my fiancée?" Sara said.

Nat rolled his eyes. "*Innocent.*"

Sara gasped. "How is it a woman can do so little, yet be judged so harshly? And by those who are closest to her?"

Nat stroked his lapel and grinned. "Sara, you must admit you've always been uncontrollable."

"Uncontrollable? *Me?* I'm *alive* is all. *Your* behavior has always been *my* definition of the word."

Nat raised his eyebrows in mock alarm. "How dare you insinuate!"

"Sara, you're risking my wrath," her father said.

Sara clamped her jaw. Nat had done it again. He'd twisted the attention away from him and his transgressions. Charming as he was, Sara hated how he always seemed to glide over any bump in the road. "And what of *my* wrath?" she spat. "Or Mary Stace's?"

"Mary Stace is a sweet womanly creature," Nat said.

"And that means she won't care that you're unfaithful to her?"

The deacon banged his fist on the table. Sara and Nat jumped. "You've got too much imagination, Sara," he said. "I've always known it. It's time you learn to calm yourself down and accept your womanly duties with grace and modesty, or you'll be out a husband as surely as you think you've landed one."

Sara blinked rapidly. Her head felt airy, like she'd sat too long in a closed room with a smoldering fire. Could it be true that despite what Charly had said, he might want her to conform to some meek and milky model of domesticity? She wouldn't believe it.

"I'm going back to finish setting this type," the deacon said. "I called you here to help me, not hinder me."

The usual wood and copper smell of the shop seemed suddenly heavier, more metallic. It was hard to take in such dense air. Sara's lungs quivered in effort.

Her father held up his hand, spreading his fingers and thumb apart about six inches. "I need this much. *Good* words. Nothing flippant. You hear?"

"Yes, Father," Sara said as he stomped to the back room, leaving her to face her smirking brother. She splayed a palm over her chest.

"Don't you hold a grudge against me, Sara Willis," Nat whispered.

Sara narrowed her eyes. "I'll never speak to you, again."

"You know I love you just as you are, and so does Charly. You've nothing to worry about."

"It certainly seemed a different story a minute ago," Sara said.

Nat smiled, the same joyous smile he flashed so many times in their youth when together they'd held swimming races in the spring-swollen creek, pitched pebbles daringly at a hornet's nest, or escaped a stifling August afternoon by pulling taffy and making limericks in the musty cool of the cellar. He stroked her shoulder tenderly. "You understand, don't you, my Sara? Father was tongue-lashing me so! I had just come in to escape Matilda Horning's flirtations and had to put up with Father's Park Street Church sermon again."

Sara took a long, quivering breath. "And just what are you doing flirting with Matilda Horning? Mary Stace is gorgeous."

"She is. And you're right," Nat said. "You won't tell, will you? I love my Mary so much and just need a little more time to figure out this one-woman-for-life business."

Sara shook her head as if to clear it.

"I saw a particular spring-green ribbon in the millinery window that had Sara Willis written all over it." Nat pulled a dollar note from his pocket. "Why don't you go claim it?"

Sara snorted. "You've always been able to smooth-talk me, Nat. You know that." She pushed his hand back toward him. "I don't need out-and-out bribes."

"And you're my favorite wild sis," he said, stuffing the bill back in his pocket and coming close enough to kiss her lightly on the forehead. "You'd better get busy on Father's filler now though. What will you write about?"

"Filial obedience," Sara said through gritted teeth. "What else?"

"That's my girl," Nat said, cocking his hat and slipping out the door.

Chapter Six

Mary Eldredge, Brighton, Massachusetts, Friday, October 9th, 1846

Before me lies a little violet, the forerunner of spring. . . . It should give me joy, and yet my tears are dropping on its purple leaves. . . . Why? Has life been such a holiday to you that your heart never grew sick at a perfume or a well-remembered song hummed beneath your window, or a form, or a face, which was, and yet was not, which mockingly touched a chord that for years you had carefully covered over? . . . Have you never rushed frantically into a crowd—somewhere, anywhere to be rid of yourself? Did you never laugh and talk so incessantly and so gaily, that your listeners asked wonderingly and reproachfully, "Does she ever think?" . . . Did you never listen to the tick—tick—of your watch, night after night, with dilated eyes that would not close, with limbs so weary that you could not change your posture, and lips so parched you could not even cry, . . . and your brain one vast workshop, where memory was forging racks, and chains, and screws, and trying their strength on every quivering nerve?

—Fanny Fern, *New York Ledger*, May 8th, 1858

Sara said she couldn't feel her fingertips, couldn't feel herself breathing, blinking, biting her tongue. She, too, must be dead, she'd said to the air or to anyone who'd listen.

Bother with her, Mary thought. The girl was as selfish as the day was long and Mary was tired of it. Thinking she was the only one who had loved Charly, the only one who could mourn him with a half-yard of hem, the deepest black gown, the longest veil. Who birthed him? Who raised him up? Who ushered him through illness and schooling and church teachings into the fine, upstanding man he was? Who sacrificed a whole life for him and his four other dead siblings? Whose heart broke five times over for her children?

So much. So much. So much had happened, Sara kept saying.

She didn't know the half of what could happen to a body. Try losing *all* of your children. Now, that's a burden. Not that Mary questioned the Lord's ways. She knew he only gave as much as a person could bear. Mary wiped her eyes. It had been a hard life and she had never been one to dwell on misery, but this—losing her Charly, the last of her babies, the best of them, too—felt crushing. Charly, who stopped in his tracks to listen to *her*, Mary, his mother, with respect and that dear grin of his. Maybe she had spoiled him just a bit, as Hezekiah liked to point out. But he had been her last one. The only one left. The only fruit left of her motherly labors.

Sara was dressed in new clothes again. Surrounded by people. As always. Everything a social event. Even Charly's funeral. And the waste of money on so many flowers. All a show, of course, without a thought to the expense. And how she sobbed so dramatically when they brought in the bouquets, heaves racking her whole body. Sara said she could smell the roses—they were just like her wedding day. The commotion turned Mary's stomach, seemed to suck what little energy she still had from her bones.

Charly and Sara had lived with Mary and Hezekiah for the first year of their married life, birthed little Mary (bless her soul) upstairs in the spare room. Had little Mary been named for her grandmother Mary? No, of course not. She'd been named Mary *Stace*, after Sara's British sister-in-law. Mary had seen enough of that woman and Sara's dandy brother, Nat, at the wedding. Frankly, they made Sara look prim as a spinster. But that wasn't saying much. Too much indulgence among young people these days. Nobody knew the satisfaction of careful planning, of saving and making do. Mary and Hezekiah were good, sober, frugal Christians. Lord knows they tried to instill those values in the children. For instance, when Charles and Sara lived with them, they'd often split two ears of corn between the four of them, so as to have two extra ears to put up. Mary told Sara that her liberal sprinkling of salt was too frivolous an adornment to common roast chicken and she routinely showed the ungrateful girl how to unravel worn-out socks to reknit the yarn into more socks, socks she'd give to Sara as a Christmas gift (and a little reminder). Mary softened the butter on the stove top before putting it on the table, cut the bread into the thinnest slices, used a scant amount of soap in the laundry water. Just as Mary did her best to save at home, Hezekiah used his doctor's fees to purchase land and acquire bank accounts like Sara's girls collected hair ribbons—if one was good, then more were better. Hezekiah waited two weeks beyond the greedy blacksmith's advice to shoe the horses, repainted the fence in just the snippets needed, turned his under things inside-out to save on wear. Together, Mary and Hezekiah had created a comfortable, secure life and Mary resented Sara for her larky attitude, the attitude that poisoned her son and pulled him away from his own mother.

To be sure, Mary and Hezekiah saved everything. They didn't *hoard*, as ungrateful Sara had spat out at them just yesterday. They protected themselves, and those they knew. And, like many of their generation, they didn't believe in lavish displays of affection. They bestowed one prudent hug apiece upon their only child, Charly, each Sabbath. Sara and the children didn't need any extra encouragement in that category. She and those little ones were already too seeped in self-indulgence to promote any more of the sensual.

When little Mary was only months old, Sara fired the nurse Mary'd hired (and paid!) to take care of the baby, certain *she* a brand-new mother, knew everything about child-rearing. I'll figure it out, Sara'd said. Well, she could make her mistakes on somebody else's grandchild. Mary tried to show her everything she knew, but Sara made Charly move away so Sara could escape Mary's domestic instruction. It wasn't so much that Sara was lazy or incapable, just undisciplined and wasteful. The Willis family's old seamstress, Miss Patty, had warned Mary about just that. With training, Mary'd hoped Sara would get better at stretching Charly's hard-earned wages, would act less like a child herself and more like the firm mother to her children she ought to be.

After they'd moved to the country, Mary couldn't believe how Sara and the children chose to spend their time. Even when little Mary was toddling and Grace was a baby, Sara always had them here and there. Did they put in the requisite hours over the Bible and stove? No. They wandered all day long out of doors. Although it was fine to take a Sunday ride to church or an occasional stroll after the chores were caught up, to make a living out of poetry and dandelion wreaths, honey gathering and bird watching, was a sinful waste of time. Just who was supposed to bake the bread, dust the furniture, sew the flour sacks together to make aprons and under things? Of course, Sara had help. Everyone did. But you had to supervise and instruct every minute or the hired hands would loaf and lumber on the sly.

Mary convinced Hezekiah to leave Boston and to move down the road from Swissdale to another little place in Brighton, so she could keep an eye on things. Those girls were her grandchildren, after all, Charly's offspring, and she had better do her best to see that they were properly raised. She tried to catch Sara in her mistakes, to better instruct, but time and time again Sara made Mary feel the fool.

Mary remembered how she had tried to surprise her daughter-in-law, one morning, with an unannounced visit to Swissdale. That the maid was new only helped Mary's purpose. Mary arrived, ready to see the house in a wreck early one weekday morning. The maid had let the "family friend" in and sat Mary, at her request, in the kitchen with a cup of tea. There were some perfectly rounded loaves rising under a dishcloth near the stove. The floor was clean-swept and the cabinets polished. A little cut-glass vase on the table brimmed with daisies and, peeking into the cupboards, Mary spied jars of preserves, pickles, and vegetables. She stepped down into the cellar and poked her fingers into the cheese and butter stored neatly in barrels.

When the maid, a jovial woman who roamed the house freely in bare feet, caught Mary in the cellar, Mary confessed that she was Charly's mother and had wanted to see their foodstuffs so she might know what to order them for next Sunday's dinner. The maid introduced herself and escorted Mary to the parlor, providing a little footstool for her and a book of poems she said were the family's favorite. Bother. Mary couldn't make heads nor tails of those words going round and round in nonsense. She sat in the expensive chair, though, with her feet up, and thought how fortunate for Sara that the sun bathed the room so nicely. She asked the maid if the furniture wasn't usually covered, to prevent fading, and the maid gave her an amazed look, as if she'd never heard of such a thing. If you hadn't noticed, the maid said, it's already faded. Missis tats so many lace throws, you just don't notice. And had she seen the new window dressings? Just plain muslin and a little ribbon, but Missis made 'em up like you see in city windows. So clever.

Mary took advantage of the maid's checking the cake in the oven to run her fingers over the picture frames and to look behind the sofa for dust balls. But Sara had out-smarted Mary. She probably guessed Mary would be by that day. When the maid came back with a slice of what she called "Missis' Applesauce Delight," something she said Sara threw together once a week before dragging the children around the meadow, she made Mary sit back down with her feet up again, insisting Sara would want to see her coddled. Mary knew better what Sara would want. It was to see her children's grandmother as little as possible. She told the maid as much. Here they'd been in the country for over two days and nary an invitation to supper or a welcome visit. The maid, of course, hushed away talk about her employer. She was smarter than she looked.

She did give her mistress away, though, in other matters. She'd told Mary that Sara sometimes couldn't calm a cranky child, and that's when she would be called on to rock one or the other of them. She also confessed that Sara took her to the market with her, to help her pick out meat and produce. Sara never could make a decision on her own, Mary offered, but the maid had said she was pretty sure her missis just enjoyed the company. Just then, Sara and the girls spilled into the house so loudly that Mary's head immediately began to ache, and she had to excuse herself from the din, taking half the applesauce cake home with her only to be polite, certain she'd feed it to the dogs as soon as she gained the peace of her own yard.

Of course, Hezekiah saw things her way. Not only had their Boston house turned a tidy profit, he didn't mind moving to the country to better keep on Charly about his fences and the barn's rusting hardware, not to mention his shambled finances. Mary didn't know much about the details, but to hear Hezekiah talk, you'd be surprised Charly was a bank employee, with the little money sense he displayed. Of course, Sara's ne'er-do-well family seduced Charly's last penny from him. They'd schemed until they could figure out how to get him to lend them thousands. Even Sara's brother-in-law tricked them all, testifying as to the security of some hair-brained investment he was chin deep into with his good-for-nothing father. Those Jenkinses were both alike that way. And, of course, Sara had probably convinced Charly to co-sign every loan those two needed, to put himself out for their shady deals. That Sara stared blankly at Hezekiah when he'd told her so just yesterday was proof of her acting skills. She'll go to her grave denying it all.

If she hadn't been so attached to luxury, Charly never would have felt any pressure to make such risky investments. Hezekiah said there was no talking to him. He'd go and sign papers behind his father's back. Sara forced them to live beyond their means. And Mary knew, too, how she cuckooed her son. She'd seen Sara in operation, had sprung upon them, once. Charly had been sprawled out on the sofa of his parents' house and Sara was sitting on his lap with her hands all through his hair, kissing him like nobody's business. Mary couldn't bear to rekindle the disgusting memory. She only allowed herself to remember the glazed-over look in Charly's eyes and to make a note to herself to watch for his spiritual decline.

After Jenkins' untimely death, though not so untimely as not to provide a handsome nest egg for Sara's smart sister, Mary, Charly seemed overwhelmed. That he felt some sort of responsibility for Mary, a perfect stranger, was beyond her. Charly simply stretched himself too thin for that able-bodied woman and her children. And, naturally, Sara was nowhere to be found when her husband needed the blessings of a comfortable home and a wife within it. She'd practically moved back to Boston to nurse her sister, Ellen, and her mother. Ellen had just delivered a baby, which died under Sara's expert care, along with the sister a few weeks later. To have Sara as a nurse apparently didn't bode well for a body. Such thoughts were sinful, Mary knew, but she just couldn't help feeling wicked when it came to Sara. Sara brought out the evil in her like nobody else could.

That Sara moped around made Mary queasy. Mary saw through it all, saw Charly getting spun tighter and tighter around Sara's little finger. Sara wasn't so grieved she couldn't get herself pregnant again, that was certain. And with Charly so worried about his finances.

It was a pity, though, about the mother, old Hannah. Mary had liked her. Even though Sara's other sisters were around to help with the nursing, she'd died just six weeks after Ellen. You'd have thought Sara was the only one in the world who'd lost a mother. The way she chided her poor upstanding father for quickly taking another wife in Susan proved how selfish she was. Everyone knows it makes sense for a still-vibrant man to have a wife.

Mary wrung her hands. Poor Charly. Sara thought only of herself for the last year of Charles's life. She was consumed with displaying watersheds of tears for her sister and mother and made a show of being sick with the pregnancy. Charles ran himself ragged doting on her. Mary'd never seen such a coward as when Sara went into labor with little Ellen. She was terrified she'd follow her sister into death. But Mary'd seen Sara deliver those other two girls like a field hand. For all of her pomp, she was about as delicate, in those ways, as a Clydesdale. But nothing Mary said appeased the spineless fool, and even after Ellen was safely delivered, Sara's weeping could be heard down the hall. In fact, Sara spent so much energy seeing to the health of the baby, she forgot all about little Mary. For a seven-year-old to be allowed to wander out-of-doors with no bonnet is unconscionable. No wonder she caught the brain fever!

And, then, for Sara to spit bitter words at Hezekiah and to imply that it was his fault little Mary died. Hezekiah was no spring chicken anymore. He had crawled from his warm bed for so many sniffles and scratches, he was certain Sara was just a nervous mother crying wolf again. How was he to know how serious little Mary's condition had become? That she could deteriorate so rapidly was a sure sign that Sara hadn't been keeping a proper eye on her sick little girl. By the time he saw her at the reasonable hour of ten o'clock, there was nothing anyone, even Hezekiah, could do.

It broke Mary's heart when her namesake, or who should have been her namesake, died. But, Sara didn't have the decency to allow people their mourning. Mary, for instance, would have liked the opportunity to sit often in the house she so warmly associated with golden memories of little Mary. She ached to visit the empty bed, finger the useless clothes. But, Sara told Charly to sell the house, even at a loss. They cut out of there faster than a cat from a rain barrel, without a thought about what little Mary's grandparents might want, or need.

And wouldn't you know it but the real Mary Stace *herself* died just about then, also in childbirth (as did the baby), leaving that foppish dandy brother of Sara's with a little girl, one he instantly dumped off for Charly to support. Mary knew it'd be a mistake trusting another child to Sara's care, but nobody would listen to her suggestions for a good orphanage. Sara probably thought she could erase her guilt about little Mary by trying her hand at nursing again, not to mention stoking her same worn-out plea about her great load of grief with the charade that she was mourning two little nephews, nephews Mary had barely heard Sara mention in the three and eight years of their short lives. Luckily, Nat's child, Imogen, only stayed under Sara's care for a few months before Mary Stace's family in England claimed her.

When they all moved back to Boston is when Charly got the bad news from the judge. He was responsible for the debt of his dead brother-in-law, Jenkins. Hezekiah had plans to win Charly back his investments, but every time he tried to get Charly to sign off on something, Charly refused, insisting he'd *earn* his own way. Who could earn back fifty thousand dollars? Hezekiah and Mary decided to let the matter settle for a little while before offering further assistance. How were they to know what Sara had in mind for the summer and fall? How were they to predict that she'd drag Charly and the children to an expensive seaside resort and insist they *live* there for months on end, without a thought about how to pay for the extravagance? Charly had weakly tried to defend Sara to Mary by saying they needed to mend their broken spirits, needed the solace of the beach and the wind and the waves. Broken spirits, my eye. Mary had mended plenty of broken spirits over a washtub sucking on a blade of grass. Charly had kissed her on the forehead then. You've come through a lot Mother, but not all of us have your fortitude.

Time is the only healing agent and when Mary'd surprise Charly once or twice a week at the bank, she'd remind him of that fact, then would always ask when they were going to move back to the city and start behaving like proper church-going folks. Mary could tell the traveling back and forth from city to ocean every day must have been getting the better of him, because he always looked wan and pale during her visits, but of course, Charly would never let on he was getting run down. He'd always slap a manly grin onto his face and insist he *loved* meeting Sara and the girls beachside after a hard day's work in the dusty, hot city, and that he *adored* spending whole weekends traipsing through the sand in search of filthy seashells and rocks. Mary begged him to take care of his health. Looking back, Mary couldn't help but think she had some sort of premonition. She shuddered, wishing she had *forced* him to stay sensibly in the city, at least some of the time.

Sara only invited Mary and Hezekiah out the one time—when she was afraid she'd killed Charly. She sent hysterical, pleading telegrams to *come, come quickly, Charly's desperately ill!* but, as always seemed the case when it came to Sara, the elder Eldredges suspected a manipulation and lingered too long. Mary had just seen Charly a few days before and, besides his usual fatigue from the split way of life Sara had concocted, he was as strapping as ever. In hindsight, she guessed he'd probably caught the fever riding in the cramped cars to the resort with all of those other exhausted, unhappy men. That Sara had hired a complete fool to prescribe the wrong medicine for him and to encourage her mistreatment of him is something Hezekiah and Mary would never forgive her for. As soon as the Eldredges arrived, Hezekiah made the proper diagnosis, typhoid fever, and threw away the archaic treatments the other quack had recommended and quickly administered up-to-date treatments to poor Charly.

But Hezekiah was too late. The damage had already been done, and he made no bones about letting that flip of a daughter-in-law understand the gravity of her irresponsibility. When Sara's "friend" in the hotel insisted on taking up a collection for Sara and the girls, Hezekiah took it upon himself to keep the funds, knowing Sara'd have no idea what to do with so much capital. And who would pay for the funeral, if not Charly's parents?

And there she sat now, her head bowed so pitifully over her brand-new mourning dress, with the girls bouncing around her in their inappropriate flounces and flowers. Mary had to agree with that wispy Nat, for once, when he'd proclaimed to everyone that Sara looked awful as a widow and should strive to get out of the attire as soon as properly possible. Mary suggested to him, that considering Sara's hand in Charly's death, perhaps she shouldn't wear black at all. Given the blanched look his face registered, Mary could see she hit the right note with him and his sentiments about his younger sister, even as she knew she had to admit that she probably also sounded like a bitter old woman.

Sara rose to begin the parade past Charly's casket before they were all supposed to march to the graveyard. Sara had insisted that Charly be buried next to little Mary on a country plot, instead of in the Eldredge family plot in the center of a nice Boston neighborhood. She'd wailed so loudly, nobody dared argue the point with her. But Hezekiah and Mary determined that Sara's wails would henceforth fall on deaf ears. They wouldn't be moved to lift a finger to help her now unless she registered a womanly modesty and maturity, and succumbed to the wisdom and experience of her own father, stepmother, and Charly's beloved parents.

Mary and Hezekiah had met with Nathaniel and Susan Willis over breakfast before the funeral to discuss the matter. Mary could see Nathaniel's point that once a daughter is married off, he should be able to wash his hands of her. Susan certainly made an excellent point that Sara had always seemed able-bodied enough to romp through forests and to climb fences, so why shouldn't she be able to use the energy as a wash girl or a maid? But even though Hezekiah and Mary stifled smiles at the thought of proud Sara rubbing strangers' clothing in cold water, they couldn't bear the thought of Grace and baby Ellen suffering for their mother's foolishness. Nathaniel said that after the creditors were paid, Sara wouldn't have one red cent to live on, and he'd already gathered one dowry for her and had suffered her flapping mouth in his house more years than any noble Christian should have to. Besides, he still had Julia at home to contend with, since he'd never been able to marry her stubborn self off.

That's when Hezekiah and Mary gathered their Christian courage and offered their magnanimous gift—they'd relieve Sara of the burden of raising Grace and baby Ellen, leaving her free to pursue washing or sewing or whatever employment she could procure to support herself. Nathaniel and Susan warmed to the idea. Julia, for instance, fairly supported herself by taking in sewing. Granted that although she lived with the elder Willises and ate like she'd been shipwrecked, she donated a portion of her earnings to help keep her in bread and butter and sewed herself the clothing she needed from remnants found at the fabric stores. In fact, Sara and Julia could share Julia's room—a room, Susan guessed, that could be closed off by the strategic placement of a decorative door.

Watching Sara slump against the coffin and break forth, once more, into her dramatic quaking sobs made Mary's insides shake. But then she only had to look at the ignored and needy girls clamoring around the mother to feel better again. Sara'd made her bed for herself. She'd lived a spoiled and frivolous life, a life that had extracted the very lifeblood of such a strong and decent soul as Charly. She should have to pay something for such wanton greed and sinfulness. She should at least have to contribute to her own support. But the children were a different story. There was still hope for their salvation. A firm hand and a firmer schedule would save them from the devil's path, and Heaven knew, Mary was just the grandmother to do it. She was secretly delighted, even though she felt a little guilty for such thoughts, that old Hannah had died after all. Susan didn't seem to care a whit about the grandchildren, and Nathaniel apparently only cared about Susan. Those darling girls could ease Mary's pain, could make up for her loss of Charly. If only she could convince Sara of the practicality of such an arrangement.

Chapter Seven

Sara Payson Willis Eldredge, Boston, Friday, December 22nd, 1848

Isn't a "seedy" hat, a threadbare coat, or a patched dress, an effectual shower-bath on old friendships? Haven't people a mortal horror of a sad face and a pitiful story? Don't they on hearing it, instinctively poke their purses into the farthest, most remote corner of their pockets? . . . Ain't they always "engaged" ever after, when you call to see 'em? Ain't they near-sighted when you meet 'em in the street?—and don't they turn short corners to get out of your way?

—Fanny Fern, *Olive Branch*, March 18th, 1852

Sara pulled the warped door closed behind her, shook her freezing fingers, and climbed the boardinghouse's steep side stairs, the very stairs she'd recently agreed to wash for five cents off the three-dollar-a-week room and board she paid the landlady, Mrs. Haufen. Deep within the folds of her pocket, the only one left without a hole, was a whole dollar and the other guilty lump—peppermint. Peppermint she'd *stolen*. She'd sewed practically round the clock for old man Schueller this week, hoping to make more than the usual seventy-five cents for the week's labor. She'd delivered one extra shirt and figured that since she was usually paid seventy-five cents for two shirts, that she'd make an extra thirty-seven, or maybe thirty-eight cents (it was the Christmas season after all). But Schueller had given her only the dollar, which made Sara tear up, as she so often did these days. When he'd asked her what she was upset about, and she'd told him, he'd smiled in that way that froze Sara's insides and had said that she could get the extra thirteen cents for as many kisses. The extra money suddenly didn't matter. Sara pulled the extended bill from Schueller's clenched grip and stumbled away from his leering grin. Later, she would blame him for her thievery.

She wished she could find other employment. After Charly's funeral, Hezekiah and her father had each agreed to give her a dollar and a quarter a week. Both devout church goers, they felt congregational eyes flutter from wretched, vocal Sara to their ample purses and knew nobody would understand their mutually agreed-upon assertion that headstrong Sara deserved to reap the hardship she'd sown. Hers was God's lesson of humility and she wasn't acquiescing a bit. Given that they knew she'd be able to earn at least fifty cents a week taking in sewing, as her sister Julia did, her room and board would be covered. Never mind the fact that the children needed shoes and clothes and the occasional book or paper toy. We understand about the needs of children, Charly's mother, Mary Eldredge often told Sara, in her many attempts to coerce Sara into giving up Grace and Ellen to Hezekiah and herself. All the more reason to allow grandparents with means to have a fuller hand in the girls' upbringing.

Sara knew what a fuller hand meant. It meant total control. It meant allowing the girls to live with the Eldredges and quite possibly giving up all her maternal rights forever. Well, she wouldn't do it. Not as long as she had strength and a steel needle. She'd get faster at sewing, better. And she'd find more moral employers than the disgusting Schueller. And she'd never steal again. In fact, she'd just applied for a teaching position at quite a nice little school in downtown Boston. Sara felt hopeful because her sister Lucy's husband, Josiah, was on the school's board. He'd been in the drafty committee room when she'd had her little interview and had steered the committee away from dwelling too long on her lack of experience with algebra at Catharine Beecher's seminary. Surely, if he had any say, the board would hire Sara. They would have to.

Sara reached the top of the three-story staircase and tapped at Widow Perkins' door.

The door opened on the hunch-shouldered, flitty-eyed old woman. "The girls went off with your sister," Widow Perkins said. "In your room."

Sara knew Julia was the only one of her sisters brave enough to visit her anymore. What a nice surprise. After her miserable day, Sara was more starved than usual for comfort.

The widow glanced down the dim hall at the closed door of Sara's room. "I've just finished," she said with a little grin and pulled Sara into the cool, dank room toward the one small window where she'd set her rickety chair to work by the light. On the chair were two pairs of small gray socks made of drab, cheap wool, but unmistakably brand new.

"Oh, thank you!" Sara said, nearly crying at the sight. Just last week, she'd had to cut the toes off of Grace's shoes because her feet had grown so. Little Ellen's shoes had been cut for a month. The worst part was not the cutting of the shoes, but looking at the raggedy, oft-mended dingy socks poking through the travesty. Another pair of new, warm socks would make the shoes seem tolerable.

Sara gave the widow her dollar and waited for her to count out change from a tattered purse she pulled from under her pillow, mostly in half-dimes. The widow was two cents short, which alarmed Sara—she wouldn't have enough for the week's board, as she'd spent her stair-washing half-dime on two extra scoops of coal. It had been so cold lately and Grace had started the week with a cough. Widow Perkins blinked and went back to search under the pillow. Sara inhaled sharply. Gently, she laid her hand on the widow's frazzled iron-gray head and proclaimed the socks to be so well made that she wanted to pay a little extra for them, after all. The widow turned from the bed, wrinkled her brow as if in pain, then rested her forehead on Sara's shoulder and cried, whether in relief, gratitude, or embarrassment, Sara didn't know. Sara, at least, could borrow the two cents from Julia.

"Merry Christmas," Sara said to the widow and kissed her good-bye. "I'll bring you a little something from father's house on Monday."

"Bless your heart," the widow said, and waved Sara off.

Sara tucked the socks into her pocket and felt, once again, the stick of stolen peppermint candy. She swallowed hard at the bile rising from her stomach. The stick had been partly crushed and was, apparently, pulled from the display jar and left on a dusty little "half-price" shelf on the grocer's back wall. Sara had slipped it into her pocket with such grace it frightened her. Other things sometimes appeared on that shelf and Sara had seen other, poorer, people quietly slip these things into their pockets: bruised apples, nearly rancid butter wrapped in paper, or sometimes, small rough pouches containing a handful or so of molding beans. But, she'd never done it before—stolen. Until that day. After enduring the nauseating leers of Schueller and the disappointment of her pay, Sara had wandered to the little shelf and spied the sad peppermint stick, which had been ignored by the shuffles of drab poverty floating past. Only Sara had pocketed the crumbling sweet. Only Sara would ruin her soul stealing candy.

Sara walked to the room at the end of the hall, the absolute cheapest room in the house, worse than even Widow Perkins' room, smaller, colder, but with a similar little window overlooking the clapboard side of the next boarding house. She poked her key through the lock and gave the skeletal door a hard push.

Julia *was* there! She was balanced on Sara's three-legged sewing stool near the window, had a girl on each knee, and was reading a book.

"Mother!" the girls cried, jumping from Julia's lap to embrace Sara.

Sara hugged her darlings close and smiled full at Julia.

"I've just come from Lucy's," Julia said, indicating the book. "She said I could borrow this to read to the girls."

"By all means, continue, then," Sara said. "I'll listen, too!"

Sara untied her bonnet and hung it on the nail, then reclined on the room's lumpy horsehair bed, still wrapped in her shawl, to listen to Julia finish a story about princesses and pudding and glittering crowns and roast beef. Decadent food. Brimming tables of crockery and wine. Lace tablecloths and bowls of flowers. Genteel manners reigning supreme. Nobody forgotten. Nobody suffering. No hunger or cold or fear. Sara's eyes fluttered, her breathing slowed, and then Sara suddenly saw Mother in the tale, sitting at the royal banquet next to sister Ellen. Oh, how radiant they looked, pink-cheeked and happy! Mother wore a turban made of ferns and she plucked one and blew it across the room to Sara, who caught it and tucked it into her bodice front. Beaming sister Ellen just ate and ate and ate.

Mary Stace was there, too, and the babies, and Lucy's boys, but where, oh where? Sara whirled in dream circles, looked madly around and around and then she saw them, Charly, magnificent in black velvet, wearing his white satin wedding vest and holding little Mary's hand. Little Mary was hopping up and down in the most exquisite shining silver shoes, pointing at Grace and Ellen sitting on Julia's knee in the corner of the palace. Little Mary had a basketful of sweets she wanted to share with her sisters and so Charly let her run before folding the then-sobbing Sara into his hearty arms and whispering to her, "All is well, all is well, all is well . . ."

"Sara!" Julia cried as she roughly shook her sister's shoulder. "Wake up! Your cries are frightening the children."

Sara shook her head at the quivering faces of Grace and little Ellen, at the pale, plain face of Julia, at the pounding at the door.

A voice boomed through the pounding. "You're loud enough to wake the dead. Are you committing murder in there?" Sara recognized the voice of the boardinghouse mistress and scrambled to her feet to open the door.

"We heard screams," the buxom woman said, narrowing her watery gray eyes. "Besides you're late with the payment, so I figured I'd have to come up."

"I've got it," Sara said. She left the landlady in the doorway while she pulled a little jar from underneath the bed and dumped the entire contents of it into the woman's palm. She rummaged in her pocket and added the forty-eight cents.

Mrs. Haufen eyed the mound in her hand. "You're two cents short."

"No she's not," Julia said, pulling a little purse from her pocket and fishing in it for two cents.

"Julia," Sara whispered.

"I owe you this from last week," Julia said evenly.

The landlady accepted the coins from Julia, then looked Sara up and down. "Schueller says you've been given to shoddy work," she said.

Sara gasped. "But, I've done more this week than usual."

"Useless rags, he says," the woman said, tapping her toe. Her quick eyes rested on Grace and Ellen's cut-away shoes. She cleared her throat, then looked toward the window. "Anyway, come down to supper. The soup's on the table."

Sara's head was suddenly throbbing. She pressed her fingers to her temples. "Do you think I could have it up here? Just this once. I'm not feeling well."

The woman shook her head at Sara, at Julia, at the girls. "Only if you fetch it up these stairs yourself. I'm not about to serve you like a princess. And you've got to wash up your own dishes before bed."

Sara nodded. She steered Grace and little Ellen to the window and pulled a small slate and a stick of chalk from a drawer in the bureau. "You girls must be good now and draw Aunt Julia a picture. We're going to go down and bring some supper up."

The girls sat on the floor under the drafty window and accepted the slate and chalk from their mother.

"What shall we draw?" little Ellen asked.

"I know," Grace said. "We'll draw the feast from the story. I'll draw the table, then you draw something on it. Then I'll draw something else, then you'll take a turn."

Grace coughed, then smiled at her mother and little Ellen smiled, too.

Sara kissed the top of each curly head and beckoned Julia to follow her and the boardinghouse mistress down the stairs. "I need you to help me carry the soup, Julia."

"And you'll have no more than usual," the woman said, casting a sharp eye on Julia.

"Don't worry about me, Ma'am," Julia said. "I've already eaten."

They descended the stairs, with the landlady twice stopping to point out mysterious stains to Sara, who promised to scrub extra hard in those spots the next morning.

When they reached the dining room, the rest of the boarders were already dunking their rye rolls into the steaming pea soup. There were eight boarders altogether; four men, Widow Perkins, and Sara and her girls. Three of the men were the rough sorts Charly had always steered Sara clear of when they'd leave the theater or some late-night gathering at one of their friends' houses. These men were dressed in saggy, thin garments that added nothing to their uncombed, unwashed presentation. Sara usually sat at the table's end, near the door with Widow Perkins and the kind-voiced, vacant-eyed William. The other three men sprawled at the table's other end, the end near the kitchen, and stabbed their choices from the platters and swiped extra bread into their pockets before passing the dishes down. Sara had felt their bright eyes on her person many times and averted her notice from their pointed comments and bold stares by busying herself cutting tough meat for the girls or chatting low with the widow and William. One of the men, Abe, whistled crudely as Sara and Julia entered the dining room.

"Behave yourself," Mrs. Haufen said. "Let these two at the soup now."

The pot had been set in the middle of the table and Sara ladled a portion into each of three bowls. She handed two of the bowls to Julia, carrying the third bowl in one hand and awkwardly holding three rolls with her other hand.

Widow Perkins flashed a bird-like smile at Sara as she was making to leave and William cleared his throat. "Miss Sara," he said, holding out a small, wrinkled apple. "I found this for you and the girls. I wish you'd take it."

Sara knew the apple had been on some or another grocer's back shelf, yet she wanted it as much as she'd wanted the broken peppermint stick. Her face reddened as she indicated her pocket to William. "Thank you, William," she said. "My hands are full, so if you wouldn't mind slipping it into my pocket."

William's eyes fluttered at the low-throated chuckles coming from the men's end of the table.

"Why I never," Mrs. Haufen said, snatching the apple from William and dropping it into Sara's pocket. "You haven't the sense of a June bug," she said to Sara.

"He's harmless," Sara said. "And my fingers are burning. Seems like it was a very practical suggestion."

"It was a suggestion all right," the landlady huffed. "I won't pity you again."

"Come, Sara," Julia said quietly. "My fingers are burning, too."

Upstairs, after the four of them had shared the three portions and the sorry apple, and Julia helped Sara tuck the girls into one end of the bed (Sara usually squeezed into the other end after sewing until the candle blurred), the two sisters sat upon the matted little rug near the dying fire, leaning back on their hands, stretching their numb toes near the paltry embers. Mrs. Haufen allowed two portions of coal or wood per day, delivered each morning by William, who then got ten cents off of his weekly bill. Sara's fire was usually cold by morning, so she had gotten good at blowing and fanning scraps of everything. Her pocket, when it wasn't weighed down with stolen candy, usually brimmed with bits of paper she and the girls found on their daily walk through the city, to the park, or down to the wharf. She only allowed the fire to blaze in the morning and after dinner because she firmly believed the girls should start and end their days in relative warmth. The rest of the time, though, the wind swept through the little room's cracks and settled in their bones.

Julia couldn't believe her sister now lived like this, like a pauper. What's more, Julia could expect the same herself anytime, should she cross her father.

That she was here now, visiting Sara, was only permitted because it was the Christmas season. Henry would be around soon to collect her in the carriage and take her back to her little room off the parlor in Father and Susan's house—her room that, though tiny, was warm and comfortably furnished. And although it was true that Julia spent a good deal of her days and most of her evenings plying her needle through muslin and silk, at least she did so with a satisfied stomach, by the warmth of a decent fire and in the light of enough candles. And, if she was careful, her weekly earnings of nearly fifty cents stretched to allow her one dress, one pair of shoes, one set of undergarments, and either a pair of gloves or a hat each year.

Julia pulled two candles from her pocket and presented them to Sara. "I took them from the pantry," Julia said. "Susan was in a tizzy for two days, but finally decided she'd been shorted and is now as watchful with the shop girls as she is with Cook. She counts every teaspoon of sugar, you know. So unlike Mother."

"Who could ever be like Mother, I'd like to know," Sara replied, fingering the candles. The dream image of her mother flashed before her—pink-cheeked, smiling, blessed. She absently smoothed the wrinkled ribbon on her bodice, where the invisible fern leaf was tucked. "Thank you, Julia," she said, her voice catching. "Now I've got you stealing, too."

In the next moment Sara teared up again and Julia sat close, patting her sister's shoulder and listening with amazement to Sara's story about the shirts, and Schueller, and the grocer's shelf, and the stick of peppermint candy. She heard about the socks and the widow and the cents and about poor William. She listened about Grace's cough and the stair washings and the scrounging for bits of paper in the streets. She saw Sara's stained and hanging dress, her rumpled, faded bonnet, her threadbare shawl. Earlier, of course, she couldn't help but notice the girls' shoes and their horrid socks, not to mention their embarrassed joy at being able to listen to her read a borrowed book.

Sara saw the pity in Julia's eyes and sat up straight. No no no Sara scolded. You mustn't pity *us*. At least there *was* a bonnet and, now, *new* socks, and a sister who would kindly lend a few cents. At least there were books to be borrowed and a back strong enough to wash stairs for extra coal. At least there was a window for some sewing light and a street that provided paper scraps. At least their supper, though often meager, was hot. At least there was the kind idiocy of dear William and the sweet widow, who would watch the girls when Sara dealt with Schueller. There was hope, too—the teaching job. The teaching job would come through very soon.

"Oh, Sara," Julia said. "Your spirit is amazing."

"I *will* keep my children," Sara said.

"Sara," Julia said gently. "I brought more than the book from Lucy's. I have news."

The way Julia said the word *news*, as if someone else had died, stabbed Sara's hope. "The teaching job?" Sara whispered.

"Gone to Agnes White," Julia said.

"Why, she hasn't half my education!"

"But she has no children to sit in on classes for free and, according to Josiah, a more . . . malleable temperament."

Sara's face burned. That her own brother-in-law hadn't spoke out for her, hadn't seen her strengths, her need.

Just then, the wind rattled through the window pane and swept through Sara, extinguishing the warm little flame of hope she had quietly been fanning.

"Samuel Farrington is coming for Christmas dinner," Julia said.

Sara shuddered. He was old and mottled and smelled like spirits. He was also newly widowed, with two mousy little girls, and was great friends with her father. Sara knew why he had been invited to spend Christmas with the Willis family. She knew what was expected of her.

"I can't," Sara said. "Charly . . ."

"Is dead," Julia said. "And you were very lucky to have had love with him. Don't you see? Samuel Farrington isn't so bad. He's well off and you'd have food and a home."

"*You* wouldn't have Simon Petudalbore!"

"I," Julia said, "didn't have two children."

Chapter Eight

Sara Payson Willis Eldredge Farrington, Boston, Thursday, January 17th, 1850

What do I mean by "legal murders"? Well, if a woman is knocked on the head with a flat-iron by her husband and killed, or if arsenic is mixed with her food, or if a bullet is sent through her brain, the law takes cognizance of it. But what of the cruel words that just as surely kill, by constant repetition? What of neglect? What of the diseased children of a pure, healthy mother? What of the ten or twelve, even healthy children, "who come," one after another, into the weary arms of a really good woman, who yet never knows the meaning of the word rest till the coffin-lid shuts her in from all earthly care and pain? . . . I could write flaming words.

—Fanny Fern, *New York Ledger*, March 12th, 1870

Sara sat on a high-backed chair in front of the broad, planked table in the big kitchen of Samuel P. Farrington's comfortable two-story house. Her sturdy buttoned shoes were new, as was her gown, a plain navy muslin with ivory grosgrain trim. She'd put on a little of the flesh she'd wasted those nearly three years at the boarding house, but not all of it. Sara had had a hard time swallowing and digesting since becoming a wife again. A spangly fire crackled in the blackened grate, casting glimmer over the gleaming oak floors, the freshly whitewashed cupboards, the stacks of flower-blue dishes stacked on shelves near the pump. Sara sighed. She was thinking of her sister Louisa's recent death, and peeling onions again. Peeling and chopping. Onions, onions, onions. They had help, of course—gap-toothed, big-boned Sally Ann—but Samuel insisted that Sara handle the onions. It was as if he wanted to brand Sara with odor, to mark her as *his*, his oniony wife. Sara felt her heart clench for Louisa but fought the urge to cry. Not in front of the children. They'd had enough of sorrow, the four of them. Sara's hands were shaking again, too. She'd found a soft onion in the heap and had to throw it out. And she'd forgotten to ask Sally Ann to pick up more onions on her rounds that morning. Now there wouldn't be enough. Not enough onions to smother the flavor of everything else. Sara prayed Samuel would be just drunk enough not to notice. Since their marriage exactly one year before, a tight, flowerless ceremony held with a blizzard raging against the church windows, Sara had discovered all three of Samuel's passions—beer, onions, and the marital act. A wave of nausea rolled through Sara and she dropped the knife and a half-peeled onion into the wooden bowl she was working over and steadied herself against the table's edge.

What if it was a baby? The idea made Sara even sicker and she vowed to maintain her practice of douching with quinine water after each encounter with Samuel. So far she hadn't gotten pregnant and that was one blessing she could think to be grateful for. To have a child in union with Samuel, a child conceived from the pickled juices of such small-hearted pettiness, might be Sara's end.

A small hand patted Sara's arm. "Mother, are you all right?" Five-year-old Ellen gazed into Sara's face and Sara rearranged her expression into a smile. Truthfully, it still delighted her to see her daughters in their clean, ironed dresses, with shoes on their feet and a little flesh on their frames. Samuel did hold a decent position as a merchant and so Sara's and the girls' material wants were satisfied, although niggardly. Even though he was a staunch churchgoer, every day wasn't the Sabbath, Samuel said. He always had plenty of money for drinking (strictly after working hours were over) and plenty of money for his weekly card games (a bedevilment left over from his wretched year as a widower), but when it came time for Sara to procure household items and to adequately dress and shoe four children, Samuel, who knew the prices of everything, always doled out exactly enough. Why pay two dollars a yard for fabric when it sells for a dime less on the other side of town? And so, along with her other lessons, Sara learned frugality.

"Ellen, don't bother Mother," nine-year-old Grace said. "Come back and play with us." Sara had given the girls scissors and the bright paper wrapping she'd saved from the few wedding gifts she and Samuel had received. The girls were cutting out figures they'd drawn of flowers and animals and houses and creating a little paper village in front of the kitchen fireplace. Later, they'd each play the role of themselves, walking their fingers through the village and interacting with each other and the paper forms for hours. All would be well unless someone got the idea to play funeral and then Grace's and Ellen's finger girls would try to outcry Nettie's and Clare's finger girls as they wept in the paper graveyard for dead fathers and mothers, respectively.

Sara was always tempted to settle the matter. It was worse to lose a mother. Especially in the case of Samuel's daughters. To lose a mother, no matter what she was like, and to be left in the care of the likes of Samuel was a daughter's worst fate. Nettie and Clare were eight and six. Sara did what she could for them. They each suffered their mother's loss more deeply than Grace and Ellen suffered Charly's death. It wasn't that Grace and Ellen didn't mourn their father—they did, as did Sara. It was just that Nettie and Clare had always known only the love of one parent, and when that mother died, they were left loveless and starvingly lonely.

They had each developed a different trick, a little way to try to pull comfort from their comfortless world. Nettie watched everything and everyone, as if waiting for the next calamity. It seemed she never wanted to be surprised, not even with an unexpected sweet or an undocumented hair ribbon. Order and precision ruled Nettie's young world. She chewed twenty times before swallowing, wore certain clothes on certain days of the week, and followed a prescribed routine for everything: washing her hands, collecting eggs, folding sheets. At first Sara had wanted to shock the brown-eyed, brown-haired girl into delight again, sure that once she'd tasted the pleasure of spontaneity and whimsy, she'd throw off her mantel of control and would act like a little girl should—singing made-up songs, begging snacks before dinner, bouncing through the sunshiny meadow collecting dandelions with no thought to getting a little of the sticky sap on her hands. If the other girls asked for a treat, Sara made sure to wait until Nettie recovered from the shock of the unexpected before doling out a sweet. And Sara knew that a sudden trip to the confectioner's on the way to buy potatoes and onions would agitate little Nettie more than the fun was worth to the others.

Clare, on the other hand, didn't care. She'd sunk so deeply within herself that often Sara didn't know if she was completely awake behind her listless hazel eyes or if maybe she suffered from some strange medical condition that didn't allow her full consciousness. Clare bumped and floated through her days, often not answering to her name unless it was repeated at least twice and often three times. Unlike her sister, if Samuel wasn't around, Clare would hum little tunes over and over again. She seemed to exist in her own misty world of air and fog and snippets of song. Whereas Nettie felt everything too sharply, Clare barely felt at all. Sara worried about them both, just as she still and always worried about Grace and Ellen. Sara noticed that Nettie and Clare's behavior worsened when their father came home—Nettie was often strung so tight, she'd explode into tears at the smallest grumble from her father and Clare sometimes rested the side of her face against the tabletop and stared at the candle, refusing to speak at all. When this happened, Grace and Ellen would gaze bewildered at Sara, their wild eyes begging for both explanation and protection. Sara shuddered to think her girls might develop such strange personalities living under Samuel's roof. She'd already seen Grace's eyelids twitch when Samuel would conduct what he called a questioning session of Nettie.

On days when he'd had enough to drink to make him drunk but not enough to make him drowsy, Samuel would come home sour. He'd jostle past Clare, who'd float out of his way, and he would corner Nettie against a wall or table. She'd wring her hands and search the sky for the answers she prayed would placate him, answers to questions mostly about Sara. Had Sara talked with anyone today? Were they women or men? If men, how many? Who were they? Did Sara laugh? Did she offer refreshment? Were there embraces exchanged? Smiles? Did Sara stay busy all through the day or did she loiter over a book? Did she bargain smartly at the market? Did she discipline the help? Did she spend Samuel's money on any frivolity or luxury? Think. A sweet? Lace? Glass beads?

If Nettie's answers appeased Samuel, he'd growl for Sara to bring him his beer and it went unspoken that dinner would be served before he would have swallowed the last gulp. It also went unsaid that he'd drink steadily through their oniony repast. Sara didn't mind the beer nor the dinner as much as she minded what came after dinner. She tried to stretch the meal out as long as possible, offering extras to everyone, hopping up to wipe some child's dripping mouth or spilled sauce—anything to prolong the actual finishing of her food. Samuel always waited until she'd finished eating. He seemed to enjoy that. Sara would cut and bite and chew like an invalid, which is sometimes what she felt like. She knew she was helpless, anyway. Completely at the mercy of Samuel P. Farrington and his beer-and-onion fevers. His alcohol-clouded eyes would ravage her from their place across the table, becoming more hazed and more calculated with each sip and each precise bite Sara took. It was a delicate balance, Sara knew, to stretch dinner just long enough to ensure Samuel was drunk, but not long enough that he was wickedly so.

When Sara finally laid her flatware across her plate and folded her napkin, a thin-lipped smile would slide across Samuel's face. He slurped whatever was remaining in his glass and rose. All four girls scattered to the parlor or out of doors, Sara was never sure where. Sara always tried to steer Samuel toward their bedroom but often his molestation began right there in the dining room. Sometimes he ripped her dress in his haste to get it off of her. Often he'd just lift it over her head and pull apart her undergarments. Sara was never sure if she should help with buttons or let his clumsy fingers attempt them. Sometimes his frustration would make him brutal, other times it seemed to delight him. Sara had developed her own trick of comfort. She'd try to make herself float up up up, out of her body, past the ceiling, past the roof, to a special safe place where Charly waited for her. There, in that lofty place that could be forest or parlor or carriage, and which often smelled of ferns and sometimes smelled of roses, her wonderful Charly would gently hold her and stroke her hair and murmur words of love and encouragement.

Sara straightened up over the bowl of onions and retrieved the knife from the pungent pile. "Grace is right," Sara told little Ellen. "Run now and play with your sisters. Mother's fine."

Ellen glanced cautiously first at her mother and then at the other girls before wrapping her small arms around Sara's waist and squeezing with all of her childish might. Sara patted her daughter's head with one oniony hand, then kissed her. "Run and play."

As Ellen bounced off, the back door slammed open. Five heads snapped to attention as each became aware that Samuel P. Farrington stood, at the unusual hour of eleven o'clock, in the kitchen doorway. Nobody moved as he surveyed the room—his wife bent over a bowl, peeling an onion for all she was worth, the four children frozen in front of a too-bright blaze, caught creating a mess with paper and scissors.

A smile played at the corner of Samuel's lips. He was completely sober. "Is this what happens when I'm gone?" he said to Sara. "I thought you said mornings were devoted to bible study and sewing."

"We've already finished," Sara said.

"How can one ever finish the sewing, or the Bible?"

"You're right. One can't. But only for today, I decided to let the girls play out a bible story so I could be sure of an extra-nice dinner tonight."

"You *decided*," Samuel said, holding up his hand to silence any retort from Sara. "Nettie, is that true? Were you playing out a bible story with that clutter over there?"

Nettie was sitting close to Grace and the two girls were squeezing hands. Nettie cast her eyes wildly to the ceiling. "Yes, Father," she said.

Sara's stomach twisted.

Samuel cocked his head and approached his daughter. "Really?"

"Yes, sir," Nettie said, squeezing Grace's fingers with both hands.

"And what story were you playing?" he asked.

Nettie glanced down at the cut-out figures of animals and people. "Noah, sir."

"Nice. Noah," Samuel said, squatting down to look into Nettie's darting eyes. "And will you show me the ark?"

"We haven't cut it yet, sir," Grace offered. "We're pretending that part."

Samuel turned his gaze to Grace. "Well, which is it?" he said. "You haven't cut it yet or you're pretending the part?"

"Samuel, leave the children," Sara said, and as soon as she spoke she wished she had swallowed her words instead.

Samuel's smile turned hard and he picked up a handful of the paper figures. "And I suppose there are flowers on board the ship," he said, dropping a cut-out blossom into the fireplace flame.

Grace stammered, "Those are—"

"I'm not speaking to *you*," Samuel bellowed.

"Samuel!" Sara said.

He turned toward her with raised eyebrows.

Sara dropped her eyes. "Please come and have a cup of tea with me in the parlor. I want to hear why you're home so soon."

Samuel gathered all of the paper figures, and fed them, one by one, into the fireplace. "I've come home early because it's our wedding anniversary."

Nettie and Grace clenched each others' fingers.

"I wanted to surprise my wife and daughters."

The paper figures caught fire quickly, curling into flame and then floating up like smoldering stars.

"And it seems I have."

Ellen had slinked her way back to Sara and held a handful of her mother's skirt.

"I've found my wife catching up on duties she should have finished hours ago."

Each blazing figure puffed a smoky soul up the chimney, before being followed by corporeal ash.

"I've found my children's education ridiculed."

Clare had long since rested her head on her knees and slowly rocked herself.

"And I've witnessed my eldest child's first lie!"

Nettie shrieked as Samuel's hand came down on her head.

"Samuel! No!" Sara rushed to Nettie's side. "She was only trying . . ."

Samuel wrenched Nettie from Sara's embrace and flung her aside. "Out!" he shouted to the children, pointing to the door leading outside. "Every one of you!"

"Samuel!" Sara said. "It's freezing out!"

"Yes, run, run, it's good exercise," Samuel called out the door at the fleeing figures.

"Run to the Winston's," Sara called in a pinched voice. "Go play with Rose and Thomas."

Samuel pulled Sara roughly back into the kitchen.

"They'll play with Rose and Thomas," she said softly.

Samuel steered Sara to the kitchen table and pushed her into the chair in front of the bowl of onions. "Of course they'll play with Rose and Thomas. They're just children, after all. Children with big imaginations and willful souls."

Sara picked up the half-cut onion. "They'll play . . ."

"Like you, my dear," Samuel continued, standing behind her, sliding his hands up and down her arms. "Sometimes I think of you as a great big child in need of correction."

". . . with Rose and Thomas."

He gripped her arms. "Point number one. Don't you ever counter me again. Especially in front of the children."

Sara jumped when a too-green log in the grate popped loud and scattered the hearth with a shower of embers.

Samuel narrowed his eyes. He'd teach her to jump from his caress. He pulled Sara out of her chair and flung her to the wood floor. Sara's head cracked hard against the table's leg. He'd teach her.

Through a swimming consciousness, Sara heard Samuel explaining other rules. Rules number three and four. The legs of the table were scuffed at the bottom. What had happened to rule number two? The comb at the back of her hair dug into her scalp. He lay on her, his hands maliciously squeezing. She had lost an important rule and she worried she'd have a hard time obeying it. She wanted to explain that she hadn't meant to jump, that she jumped from the sudden popping of the fire, but it was hard to talk, hard to think. His hands were around her neck. It was hard to breathe. He'd teach her many things. Rule number three. What was rule number three? His hands were ripping away her clothes. He'd teach her how to be a wife. No, they weren't his hands; he was using the scissors. A good wife. A wife he could be proud of. There was a loud snip near her ear and she saw a handful of golden hair dangle before her eyes. She couldn't remember rule number two. He'd teach her to flaunt her beauty. Rule number four: never ever ever. The smell of burning hair permeated the kitchen. Small popping sounds came from the hearth. All day long and whenever there was company she displayed her nimble tongue too freely. Please, please, Samuel. He lay on her, pumping painfully. Teasing men and boys alike with those frank eyes, that bold tongue. Her skirt lay smoldering in the flames, the ribbon and muslin steaming. Something sharp stabbed her side. Never cry out, you wench. Rulenumbertwo. Rulenumbertwo? Rulenumbertwo. He'd strip her naked if that's all she wanted. See how easy. The table legs were scratched. Had she used her nails? He'd see to it she never had a stitch on. Her corset was on top of the skirt. In the fire. Far away. What was she learning? Speak, dammit! Samuel balled wads of Sara's dress sleeves and tossed them into the smoldering pile. He'd teach her to appreciate how fine she had it. How he'd saved her from death's door, cared for her as dutifully as expected. And for what? To be ridiculed in public. Rules are meant to be followed. Rules must be remembered. What *are* the rules? The table legs needed polish, maybe sanding. To lose face in his home. Everywhere people jeered. He'd lost control of this second wife. He'd lost his hand in things. A sudden draft. Gooseflesh. The clothes whooshed into a blaze that threatened to tumble onto the hearth. Rule number one, in front of the children. A snip by Sara's other ear and another golden handful swung from Samuel's grip. *No simpering.* In front of the children. Rule number two? He tossed the hair into the fire and Sara smelled it melt, smelled herself melting, liquefying right there on the kitchen floor. Something wet ran down her forehead, down her leg, down her side. He knew she didn't love him. Did she think him an imbecile? The flames were roaring hot. The question, then, was who she *did* love. There had to be someone. Speak! Sara smelled her fear and the children's fear, Nettie, Grace, Clare, Ellen. He would get it out of her, or out of the children. *Her* children! Ellen and Grace.

"They're my children, too!" Sara cried.

Samuel's trousers were wrapped around his ankles, his wrinkled shirt was full of soot and dark stains. He was off of her (when had that happened?), out of her, standing in front of the kitchen fireplace, poking at Sara's ravaged clothing, mumbling and cursing. At Sara's words, Samuel turned, dropped the scissors he was holding with a clatter to the kitchen floor, and burst into rolling laughter. Her clothes continued to blaze in the fireplace behind him as Samuel laughed and laughed and laughed.

Sara was suddenly cold, lying on the kitchen floor. Cold but thinking clearly. She had just made another mistake, she knew, but she wouldn't change her words even if she could. She pulled herself to a sitting position and wrapped her arms around her bare legs.

"Look at you," Samuel said, still chuckling. "You are starting to look like Clare, a disheveled heap on your own kitchen floor. What sort of mother keeps herself this way?"

Sara's head ached with every movement, yet she pulled herself up by the table leg to a standing position. "They're my children, too."

Samuel's jaw tightened. "Oh? Did you give birth, then, to Nettie and Clare?"

"Of course not," Sara said. "But I certainly birthed my own."

Samuel raised his eyebrows. "And such a fit mother you are," he said. "Everyone can see that. Sally Ann is going to walk in here and see that you've stripped yourself naked, flung your clothes into the fire, cut your hair and sent your children out to the elements."

"Sally Ann will see exactly what's happened."

Samuel took three strides and clenched Sara's chin in his hand. "Sally Ann will remember her master's strict working hours. Sally Ann will add her lowly testimony to mine committing you to the asylum if you continue on as you are. Then what will become of your orphaned daughters?"

Sara shivered. The asylum! Rules and numbers and one, three, four. Sara was suddenly so cold her teeth chattered.

And then Samuel was stuffing chopped onions into her clattering mouth. "Bite down on those. That'll clear your head. Make you think."

But Sara's vision was swimming again. The asylum! "Samuel no," she mumbled, through a mouth of onions. "Samuel no Samuel no no please."

And his arms were suddenly around her and he fished his fingers into her mouth to scoop out the onions. "Why you are a woman after all, my love," he said. "There *is* hope."

Sara nodded her head, coughing out onion juice.

"Such humility is very becoming."

Sara shook her head wildly. "No Samuel no no."

"Shhh," he croaked into her ear. "I won't send you away. Who would tend to the children?"

"The children."

"Who would see to it that dinner is made properly?"

Sara shuddered in the cold air, despite the blaze of clothing in the fireplace.

"Now you see," Samuel said. He ushered his shivering wife out of the kitchen and into their bedroom on their first wedding anniversary. "There's hope for us, yet." He sat her upon the bed, their marital bed, and covered her shoulders gently with a blanket as he explained everything. He'd so happily take care of them all. Couldn't she see? He didn't want to play the role of the disciplinarian, the ogre, but she was so unruly. She had to see at least *that*, couldn't she? Even her father called her a handful. She must know that. Everyone did. Her brother had also warned him. Nat, of course. Samuel had had nothing but warnings, really. But he was not discouraged. He was up for the task. He was man enough, he knew, to corral Sara's wicked soul. Was she woman enough to allow it? Did she think she could change? All he wanted was womanly love and respect. All he wanted was the simplest of things. His dinner. His beer. His wife's love. Piety. Reverence. Dutiful, graceful compliance. Was that too much to ask? Was it now? With all he'd given her and her daughters? With the trust he gave her regarding his home, his girls, Sally Ann? Couldn't she find it in herself to follow the rules, to try to be good?

Sara felt warmer with the blanket wrapped around her shoulders and Samuel's voice smooth and calm in her ear, yet she knew she could no more try to be *good*, if that's what Samuel called it, than try to be an elephant. She'd struggled her whole life to fit some mold of purity she just didn't fit, and what's more, was happy not fitting. Some people had thought she was fine just as she was—Mother, Miss Beecher, Charly. She raised her eyes to Samuel's smiling face.

"What do you think, my Sara," he said. "Shall we put an end to this quarrel?"

Sara blinked and a tear slipped down her cheek. "Samuel, I'm afraid I . . ."

Samuel stiffened. His eyes glinted like steel and his smile hardened on his face. "Have it your way, then," he said. "It's back to the boardinghouse with you."

Chapter Nine

Sara Payson Willis Eldredge Farrington and Harriet Jacobs, Boston, Friday, January 10th, 1851

I hereby forbid all persons harboring or trusting my wife, Sarah P. Farrington, on my account, from this date, having made suitable provision for her support.

—Samuel P. Farrington,
notice in the *Boston Daily Bee*, February 25th, 1851

Perhaps you ask would I have a woman, for every trifling cause, "leave her husband and family?" Most emphatically, No. But there are aggravated cases for which the law provides no remedy—from which it affords no protection; and that hundreds of suffering women bear their chains because they have not courage to face a scandal-loving world, to whom it matters not a pin that their every nerve is quivering with suppressed agony, is no proof to the contrary of what I assert. What I say is this: in such cases, let a woman who has the self-sustaining power quietly take her fate in her own hands, and right herself. Of course she will be misjudged and abused. It is for her to choose whether she can better bear this at hands from which she has a rightful claim for love and protection, or from a nine-days-wonder-loving public. These are bold words; but they are needed word—words whose full import I have well considered, and from the responsibility of which I do not shrink.

—Fanny Fern, *New York Ledger*, October 24th, 1857

"Hatty, you've come," Sara said as she opened the door of her boardinghouse room early one afternoon to her old friend, Harriet Jacobs, and Harriet's daughter, Louisa, who'd recently bloomed into a young woman. "I wondered if you would."

Louisa ran directly to reacquaint herself with Grace and little Ellen. Hatty and Sara held each other in a long, swaying embrace. When they finally pulled back, Hatty was stunned by the changes she saw in Nat's sister. Sara was pale and thin and had the remains of an old bruise on her jaw. Her eyes were red-rimmed and puffy and her hands shook as she closed the door. Her shoulders were stooped like an old woman's underneath her drab, cheap dress and the blue veins near her temples pulsed visibly.

Hatty had first met Sara back when Mary Stace was still alive, bless her soul, and Hatty worked for Mary Stace and Nat in their fancy New York brownstone. Sara was bright and bouncy and had proven to be as warm and accepting to the runaway slave as Mary Stace was. Naturally, Hatty was careful who she told her story to. Her master still combed the country in search of her and Louisa. But Hatty knew she could trust Sara, as she had trusted Mary Stace. And even though it had been sixteen years since Hatty had been under her master's power, she still didn't feel free. She'd first spent seven years hiding out in her grandmother's attic, a stranger to even her own two children, waiting for her owner to lose interest in recovering her so she could make her way north more safely. But that day never came; he was obsessed with reclaiming her. Eventually she was able to flee, with her children in tow, and had played fox and goose with that wretched piece of humanity who claimed to own her for the past nine years. She'd come north and supported herself and her two children. She worked quietly these nine years, fearfully, as a seamstress, a nursemaid, cook, and as general help to good women like Mary Stace, rotating around New England, never staying too long in one place.

After Mary Stace's death, Nat had hired her to take care of Imogen. He was lucky Sara was so willing to help him at first, because it took him three months to find Hatty, again—her tracks were that well covered. Still, it shook Hatty that anyone could find her at all and she worried that if it only took Nat a few months, how long would it be before her disgusting old master came knocking on her door to claim his rights with her, as he called the way he had treated her since she'd been thirteen. Now Nat was planning on taking her to England again in a few weeks to help out with Imogen. Hatty was glad to go, mostly to avoid the panic this new Fugitive Slave Act was causing. It was hard to know who to trust anymore. The North was no longer the safe place it used to be. Hatty could be returned down south any day and her beautiful Louisa could be subjected to the defilement that slaves of her beauty could always expect.

Hatty's stomach squeezed in on itself when she thought of her old master's dry hands on her child's body, as they'd been on her own body as a child younger than Louisa. Hatty had suffered such ill-usage at those dry hands her body had become numb. She'd walk days before realizing she had a blister, would drink down hot soup that everyone else blew on. And now, from the little she could piece together of her meeting with Sara the day before, she understood that it could be the same for white women. That someone as capable as Sara could be in the same predicament as a slave stunned Hatty. White men didn't only misuse black women, but also misused white women, even their own wives. *Some* white men. Hatty must be ever careful of too broad a categorization. Still, Hatty had a sudden new sympathy for her former Southern mistress, who would often order her around cruelly and, then, would suffer bitterly of headaches and vomiting. The woman was likely as unhappy as Hatty had been! Who knew what sort of treatment her mistress had had to face? Social class didn't necessarily protect a woman from a man's dry hands. It didn't protect a woman from a man's brutal embrace or razor tongue.

Hatty touched Sara's bruised face.

Sara flinched.

"Poor dear," Hatty said, and Sara's eyes instantly brimmed.

"When I saw you and Mr. Farrington on the steps the other evening, with him pushing you ahead of him and calling you those base names like he was," Hatty said.

"Never mind that," Sara whispered, casting an eye on the girls chatting on the bed. "Oh, Hatty, that's not the worst of it!"

Hatty's stomach twisted again. She was afraid to hear any more in front of the girls. She hurried to Louisa and gave her hand a meaningful squeeze, then told the girls that she and Sara were going to go out for air and would be back shortly. Louisa nodded. She'd be in charge. Hatty flung Sara's shawl over Sara's shoulders, scooped her bonnet from the nail by the door, and pulled her out into the hall. "Those girls shouldn't hear whatever it is you've got to tell," Hatty said.

"You're right," Sara said. "Though mine have *seen* it. What could be worse?"

"Louisa, too, when she was little," Hatty said. "And Henry. Thank God he's finally safe in Canada. But the less memory of those days, the better. Come, now."

Hatty tied Sara's bonnet under her chin, placed her own gloves on her friend's hands, and steered her down the stairs and out the front door of the boardinghouse. The weather was unusually warm for January, in the high thirties and with no wind. The bright sun made the day feel even warmer, so it would be a fine day for a walk, despite whatever difficult topic Hatty knew Sara had to discuss. "Tell me," Hatty said as the two women descended the three steps to the Boston street.

Sara told Hatty how she'd felt pressured to marry Samuel, even though she didn't love him, even though she told him she didn't love him. That had been her first mistake—being honest.

"Men don't like knowing something like that," Hatty agreed. "If the world doesn't revolve around them, at least they have to believe it does."

"Not Charly," Sara said.

"No, not Charly," Hatty agreed. "But he was always the exception."

Sara burst out crying when Hatty said that, about Charly being the exception, and they had to sit on a little iron bench in front of the hat maker's shop for a few minutes until Sara could compose herself again. Sara told Hatty how this happens to her all the time now, this crying.

"So unlike the Sara I always knew," Hatty said.

Sara nodded. "Now I cry," she said, suddenly studying the milliner's sign next to them, "at the drop of a hat."

Hatty squeezed Sara's hands and the women smiled together.

"Oh, Sara," Hatty said. "You're in there somewhere after all."

"Hatty, I swear that's the first little joke I've made in two years."

Hatty's face grew serious again and she slowly shook her head. "I think you and I have more in common than we ever could have predicted."

Sara's eyes brimmed again.

"Go slow," Hatty said. "Tell me what you can. Believe me, it'll hurt all over again, but it'll feel better after. I've got all day and Louisa's got the girls. When you expecting *him*?"

"After supper."

"We've got the afternoon then."

Sara decided she felt well enough to walk again and so they did. Sara and Hatty walked up and down the streets—the busy ones and the pokey ones. They walked slowly, swinging their skirts in rhythm, arms linked, looking mostly straight ahead so as not to arouse curiosity. Hatty listened and murmured poor dear and lord, no. Sara talked. She told how she never consented to marry Samuel. She had vacillated so long that finally someone—she had never quite figured out if it was Father or Samuel—just put a marriage announcement in the paper. Well, of course, after that, she *had* to marry him, cruel hoax or not. What else could be done? Sara submitted. She told Hatty about the hope she courted early on that maybe she would fall in love again and have another Swissdale mirage of a life. She'd dreamed of raising four lovely daughters in a home brimming with laughter and love. She'd imagined Samuel and her piecing together the bits of their broken hearts to form stronger ones, hearts immune to further damage. She'd never guessed that married life to a wealthy merchant could actually be worse than nearly starving as a seamstress. She'd never foreseen that there were worse ills for a child than cold fingers and toes.

Sara told how she had learned to handicap herself, to turn down her smile, to wrap cotton around her wit, and to shrink her thoughts to better fit Samuel's ideas. At first, things went better for her when she'd float silently by his side at gatherings, when she'd nod approvingly when he'd speak about his obvious purchasing bungles, when she'd fix her eyes on the water stain on the ceiling over the bed and imagine it was Charly's face smiling down on her. But sometimes, she just couldn't keep herself shrouded. She'd laugh at some gentleman's joke or would banter with Sally Ann or would sing slap-hand songs with the girls, and then Samuel would raise his eyebrows and the sooner Sara shrunk again, the better.

After a while, though, it was not enough for Sara to be diminished. It seemed Samuel would only be happy if she became invisible. He had started hitting her about a year before.

"I knew," Hatty said, sliding her fingertip gently along Sara's jaw.

Sara bit her lip.

"Don't take that into you," Hatty said. "That's proof of *his* shame, not yours."

"I know it," Sara said. "But it's getting harder."

"You've got to hide. That's what I did. Even my grandmother's attic wasn't much worse than this place he's got you holed up in. Why you living here?"

Sara explained how Samuel had moved her and Grace and Ellen back to the boardinghouse last year. No water. No coal. Very little food. She told Hatty about the day of their first wedding anniversary when he'd knocked her down and stuffed her mouth with onions and stripped her clothes off and burned them. She told how he'd raped her. She told how he'd chased the children out of doors in the freezing weather and how later she'd found out they'd hunkered together in the chicken coop to stay warm, too embarrassed to run down the road to the Winston's. She told how Samuel seemed sorry, at first, to have mistreated her and actually was softer and kindly for a month or so after that day. But then he'd struck her again one evening after they'd come home from a party. Samuel had been drinking, as usual, and had it in his head that she was in love with their neighbor, Joshua Winston, because she'd asked him about his sick mother and had offered to send over some fresh eggs the next morning. Sara told how Samuel had dragged her out to the yard to watch him break apart the chicken coop, scattering the hens and smashing the eggs. He sent Sara and the girls to the boardinghouse the next day, supposedly to keep Sara from the arms of Mr. Winston.

"Did you and Mr. Winston?"

"Of course not," Sara said. "Mr. Winston is a hundred years old if he's a day. He was a listening ear, though. A gentle heart to hear my grief."

Hatty patted Sara's arm. "I know how a body needs that. And you've been here a year?"

"Almost. Samuel comes round every night and . . . well." Sara shuddered.

"I don't have to hear no more."

"I send the girls downstairs," Sara said. "Often he doesn't say a single word to me, Hatty! He just sates his appetite, throws a dollar or two on the table, and leaves. I worry about Nettie and Clare. I wonder . . ."

"Oh, precious. You can't afford to worry about them girls now!" Hatty said. "You've got to save yourself and yours. Has he touched your girls?"

Sara startled. "No!"

"Don't be surprised if they're not next."

Sara blanched. "He's threatened me with the asylum again," she said. "Lately. And more often. Who would look out for the girls if I were gone?"

"The asylum?! Heaven help you if you go in there! Heaven help the girls."

Sara's eyes darted up and down the street. "I know, Hatty. I knew one woman, a friend of mine, Diana, with the most gorgeous sapphire-blue eyes. She couldn't bear children and became more and more despondent about it until one day her husband decided she needed to be committed. Had lost her mind to worry, he said, but everyone knew she was sick with nerves trying to please a displeased man. He was married to a plump young thing within a month. And didn't the new one have a child not six months later."

"And the woman?"

"Diana? I went to see her once, after she'd been there only a few weeks. Oh, Hatty, she wasn't crazy when they put her in. She wasn't. But she *became* so. It's the place that does it. They put chains on your ankles and bars on the windows and who knows what."

"You can't go there. You wouldn't survive! What about your brother?"

Sara snorted. "Nat? He won't help. He won't listen to a word I say. He and father both say I'm finally getting the correction I've always needed."

"If Mary Stace were alive . . ."

"But she isn't," Sara said sternly. "She isn't, Hatty! And neither is Mother nor Charly nor sister Ellen. I haven't a friend in the world it seems . . . except for you."

Hatty squeezed Sara's arm. "Oh, Sara, you've always been a friend to *me*. All those years helping me find work, helping me move and hide and raise my children. Now I've got to help you. We've got to find you a place to hide!"

"I can't hide, Hatty," Sara said. "It won't work that way for me. Everyone knows me. I can't become invisible."

Hatty stopped walking and folded her chin against her chest. "I guess you can't."

"But I'll tell you what I am going to do," Sara said with a tiny smile. She pointed to a little café they were passing. "Come, let's stop for a cup of tea. I'm getting chilled and you need to be sitting to hear what I've got to tell you."

The two women bustled into the café, ordered black tea, no pastries, and sat at a little table near the back. "I'm leaving him," Sara said, shortly after the tea arrived. She sipped her scalding tea and nodded once. "I am."

Hatty gasped. "How?"

"Everyone will know. It'll be awful. Who knows what he'll say. But I'm leaving him. I've decided. Tomorrow."

Hatty squeezed her eyes. She cringed thinking of the public scandal Sara had ahead of her. A woman just couldn't up and leave her husband. Not if she wanted to lift her head again. Not if she wanted to eat. Marriage vows weren't to be broken or even stretched, especially by a woman. Sometimes if men had good cause, they were known to divorce a drunken or fallen wife (and he was the one who decided about both), but a woman had no means of support, and once married, no claim to a family's protection. She was her husband's, for better or worse, and her lot reflected her spiritual character. If a woman couldn't make her husband happy, couldn't be content with the family God had chosen for her, then she was lacking in more than earthly happiness. She lacked morality, virtue, and a woman's true spirit. Hatty knew the judgment would come down squarely in favor of Samuel if Sara left him and Sara would be hard pressed to work even as a seamstress.

"Have you thought this through?" Hatty said. "How will you live?"

Sara pulled a black velvet purse from her pocket. It was stuffed with coins and wads of bills. "I've got this. Fifty-four dollars and eleven cents. I've saved it over these last two years, and when that's gone, I can sell my wedding ring."

"But even living small, that's not going to last you and the girls half a year!"

"It'll be better than this, Hatty! Anything would be. And it'll give me time to find employment and a place to live . . ."

"I wish I had a place for you. You know Louisa and I are leaving with Nat next week for England. Maybe you could come with us?"

Sara pressed her lips together. "I've already asked Nat. He said he'd have nothing to do with helping me if I left my husband."

Hatty's mouth dropped open. "And him bragging about helping that actor's wife?"

Sara's eyes brimmed and she bowed her head. "Exactly," she whispered.

For the past month, Nat had been widely written about in the newspapers for his chivalrous defense of actor Edwin Forrest's slandered wife. Apparently Forrest wished to divorce her and fabricated adultery claims to gain the necessary grounds. Forrest's method wasn't unheard of, but the defense of his wife by someone other than a blood relative was. As a prominent New York City poet and editor, Nat's actions rocked the society pages.

"I wonder what the papers would say if they knew what he said to his *sister*. If they knew how he constantly chided me to take my womanly medicine with a grin," Sara said.

"Nobody should have to suffer so," Hatty said.

"Not actor's wife nor merchant's," Sara said.

"Nor slave," Hatty added.

Sara sighed. "Amen to that, my dear Hatty."

Hatty patted Sara's hand. "There's hope, though, always hope!"

"That's what Mother would say," Sara said.

"Listen to what I'm going to do," Hatty said. "I've been talking to some of those abolitionists and to hear them talk, you'd think what I did by hiding and escaping and darting here and there to protect my children makes me some kind of hero."

"It takes the courage that most people can't possess."

Hatty shook her head. "I don't believe it! Everyone's got the same courage deep down if they just look. It's courage based on love for my children and love for my dignity. You can't say the Lord would want my little suffering in this big ol' world."

Sara sat straighter in her chair.

"The abolitionists think I'm on to something. That I could help people stir up the courage they've got hidden deep down."

"I believe they're right!" Sara said.

"Listen, Sara. I'm going to write a book! A *book*, Sara. About my time in slavery and hiding and running all these years."

"Hatty, how proud I am of you!"

"It'll take some time, I believe. And I'm going to need a heap of help, but they say my story can aid the cause. They say my one voice can help."

Sara smiled gently at her friend and Hatty smiled back.

"And that said, I think it's a fine idea, your leaving Mr. Farrington," Hatty said. "If I can write a book, you can leave a husband. You're Sara Willis! You'll find a way out!"

Sara smiled and took a sip of tea. "You're right, Hatty. There's got to be a way."

Chapter Ten

Grace Eldredge, Newton, Massachusetts, Wednesday, February 19th, 1851

[Christian Charity.] Don't you believe it! They would run from you, as if you had the plague. "Write your brow" with anything but your "troubles," if you do not wish to be left solus. You have no idea how "good people" will pity you when you tell your doleful ditty! They will "pray for you," give advice by the bushel, "feel for you"—everywhere but in their pocketbooks; and wind up by telling you to "trust in Providence"; to all of which you feel very much like replying as the old lady did when she found herself spinning down hill in a wagon, "I trusted in Providence till the tackling broke!" . . . Now listen to me;—just go to work and hew out a path for yourself; get your head above water, and then snap your fingers in their pharisaical faces! Never ask a favor until you are drawing your last breath; and never forget one.

—Fanny Fern, *Fern Leaves from Fanny's Portfolio*

It was cold out. Bitter cold. The air was so dry it sucked the vapor from one's lungs and whirled it skyward only to come back again, that afternoon or evening, in the form of a few more brittle flakes of white. The snow crunched beneath almost-ten-year-old Grace's boots as she and Mother and Nelly (Grace's new nickname for her sister) walked the narrow path to the Eldredges' front door. Grace had on all of her clothes—her underthings, two dresses, two pairs of stockings, her cloak, two hats, and her gloves, yet she was still cold. She hoped there'd be a roaring fire inside the large stone house they walked up to. And she hoped there'd be tea.

Papa and Nana had called a family meeting at this, their new country house, Mother said. Grace knew that Papa Willis would also be inside because she'd seen his smart carriage and his fine horses (with polished bells hanging from their jaunty necks) pass by the train station as they were calling for a ride. Grace asked her mother why Papa Willis didn't drive them and mother said that he must not have seen them. Other people had not seen them lately either. Mother's sisters on the other side of the street, father's jovial business partner, old friends from their days at Swissdale. So many people walking with their heads down. It was a puzzle.

Mother had left Mr. Farrington and for that Grace was thankful. Mr. Farrington frightened her. He had a pungent cloud around him that made Grace breathe through her mouth. A fume, fetid, like the smell that covered the yard when they made soap or that floated out of some taverns on Saturdays. Another thing about Mr. Farrington was that he was always watching. He looked at Grace with eyes the color of flint. Grace felt that if something would scratch those eyes, say a fingernail or a knife, a spark would start and Mr. Farrington's fumes would make him burst into flames. She worried that she had these thoughts and at first prayed to be able to love her stepfather. But when Grace saw that Mother couldn't even love him—and this she could tell by the way Mother searched the tabletop for answers to Mr. Farrington's questions, the way she'd bustle Grace and the other girls through every imaginable task when *he* was around, but would close her eyes and draw heavy sighs when the door would close behind him—then Grace decided that it might be all right if she couldn't love Mr. Farrington either.

They were living in a boardinghouse again. The worst one yet. In Cambridge. Not even Boston. They weren't even allowed downstairs for dinner. Mother broke up pieces of bread into little bowls of milk, instead. Grace loved bread and milk, but she was getting tired of having it every day. Her feet went crunch crunch crunch in the snow. It sounded like teeth chewing carrots. Or apples. Even rutabaga. Did she smell roasting meat? Potatoes? Grace's stomach growled as Papa and Nana Eldredge opened their front door. Nana took their cloaks and hats and frowned when she saw Grace's two dresses. "It's awfully cold out, Ma'am," Grace said in explanation. Mother kissed Grace's cheek and took both girls by the hand and led them to the parlor.

There were meat sandwiches on a tray and a bowl of cut fruit on a heavy carved table by the roaring fire where Papa Willis and Papa Eldredge were already sitting and eating. Papa Willis had his boots off and was stretching his toes toward the flames. "Mother!" Nelly said aloud, and mother murmured something to her and squeezed Grace's hand. Grace knew Nelly wanted a sandwich and Mother was telling her to be polite and wait until one was offered.

A maid came in with some straight-backed chairs that Grace and Nelly and Mother were to sit on. Nana spoke to Mother and soon Grace was settled on her chair, not near enough to the fire as she'd like, but with a heaping plate of food balanced on her lap and a hot cup of tea on the little table by her side. She felt like a queen. To have such a scrumptious meal served by a real maid in front of a fire that must have cost a fortune! The rug on the floor was thick beneath Grace's boots and the chair she sat on was sturdier than many she'd balanced on lately. It was the most pleasant visit to Nana's and Papa's yet.

Grace sneaked a look at little Nelly's face, sure she'd see rapture. There it was. Nelly had a huge bite of beef sandwich in her little mouth and was chewing it like it was so much butter toffee. Nelly was like an open book, Mother always said, not like Grace who'd developed a womanly smile, a smile mother said sometimes hid her true emotions. Mother would stroke Grace's hair when she'd say such things and would give her an extra long hug. Grace didn't like adding to her mother's worry. She started glancing at herself whenever she passed by looking glasses or large expanses of windows and was surprised to see the corners of her lips perpetually pinned up, like handkerchiefs on a line. Grace thought it strange that her mouth did this, whether she was feeling happy or not. That must be the womanly smile. It must be a smile that is pinned on.

As she chewed her own beef sandwich and savored bites of canned berries and pears, Grace knew her smile was real. Mother was eating, too, but was listening to Papa Willis and Papa Eldredge with that stern wrinkle between her eyebrows. They were talking about money again, a subject that both worried and bored Grace to tears. Every pleasant time could be spoiled by talking about money, by thinking about money, by Mother taking out her little velvet pouch and counting, counting, counting her money. Mother had been sewing again, plying her needle day and night. That left Grace to manage Nelly a good deal more than she cared to. Sometimes, when the weather allowed, they'd walk to the square and back to get some air. Sometimes Aunt Julia would visit with a little sweet or some folding paper to play with. Often, though, Grace and Nelly would only have each other, which was mostly enough, not counting the times Grace wished she were in school with the friends she'd made while living at Mr. Farrington's house.

Papa Willis and Papa Eldredge showed papers to Mother, papers that made her angry. No womanly smile for her mother, that was certain! When her mother was upset, everyone knew about it. And something in these papers made her furious. Nana Eldredge smiled at Nelly as Nelly gobbled down her plate. Someone will have to learn her manners, Nana said, which made Mother even angrier. Nana smiled at Grace, too, and Grace was aware that her pinned-on smile smiled back. It made her wonder if Nana's smile was a womanly smile or if she was really happy they'd come to visit this time. Mother threw the papers into the fire, which made Papa Willis shake his head severely. He'd have nothing to do with her, he said. She was incorrigible and unruly and he was finished finished finished.

Mother didn't seem to care if Papa Willis was angry. She was the angriest of them all. She went through the door to get their cloaks and Nana Eldredge jumped up to follow her, pulling on her fingers like she was struggling out of imaginary gloves. Grace could hear them talking in the kitchen, Nana's steady monotone and Mother's yelps of emotion. Was she still angry or did she sound afraid? Grace felt the corners of her mouth with her fingers and found the corners turned up. This was a serious situation. She shouldn't be smiling. Grace rubbed her lips until they relaxed into a straight line like Nelly's. Papa Eldredge stared into the fire, his head cocked toward the voices from the kitchen. Nelly and Grace each took a biscuit from the tray and ate it with their tea. Then Nelly sauntered back to the heavy carved table, crinkled her eyes at Grace and swiped two more biscuits and hid them in her pocket. Grace burned her eyes into her sister. What would Mother say?

Mother and Nana finally came out of the kitchen. Nana was smiling proudly. Mother's eyes were red and puffy, a sure sign she'd been weeping. Grace felt her lips turn up in response—poor mother! Nana went to Nelly and was dressing her and prattling on. Nelly had a big smile on her face and Grace knew it was because she was proud she'd taken the biscuits. Mother took Grace's hand, softly, tenderly, and led her into the kitchen where a low fire smoldered and a single lamp glowed from a corner table. Mother sat Grace in a chair, a chair much like the one she'd sat upon in the parlor, and knelt before her. Mother told Grace that she was to stay with Papa and Nana Eldredge for a little while. She couldn't afford to pay for them all anymore and little Nelly was too young to be alone. Grace thought she was too young, too, but mother told her she was a big girl now, big enough to remember all the things she'd been taught. Big enough to be alone for a little while so mother could earn enough money for all three of them.

Grace asked how long a little while was and Mother started to cry. She said she didn't know but would be back to visit often. *Visit!* Grace didn't want her mother to visit. She wanted to live with her mother. But she was going to live here, like a brave girl, with Papa and Nana. She wasn't going to live with her mother anymore? No, no, Mother said. It is only for a little while. You'll be staying here, but you'll always live with me, she said, in spirit. Grace's smile dissolved. It was turned completely down and she and Mother both started to cry. Give me your hands, Mother said, and when Grace offered her hands up, Mother held them to her own heart and said this is where you live—in my heart as I live in yours. As your Papa lives there and sister Mary and Nana Hannah. Grace's tears streamed down her cheeks. She didn't want to live in her mother's heart. She wanted to live in her house!

My darling, my darling, my darling, Mother said over and over again as she held Grace close and kissed her and stroked her hair. I promise you a thousand times that I will visit you every chance I can and that I will work so hard to get enough money so we can all be together. When, Mother, when, when, when? Soon. Grace didn't like the sound of that word—soon. It sounded like *never* to Grace and right then and there, in Nana Eldredge's kitchen, Grace felt a strange flutter in her chest. It was as if she had somehow swallowed a tiny bird and it was trapped. Maybe it was a bluebird. Mother always said bluebirds portended happy days. Grace hoped it was a bluebird.

Papa Willis came into the kitchen holding Nelly's hand. Nelly had on her cloak and hat and stared at Grace with her mouth open. Papa Willis pulled sobbing mother away from Grace and steered her toward the door. Nana Eldredge fastened Mother's cloak on her and placed her bonnet crookedly on her head. Mother's hair stuck out of her bonnet on one side and Grace felt the bird sputter madly against her lungs. Grace folded her hands over her chest. She couldn't breathe! The bird's feathers must be getting into her windpipe! Mother was sobbing and calling out things to Grace as she backed her way out the door. Mother! Grace sprang from her chair and ran to her mother for one last tearful embrace. Don't leave me, please, Grace whispered into her mother's ear, I won't eat much and you need me to care for Nelly while you sew and I can learn to sew, too, or I could wash the boardinghouse stairs or carry coal or . . .

Mother held Grace's head between her two hands. There was no sign of a womanly smile on either face. Mother's eyes were sad, but her mouth was strong. I will visit every chance I can and I will come back for you as soon as I earn enough money, she said. I promise you, Grace. I promise you. And then she was crying and then she was gone and Grace was screaming and pulling against Papa Eldredge who held her around the waist. Mother was hunched over and sobbing on Papa Willis' arm as she walked down the path, away from Nana and Papa's house, away from Grace. Nelly clung to Mother's skirts and looked back, open-mouthed at Grace. Then Nana Eldredge closed the door and told Grace she had to calm down now, she was too old to be acting like a baby. She was too old for a lot of things, but they'd talk more about that later.

Papa Eldredge pulled Grace back into the parlor and bade her sit in the chair Papa Willis had just vacated. Grace sat in the big chair by the roaring fire and felt too hot. If she'd only appreciated how perfectly comfortable she'd been in the drafty boardinghouse eating bread and milk with Mother and Nelly. This chair was too lumpy, the fire too strong, the meat and fruit made her insides work too hard at digestion. I don't feel well, sir, she told Papa Eldredge. Then maybe it's time for bed already, Nana scolded. Yes, Ma'am, Grace said and Nana blew out a breath of exasperation. Why you dickens, she said and yanked Grace up the stairs to the little room that would be hers, as Nana said, from now on. But mother promised she'd come back for me soon, Grace protested. Soon has different meanings for different folks, Nana said, and the bluebird in Grace's chest fluttered wildly.

Grace changed into the dressing gown Nana had already laid out on the bed and brushed her hair with the brush on the vanity top. Grace washed her face with the cold cold water in the basin and thought it strange that her fingers didn't feel tingly numb like they usually did. Why she'd ever complained to mother about the cold water before, in the boardinghouse, was suddenly a mystery. Nothing was really so bad, then. Nothing. She would sleep in this little bed and eat her meals and wash her face with cold water and before she knew it, Mother's velvet pouch would be bursting with money and Mother and Nelly would come back for her. They'd all eat bread and milk together and would splash each other with the cold cold water from the basin. And nobody would mind a bit. Especially Grace.

Grace could feel the smile form on her lips. Off to bed, if that's what you want, Nana said, and pulled the coverlet back. Grace went to kiss her grandmother good-night, as she always kissed her mother and sister and even sister Mary and Father, when they were still alive. But Nana pulled back her cheek with a look of horror on her face. Tut, tut, child, she said, Judas betrayed his master with a kiss.

Chapter Eleven

Sara Payson Willis Eldredge Farrington, the Road from Boston to Newton, Saturday, April 26th, 1851

Has a mother a right to her children? MOST UNQUESTIONABLY, law or no law. . . . Shall any virtuous woman, who is in the full possession of her mental faculties, how poor soever she may be, be beggared by robbing her of that which has been, and, thank God! will be the salvation of many a down-trodden wife?

—Fanny Fern, *New York Ledger*, April 4th, 1857

Sara had a sore foot. The week before, the heel of her boot had loosened and she'd fixed it herself with a nail she'd found in the street. But the nail had been a little too long and poked through the shoe, scraping her foot with every step. Sara covered the nail tip with folded wool, which helped immensely, except when she had to walk long distances. Then the tiny hard bump in her shoe felt like a dagger.

Sara was walking the ten miles to Newton to visit Grace. It made her stomach ache to think this was only the third time in over two months she'd managed to visit her daughter. The first time, she and Nelly had taken the train. The second time, to save money, they'd walked, with Sara carrying Nelly most of the way on her back. That had proven more difficult than imaginable with Nelly cold and squirmy and hungry, so this time Sara had left Nelly in the care of a kindly conductor to ride to Newton at half-fare, while she walked the distance by herself. She glanced now and then down the road, looking for the train to come up behind her. She'd told Nelly to wave a red ribbon out the window at her mother so Sara would know she was safely aboard. Sara hated leaving Nelly, even though the conductor had promised to keep her close and safe. Sara hated leaving her children in the care of others.

She had had to leave Grace with the Eldredges because she was quickly running out of money and was hard pressed to buy food enough for the three of them. Leaving Grace, temporarily, was the best solution Sara could consent to. The Eldredges had first wanted to adopt both girls, then had pressed for just Nelly. But, seeing the way Mary Eldredge's eyes lingered on innocent Nelly like a wolf on a stray lamb made Sara's heart race. She'd no sooner allow Mary access to her baby than she'd willingly take a sharp stick to the eye. She'd thrown the adoption papers straight into the fire. Shameful how her in-laws, not to mention her father, had tried to worm their way into her heart and frighten her into giving up her motherly rights with a few creature comforts and a sickly spin of warm-sounding lies. Sara knew that if she would have signed those papers, there would never be a re-adoption back to her, there would never be weekly overnight visits or joint decision-making. The Eldredges were looking to steal her girls in hopes of plugging the hole Charly's death had left in their worlds. Sara knew all about holes left over from loved ones' deaths. And she was keen enough to realize you couldn't jam other people into those holes. They simply didn't fit; in fact, made the pain of the loss even greater. She'd learned that in her marriage to Samuel. She'd learned a great deal since Charly had died.

When Mary had sat her down in her kitchen and pleaded with her to at least leave the girls, just until she could improve her finances, Sara broke down and agreed to leave only Grace. She was getting desperate to support the three of them. That she wept as quietly as possible every night into her pillow couldn't possibly escape the girls' notice either. Sara had finally agreed to allow Grace to stay, only because she hoped Grace's age would steel her from any lasting harm the Eldredges could inflict. She'd hoped Grace would be strong enough to understand Sara's desperate straits and would keep herself whole for the little while it would take Sara to figure out how to earn a living.

Over three months later, though, Sara's financial situation hadn't improved. She had only twelve dollars left in her velvet pouch and not much hope for future earnings. At first, she'd started out sewing for Mr. Schueller again and had earned the usual rate of between sixty and seventy-five cents a week. Her room cost a dollar a week, so she had to borrow regularly from her velvet pouch before she even got started. Food was at least another dollar a week, more if they wanted anything substantial. They often went without a fire. Coal and wood were just too expensive. But after the day of the blizzard, the day Mr. Schueller backed her up against a wall and pressed his tongue into her mouth and roamed her body with his pulpy hands, well, Sara couldn't look at a shirtsleeve without shaking. She'd pushed Mr. Schueller fiercely and had run from the room. She flew down the stairs and out into the street. She had *gotten away* and all in all, the whole ordeal had only lasted a few minutes. But, still, Sara had a hard time forgetting about it, the day of the blizzard in Mr. Schueller's office with nobody else around and her velvet pouch, where she'd just deposited three quarters, balled uselessly in her hand. To run out into the wailing wind was a relief. She had felt close to fainting. She had gladly let the snow slap her face like a cold hand. It was that day, the day she ran crazily down the street in the blizzard, that she had likely damaged her boot. It took another week or so for the heel to loosen. And walking as she was on the ten-mile road to Newton to visit dear Grace, her boot, her foot, and that day of the blizzard were all she could think of.

But she could think of Grace. Sara had gladly paid the sixty cents for her and Nelly to take the train to visit Grace that first time, on Grace's birthday, just five days after they'd left her with the Eldredge's. Sara had even spent a whole quarter on a little cake she carried all the way on her lap. She had expected Grace to be wild with excitement—for their visit, for her birthday, for the cake—but she'd sat demurely and politely thanked her mother and sister for their "company" while she ate her cake like a ghost child. For their *company*! It had only been five days with the Eldredges and Sara could see Mary Eldredge's dour severity already spread over Grace like fog. She would have to work fast to think up a way to make a living. Even strong, capable Grace wouldn't last long in that stifling environment. Sara knew. Mary only had compassion for Charly. Only her son caused her smiles, only *he* touched her heart. Sara shuddered, remembering her year as a newlywed living with her in-laws, a year that frequently found her, a grown woman, reduced to tears in the face of Mary's stern cruelty, a cruelty Charly couldn't understand any more than Sara did. It hurt to think of sweet Grace facing the same treatment. She *must* find a way to earn a decent living!

The week before, Sara had tried her hand at millinery work. She'd finally convinced Mr. Kelsey, the hat shop's owner, to let her try the craft. She, after all, was creative and bright and handy with her needle. Surely, she could learn how to put together a stunning hat. Surely she could learn quickly enough not to be a bother to anyone and to add to the little store's profits. But Sara wasn't allowed more than a few days at hat-making. She would sit, with Gertie and Mam, in the back of the store surrounded by ribbon and lace, feathers and silks, humming her way through her creations, when she'd become aware of the whispers. Women would walk into the millinery and instead of exclaiming in rhapsody over Mr. Kelsey's French blue satin or deep raspberry trim, they'd take one look at Sara working and would either shake their heads and leave or commence with that grating whispering.

Sara was no fool. She knew what was being said about her. Her divorce lawyer had warned her but good to be careful about whom she talked with and where she was seen—in essence, to avoid the attention of any man, known or a stranger. Samuel was spreading slander. He was implying she was adulterous and that he was the one seeking a divorce. He wished to ruin Sara in the easy way men could ruin any woman—by questioning her morality. He no longer had the power to claim her insane, but he certainly had easy access to her social reputation, and that was a power he wielded with glee. He had even hired one after another in a line of unsavory men to follow Sara and to accost her outside of her boardinghouse in order to prove her lack of virtue. Thankfully, Sara had witnesses who spoke of her unwillingness to engage with these men. Thankfully, Samuel's own brother had written a letter to the newspaper in honor of Sara's purity in light of Samuel's lies. But most people hadn't seen Thomas Farrington's letter denying he'd ever said she'd been in the habit of receiving overnight visitors. Most people only saw, and remembered, Samuel's notice in the *Boston Daily Bee* publicly denouncing Sara and withholding all financial support of her sinful self. Nobody but Sara, of course, knew about the drawer full of letters he'd sent her, letters beginning with *My dear Wife*, letters full of false pronouncements of love and longing, letters begging Sara to join him in Illinois or Ohio or Iowa, wherever it was he was roaming. Sara's lawyer told her never to answer the letters or counter his public statements, especially angrily. Samuel could use the smallest sentence as proof of insubordination, adultery, or desertion. It infuriated Sara to be the victim of Samuel's vicious lies, but she was clear-headed enough to fear his power.

Mr. Kelsey had surely heard the rumors, too, and had given Sara a chance. But even he couldn't bear to lose the city's most well-heeled customers in defense of a headstrong widow, and *scandalized second wife*, whose work would take months to polish into real artistry. He'd sadly shown Sara right back out the door on her fourth morning of work and Sara had left, with fifty cents to add to her velvet purse and another layer of grief to add to her burdens. She'd collected Nelly from the woman who'd promised to watch her, along with a dozen other little waifs, for a dime a week, paid her the week's bill, and trudged back to the boardinghouse to crumple into tears. That was Thursday, and Sara had, indeed, shed more than a few droplets onto her pillow. On Friday, she'd decided that no matter the trouble or the cost, she had to see Grace. She needed at least a day to see her family whole.

Walking along the road to Newton with her foot throbbing, Sara looked again and again over her shoulder for the train. She'd left the station a full two and a half hours before the scheduled departure time in hopes of meeting the train exactly at the Newton station. Overhead, the fruit trees were in full blossom, with scores of white and pink and red petal froths perfuming the air. The lilacs were also at their peak and Sara breathed deep of their purple wonder.

The scents reminded her of better days—days at Swissdale, days at Catharine Beecher's seminary, days as a child walking *somewhere* with Mother. Flower play with her girls. Weaving wreathes of daisies with beautiful little Mary Stace. Flower play when *she* was a little girl. She'd made a church, a flower church, then went to visit one with Mother.

Sara breathed deeply and allowed the tears to slip from her eyes. She'd counted the types of weeping these last five years. There was the shivering kind that made her feel as if she were being run through by lightening. There was the hulking, wrenching sort that heaved its way out of her like a demon. There were the muffled squeaks that escaped onto her pillow in the moonlight. And then there was this kind, the silent, effortless spill that ran free with each blink. This quiet crying puzzled Sara. That she could weep as a matter of course doing nothing more than walking down a springtime road, sans children, was certainly strange for someone who'd once been known for her dazzling vivacity. What had happened to her, to *her*, these years? Where had Sara Willis shrunk off to?

She'd lost just about everything a person could possibly lose, that's what had happened. She'd lost her youth—she was forty years old! She'd lost her husband, her mother, her child. She'd lost her home and hope for one in the future. She'd lost her family's support. She'd lost weight. She'd lost hair. She'd lost a tooth in the back on the left. She'd lost hats and gloves and manners. She'd lost her public reputation. She'd lost her smile and the twinkle in her eye. She'd lost her sister and sister-in-law. She'd lost nieces and nephews. She'd lost her father to Susan. She'd lost friends and acquaintances. She'd lost more money than she even realized she had. She'd lost her big brother. She'd lost courage. She'd lost faith. Now she was thinking she might lose hope. She might lose hope because very soon, she might lose her children.

Sara blinked and allowed the tears to wash down her cheeks. She didn't even need to push them out anymore, to heave and shudder them out. They flowed out as easily as water over the top of a flooded dam. Soon the dam would break and the tears would ravage this springtime countryside. Then, Sara guessed, all would be calm. The water would drown everything in sight. It would seek a silent level, with the dead caught among rocks beneath the smooth reflecting surface. Yes, that's how it might be. She had twelve dollars in her velvet pouch. The pouch itself might then be sold for five cents. Sara had six weeks.

Sara walked just a little way off the road and crumpled to the ground for a rest. Her head ached, her foot throbbed, and she was suddenly more tired than she'd ever been in her life. She needed a few minutes repose to revive enough to finish her journey, to see her Grace. She laid her head back on a fragrant patch of soft tender shoots and allowed the tears to slide down her cheeks to the earth. A tree dappled shade over her face. The sun shone hard on her throbbing feet, warming her toes and ankles and calves. Her body nestled in the soft mossy green. A light breeze blew her hair in tickles around her temples and caressed her face with flower scent. A lone ant walked tenderly over her fingertips. A bee droned a soothing buzz somewhere over her head. In the distance, beyond the scent of lilac and crab apple blossom, a low rumble sounded. The earth beneath Sara vibrated, shaking the tension from her muscles and the last of the tears from her eyes. Birds chirped to each other in the branches over her head and Sara took several slow even breaths. For the first time in such a long time, she felt a flutter of peace. Even though she only had twelve dollars left, was walking to see Grace for probably the last time, was counting on the benevolence of strangers to protect Nelly, and was fast fading in body and spirit, Sara felt the unmistakable flutter of peace.

She laughed. Funny to find peace now, when there was nothing left to hope for. Maybe she was dying. Maybe this is what it felt like. Sara nestled into the soft cocoon of green and turned her head this way and that in search of—what? *Something.* In search of something she ached to find. It was elusive, just an aroma that came now and then amid all the flower scents. She knew it. It was that special smell. That special smell coming from over her right shoulder. She sat up and raised her nose to the wind. It wasn't lilacs, or flowering crabs. It wasn't viburnum. It was greener, earthier than that. It wasn't a flower after all. It was sturdier, franker. A smell of strength. Sara pushed herself up and followed the scent, coming here and there whenever the breeze stirred up. Was it the earth? No, too crisp for that. Water, nests, evergreens? No, no, and no. Sara tripped on a rock half stuck in her path and swung her arms for balance. The wind picked up just then, at that moment of her teetering, and rustled the fronds she knew so well. Wild ferns! That was the smell. The husky, bright smell of health and power. Sara bent over the prolific plants and pulled the leaves to her face. Their smooth, cool leaves soothed her skin, seemed to reach deep within her to release a healing elixir.

Mother was near! Sara whirled around, half believing she'd really see her mother, laughing at herself for how silly she must look—searching for ghosts on the country road from Boston to Newton. Sara smiled. The breeze brushed her hair gently back and forth across her temples and floated the ripe scent of ferns over her. Mother *was* near. And for the first time in a long time, Sara understood how fiercely her own mother must have loved her to steal her off to her woman's prayer meeting, to whisk her into the care of confident Catharine Beecher, to encourage her to take her time in marrying and to marry only for love. Mother never cared that Sara couldn't seat a pair of trousers. Mother didn't care that Sara laughed too loud. Mother had always approved. She had! She'd sat quietly with her needle hovering just over her work, listening to Sara's stories and anecdotes and songs. Mother had given all she could of her strength to Sara and foolish Sara had always assumed she'd invented her own personality.

Without Mother silently egging her on from the corners, Sara would never have developed any courage.

And courage is what Sara needed now. She was not ready to give up. She was Sara Willis and she would find a way. Sara plucked a bright bit of fern frond and stuck it jauntily in her bodice. "Like that, Mother?" she said to the breeze, the sunshine, the scents.

The ground continued to rumble, to send a tingle through the earth to Sara's feet. The train! It must be close to gaining on her. Sara dashed back to the road and walked briskly toward the Newton station. Surely it was only a mile or two further. She breathed deeply of the fern as she strode along, lifting her face to the warm sun. She was going to see Grace. She was going to reassure her daughter that all would be well, all would be well, all would be well. Where had she heard that phrase lately? Sara shrugged. It didn't matter. The important thing was to have hope. There were so many people who'd survived worse than Sara. There was the generous Widow Perkins, knitting socks on her tippy chair near the boardinghouse window, the simple William, stealing a holiday apple for Sara's girls. There was Julia, striving to earn her living sewing under Susan's and Father's sharp eye. And there was Hatty, who'd lived seven years in her grandmother's attic, watching her children grow up from a distance, waiting patiently for her chance at freedom.

Hatty's face floated in Sara's memory. "I'm going to write a book!" Hatty had said. Hatty Jacobs was going to write a book about her hard life in order to open people's eyes to injustice. Slavery was injustice, to be sure, but so was this prison Sara was confined to. The prison of a woman's lot! The prison of needing to earn a living and not being able to, not being allowed to, and not having public approval to do so. All Sara wanted was to take care of herself and her children, surely no more than any father wanted. Why, in all of her years of education, hadn't she received a bit of useful training? Why hadn't she been able to boil down all that learning into a means of support? She wasn't even qualified to teach, yet she'd out-read most teachers around. She wasn't allowed to preach, though she'd plenty of anecdotes and a pulpit personality. She wasn't even allowed to voice her beliefs in writing, as female writers were confined to writing about *womanly* interests. Fine idea if one led the protected myth of womanly life. But few women Sara knew really fit that profile—the image of the smiling, peaceful maiden gently raising God-fearing children in a tidy home smelling of bread and chestnuts. The image of a woman who needed nothing for herself, not love, not challenge, not pride. What about the women in boardinghouses, the women sewing and making hats, the women in asylums making room for their husbands' new loves? What about the women who never married, the women who were widowed, the women who were divorced? What about the women who did marry, comfortably, and who rocked their senses away in little dark corners of self-sacrifice? What about the women who married men like Samuel? What about women like that?

Hatty's face floated in Sara's memory again. "I'm going to write a book!" Sara smiled. That's it. She could write. She could always write. Sara wrote as well as she spoke. She wrote at Catharine Beecher's, so well the newspaper often printed her little essays. She wrote for her father's paper for so many years, all without acclaim. She wrote out stories in her mind all the time. She saw life as stories. She told her daughters stories. She told herself stories. She had *just now* written a story about a woman's lot in her head! Walking along the road to Newton, Sara had written a fine newspaper article. She could see it, could almost read it.

The train was coming. Sara heard the distant shriek of metal against metal, the heavy bear-like lumber of wood rising up and coming down upon itself in a rattling, rhythmic pounding. She smelled hot, dark salt or maybe rust; oily, burning coal; pulpy, sweltering timber. Then, the too-loud blast bleated through her body and she felt the pumpa pumpa heartbeat of the beast as it shook and pounded closer. The train burst over the hill behind her and rumbled near—sleek, black, and steaming. Nothing would stop that train, once started, and inside its protective armor scores of warm, peaceful passengers snuggled, riding along with hope. They were so close to their destination. Their adventures were only beginning. Sara trudged along more quickly, determined to arrive in Newton before the last passenger stepped onto the platform. The train huffed closer and closer to Sara who didn't even wince when her foot nudged the nail in her boot, didn't slow her pace a bit as the rumble grew louder and louder.

The little shelter that served as the Newton train station appeared in the distance just as the train started to pass Sara. Sara turned around, walking backward, in order to better see the red ribbon she hoped would fly from some window. There it was, streaming from the first window in the conductor's car, just in front of the coal box. The train puffed violet smoke into the air as it passed Sara, yet, through the haze, Sara could make out Nelly's jubilant face and the beaming face of the kindly conductor hovering protectively over her. All *would* be well. Sara picked up her skirts and ran. She had to pick up Nelly. And then, they were going to see Grace.

Chapter Twelve

Sara Payson Willis Eldredge Farrington, Boston, Friday, June 13th, 1851

If a poor wretch—male or female—comes to you for charity, whether allied to you by your own mother, or mother Eve, put on the most stoical, "get thee behind me," expression you can muster. Listen to him with the air of a man who "thanks God he is not as other men are." If the story carry conviction with it, and truth and sorrow go hand in hand, button your coat up tighter over your pocket-book, and give him a piece of—good advice! If you know anything about him try to rake up some imprudence or mistake he may have made in the course of his life, and bring that up as a reason why you can't give him anything more substantial, and tell him that his present condition is probably a salutary discipline for those same peccadilloes! Ask him more questions than there are in the Assembly's Catechism, about his private history, and when you've pumped him high and dry, try to teach him—on an empty stomach—the "duty of submission." If the tear of the wounded sensibility begins to flood the eye, and a hopeless look of discouragement settles down upon the face, "wish him well," and turn your back upon him as quick as possible. . . . People shouldn't get poor; if they do, you don't want to be bothered with it. It is disagreeable; it hinders your digestion.

—Fanny Fern, *Olive Branch*, June 5th, 1852

"*Mother*, I'm awfully warm," Nelly said to her mother as they climbed yet another set of tall steps, this one four stories high and dustier than most, to bake in the gritty front hall of yet another Boston newspaper office.

77

"This is the last stop before some lunch, darling," Sara said. "I promise." She fingered the two slices of bread in the pocket of the black mourning attire she had gone back to dressing in, at least while she was out on the streets peddling her writing. She found a peaceful anonymity in the sad costume. Although it reminded her of Charly's passing, it also provided her and Nelly real protection from the constant waggling of malicious tongues that her presence in public always seemed to produce, the bitter gossip Samuel continued to encourage. Thank goodness the mourning gown was made room for in public, respected, pitied, but seldom scrutinized enough to identify one wearer from the next. In it, Sara could breathe a little easier, even if it did bring her closer to the heartbreak of Charly's death.

It was a dry, sunny day. The sort of day that one longed to be lounging in some fragrant meadow under ample shade, a cool glass of lemonade within arm's reach. Not the kind of day to be tramping up and down the dusty streets of Boston with a weary child in tow. In front of the *Olive Branch* office, Sara wiped perspiration from her forehead with her already too-damp handkerchief. She had told the newspaper's editor, the Reverend Thomas Norris, that she'd be back at the end of the week to see him, as he hadn't had time the other three times she'd called on him to talk to him about her writing samples.

Sara was getting used to newspaper editors who hadn't enough time to see an unknown female writer. However, she was not getting used to the rude inquisition she inevitably received when and if some editor eventually made a few moments for her. Sara had been furiously dedicated to getting something, some little tidbit, published for almost two months. She'd bought an old inkstand at a secondhand shop, along with a meager supply of paper, nibs, and ink, and started writing. She'd get an idea for an article or essay, and after thinking about it for a few hours, the whole piece would flow straight out of her, from her heart to her pen. It had to. She couldn't afford to waste any ink or precious paper on writing that wasn't quite right. So she thought everything through, very carefully, before committing it into existence.

Sara was thinking all the time, lately. If she wasn't lost in thoughts of yet another exposition, she was calculating how far her last coins might stretch. She'd been so careful, often skipping dinner altogether so Nelly could have a bit more bread and milk. Still, the money was nearly gone, and the last few nights, even Nelly didn't have any milk. Sara had a dollar and a half left—enough for one more week's living, barring calamity.

Sara tucked stray wisps of damp, curling hair back into Nelly's bonnet and gave her darling a squeeze. "This might be the lucky stop," she said. "Cheer up, now!"

"Nothing's lucky today Mother," Nelly said. "Don't you know it's Friday the Thirteenth?"

"It's just another day as far as I'm concerned," Sara said.

Sara was getting ready to knock on the slightly ajar door when she heard a booming voice pontificating amid a flutter of laughter. Perhaps she'd come at an inconvenient time? She shushed Nelly with a look and stood listening to the commotion, hand still half ready to knock, when a young man in a straw hat flung open the door and pushing past them, bolted down the stairs. The door open, Sara couldn't help but look inside at the gaggle of newspaper employees surrounding the Reverend himself. The newspaper editor was elderly, a bit frail looking, with sparse white hair and shaking jowls. Still, he commanded the brightness of a younger man and the attitude of someone who was nobody's fool.

"Ah, you've finally come back," Reverend Norris said to Sara when he'd spied her in the doorway. "Come in, come in. We were just reading the article you left."

"*This* is the writer?" a tall, wiry assistant said. "I just assumed it was a . . ." He coughed.

"A man?" Norris said. "Is that what you were going to say?"

"Yes, sir."

"I must agree with you. Quite pointed writing for a . . . *lady*."

Sara's face reddened. "I have other samples," she said. "Pretty ones."

"I saw them all," Norris said.

Just then, a woman who'd been placing an advertisement whispered conspicuously with the clerk taking her order. The clerk's face paled and his eyes bugged out. "Sir. Reverend Norris," he said, beckoning the editor to his desk. "May I have a private word with you?"

"Can't it wait a minute, Higgens? I'm in the middle of a meeting."

"I'm afraid it can't, sir."

The Reverend rolled his hazel eyes. "If you'll excuse me a moment," he said to Sara and patted Nelly on the head as he passed by.

Sara murmured agreement and tried not to panic at the muted exchange she saw taking place between the woman, Higgens, and Reverend Norris. All three pairs of eyes shifted her way. All three faces registered the shock and outrage Sara had continued to evoke since leaving Samuel.

Eventually Reverend Norris adjusted his braces, smoothed his shirt collar, and strode back to Sara. He glanced down at Nelly, then to the wiry assistant. "Perhaps the little one would like a draught of water in the back room?"

Sara nodded quickly and a smiling Nelly went off with the assistant.

"You sign your work Clara. Is that your name?" the Reverend asked.

"No, sir. It's Sara."

"A nom de plume for so similar an address?"

Sara bit her lip.

"What's your last name, Sara?"

"My surname is Willis," Sara said quickly.

"Any relation to the famous poet?"

"My brother."

The Reverend raised his eyebrows. "And your name by marriage?" He paused a second, running his eyes up and down Sara's black dress. "I see you are a *widow*."

"Eldredge."

"Eldredge?" Reverend Norris cast a puzzled look at Higgens, who was making himself look very busy with the woman placing the advertisement.

"And Farrington," Sara said softly. "But I must protest that the accusations made by my former husband are utterly false."

"So false that you choose to write under 'Clara'?"

"I thought it would be best, sir," Sara said. "Isn't that quite the fashion these days?"

"I suppose it is," he drawled. "Keeps the readers guessing."

"Yes, sir."

"About identity, of course. Sex. Position."

Sara nodded. A droplet of sweat trickled from her forehead slowly down her temple. "If Clara won't do, I could go by Tabitha," she said. "Or Olivia. Anything really. Whatever you'd prefer."

Just then, Nelly and the tall assistant emerged from the back room. Nelly was prattling to the young man who had a look of bemused indulgence on his face.

The Reverend took the whole scene in—chattering Nelly in her rumpled dress and faded bonnet, Sara in her widow's weeds and scuffed shoes holding the tattered reticule presumably containing more writing samples, the whispering woman with her head close to Higgens—and cleared his throat. "We'll take this one, 'The Model Husband.' I'll pay you fifty cents for it."

Sara beamed. She could almost feel a piece of sausage melting in her mouth. "Oh, thank you, sir. Thank you so very much!"

"When it runs," he added. "I've got a two week backlog of these sorts of things. At least two weeks."

Sara's smile drooped. "Two weeks?"

He looked at her in all seriousness.

She adjusted her features back into a smile. "Well, fine. That will be just fine. I have no idea how these things work. So, I'll keep my eye out for it, then."

"And come back for your payment when you see it," he said, steering her toward the door with her elbow. At the door, he held out his hand to her. "We'll see how things go."

"Thank you, again, sir!" Sara said, shaking his hand.

She and Nelly tripped down the steps out into the dry hot afternoon, holding in squeals of excitement.

"Mother, you sold an article!" Nelly said. "And for fifty whole cents. I think we should get ice cream!"

Sara's smile faded. Just fifty cents. Payable when it runs sometime at least two weeks away. She looked for what seemed like a long while at the bright smile on her daughter's face. Little pearly teeth lined up like a necklace, sparkle flashes at the corners of her eyes, a dash of pink flushed over the tops of round cheeks. What a beautiful thing—a child's smiling face. Ice cream. Would one treat be so bad? Sara took a shaky breath. "Absolutely, my love," she said to Nelly. "But just a small one for you. Mother is too excited to eat anything."

Sara's article ran two weeks and one day later, on Saturday, June 28th, 1851. Every morning since she'd shaken hands with the *Olive Branch* editor, Sara walked the streets and parks with Nelly on the lookout for forgotten newspapers. If they found a copy of the *Olive Branch*, Sara rushed back to their Brattle Street boardinghouse in Cambridge to scan it for her article, just in case Reverend Norris decided to run it early. Time after time, Sara was disappointed not to see her work. But she read the other articles submitted by other correspondents—men and women alike—and spent afternoons and evenings writing new pieces in response to what she read. How annoying most of the women's pieces were! All about trivial household tips or sentimental rhapsodies about fruit flies and flowers. Now Sara enjoyed the finer things in life as much as the next woman—the aesthetic, the artistic, the genteel—but it seemed as if many of the women writers had no connection to life's realities. When they advised readers to bathe their temples daily in lavender water, didn't they realize that on a widow's small budget, lavender water was the last item on the grocery list? When they made distinctions between confectioners' sugar brands, didn't they know that more than a few women hadn't tasted a sweet in ages and, furthermore, wouldn't care a whit which brand of sugar she'd finally been able to sprinkle into her tea?

On the other hand, Sara found the male-authored articles fascinating. They seemed to fall into two categories. One type she read with great interest because it offered ideas and solutions to the broken wheel of modern society. Such articles discussed the growing groups of poor, widowed, orphaned, maimed, sick, committed, jailed, homeless, and hungry people. Sara devoured such articles, searching for voices of reason among the heap, looking for the compassionate brilliance she knew was needed to set this world right. Yet, many other male-authored articles angered Sara. More than a few people—educated people, prominent people, people who should know better—blamed a raw circumstance on the virtue of the victim. In these writers' minds, the unfortunate deserved their misfortune. It was God's judgment for sins, known or unknown. When Sara read such pieces, she paced the tiny length of her attic room and murmured retorts. That she could write against civil ignorance, that she could write against inequality and hard-heartedness! This was her wish.

Sara also continued to hike into downtown Boston and make her black-garbed rounds among the city's other newspaper offices, but still hadn't gained another interview or garnered any interest in her work. The continued rejections didn't really bother her, though. She felt steered by the hand of Providence, a mysterious, golden hand that had fortunately opened to her in generosity at the ice cream shop on the day she'd sold "The Model Husband."

Sara still smiled when she remembered handing the small paper dish filled with strawberry ice cream to little Nelly that oppressively warm day. She was searching through her velvet pouch for a penny to pay when the gentleman behind her said, "Allow me, ma'am." He handed the grocer three cents and instructed the clerk to produce two more "Penny Licks" along with two more flat wooden eating sticks.

Sara's mouth dropped and she blinked rapidly. Who was this man?

The man smiled at her confusion. "Sara? It *is* you, isn't it?" the man asked, looking gently into her eyes. "I was friends with your husband."

Sara smiled a bewildered greeting.

"With Charly, I mean," he quickly added.

Sara blushed.

"He was a fine man," the man said. "A great friend to me."

"Well, I'm glad to hear that," Sara said as the smirking store clerk handed her an ice cream. "Thank you for this, ah . . . Mr.?"

"Mr. Smith," the man said. "And you're more than welcome. It's the least I could do."

Sara nodded.

He took her hand and squeezed it. "God Bless you, Sara," he said. "Charly thought the world of you. He was always talking about you and how happy . . ."

Sara's chest ached with heaviness.

"How happy you made him," the man said softly. He released Sara's hand, held his own ice cream up to her in salute and hurried out the door.

Outside the store, Sara's eyes brimmed as she and Nelly ate their ice cream sitting on a side-street bench. Even though the cool strawberry was the best thing she'd tasted in months, Sara's throat was so tight, it was hard to swallow. "Here, darling," she said, giving the remains of her treat to delighted Nelly. "I told you mother's too excited to eat."

It wasn't until later that day, after they'd walked back to Cambridge and climbed the two stories to their broiling attic room in the boardinghouse, that Sara realized what a kind and generous man "Mr. Smith" was. Nelly removed her bonnet and was emptying her pocket of pebbles she'd collected on their sojourn when her face suddenly hung blankly. She approached Sara with a folded piece of paper addressed to Sara Eldredge. "I found this in my pocket," Nelly said.

Sara unfolded the paper and out popped a real five dollar note. On the paper itself was a hastily scrawled "God bless you."

Sara held the bill to her chest. "And God bless you, too, Mr. *Smith*," she said, breaking down in tearful relief.

Sara wept full out that day. Not only had she secured a place for her first article, but she'd received guaranteed sustenance for a few more weeks. That five dollars meant survival for Sara and Nelly, and Sara used it as carefully as possible. In fact, she still had nearly three whole dollars left two weeks later. Better yet, each time she opened her velvet pouch, she was reminded that there was still some good left in the world, a reason to hope, a reason to smile.

She'd yelped when she found her article, *her article*, that Saturday morning, just one day after the promised two-week delay. There was an introduction to it, presumably written by the Reverend, which melted Sara's heart as it assured her anonymity. Sara Payson Willis Eldredge Farrington's first article followed Reverend Norris' introduction.

As the following account of a "Model Husband" is from a lady in good position in society, we can but suppose her model husband is the true style of husband, and what all good married men should be. In looking over our nearly forty years of married life, we find that our good wife has never exacted quite so much of us, but she merely waived her rights, I suppose.

The Model Husband

His pocket-book is never empty when his wife calls for money. He sits up in bed, at night, feeding Thomas Jefferson Smith with a pap spoon, while his wife takes a comfortable nap and dreams of the new shawl she means to buy at Warren's the next day. As "one good turn deserves another," he is allowed to hold Tommy *again* before breakfast, while Mrs. Smith curls her hair. He never makes any complaints about the soft molasses gingerbread that is rubbed into his hair, coat, and vest, during these happy, conjugal seasons. He always laces on his wife's boots, lest the exertion should make her too red in the face before going out to promenade Washington St. He never calls any woman "*pretty*," before Mrs. Smith. He never makes absurd objections to her receiving bouquets, or the last novel, from Captain this, or Lieutenant that. He don't set his teeth and stride down to the store like a victim every time his wife presents him with another little Smith. He gives the *female* Smiths French gaiter boots, parasols, and silk dresses without stint, and the boys, new jackets, pop guns, velocipedes and crackers, without any questions asked. He never breaks the seal of his wife's billet doux, or peeps over her shoulder while she is answering the same. He never holds the drippings of the umbrella over her new bonnet while his last new hat is innocent of a rain-drop. He never complains when he is late home to dinner, though the little Smiths have left him nothing but bones and crusts.

He never takes the newspaper and reads it, before Mrs. Smith has a chance to run over the advertisements, deaths, and marriages, etc. He always gets into bed *first*, cold nights, to *take off the chill* for his wife. He never leaves his trousers, drawers, shoes, etc., on the floor, when he goes to bed, for his wife to break her neck over, in the dark, if the baby wakes and needs a dose of Paregoric. If the children in the next room scream in the night, he don't expect *his wife* to take an air-bath to find out what is the matter. He has been known to wear Mrs. Smith's night-cap in bed, to make the baby think he is its mother.

When he carries the children up to be christened, he holds them right *end up*, and don't tumble their frocks. When the minister asks him the *name*—he says "*Lucy—Sir*," distinctly, that he need not mistake it for *Lucifer*. He goes home and trots the child, till the sermon is over, while his wife remains in church to receive the congratulations of the parish gossips.

If Mrs. Smith has company to dinner and there are not straw-berries enough, and his wife looks at him with a sweet smile, and offers to help *him*, (at the same time *kicking him gently* with her slipper under the table) he always replies, "No, I thank you, dear, they don't agree with me."

Lastly, he approves of "Bloomers" and "pettiloons," for he says women *will* do as they like—he should as soon think of driving the nails into his own coffin, as trying to stop them—"cosy?"—it's *unpossible*!

—Clara

Sara smiled when she read it. It was fun enough, she supposed, but most impor-tantly, it was her writing in print. She'd often seen her scribbles reproduced as type in her father's paper, but *this* was different. *This* involved a signature (next time she just might be Tabitha) and cash payment.

Sara and Nelly spent that whole beautiful Saturday lolling on the Boston Common. Nelly had decided she'd make the longest dandelion chain ever and Sara decided she'd spend the entire day with eyes only for Nelly. It was one of the first days in so many months that Sara hadn't felt burdened with the weight of worry. The happy bloom spreading through her reminded her of the day she'd walked to visit Grace, the day she'd felt her mother's presence near, had picked the wild fern, and had first felt the inspiration to write. Yes, it was only fifty cents, but Sara saw it as more than the bit of money. It proved she could sell her writing. She could sell her writing forever and would somehow be able to piece together enough quarters to feed and clothe herself and her *two* children.

As if Nelly read Sara's thoughts, she said. "I wish Grace were here, too. She loved making dandelion chains."

Sara's throat tightened. "She'll be back with us just as soon as I can manage it."

Nelly smiled. "I know, Mother. You've got loads of articles in your reticule." It was true. Sara was writing all the time.

The next day, while Nelly napped, Sara wrote another two pieces and added them to her pile. She planned on visiting Reverend Norris first thing on Monday for her payment and wanted to be ready with a wide variety of pieces for him to choose from, should he wish to purchase something else. Late in the afternoon, Sara decided to take a break and, taking the refreshed Nelly by the hand, headed down the boardinghouse stairs for a turn around town. In the parlor, Mrs. Griffin was entertaining a few women visitors. As Sara passed the parlor door, she overheard one of the women reading aloud. She caught the words . . . " 'cosy?'—it's *unpossible!*" followed by uproarious laughter from the group of women. Sara froze. They'd been reading her piece! And enjoying it! Nelly beamed at her mother and squeezed her hand.

"Excuse me," Sara said. "Were you just reading from the *Olive Branch?*"

Mrs. Griffin shook her curls in irritation. "The what? Never heard of a pulp by that name."

Sara was confused. She had been *sure* those were her words. "But I thought I recognized that piece. I mean I just read something like it."

The woman opposite Mrs. Griffin, the one holding the newspaper, folded it and held it up for Sara to see. "You see? It's the *Boston Transcript*. And this writer, *Clara*, is new to me. Isn't that right, ladies?"

The women nodded in agreement.

"Clara, you say?" Sara asked.

"Come see for yourself," the woman said and opened the paper. There was Sara's article, faithfully reprinted one day later in Boston's most celebrated periodical.

Chapter Thirteen

James Parton, New York, Monday, July 14th, 1851

I wish all reviewers believed me to be a man; they would be more just to me. They will, I know, keep measuring me by some standard of what they deem becoming to my sex; where I am not what they consider graceful, they will condemn me.

—Fanny Fern, in response to Charlotte Brontë's comments about critics' standards for female versus male writers, *New York Ledger*, June 13th, 1857

James Parton alighted from the cab and gave the driver his pay. As the horse clopped away, James turned and stared at the lavish red brick building in front of him. He was in one of the most fashionable residential areas of Manhattan, in front of the legendary N. P. Willis' house, and even though the sun blazed, early afternoon as it was, Parton felt significantly cooler here among the waving green of so many trees and pots of flowers. He wiped his brow with a linen handkerchief and replaced his hat, then took a healthy breath and strode up the three steps to the door. He'd promised himself all weekend that today would be the day, the day he'd muster the courage to introduce himself to the heady poet and editor, the day he'd beg Mr. Willis to read his carefully written article.

Naturally, he had stopped by the *Home Journal* office first, but the assistant editor, a dark-haired, fast-blinking Mr. Murphy had sent him directly to his editor's home, loaded with a packet of papers and the strictest assurance that *Nat* would be sure to see him, if only to accept the delivery. James had hesitated to take the packet. "Do you know who I am?" he'd asked Mr. Murphy. "How is it that you trust just anyone with what must be valuable documents?"

"You have the look of a writer, an intelligent look, certainly," Murphy said. "Why wouldn't I trust you? Besides, the correspondence here isn't particularly valuable—just some writing samples from the swarm who want to be in our pages, and a few bills."

James's smile faded.

"Don't look so glum," Murphy said. "It'll get you in the door."

And so James stood and pounded the knocker against the glossy white front door. It was opened by a formally dressed young man who barely had a moment to greet James before they both heard bellowing from some near room, "Jacques! Who is it? Have they come with the packet from the office?"

James lifted the packet, tied securely with string, as an answer, but again before Jacques could speak, his master pushed past him to see for himself. James's mouth dropped open when he saw those famous blue eyes, that head of well-known curly hair, N. P. Willis himself standing before him in a gold satin dressing gown and embroidered slippers. "You'll excuse my dress," Nat said. "I'm a bit green around the gills today."

"Of course," James said.

"You have the packet from Patrick?" Nat said, eyeing the parcel James held. "Yes."

"Well, what's the delay? Hand it over," Nat said.

James bit his lip. "Of course. But first, sir, if I could have a minute of your time."

Nat wrinkled his brow.

"I did bring your papers here and I believe I've earned at least—"

"Go on," Nat said. "What do you want?"

James cleared his throat and gave a slight bow. "My name is James Parton and I'm a writer."

Nat groaned.

"I'm sure you meet quite a few in your position."

Nat reached for the packet. "You have no idea. Now if you'll just—"

"But if you'll only listen for a moment. You see I've written a piece about the British writer, Currer Bell."

Nat frowned. "He wrote that book about the governess?"

"Actually, *she*, sir."

"Well, he, she. Everyone's already been all over that."

"But it must be a she, sir. And my article proves it. Not that the writing is lessened a bit for the knowledge," James said. "In fact, she must be a great woman. Strong. Intelligent. To write so powerfully, I mean."

Nat assessed James, standing earnestly on his front porch, his dark beard neatly trimmed, his nails clean and buffed, his shoes recently shined.

"*Jane Eyre* will become a classic. It's a masterpiece," James said, his dark eyes glowing with passion. "And although it's been written and written and written about, I've put everyone's theories in order and found holes in some and strengths in others until I've come up with my own views—"

"And who are you to write about your views?" Nat said.

"I've written various little articles here and there, worked as a schoolteacher for some time, have read scads of books, and am a fair hand as an editor."

"Not to mention, by the sounds of that hint of accent you still carry, that you've come from Currer Bell's motherland."

"Yes, sir. Born in Canterbury."

Nat smiled. "My wife's from England. So, of course, she'd have me flogged if she ever heard I'd turned out one of her kinsmen."

James smiled and pulled a folded manuscript from the inside pocket of his coat. "So you'll read it? My article about *Jane Eyre*?"

"I shall. But beyond reading, I cannot promise a thing." He pointed to the packet Murphy had sent from the *Home Journal* office. "Those are more of the same, you know."

"So I was told."

"And you didn't lose them to some ferocious windstorm on the way here?" Nat said with a grin.

"No, sir."

"Well, you earn high marks for honesty, at any rate," Nat said, taking both the packet and James' manuscript. "Keep an eye out in the paper. If you see your piece in print, you'll know I liked it."

Chapter Fourteen

Sara Payson Willis Eldredge Farrington, Boston, Monday, July 14th, 1851

Women are getting altogether too smart now-a-days; there must be a stop put to it! people are beginning to get alarmed! I don't suppose there has been such a universal crowing since the roosters in Noah's ark were let out. . . . Well, I hope it will be a warning! the fact is, women have no business to be crowding into the editorial chair. Supposing they know enough to fill it (which I doubt! hem!) they oughter "hide their light under a b"—aby! I tell you, editors won't stand it, to have their masculine toes trod on that way. They'll have to sign a "quit claim" to their "dickeys" by and by! I wonder what the world's coming to! What do you suppose our forefathers and foremothers would say, to see a woman sitting up in the editorial chair, as pert as a piper, with a pen stuck behind her little ears? phew! I hope I never shall see such a horrid sight!

—Fanny Fern, *Olive Branch*, October 23, 1852

It was another sizzling day in Boston. The sun blazed high in the sky, baking the city that had been rainless, and nearly breezeless, since a downpour had ruined hundreds of Independence Day picnics. People walked in slow motion in and out of shops, lingering at street corners, holding handkerchiefs to their noses to avoid inhaling the clouds of dust stirred up by passing carriages. Even the horses plodded, heads down, sweat dripping down their sides. Sara was stifling in her widow's weeds. But she knew it was better to be inconspicuous on the streets as a pitiful mourner than to be recognized as Mrs. Farrington. The divorce had still not been made official and Sara couldn't afford to keep checking with the lawyer. Each three-mile trip from her boardinghouse in Cambridge to the lawyer's office on the outskirts of Boston wore her out, physically and emotionally. She had to trust that Samuel would eventually tire of abusing her name in public. She had to trust at least that. And she had to hope that maybe one day, he'd officially set her free.

Today, Sara walked, but she wasn't walking to the Munroe & Company firm on Washington Street. She was walking to the *Olive Branch* office—again. She held Nelly's sweaty hand and led her, for the fifth time in a little over two weeks, up the four dusty flights to the newspaper's office. The relentless heat had put the usually cheerful Nelly in a foul mood. Sara had thirty-six cents in her velvet pouch and still hadn't received payment for her article. She was in a foul mood, too. The good Reverend, coincidentally or not, had been unavailable to meet with her each time she'd stopped. Each time she'd stopped, the wiry assistant, or Mr. Higgens, instead, had told her it'd be best if she could come by again a few days later. It'd been a month since she sold "The Model Husband" and Sara vowed she would not leave the office again without payment. Nelly needed a good meal. Nelly needed so much more than that, but a good meal would do for now.

When they reached the top of the stairs, Sara straightened her dress front and knocked on the door. There was no answer. It was mid-afternoon on a Monday. Surely the office was open for business. Sara knocked again. There was still no answer. She put her ear to the door and heard the murmur of voices. "Why, the nerve," she said, thrusting the office door open.

The tall assistant was sitting at the desk closest to the door. He jumped up when Sara exploded through the doorway and strode straight to the editor's desk behind a glassed-off partition. "Ma'am, ma'am," he said, hurrying behind her. "The Reverend isn't in. I'm afraid you'll have to come back to see him."

"And aren't you in either?" Sara said. "How is it nobody can be bothered to open the door to me, let alone see me to pay me my wages?"

"Certainly nobody intends to inconvenience you, ma'am."

"It is not an *inconvenience* at all," Sara said.

"Wonderful! Then, of course, you wouldn't mind—"

"It's my living," Sara said.

"Well, surely you can't be getting by on quarters picked up here and there."

"I am and I will." Sara said.

Just then Reverend Norris peeked his head out from behind the glass partition. "What seems to be the trouble?"

Sara said, "Ah, so you are in," at the same time the assistant said, "Sir, I tried to tell her . . ."

"Never mind," the Reverend said. "I'll see her presently."

Sara sat Nelly in a waiting chair near the assistant's desk and told her to sit quietly while mother had a meeting and if she were offered a nice glass of water by the gentleman, she was allowed to drink it. Sara gave the assistant a pointed look and he shrugged, bug-eyed, at his editor, then scurried off to the back room for Nelly's refreshment. Reverend Norris held the door to his office open for Sara and when they'd both entered and sat, he behind his desk and she just next to it in a broad walnut chair, the editor procured a pitcher of water and two glasses from somewhere under his desk and proceeded to pour them each a glass which they both drank completely down without saying a word.

Sara set her glass on the edge of the desk. "Thank you for the water, sir, but I've come for my payment."

"Payment? What payment is that?" the editor said.

Sara's eyes flew open. "Payment for my article 'The Model Husband' which ran in your pages over two weeks ago."

"I know the piece, of course. I remember it . . . and you . . . Sara," he said, pointing to her. "But this office is accustomed to rendering payment when an article is printed. You say it's been two weeks, so I'm sure we've already paid you, my dear."

Sara narrowed her eyes. "Oh, is that how it goes?" she said.

"I beg your pardon?"

"You aim to swindle me, a woman, innocent in the ways of business."

The Reverend Norris chuckled. "If I may say so, you seem anything but *innocent*, Ma'am. Tramping the streets, selling your thoughts, with your little child in tow." He lowered his voice. "Honestly, isn't there any other way?"

Sara raised her eyebrows. "No, there is not," she said deliberately. "I've chosen *this* way and if my writing is good enough to appear in print in your publication, not to mention the *six* other places that have copied it thus far, then it is certainly good enough to render me the wage promised me. You did *not* pay me, sir." Sara took a shaky breath. "I keep careful account of my finances and I *know* I haven't yet received payment. I've stopped by here faithfully since the day my article was published two weeks ago and have always been met with resistance from Mr. Higgens or . . ." She pointed her chin at the closed door. "Or that tall fellow, who've both told me you weren't in or were unavailable, unreachable, out of town, whatever they had to tell me to get me to cow my head and drag my little darling back down those stairs. Well, I am not leaving here today—"

"O'Connor!" Reverend Norris suddenly shouted.

Sara jumped.

A few seconds later, the tall assistant cautiously opened the door. "Yes, sir?"

"I want to introduce you to our writer, Sara, ah . . ."

"Just Sara is fine," Sara said.

"I'm Sean," the assistant said, tentatively offering his hand to Sara, which she shook.

"Good," the Reverend said. "Now we all know each other. O'Connor, get the cash box."

Sean nodded and hurried out.

"Thank you, sir," Sara said.

"It seems we've slipped up in our accounts," Reverend Norris said. "I cannot fathom who would display a case, as you just have, if it weren't true. You speak directly and firmly." He tapped some papers on his desk with the tip of his index finger. "Just as you write. I like that. Sara. Clara."

Sara nodded.

Sean came back with the cash box and the Reverend opened it and counted out five dimes which he placed in Sara's outstretched palm. "It's seven, by the way," he said.

Sara cocked her head. "I beg your pardon?"

"You've been copied in seven papers. Six here in Boston, true. But also by one in New York. The *Home Journal*. That's quite a feat for a new writer."

Sara blanched. The *Home Journal* was where Nat served as editor. Did he know it was his sister's writing he pirated? Was he striving to pave a way for her after all, even though he'd sent her that rude note utterly dismissing both her and her writing just a few days before?

"Thank you," Sara said, pouring the dimes from her palm into her velvet pouch. She opened her reticule and pulled a sheaf of papers from it. "Perhaps you'd like to purchase another?"

The Reverend smiled slowly, took the pile and looked through it. Eventually he picked out six pieces, all to be printed within the month. "We'll switch it up a little," he said. "We'll call you Tabitha sometimes and something else for these children's pieces."

"I like 'Aunt Emma,' " Sara said.

"Fine."

Sara inhaled sharply. "I'd also like to be paid up front," she said. "Just so there are no further misunderstandings about payment."

The Reverend's smile faded. What behavior! How unwomanly. How strange. His mouth hung open slightly as his eyes darted over Sara's face searching for peevishness or insubordination. Sara's black head covering had slipped enough to show damp flaxen curls framing her pale face. Her mouth was set in a line, neither bitter nor angry, but firm. Her blue eyes blinked a little too rapidly for someone sitting so still. The Reverend Norris had never paid up front. He'd always paid on publication. That was standard procedure. Common practice. Yet, there was something about this Sara that baffled him. He wanted to slap her down yet at the same time he wanted to rally behind her. It was as if she didn't quite understand social protocol, like she was somehow still a child, willful, boisterous, a little too idealistic. He again noticed her worn shoes, the clutched velvet purse in which she'd slid her little earnings. He came back to her eyes, vivid blue and leveled his way for the most part, yet revealing her discomfort with their occasional fluttering. Was she holding back tears? Annoyance?

He didn't know what he was doing when he again reached for the cash box and pulled a three-dollar note from under the cast iron paperweight he'd had since he'd started his career some twenty two years before. His father had given him the paperweight, the replica of a sailboat, assuring him he'd be successful because he was a man of vision and sense, because he knew what he wanted, could steer his own course. As Reverend Norris held the bill out to the now slightly smiling Sara, he realized he saw those same qualities in this woman writer—those qualities of quiet determination his father had seen in him and that had sustained him in those early rocky years of his career so many decades earlier. Reverend Norris' father was long dead, buried next to his mother not two miles away. Yet, as the woman writer, Sara, tucked the bill into that sorry velvet pouch, retied her reticule, and collected her handkerchief and daughter, from the chair she'd been sitting on and from Sean's care, respectively, the Reverend felt his father's presence fully, shining down on him from some peaceful place. Reverend Norris next found himself shaking Sara's hand, smiling into those now-steady blue eyes and not only requesting that she stop by soon, as soon as she'd written some more articles, but also writing a quick letter of reference for her to his editor friend, William Moulton, at the *True Flag*. This woman was determined to make her way. After he'd so underestimated her, the least he could do was give her a hand up. After he'd sealed the letter of introduction and handed it to her with directions about Moulton's visiting preferences, he offered his arm to her, which she took, and he led her, lady-like, to the office door. He'd just purchased, up front, six articles from a scandalized female. Six pieces he knew his readers would love.

Chapter Fifteen

Louisa Jacobs, New York, Monday, July 14th, 1851

The man over there says women need to be helped into carriages and lifted over ditches, and to have the best place everywhere. Nobody ever helps me into carriages or over puddles, or gives me the best place—and ain't I a woman?

—Sojourner Truth, May 1851.

Louisa hummed as she scrubbed the railing on Nat Willis' front porch. *Praise be! Praise be!* A cool breeze blew up from the road and bathed Louisa's sticky forehead with relief. She was overheated, true, from bustling around with Mother, preparing for one of the frequent dinner parties Mr. Willis reigned over. But she wasn't dour. She didn't think she'd ever feel downhearted again, no matter her workload, no matter her circumstances. Louisa had been transformed. It had happened weeks ago, and, yet, to Louisa, it was as pure and clear in her head as if it had just happened. She could draw on it anytime she wanted. Just pour it through her body like sparking cool water from a crystal pitcher.

It was at a convention, of course. It was a speech. A woman. A speech from a woman, so powerful, both, that Louisa would never be the same. Louisa's mother, Hatty, had taken her to the convention and soon was absorbed in talking with her new friends, the abolitionists. They were helping Hatty prepare to write her book about being a slave, a book everyone said Hatty must write.

Whenever they could, Louisa and Hatty attended conventions, some meant to raise the real horror of slavery to the forefront of white people's minds, some meant to promote women's rights, many to do both. That's when it happened—the speech Louisa couldn't forget—at the women's rights convention. The same people were there who were often at all of the conventions and the same speakers spoke who often spoke. Mrs. Gage was presiding. She let speakers have their turns at the podium and signaled when it was time for the next one to come forward.

Louisa didn't think she belonged at the strictly women's rights conventions. In spite of the fact that her mother insisted that women's rights included colored women's rights, Louise saw mostly fair faces in those audiences. They were different battles, she supposed. Both necessary, both unfathomably difficult, but each battle stemming from very different roots. Despite her own fair complexion, Louisa had a hard time feeling a part of the mostly white audience at the women's rights conventions. On the other hand, Louisa didn't need a convention at all to remind her of slavery. She'd *been* a slave. Though a privileged one, she knew. But she'd seen the horror of it—whippings, lynchings, shootings. Mother had to hide out from Mister in Granny's attic for seven years, and the worst of it was that even though Granny hinted otherwise, Louisa thought her mother had been dead the whole time.

When it happened, the speech Louisa couldn't forget, Mother had been talking with her friends and Louisa had been lost in thought, remembering, thinking of those times when she lived with Granny, those times Mister would sometimes ride his carriage too close to her when she was walking to town and ask her where, *gal*, her mother was. He'd find that bitch and shoot her dead. He would. Mark his words. He wouldn't rest until he either brought her back or killed her. *Keeled* was how he said it. Until he *keeled* her.

Louisa shuddered and tried to turn her attention to the convention speakers. A giant of a woman, dark as night, sat on the steps at Mrs. Gage's feet, waiting patiently for her turn at the podium. Her skin had the same blue highlights as Aunt Tilsey. She had the same great beautiful eyes as Uncle George. Louisa missed them both. And Granny. And cousin Bib and Nancy and all the rest. Louisa's eyes stung. She and Mother would never see any of them again. Mother said they could never go back, *ever*, and Louisa knew it was because of Mister. She knew it was because he'd shoot them *all* dead if he ever found them. *Keeled.*

There was a hissing sound from the audience and Louisa didn't know if it was because of the last speaker, a clergyman, or because of what Mrs. Gage was saying. "Sojourner Truth!" she said and the huge woman stood up next to, not behind, the podium. The woman was quiet for a moment. She calmly scanned the audience and the hissing died down. She raised her great arm and pointed to the back of the hall, pointed to someone Louisa couldn't see and in a booming voice said *that man* said women were given special treatment, they were helped into carriages and over puddles. The audience murmured. Louisa smiled, thinking of her days at Mister's when he'd just as soon push a colored woman *into* a puddle as help her over it. That's what Sojourner Truth said, too. It was the myth of women's protection. The myth of women's sheltering. The myth that all women were pampered darlings perched on velvet lounges, a china cup in one hand, a lacey fan in the other. It was something everyone knew, in the periphery of consciousness, but something nobody admitted out loud. Women suffered like men did. Women held the whole range of human emotions and should also participate in a full portion of human experiences. To deny was not to protect. It was to subjugate. To enslave. Sojourner Truth made the truth known, not in so many words, but in enough words and in the right words.

And that's when it happened, when Louisa was transformed. She, and everybody else, listened to Sojourner's deep, steady voice and understood, really understood, the web these two causes wove together—the abolitionist movement and the women's movement. The faded hissing was replaced by silence, a breath-holding, chest-aching quiet that shook Louisa's insides even as it calmed her. Sojourner Truth pulled up her sleeve and showed her bare skin to the audience. Her skin was dark and a little ashy but covered a surprisingly muscular frame. Sojourner Truth bent her elbow to make her muscles jump and told how she'd planted and ploughed like a man, had borne the whip like a man, but had never had the protection *that man* claimed all women had a day in her life. Not one day. And Louisa knew it was true. Everyone did. *Keeled.* There were hardships in women's lives, painful ones, unwomanly ones, and now Sojourner Truth had said it aloud. *She* was a woman, and proof, too, how women *weren't* treated like men swore they *were*.

The quiet burrowed into the listeners and shook them. Louisa felt her insides quivering, a hopeful trembling that turned volcanic. It rumbled inside her, building like steam. The hall suddenly exploded with cheers and Louisa clutched her hands over her chest, opened her mouth wide as the Mississippi and bellowed with the others. *Praise be! Praise be!* This was the connection they'd all been hunting for. The connection they needed to understand these causes as one cause. Here, in this crammed hall, an old ex-slave had been able to make it clear. The fight for women's rights and the fight for colored's rights was the fight for people's rights. A colored woman and a white woman were not two different kinds of women; a colored man and a white man were not two different kinds of men; coloreds and whites were not two different kinds of people. Sojourner Truth turned her telescope full on the crowd. She showed this audience its heart and let the crimson knowledge beat its way through the body. And here was Louisa, a colored woman. In the unspoken social pyramid, she surely occupied the bottom step. White men on top, colored women on the bottom, colored men and white women hashing it out somewhere in the middle. It was ridiculous, this ranking. And this audience knew it.

Louisa howled and clapped with the crowd. *Praise be! Praise be!* Louisa joined the chant and swung her head to try to catch her mother's eye. But Hatty didn't look toward her daughter. She gazed full at the podium and at the magnificence of Sojourner Truth next to it. Hatty's arms pounded the air in time to the chants—chin tipped up, cheeks and nose and forehead shining. Her mouth formed words with soft edges, loving edges, the corners of her eyes glittering moist. Hatty, too, felt the quaking. The rocking of the world off its axis. All would be well now. It had to be. Who could forget this awakening? Who would refute it? Louisa raised her own arms and clapped along with the chants. *Praise be! Praise be! Praise be!*

Chapter Sixteen

N. P. Willis, New Orleans, Monday, August 16th, 1852

[N. P. Willis]'s tastes are very exquisite, and his nature peculiarly sensitive; consequently, he cannot bear trouble. He will tell you, in his elegant way, that trouble "annoys" him, that it "bores" him; in short, that it unfits him for life—for business; so, should you hear that a friend or relative of his, even a brother or a sister, was in distress, or persecuted in any manner, you could not do [him] a greater injury (in his estimation) than to inform him of the fact. It would so grate upon his sensitive spirit,—it would so "annoy" him; whereas, did he not hear of it until the friend, or brother, or sister, were relieved or buried, he could manage the matter with his usual urbanity and without the slightest draught upon his exquisitely sensitive nature, by simply writing a pathetic and elegant note, expressing the keenest regret at not having known "all about it" in time to have "flown to the assistance of his dear"—&c. [He] prefers friends who can stand grief and annoyance, as a rhinoceros can stand flies—friends who can bear their own troubles and all his—friends who will stand between him and everything disagreeable in life, and never ask anything in return. . . . From all questionable, unfashionable, unpresentable, and vulgar persons, Good Lord, deliver us!

—Fanny Fern, *Musical World and Times*, June 18th, 1853

It was already almost nine in the morning and, sitting at the breakfast table in their rooms at the Landmark Hotel, Nat wasn't feeling well, again. Despite drinking his usual pot of coffee, he felt sluggish and slow in this hot humid

swampland, but so did everyone, judging from the drawling speech and saun-
tering step that hailed from both natives and visitors of this annoyingly slow
city. Even Nat's thoughts had slowed, he noticed, since his arrival some two
months before with Cornelia on their way back to New York via Bermuda. He
snorted. His head was stuffed, probably with inhaled cotton wisps from flying
past field after field in his claret, gold-striped sulky. That had to be it. That and
this heavy air that didn't let anything circulate—not heat, not odor, certainly
not thoughts. It was as if New Orleans was a colossal simmering skillet full of
peppers and onions and sausage. Some giant Creole had flung in the required
heaps of crawfish and shrimp and *bam* down came the lid that covered—and
stifled—everything.

Nat loosened his blue satin cravat and rang for Jacques. He needed a
stomach bromide before he could even think of whatever spice-heaped concoction he'd be too starved to refuse for dinner. Everything always tasted fine going
down. It was the digestion that bothered him. And so he would irrigate the
spices with plenty of wine or iced bourbon, which always helped immensely,
except for these sour mornings he'd been slogging through lately. Something
wasn't right. Nat would get to the bottom of it, too.

The quack physician he'd seen the day before had given him a nasty
lecture, punctuated in French, telling him to coddle himself, telling him that
he was old and that he should go easy on the rich food and wine in favor of
plain eating—porridge and tea, he supposed. *Old!* He was forty-six. He had a
good twenty years ahead of him. *Old.* Age was a state of mind, a condition of
will. Maybe he'd write a poem about it. Yes, that was it. About how *old* can
be staved off like sleep and marriage with the proper will and enough money.

Nat chuckled. After Mary Stace's death he'd been depressed, worried
even, about his financial affairs. The inheritance he'd expected from her parents
surely wouldn't be coming and her dowry was almost gone. Thank Heaven he'd
grabbed Hatty and taken Imogen on that trip abroad, the trip where he'd met
Cornelia. Things had a way of working out for Nat. Pleasant things happen to
pleasant people. Cornelia Grinnell's family made Mary Stace's seem like poor
relations (God knew how he hated those!). And the Grinnells didn't believe in
inheritances. They divided things up in the present, a practice much more to
Nat's liking. Not that he hadn't earned a handsome income in his own right.
Still, a newspaper editor, even a riotously successful one, was no match for
scads and scads of interest-generating old fortunes.

Nat rang again for Jacques. Lazy as the day was long! He'd have Jacques
ready his cream-colored coat, the matching gloves, and that too-perfect little
box of a gray hat he'd just purchased. Perhaps his blue velvet waistcoat should
be brushed, too. On second thought, velvet was too heavy for the steamy day;
he'd go with the blue and gray tapestry waistcoat, sans jacket, but with a blue
feather in that handsome hat. What a picture he'd make dashing by, his silk

shirt sleeves ballooning in the breeze and his black Wellington boots polished to a dazzling gleam. He'd stick his new breast pin into the tapestry just so— that lovely pear-shaped pearl surrounded by the cup of diamonds begged to be flawlessly presented. And he'd offset the look with his gold wedding watch and chain, a steady, yet elegant, year-round accompaniment to his wardrobe. Thinking of his ensemble, Nat already felt better. Coddle himself indeed. He was still a vibrant young man, an important literary talent, a noted citizen of New York City.

A tap on the door startled Nat from his reverie. Hatty stood in the doorframe, wringing her hands in that irritating way she had. Ex-slaves simply didn't have the deportment of Northern-raised servants and the sad truth was, no amount of late-life freedom could procure it. Personally, Nat appreciated Hatty's maternal way with Imogen, but liked her best when she made herself scarce. Although still handsome, as colored women could be, Hatty's scared-rabbit look drove Nat to fury and reduced her womanly good looks to the gangly discomfort of a country adolescent. Hatty darted a look at him.

"Well, now, Hatty, what is it?" Nat asked. "And where is Jacques? I've rung twice for him."

"Jacques's coming. He was with the horses," Hatty said. "But, sir, I was wondering something."

Nat picked up the last pecan pastry from the serving platter and took a vicious bite. *Old.* "Yes, go on, Hatty," he said with his mouth full. "What are you wondering, now?"

"Have you heard anything from Sara, sir?"

"Sara who?"

"Your sister, sir."

Nat rested his elbows on the table. Where was Jacques? He had to get out of this stifling room.

Hatty continued, "It's been a while since I've had any word and I've been worried—"

Nat shook his finger in Hatty's direction. "Don't you go believing her sob stories. She's as fine as a headstrong widow ought to be. Widow and marital *deserter.*"

Hatty flinched.

"I told you I didn't want her name mentioned in my presence and I meant what I said. What a *sister!* To try to manipulate me with her tears and groans, to try to get me to publish the sop she calls writing. Why my sentiments were so sorely bruised by the pitiful begging she made to me, *via post,* that I'll be loathe to speak to her again."

"Is she bad off, sir?" Hatty said. "I've always been, well, *fond* of her."

Nat wiped his forehead with his monogrammed handkerchief. "You're fond of the fair-weather Sara, as everyone is. This new version, sister Lucy says, is a downright embarrassment. Traipsing around Boston peddling her writing like a beggar, without a proper thought to the family name, especially considering how she's dragged that name through numerous mud puddles. She has no thoughts of anyone but herself. All she wants is her spoiled life back, no matter the cost to her or the family's reputation."

Hatty started backing through the door. "Yes, sir."

"I don't want her mentioned unless you've come with her written apology," Nat said. "It's about time she learned her place. Heaven knows no man has ever been able to teach it to her."

Just then a breathless Jacques stepped around Hatty. "I heard you called, sir. I was brushing the chestnuts, like you asked, and didn't hear the bell."

"I'll take the sulky today. Make sure it's clean. I splashed through a few puddles yesterday, as you probably noticed on the cuffs of my trousers."

"Yes, sir."

Nat waved Hatty away with short rapid fans from his hand and turned, red-faced and sweating, back to Jacques. "And tell Cornelia we'll have dinner in town tonight. On the way to the theater. We're going to celebrate our health!"

"Yes, sir!"

Chapter Seventeen

Lucy Bumstead (nee Willis), Boston, Monday, August 16th, 1852

Never mind back aches, and side aches, and head aches, and dropsical complaints, and smoky chimneys, and old coats, and young babies! Smile! It flatters your husband. He wants to be considered the source of your happiness, whether he was baptized Nero or Moses! Your mind never being supposed to be occupied with any other subject than himself, of course a tear is a tacit reproach. Besides, you miserable little whimperer, what have you to cry for? A-i-n-t y-o-u m-a-r-r-i-e-d? Isn't that the summon bonum—the height of feminine ambition? You can't get beyond that! It's the jumping-off place! You've arriv!—got to the end of your journey! Stage puts up there! You've nothing to do but retire on your laurels, and spend the rest of your life endeavoring to be thankful that you are Mrs. John Smith! Smile! you simpleton!

—Fanny Fern, *Olive Branch*, August 28, 1852

Lucy Bumstead would arrange the desserts herself. She'd told Millie to polish the large silver serving platter after breakfast and it sat gleaming on the sideboard next to the just-delivered box of fruit tarts, miniature custard cups, biscuits, and petit fours. Lucy was a master of artful arrangement. In fact, she'd already arranged the party flowers—the table centerpieces and the smaller bouquets of roses, lilies, and delphinium for the entryway, parlor, and keeping room tables. She was especially excited about arranging the desserts, though. She couldn't wait to see the gaping mouths of her fellow whist club members when they'd seen she'd ordered such perfect blueberries to be used for the tarts or how light the specialty key-lime custard was juxtaposed with the equally magnificent hazelnut biscuits or the almond and chocolate petit fours. Mrs. Hathaway, especially, would have to admit to being impressed. True, such a display would only be better if Lucy's own Millie had been able to create such lavish edibles. But, surely, everyone would attest to the sumptuous expertise of Toma's Bakery and would be awed that Lucy could afford to purchase so many fine treats.

Lucy snipped bits of fern leaves to tuck under and around the desserts. Fern leaves always reminded her of her mother—fresh, fragrant, and not so delicate as to need excessive coddling. Lucy was like that, too. She'd married early and well. Josiah certainly knew his way around the mercantile industry and his business savvy had earned him regular bonuses and what he called benefits. When they'd moved to their breathtaking Beacon Street home, Lucy thought herself the luckiest woman in the world. Smooth, polished marble; thick, hand-turned woodwork; gleaming chandeliers; two kitchen stoves; thick, brightly patterned carpets, sumptuous velvet draperies and tapestry furniture—this and more was her world to govern and order, to decorate and arrange. Her head spun the minute she started unpacking. She'd put the crystal statuette here. The carved-ivory box there. And, of course, the shops were brimming with all the extra niceties she needed to make this house an elegant home.

Josiah thought her taste impeccable and she'd immediately set to work, with his blessing, creating the sanctuary she saw in her mind's eye. Yes, she'd taken good care to secure her future. That was one of the first jobs a smart woman had better figure out. Lucy smiled at her use of sex and mildly corrected herself. Smart *people*. Smart people had to figure out how to secure a good future, Nat would say to her, tipsily, over some excellent glass of red. They were two peas in a pod, she and her brother. The two oldest Willis children and the two with the most sense. They both understood what it took to make it in the world. Yes, grace and charm counted. So did a healthy intellect. But what really mattered was money, vulgar as that sounded when spoken aloud. Without it, life was just plain miserable, despite the pulpit groaners who swore that earthly suffering would be rewarded in the afterlife. Lucy and Nat figured that one could be a good citizen, a conscientious social crusader, without living in poverty.

Take, for instance, all the charity Lucy'd doled out to her sister, Sara. Now that's *one* who didn't know the ropes when it came to making a good marriage. Sara had lucked out with Charles Eldredge, all right. The two of them seemed happy enough and Charles looked like he was making a good living. What a surprise to find out he was a reckless financial manager. True, it was a shame to leave Sara so unfit to negotiate the world and its myriad of living expenses, but Sara had an equal blame in what had become her lot. She had a second chance. She married the well-to-do Farrington, yet practically spit in his generous face. Who could blame him for disowning someone as brazen, as unwomanly and indelicate as Sara could be? It was all benevolent Lucy could do to tuck a stray dime into Sara's rough hand when she'd come over to wash her clothes in the back kitchen like a servant. Lucy just couldn't bear to watch Sara's charade of poverty. How expensive was it really to have one's laundry taken care of? Lucy'd seen countless little stands where the foreign-looking proprietors practically begged to do heaps of wash for almost nothing. How embarrassing of Sara to trot her underthings across town to swish them around in Lucy's basins. And then, to hang them all over the kitchen! Lucy'd finally delicately suggested that Sara take her unmentionables up to the attic to dry, if she insisted on rough drying them at all. She herself had Millie steam her own with the iron when they were just this side of damp and they were ever so soft and fresh. Lasted longer, too. But Lucy had tired of arguing about social norms with Sara. Sara apparently liked to chafe her thighs with rough-dried pantaloons because, inevitably, after drinking tea and eating as many tea sandwiches as she could stuff into her stomach (and after Lucy, as any older sister had an obligation to do, would kindly reprimand Sara for her bad manners), Sara would snatch her board-hard laundry from Lucy's attic rafters, snap up that little urchin of a daughter she carted here and there with her, and would storm off into whatever weather—rain, snow, wind, or blazing heat—without gloves or hat, sometimes without even a shawl. Lucy could only shake her head in dismay and hope that her friends weren't riding by at just that moment in their carriages. Lucy would never be able explain Sara to them. All she could do was wish Sara speedily away.

Lucy had never been able to explain Sara to anyone except Nat. He was the only one Lucy knew who understood Sara's manipulative ways. Lucy and Nat agreed that father and Dr. Eldredge were probably doling out money by the fistful to Sara, but that she, as she'd always done, was probably wasting it on too many yards of French lace, too many chocolate cups at the confectioner's, or too many replacement gloves. Lucy and Nat had no patience for such waste, nor for the entitled attitudes that preceded such behaviors. *They* knew Sara and her predicament. Sara had always been flighty, had always thought she could get by with a whistle and a dimpled smile. Well, it was time she grew up, like Lucy and Nat were forced to do so long ago. Being the eldest made one race through childhood, to be sure, but sometimes, such training guaranteed a little ease in one's middle years.

Lucy placed the last bright tart on the gleaming silver tray. She would tell Millie not to allow Sara in if she came with her bundles of laundry. Sara would simply have to budget her income for necessities. She needed a push into the grown-up world and, as usual, Lucy would have to be the one to push her. Lucy would tell Millie that Sara was to visit, like a normal sister, and a *lady*, when Lucy was *at home*, in the parlor, orchestrating polite conversation. She could bring her daughter, if Nelly was ready for society and the demands of gracious deportment. Sara could partake of any and all refreshments that Lucy made available to all of her guests, with the usual restrained good manners. Lucy shook her head as she positioned the stunning dessert tray between two brimming vases of roses. How absurd that she should have to teach her grown sister such social basics. But absurd or not, Lucy wouldn't shrug her duties. She'd arrange to guide Sara into the world of the genteel or Sara would face her own fate. It's all any sister could be expected to do.

Chapter Eighteen

James Parton, New York City, Monday, August 16th, 1852

"Now girls," said Aunt Hetty, "put down your embroidery and worsted work; do something sensible, and stop building air-castles, and talking of lovers and honey-moons. It makes me sick; it is perfectly antimonial. Love is a farce; matrimony is a humbug; husbands are domestic Napoleons, Neroes, Alexanders,—sighing for other hearts to conquer, after they are sure of yours. The honey-moon is as short-lived as a lucifer-match; after that you may wear your wedding-dress at the wash tub, and your night-cap to meeting, and your husband wouldn't know it. You may pick up your own pocket-handkerchief, help yourself to a chair, and split your gown across the back reaching over the table to get a piece of butter, while he is laying in his breakfast as if it was the last meal he should eat this side of Jordan. When he gets through he will aid your digestion,—while you are sipping your first cup of coffee,—by inquiring what you'll have for dinner; whether the cold lamb was all ate yesterday; if the charcoal is all out, and what you gave for the last green tea you bought. Then he gets up from the table, lights his cigar with the last evening's paper, that you have not had a chance to read; gives two or three whiffs of smoke,—which are sure to give you a headache for the forenoon,—and, just as his coat-tail is vanishing through the door, apologizes for not doing 'that errand' for you yesterday,—thinks it doubtful if he can to-day,—'so pressed with business.' Hear of him at eleven o'clock, taking an ice-cream with some ladies at the confectioner's, while you are at home new-lining his old coat-sleeves. Children by the ears all day, can't get out to take the air, feel as crazy as a fly in a drum; husband comes home at night, nods a 'How d'ye do, Fan,' boxes Charly's ears, stands little Fanny in the corner, sits down in the easiest chair in the warmest corner, puts his feet up over the grate, shutting out all the fire, while the baby's little pug nose grows blue with the cold; reads the newspaper all to himself, solaces his inner man with a hot cup of tea, and, just as you are laboring under the hallucination that he will ask you to take a mouthful of fresh air with him, he puts on his dressing-gown and slippers, and begins to reckon up the family expenses! after which he lies down on the sofa, and you keep time with your needle, while he sleeps till nine o'clock. Next morning, ask him to leave you a 'little money,'—he looks at you as if to be sure that you are in your right mind, draws a sigh long enough and strong enough to inflate a pair of bellows, and asks you 'what you want with it, and if a half a dollar won't do?"—Gracious king! as if those little shoes, and stockings, and petticoats could be had for half a dollar! Oh girls! set your affections on cats, poodles, parrots or lap dogs; but let matrimony alone. It's the hardest way on earth of getting a living—you never know when your work is done. Think of carrying eight or nine children through the measles, chicken pox, rash, mumps, and scarlet fever, some of 'em twice over; it makes my head ache to think of it. Oh, you may scrimp and save, and twist and turn, and dig and delve, and economise and die, and your husband will marry again, take what you have saved to dress his second wife with, and she'll take your portrait for a fireboard, and,—but, what's the use of talking? I'll warrant every one of you'll try it, the first chance you get! there's a sort of bewitchment about it, somehow. I wish one half the world warn't fools, and the other half idiots, I do. Oh, dear!"

—Fanny Fern, *Olive Branch*, December 6th, 1851

James Parton clipped the little article from the Boston newspaper and put it on the pile next to his inkstand to be copied sometime this week for the *Home Journal*. What a spunky, funny piece. Strange though, how it was hard to determine the writer's sex. The style was snappy and bold, very masculine, actually. But the signature, Fanny Fern, was one of those maddening alliterations meant to confuse. He'd seen scores of them lately. In fact, one of Nat's pet projects was to find one or two writers just starting to produce sparks and gently fan their careers into billowing flames. All involved parties benefited. The new writers' careers blossomed and Nat could take the credit for *discovering* them, for nurturing their innocent (usually female) talent amid the harsh brutalities of the New York business world. Lately Nat'd been promoting Grace Greenwood and Fanny Forrester as his special protégés. Another, a Sally Sunflower, had proved to be a man—something James suspected from the beginning, because of the author's awkward attempts at writing the sentiments of a womanly heart. Nat, of course, would have nothing to do with the writer's ruse, although James was willing to give him a chance; he was a decent writer, when he hit the nail on the head. But that was neither here nor there anymore. Nat had decided against him. James chafed at the decision. It felt unjust and he had always had a hard time letting an injustice alone. He had rallied for the underdog since he could remember. What did sex matter if a writer was good? If a writer was good, what did anything matter?

Nat had been gone for months on a recuperating holiday with Cornelia. Even though the doctors had been warning Nat for years that his reckless lifestyle would eventually take its toll, Nat lived in a bubble of disbelief. He considered himself immortal and would drink and smoke and eat and dart around like a fly in a bottle until the world believed him immortal, too. The world didn't quite believe N. P. Willis to be immortal, at least not yet. But they rightly recognized a powerful presence in him. James was always sorry when Nat couldn't rely upon his very good writerly reputation and would take to garish self-promotion and indelicate social posturing. Even the biggest buffoons soon saw through that tired maneuver, yet, because of Nat's social standing, most everyone usually winced and looked kindly away from Nat's antics. What a shame Nat didn't have more real confidence in himself. He *was* a talent and if he'd just apply himself as diligently to his writing as he did to promoting his writing, he'd be as powerful a voice as Hawthorne or maybe even Emerson.

Even that morbid writer, Edgar Allan Poe, the one who'd occupied James' very desk and assistantship with Nat but a few years before, had received adequate reviews. James sometimes still came upon copies and notes in Poe's hand and never failed to shiver at the even, too-perfectly drawn script. *That* one wrote from the edges of lunacy, yet with a clarity that was hard to replicate. James admired Poe even as his work made him cringe.

James felt he could speak from authority about writers, being a writer, too. He wrote every free moment and he understood the strange fever writers have when the need to put pen to paper overwhelms every other desire. James had penned the usual articles, columns, and the occasional whimsical story or anecdote expected of a newspaper assistant editor. But he also had a strange fascination with chronicling the lives of others. He was working on a fascinating study at the moment, interviewing *New York Tribune* editor Horace Greeley and taking as many notes about the maverick as his aching hand allowed. It'd been months since they'd started their conversations and James couldn't wait to put this living legend's life onto paper so that the public could benefit from his courage and inspiration, as James, indeed, had, just in this little interviewing process. James hoped Nat wouldn't be angry when he found out he'd been diverting his interest from the daily happenings of the *Home Journal*. Chances were that as long as the paper's circulation stayed high, Nat wouldn't give a whit what James did in his off hours.

Truthfully, Nat hadn't shown any real interest in the paper, aside from nursing the new writers, in at least a year. His health hadn't allowed it. James remembered the day Nat and Cornelia left for Bermuda. Nat had handed James the office key and, wheezing into one of his over-embellished handkerchiefs, had scarcely looked over his shoulder as he hurried back to his waiting carriage. That was fine with James. He'd let his own tastes and viewpoints seep into the periodical's pages. He picked up the Fanny Fern column again and smiled. The world needed more writers like this. Writers who weren't afraid of stepping on a few toes. Writers who knew how to write to the point. Writers who could melt the iron judgment of social propriety with ironic, humorous charm. Fanny Fern. James would have to keep an eye out for this one.

Chapter Nineteen

Sara Payson Willis Eldredge Farrington, Boston, Friday, September 17th, 1852

Ah! The modern old maid has her eye-teeth cut. She takes care of herself, instead of her sister's nine children, through mumps, and measles, and croup, and chicken pox, and lung fever and leprosy, and what not. She don't work that way for no wages and bare toleration, day and night. No, sir! If she has no money, she teaches, or she lectures, or she writes books or poems, or she is a book-keeper, or she sets type, or she does anything but hang on to the skirts of somebody else's husband, and she feels well and independent in consequence, and holds up her head with the best, and asks no favors. . . . She carries a dainty parasol, and a natty little umbrella, and wears killing bonnets, and has live poets and sages and philosophers in her train, and knows how to use her eyes, and don't care if she never sees a cat, and couldn't tell a snuff-box from a patent reaper, and has a bank-book and dividends: yes, sir!

—Fanny Fern, *New York Ledger*, June 5th, 1869

Kicking through the season's first crackly leaves, Sara walked Nelly to school. She kissed her daughter good-bye, rambled back to the boarding house, and soon sat at the boardinghouse's dining-room table paging through the day's newspapers and enjoying a finger-warming second cup of coffee. She had *two* articles out at once—one in the *Olive Branch* and one in the *True Flag*. Sara's purse grew heavier by the week. It was hard to believe that a year before, she'd sometimes strung pennies together for a daily morsel of food for herself and Nelly. Considering that the two of them had practically lived on bread and milk for months, one would think that the mere thought of the concoction would turn Sara's stomach. But the contrary was true. When she thought of the dish, or occasionally still ate it, she'd brim over with pride that she'd survived what she hoped was the worst period of her life. Not so with Nelly, though. Even when Mrs. Dougherty would bring a steaming pudding from the kitchen for dessert, hardly bread and milk but a distant cousin of the dish in any case, Nelly's face blanched and she'd make excuses to leave the table as quickly as possible. Sara cringed when she thought of the long-term childhood memories her poor Nelly had formed. She cringed even more when she allowed herself to wonder the same things about Grace.

So much had happened in the past year. She had forged a wonderful, respectful partnership with the dear Reverend Norris and the *Olive Branch* was printing several of her articles a week. She'd also entered an agreement with the sometimes shifty William Moulton of the *True Flag* and wrote equally for his paper. Each periodical was now paying her by the column, not the article—two dollars a column—and Sara couldn't believe that she now wrote seven, eight, at times, ten articles to fill three and sometimes four columns and, so, *earned*, completely in her own right, at least six dollars a week. It was certainly no fortune, but she could finally afford most of life's necessities.

Her earnings hadn't improved overnight. She'd worked that first winter, day and night, scratching away with her pen every free minute. Nelly had fallen sick early in the fall and relapsed off and on the whole season. Sara knew the cold room and meager meals of the Brattle Street attic room didn't help the child's health. Since she was still being paid fifty cents an article, she'd often stay up deep into the night and try to dash off an extra article or two so she could afford to buy Nelly an occasional bowl of warm broth or slightly soft apple. Each day, Sara tried to keep Nelly's spirits bright with play and stories and bundled-up walks to tend to their errands. Every night, Sara would cover little Nelly with a ridiculous heap of blankets and shawls—all they owned—and would stroke her hair, singing softly, until Nelly's tortured breathing eventually gave way to a soft wheezing, regularly interrupted by that awful hack hack hack of her lingering cough. Then, Sara would ply her own freezing fingers, would light a candle and would take it to the shaky little table and chair next to the window, hoping for moonlight or starlight to ease the late-day strain on her eyes. There, she'd rub the inkstand between her palms for a minute, hoping to warm both the ink and herself as she thought through her ideas. She dashed off article after article, occasionally lifting her eyes to focus on the pearly moon or pausing to listen as the city clocks chimed one, two, and often three, from some faraway place. More than once, she'd startle herself awake, forehead smack down in a puddle of ink, her limbs aching with cold and stiffness from having fallen asleep over her work. She'd either try to salvage the piece by blearily reworking it or would try to salvage her slumber by crawling into bed next to the then-warm rasping Nelly.

The winter passed slowly and by spring Nelly was no better. Sara took her little pile of coins and called a feeble, half-witted doctor to look at her daughter. He took all of her money and gave her a bottle of medicine, which did absolutely no good. It was then, one wild night, half way between winter and spring, a season that alternately gusted rain and snow against the rattling shutters, that Sara realized that she'd have to write dozens of articles, at fifty cents apiece, just to survive. That pace would kill them both. After wallowing in despair for most of the night, frantic already about losing Grace to the Eldredges and terrified about losing Nelly, too, Sara sprung, red-eyed, from her sleepless bed and dashed off a piece about too many mothers losing children to death and circumstance, then hurried as soon as business hours began, to Reverend Norris. There, she laid out her plight and, straight-faced, insisted upon a raise.

"But your pieces are getting shorter," he'd protested. "Soon, I'll be paying you to think of them."

"I'll be able to write more clearly if I can limit myself to writing a reasonable amount for a living wage."

"But we," Norris said. "We've always. Nobody else—"

"Is copied at the rate Fanny Fern's work is," Sara said. "You yourself said your circulation has dramatically improved."

Reverend Norris nodded and stroked his beard. "Your articles had better be longer."

"They'll be the length they should be. I won't add filler to your pages. You've got plenty of that if you need it. But I suggest you pay me by the column. I write as many articles as needed to fill them up, you pay me for as many columns as I can scribble."

Reverend Norris snorted. "But a column only holds two of your pieces. Maybe three of the short ones."

"Exactly. I cannot write enough now to live on. Nelly's sick and the medicine . . ."

He blanched.

Sara wrung her hands. "And if it isn't the medicine, then it's shoes. And if it isn't shoes, it's ink and paper." She gathered up her shawl and empty reticule, then stood next to his desk with her hand open. "I've already given a piece to Higgens on the way in," she said, her face reddening. "A long piece, one that will surely take up a whole column at least. So, that will be . . . two dollars."

Reverend Norris shook his head reproachfully, though his hazel eyes twinkled. "*Two* dollars? For one article?"

"For one *column*." Sara stood for what seemed like the whole day with her eyes on the floor and her hand held out for payment. The words *two dol-*

lars had sprung from her lips on their own. She'd meant to say one dollar. She had! But after her speech about the medicine and shoes and ink, the words seemed to have formed themselves and jumped from her parted lips. She had no choice now but to stand there and see what would happen.

After a time, she heard the Reverend pulling out the cash box and opening the lid. She heard him muttering a bit as he shuffled his fingers through the paper and coin sections. She felt him place two notes in her hand and she slowly brought her eyes from the floor.

He smiled at her then, in a fatherly way she hadn't seen from anyone in ages. "Get Nelly some oranges, won't you?" he said and Sara nodded briskly, wiped her leaking eyes with the back of her hand.

Sara didn't have as easy of a time convincing Moulton to increase her pay, until he heard that Norris had already agreed. Then he smiled that tight flat grin of his and pumped her hand like a well handle. The way Moulton ran his mouse-brown eyes up and down her reminded Sara of Mr. Schueller. Try as she would to forget that wintry day Mr. Schueller had manhandled her with his pulpy hands and sour tongue, sometimes the smallest detail—a tight bookish smell, the heavy cold of snowy days, or, as was the case with Moulton, a skittery *look* in a person's roving eyes—would cause some sort of snap in her brain and it was almost as if she could feel Schueller's wet breath on her ear again.

The day she told him of her raised rates, rates that were still lower than almost all of the paper's male correspondents' rates, Moulton's look changed from appraising to calculating. He didn't want to lose in his longstanding competition with Norris, but at the same time, to be spoken to so brusquely, to be almost commanded to increase his payment, to be so nearly cornered by this *female* was something William Moulton was not at all used to. And it was something he didn't like. He'd give in to Mrs. Sara Farrington (well, yes, of course he knew who she was!). He'd give into her demands, but only because he needed her work. The minute her little well ran dry, why, then, *he* might just use his inside knowledge about the notorious Fanny Fern, as she had taken to signing herself, to sail his own ship. It was all well and good to keep her filthy little secrets for now, and really, what did it hurt to protect her sordid identity as long as her writing sold his papers? But she wouldn't be able to hide behind black veils and parasols forever. And, *then!* Then, he'd earn back every dollar tenfold.

After both Reverend Norris and Mr. Moulton agreed to Sara's requested pay raise, life was easier for her and Nelly. Just after Thanksgiving, she and Nelly had moved to a better boardinghouse, one that included a load of wood and a basin of water a day, and three real meals. Sara was finally able to purchase new shoes for each of them and had sewed them one new dress apiece. Nelly was enrolled in a modest little Cambridge school not far from the boardinghouse and on the way to Boston, which was very convenient, as Sara was still walking into town several times a week to drop off articles or pick up her earnings.

That she still couldn't have Grace near was the thorn in her side. Retrieving her daughter had proven trickier than Sara had ever expected. Hezekiah was critically ill and every time Sara wrote inquiring when she could come to retrieve Grace she was blasted with an icy reply claiming that Grace was desperately needed to help nurse her grandfather and to keep his spirits up in what were presumed to be his final days. That Sara could even think of ripping this cherished child from the nest her grandparents had built for her was more than could be endured and they all simply needed more time to get used to the idea. Sara, of course, doubted every word of Mary Eldredge's plaintive letters. Her own letters to Grace went unanswered and Sara was sure that Grace wasn't receiving them. When Sara had arrived on the Eldredges' doorstep, some four times in the past year, she'd only been allowed to see Grace once, and that visit lasted a trifling hour and was under the constant supervision of Mary. Sara tried to console herself with that last image of Grace, sitting quiet and seemingly peaceful in front of the fire, sipping a cup of tea like an almost-young-lady, answering her mother's inquiries with a polite and pleasant tone. But try as she would, Sara would never be consoled that her daughter was not with her, that her daughter was living with grandparents who were likely thwarting her sensibilities and poisoning her heart.

One of Mary's recent letters had unsettled Sara more than usual. Mary informed Sara that she and the doctor had rewritten their wills, bearing in mind Sara's "inability" to provide long-term financial stability for her daughters. Grace and Nelly would each receive $5,000, payable to them upon marriage (so their funds would be managed by their husbands—a point not lost on Sara), provided that upon Hezekiah's death, Grace continue to live with her grandmother to keep Mary's "heart company." What sop! Although Sara worried about providing for her girls—Heaven knew how long it'd take to save $10,000 on the leftovers of six dollars a week—she worried more about their long-term emotional stability. In times of trouble, sometimes all Sara had were memories of her mother's strength and love and quiet encouragement. To think that Grace might not have those resources, *inner resources*, frightened Sara to death. How would Grace cope with hardship with only money to aid her? How would she survive in this world without the bubble of protection from her mother's heart? Sara saw through Mary's sentimental dribble like a window. She could honor the need for Hezekiah to die in peace. But despite the lure of small fortunes for her girls, Sara could not be forever parted from her darling Grace. In fact, they couldn't be reunited too soon. Even if it meant another period of monetary stretching for them all, Sara already knew she could live through anything if it meant her little family could be together again.

Charly would certainly approve of her motives. His love, even from that other place, had buoyed Sara these past years. He'd always believed in her, just as he'd always accepted her, *exactly as she was*. She supposed her heart would never fully recover from losing her Handsome Charly. Although she was told she was still attractive in form and face, especially since putting on the flesh she'd lost during those sad, lean months, she doubted she'd ever marry again. Sara simply couldn't easily forget the Samuel disaster. She'd rather work her fingers to the quick until her last breath than be under the thumb of such an ogre again. Why women didn't provide for themselves more often was baffling. Sara found such immense satisfaction thinking of her articles, dashing them down, delivering them, albeit incognito, seeing her work in print, and collecting and managing her funds. Sara was still astonished that she *could* compete with and earn the same rate as many of her male counterparts. How funny that the general notion was that women weren't capable of higher thought, weren't mentally able to budget funds or negotiate working conditions, weren't physically capable of earning their own livings. Sara guessed that if she were proving to be a satisfactory writer, that there must be plenty of other women who, given the proper circumstances and training, would be able to function as business leaders, political thinkers, maybe even physicians.

Sara's thoughts were interrupted by a conversation among the gentlemen seated in the adjacent keeping room. They were smoking a morning cigar or pipe each and bantering ideas around before they left for their various positions as clerk or apprentice. Sara sometimes listened to their conversations, especially if they involved social issues or politics. She seemed to want to learn all she could lately about what made society work the way it did. This morning, though, her ears hadn't been teased by either subject. Rather, she couldn't help but be interested because they were contesting the issue that was at the forefront of many a Bostonian conversation these days—the identity of Fanny Fern.

Sara had tried out the nom de plume last fall and it had immediately felt right. After playing with a variety of signatures—always bent on ensuring her anonymity, as Samuel hadn't stopped, and likely would never stop, circulating his scathing stories about her and her character—Sara had dreamed up the name in honor of her mother, and the constant image Sara kept of her plucking the hearty wild fern leaves and tucking them into her bodice to inhale the strengthening and heady fragrance. Sara had decided to use an alliteration, mainly to blend with the masses that were doing the same and to further divert attention from her identity. She'd decided on "Fanny" because she'd always liked the name. As far back as she could remember, she'd associated the name with loving wisdom. The combination of Fanny Fern felt good to her and as soon as she'd hit upon it, she told both Norris and Moulton that she'd write under nothing else.

It surprised her to hear herself hotly debated, as she often was these days. That slyboots Moulton even fanned the flames of public curiosity by printing an article a few days before entitled, "Who is Fanny Fern?" In the article, he proceeded to list the numerous rumors about the identity of the fascinating new writer. Many suspected that this "woman writer" was likely a male writer, perhaps Moulton himself, or Reverend Norris. Maybe Fanny Fern was the pseudonym of New York City journalist Park Benjamin or the blockbuster abolitionist writer Harriet Beecher Stowe. A Mrs. Ellet of Cincinnati claimed to be the popular writer but after reading her pathetic imitations, most released that rumor back to the wind it rode into town on. Some said Fanny Fern was the wife of a famous Southern politician or maybe the New York poet, N. P. Willis.

"She can't be Willis," Sara heard the corn-cob smoking Irishman say from his plush chair in the boardinghouse keeping room. He sucked a deep draught and flicked his newspaper. "This writing is too fierce to come from such a namby-pamby."

"And vulgar!" agreed his tall, black-haired friend. "Did you see the article where she said she didn't mean to make her writing sound humorous, that that was the way she wrote when she couldn't 'find a razor handy to slit her own throat!' "

The blonde German with the thick fingers cleared his throat. "Words like that make me think this 'Jill' is a 'Jack.' "

"But that Jack can't be Norris," the Irishman said. "He's got one foot in the grave and the other in the church."

"It's Moulton," the black-haired gentleman said with a nod. "Have you ever met him? He looks like the type who always has a card up his sleeve."

The German again cleared his throat. "I heard a young reporter stationed himself for a week first by the *True Flag* and then by the *Olive Branch*. He says it's definitely a woman, or he ain't the man he always knew he was. A fine looker, too, from what he could see poking out of a swarm of widow's weeds."

"So that's the trick," the Irishman said, tapping his spent pipe into the little tin cup on the table. "Women in those costumes all look alike. You could put a man in one of those get-ups and nobody'd take the time to see the sham."

Sara slowly closed the section of the *Olive Branch* she'd been reading, swallowed the last of the coffee in her cup, and quietly rose from the table. She kept her eyes lowered as she passed the keeping room door and tried to keep her step even as she headed toward the stairs and to her room on the second floor.

"Like that one," the German whispered none-too-quietly as Sara passed. "Wouldn't it be something if Fanny Fern were dining with us every night?"

The three men broke into laughter.

"We'd have known Fanny Fern if we'd have seen her," the Irishman said. "She's probably as big as a wagon, brown, weathered, and with a rolling pin over her shoulder for good measure!"

Mrs. Dougherty jotted from the kitchen, intercepting Sara at the foot of the staircase. "Ma'am, a letter's just arrived for you."

Sara's heart leapt, first thinking she'd finally received a note of apology from Nat. But a quick glance caused her even more surprise. It was a letter from her Richard! He was, apparently, settled in New York. Her dear absent little brother must finally be home from Germany!

Sara took the letter to her room. Before opening her mail, she took off her shoes and placed them carefully in the corner, loosened her corset, and fluffed her fingers through the bits of curling honey-colored tendrils that always escaped the pins.

Richard had indeed arrived home from Germany where he'd gone to live the artist's life and to further his interest in music and composition. The surprise was that he'd been stateside for nearly a year, but hadn't been able to get information from Father or Nat about where to find her. Sara fumed. When would she ever be seen in a just light by the likes of either of those two? Richard had been working as a music teacher, just scraping by in the city. He had great news. He was soon to marry one of his students, which apparently Father disapproved of, but which would allow him, by virtue of her personal fortune, a much easier lifestyle than the impoverished one he'd held for so long. Dear Richard! He felt sorry he hadn't known of Sara's troubles and was offering his hand to her (albeit after the worst of the crises, Sara thought) in whatever way she could use it. What's more he had a burning question—was *she* the writer Fanny Fern that everyone was talking about? He'd seen the articles reprinted in a variety of New York papers and couldn't shake the idea that the writerly style was that of his own witty sister. He'd mentioned as much to Nat (who'd become reacquainted with Richard after learning of his favorable marriage plans) and Nat had scoffed. "He told me he'd seen your writing, a year or so ago, and it was indelicate and immature. Certainly nothing close to this Fanny Fern's, who is causing so much speculation," Richard wrote.

Sara blew an exasperated breath. Nat! She guessed she wouldn't be receiving a letter of apology after all. He had, indeed, seen samples of her writing—last summer when she had but a few cents to her name and was growing faint from walking the hot, dusty streets looking for a means of support. Sara still had his selfish reply, a letter bemoaning his annoyance at being harassed by her and with retorts to stop both writing and bothering him. She pulled it from its cache among her papers.

Dear Sara

I am suffering intensely from tooth-ache, in addition to my other ills, but I will try to answer your letter. New York is the most over-stocked market in the country, for writers, as we get a dozen applications a day from authors who merely wish to have the privilege of seeing themselves in print—writing for vanity only. Besides all the country flock & send here for fame etc. I have tried to find employment for dozens of starving writers, in vain. The *Home*

Journal pays for no contributions, being made up of extract, & so with all the papers, & many magazines.

Your writings show talent, but they are in a style that would only do in Boston. You overstrain the pathetic, and your humor runs into dreadful vulgarity sometimes. I am sorry that any editor knows that a sister of mine wrote some of these which you sent me. In one or two cases they trench very close on indecency. For God's sake, keep clear of that.

The most "broken reed," I know of, to lean upon for a livelihood, is amateur literature. The only chance is with the religious papers, which pay for a certain easily acquired kind of writing. Your education might enable you to do something of this. But in other literature I see no chance for you—unless, indeed, you can get employed by the editors you write for already.

I am sorry that I can write no more encouragingly, but I must speak honestly, & I would not keep you on a mistaken track.

I write in great pain,—you will excuse my abruptness.

Your affectionate brother

Sara's face still burned whenever she read Nat's cruel words. Not only would he not help her get a leg up in the publishing world, he was fairly certain her meager talent should be confined to small, unobtrusive ends. How, Sara wondered, did he believe she could eat on the wages of a hobbyist? How could she rear two daughters on pocket change? And why did he insult her with notions that she wrote from the same vain needs that likely drove him? She strove to keep her identity concealed even as she burned with the need to write frankly about all the injustices and insanities of society, including this one—the strange notion that no woman really needs any earnings because all women everywhere were soundly and comfortably kept by a system of filial love and obligation. Humbug to that! Boardinghouses and *the streets* were filled with female testaments to the opposite. But, of course, society turned a blind eye to such women in need, justifying this blindness with the little noble belief that somehow these women *deserved* their misfortune as divine repayment for sins and inadequacies, public or private.

As was usually the case when Sara read Nat's last words to her, she felt the pointed urge to throw his insults into the fire. Once, she'd even flung "To My Wild Sis," the beloved poem he'd written in her honor, to the flames, but had snatched it back again, the paper only receiving mild scorches along the edges. Sara composed herself and carefully folded the scorched poem, *a reminder*, and the letter, back into the envelope. She would not react in anger, tempted as she was. Deep down she still had the little-sister admiration and love for her big brother, Nat. Little brother Richard could stoke her up all he wanted and, for some strange reason, it would never mean as much as one puff from the lips of Nat.

Sara sighed, then reread Richard's missive. She smiled at the clear, strong script, and especially at his question, "Are you, dear Sara, this Fanny Fern?" His postscript informed Sara that he'd taken a position as editor with a New York paper, the *Musical World and Times*. He waxed on about the paper's owner, Oliver Dyer, an original thinker, good, sincere, frank, and independent, just the sort of person who heartily appreciated writers like Fanny Fern. He signed his letter with love and warmth and Sara was overcome. How long had it been since she'd felt such a balmy arm of encouragement from anyone in her family but Julia? Dear, dear Richard. She felt such a swelling of gratitude that she would do anything for him.

Sara finished reading Richard's words, then opened a second page he'd enclosed in the envelope. It was a sheet of music with a penciled inscription. "Wrote this a few months ago. What do you think?—Richard." Sara looked over the composition and hummed it as she read. How lilting. How beautiful. What a gorgeous Christmas carol this would make. Sara dashed off a little note of appreciation to him, both for the long-awaited correspondence and for the musical score. Before signing the letter, Sara wrote, "I hope, dear Richard, that you try very hard to publish your wonderful new composition, 'It Came Upon a Midnight Clear.' As a whole, it is so beautiful, so well crafted and so carefully written that I just know it will be well received."

Chapter Twenty

※

Oliver Dyer, New York, Friday, September 17th, 1852

Isn't it the funniest thing in life, that a woman can't be vital and energetic, without being thought masculine?

—Fanny Fern, *New York Ledger*, November 19th, 1870

Oliver Dyer, publisher of the New York *Musical World and Times*, settled his large frame in his chair, rolled up the cuffs of his shirtsleeves, loosened his crimson silk cravat, and spread the latest pages of circulation figures on his desk. He'd just come from another executive board meeting and, once again, didn't like the news. Advertising was down, overhead was up, and circulation hung disappointingly at the same level it'd been at for two years. Something had to change. This paper needed a boost, a punch, a shock of some sort, to jar it from its apathy into vibrancy again. True, Oliver felt fabulous about hiring the bright new editor, Richard Willis (who, thankfully, was nothing like that social-climbing brother of his), but even *he* couldn't make wine out of water. The paper needed life. It needed energy. Soaring, melodious articles, thought-ful reviews, and serious essays were important. They were the lifeblood of the musical world and Oliver was ever dedicated to serving that world and the talent within it. But talented people also wanted mental challenges. Beautiful souls produced new visions not only from places of light, but from the edges of light, and even from places of pain, frustration, and risk. Every musician, every artist, knew that. But how could he infuse his safe, solid paper with such a vague aim?

"Willis," Oliver called. "I need some thinking help."

Richard hurried over to his boss' desk and sat down in the wooden chair opposite it. "Yes, sir. I'll do what I can."

Oliver took in the sight of Richard Willis—neatly trimmed hair, brushed jacket, shined shoes. Richard was a man who took pride in his appearance, true, but also took pride in his character. He taught music on the side, as many of Oliver's employees did, and Oliver guessed Richard Willis was one of those teachers whose students left with new practice techniques and perhaps a joke or two, a teacher who made a true difference in his students' lives, a teacher who liked to teach. Oliver cleared the garble in his throat and shifted his weight in the broad, creaky chair. "You're generous, Willis. I like that about you. With your time, your thoughts. Generous."

"Thank you," Richard said. His clear eyes beamed. His cheeks puffed in a grin.

Oliver stroked his salt-and-pepper beard. "Circulation hasn't moved."

Richard's face fell softly. "I'm sorry, sir."

Oliver shrugged his shoulders. "We need something brighter for the pages. Livelier. Spunky but not coarse."

"I agree," Richard said. "Something irresistible to the readership."

"Yes, you see what I mean. What do you think?"

Richard swallowed, then excused himself for a moment. He hurried to his desk and came back with a stack of other New York newspapers. "If you look here, sir," he said.

Oliver held up his hand. "Stop right there. I know what you're going to say."

"But, sir."

"I know everyone clips and copies anything and everything these days, but I won't do it." Oliver shook his head briskly. "It's stealing, seems to me. Stealing ideas, sure, but stealing just the same."

"But nobody minds."

"You think not?" Oliver raised his eyebrows. "Do you think if you wrote your very heart into an essay or article and sold it for the pittance authors get from even the finest periodical that you wouldn't be the least bit perturbed to see that two-dollar piece copied and copied and copied until added up, each printing actually could be said to have netted you but a few pennies each?"

Richard nodded. "I agree with you, sir. For the most part."

"Good. What do you mean 'for the most part'?"

"I think we should clip and copy Fanny Fern's pieces. Her work is just the energy this paper needs. And I've talked with others. Whenever her pieces appear in a publication, no matter that they're copied, the publication's circulation climbs. *Climbs!* We could just use her once in a while, just until we've got a few more readers used to our pages."

Oliver stroked his beard. "I know what you mean about her. I've seen the pieces, too—and I never tire of them. But I can't get the idea out of my head that clipping and copying are a socially sanctioned form of piracy."

Richard nodded. "Your values are stronger than most men's. It's inspiring, sir."

"Inspiring, eh?" Oliver snorted. "Strong values don't necessarily improve circulation figures," he said.

Richard wrinkled his brow. "What are you saying?"

Oliver smiled, twisting his fingers through his beard. "I'm saying that I won't clip and copy Fanny Fern's work. But, I'll see if she will write some original pieces, just for us. Just like our other artists write music and lyrics, we could solicit her to contribute, too!"

"But, how? Nobody knows who she is."

"Leave that to me, Willis," Oliver said, dismissing the editor with a friendly wave. As Richard Willis shuffled back to his desk, a thoughtful smile playing at the corners of his lips, Oliver Dyer pulled a piece of stationery from his desk drawer, uncorked his ink, and wrote to Fanny Fern, in care of the Reverend Thomas F. Norris, the *Olive Branch*, Boston. In his letter, Oliver asked Fanny Fern to write exclusively for the *Musical World and Times*. "I'll pay you double your combined earnings from all of your sources and will honor and protect your anonymity," he wrote. "Please give this offer serious consideration. We are a paper dedicated to the aesthetic and the progressive and are led by a young genius of a musician and editor by the name of Richard Willis. I've enclosed copies of our latest issues for your perusal and hope our earnest desire to have your work showcased exclusively in our pages will become our happy reality in the near future." Oliver Dyer signed the letter and directed the mysterious Fanny Fern to address correspondence to himself or to Richard Willis, whomever she preferred.

Chapter Twenty-One

Sara Payson Willis Eldredge Farrington, Boston, Tuesday, February 1st, 1853

As a general thing there are few people who speak approbatively of a woman who has a smart business talent or capability. No matter how isolated or destitute her condition, the majority would consider it more "feminine" would she unobtrusively gather up her thimble, and, retiring into some out-of-the-way-place, gradually scoop out her coffin with it, than to develop that smart turn for business which would lift her at once out of her troubles; and which, in a man so situated, would be applauded as exceedingly praiseworthy. The most curious part of it is, that they who are loudest in their abhorrence of the "unfeminine" trait, are they who are the most intolerant of dependent female relatives . . . "Do something for yourself," is their advice in general terms; but, above all, you are to do it quietly, unobtrusively; in other words, die as soon as you like on sixpence a day, but don't trouble us! Of such cold-blooded comfort, in sight of a new-made grave, might well be born "the smart business woman." And, in truth, so it often is. Hands that never toiled before, grow rough with labor; eyes that have been tearless for long, happy years, drop agony over the slow lagging hours; feet that have been tenderly led and cared for, stumble as best they may in the new, rough path of self-denial. But out of this bitterness groweth sweetness. No crust so tough as the grudged bread of dependence.

—Fanny Fern, *New York Ledger*, June 8th, 1861

Sara sat in the café alone, at a small table near the back, sipping fresh tea and picking pieces from the edges of the walnut raisin pastries she'd ordered.

Late-winter sunshine bathed the café's pale yellow walls, warmed the heads of the patrons bent over newspapers along the counter. The café's tables were filling up with the post-breakfast crowd, clusters of clucking women gossiping and getting ready to shop. The shelves that held bakery were thinning and many a click and clack of china cup could be heard as coffee and tea were drunk in the low-burning glow of double cream-tiled fireplaces. Sara checked the clock on the wall behind the counter. Quarter past nine. How odd for Julia to be late.

Sara had walked Nelly to school, proud, as usual, to slip the warm woolen mittens on her little darling's fingers, to help her position her feet in the well-fitting, sturdy boots, to wrap her in a heavy shawl. Such pleasure from such simple things. Sara loved the feeling of being able to provide for herself and Nelly, loved being able to earn her own way. She was beginning to understand the world of men, the heady pull they must regularly feel toward career and earnings and self-reliance. It was a secret kept too long along sex lines, this secret of independence, this secret of self-accomplishment.

It was funny, though, how she was viewed by others—the head-shaking school mistress at Nelly's school, the throat-clearing shopkeepers, the quick-blinking boardinghouse keeper Mrs. Dougherty, and just about everyone else she happened to come in contact with. They didn't admire that she bustled down the street with purpose and a packet of business. They felt pity, or worse, for the poor widow forced to worry about the material, forced to engage in life. Sara smiled to herself. Ten years before, she might have shared these same views, might have fiercely defended her existence as wife, mother, and administrator of Swissdale—in charge of bread making and cake baking, flower arranging and pillow plumping. But *now.* She had mixed feelings. She had to admit that the strain of writing and chasing and collecting and figuring sometimes frazzled her edges to the point that she collapsed with an exhausted headache. Then she was no good to Nelly who wanted to play. Then she was no good for anything. But when she woke the next day, headache free, and felt her own strength running through her veins, and sold her own work, and collected her own wages, and paid her own bills, and provided for herself and her child, then the immense feeling of *purpose* blotted out any fatigue or wish for indolence, however momentarily pleasant. She had her independence, and that was a gift more women should experience.

The fact was that Sara found herself positively ambitious sometimes. Yes, it was true. As unfeminine and unflattering as that was thought to be, Sara was ambitious. And she was proud of it. She had happily accepted good Oliver Dyer's proposal to write for the New York *Musical World and Times* at double her combined Boston earnings. How could she refuse such a generous and flattering offer? At first she'd felt strange writing under a pen-name for a paper where her unsuspecting brother served as an editor. But she soon realized her persona of Fanny Fern was so immense in many people's minds that it couldn't reasonably be fit to a single person, let alone a person already in one's circle of acquaintance. Oliver Dyer had, indeed, doubled Sara's Boston salary. When Reverend Norris and Moulton heard that she planned to write exclusively for Oliver, they, in turn, raised her pay, too, hoping she could write for all three papers. Oliver proved to be a fair and understanding man and agreed to allow Sara to write an occasional column or two for each of the Boston papers, despite Sara's having signed an exclusivity agreement. "I want the best for you and your career," he'd written to her.

Sara was grateful for her opportunities, as she was grateful for her ambition. She would go on writing, Heaven knew there were unlimited supplies of ideas to write about, and she would continue to take care of herself and Nelly, and she would earn so much that she'd be able to wrench Grace from the Eldredges once and for all. It wouldn't be long now. Sara could feel it. Mary's last letter indicated that Hezekiah was very near death. Mary scolded, even with her pen, telling Sara that her mother's feeling came after a granddaughter's duty to a dying patriarch. Sara snorted at the letter, but acquiesced. Soon, nothing and nobody would keep her from cradling her lovely Grace again in her arms, in her home. She suspected there'd be other objections, other obstacles, even after Hezekiah passed. Mary was cunning as a fox. But Sara would not be kept from Grace any longer than necessary. As soon as Hezekiah breathed his last, she'd claim her daughter and would take care of her as well as anyone.

Fingers snapped in Sara's face, startling her from her thoughts. "Good morning!" Julia said. "My dreamy sister. I'm so sorry I'm late."

"Julia!" Sara rose and embraced her sister. "I was worried."

"I have interesting news," Julia said, untying her bonnet and seating herself on the bent-back chair. "But, first, let me look at you."

Julia appraised her sister, glad to see her figure filled out to its previous beauty, glad to see the pink in Sara's cheeks again, and the hint of gold light up her blue eyes. "You look well," Julia said.

Sara nodded. "As do you." And she meant it when she said that Julia looked well. True, Julia's eyelids were forever pink from too much reading and she could never manage a flattering hairstyle nor chase the pallor from her cheeks, yet Sara loved the spark of life in Julia's eyes that morning. It was a spark that came and went for Julia, depending on how oppressive her situation and how much hope filled her heart. Sara patted her sister's thin, pale hand.

"And Nelly?" Julia asked.

"Fit as ever."

"Dare I ask about Grace?"

Sara's mouth tightened. She had seen little of Julia since she'd left Samuel, so hadn't the luxury of a steady sisterly confidant regarding her heartbreaks.

Her father forbade Julia's taking a carriage to visit Sara in the shabby lodgings she'd been forced to take. He probably hoped that loneliness would add to the pressure he and Hezekiah bestowed on Sara to get her to see things reasonably, to get her to swallow her unwomanly pride and, perhaps, to give up rights to Grace forever. Julia was practically Sara's only support. Even though they rarely could sneak a visit together—the last being nearly a year before when Sara was almost penniless—when days were especially bleak, Sara relied on the memory of her sister's love and acceptance. When Sara received the note yesterday asking her to meet Julia at the café, she danced around the room. She couldn't wait to gaze into friendly eyes, to embrace real family devotion.

Sara told Julia about Grace, about the pressure to let her continue with the Eldredges, and about having so much trouble communicating and visiting with her, especially lately. Sara quickly thwarted Julia's baleful expression with her assurance that she *would*, very soon, put the situation to rights. She explained about her year's adventures in the world of writing. And, with a cat-who-ate-the-canary smile, Sara divulged her nom de plume.

Julia gasped, "*You're* Fanny Fern? How astonishing! I should have known it!"

Sara nodded brightly.

Julia grasped her sister's wrist. "You mustn't tell Father," she said. "He thinks she's shameful!"

"I don't doubt that."

"How reckless! The things you write about. Why you poke your fingers in all of our eyes then squeeze in a little lemon juice for good measure."

Sara arched her eyebrows. "I write from my heart. That's all I know."

"I should have known," Julia said again. "Well, *Fanny Fern* . . ."

"Shhh," Sara said, looking around the café. "You've no idea how many people are trying to find out my secret."

"I imagine as much," Julia said.

"I can't help worrying about what would happen if, if . . ."

Julia knitted her brows. "I know," she said. "That blackguard Farrington. It's a crime what a man can do to a woman's reputation."

Sara felt a knot clench tight, deep within her abdomen. Her cheeks reddened. "You've no idea."

Julia clasped Sara's hand. "And I don't need to know anything you don't want to tell. But I'm just sorry I encouraged you to marry that beast. And sorrier that our cowardly father and brothers aren't quick to defend your honor."

Sara's eyes brimmed.

Julia darted glances around the café. "It's disgusting," she whispered. "Susan has father wrapped around her shrill finger. And *Nat!*"

"Don't mention his name."

Julia nodded quietly. "I'm moving out, you know."

"Julia! How?"

Julia held a finger to her lips. "Not now, but soon. As soon as I can afford to. I need to escape Father and Susan's suffocating restrictions. I'll never marry."

"Julia."

Julia sighed. "No, it's true. And I don't care. But I won't give up my life because of it. I've decided I will have to support myself. I want to! I do."

"I know exactly how you feel," Sara said.

"I want to travel and I want to . . ." Julia hesitated. "This is going to sound silly after what you've just told me, but . . ."

"Go on!" Sara said.

"I want to write," Julia said. "Already I've got Father paying me for my *Youth's Companion* pieces."

"And why not? He pays other writers!"

"Exactly."

"Oh, Julia, how wonderful for you, for us," Sara said. "Don't you feel you've stumbled upon some great secret world?"

"Yes! But I am a little afraid, too."

"With the experience of freedom comes the insecurity of it," Sara said.

"I've been writing for other publications," Julia said. "Little ones. Little pieces. But, just the same, I am earning more than I ever could sewing."

"Yes. And good for you," Sara said. "Women, despite the idea that the world shelters them, are too easily exploited if they need to earn a living."

"I couldn't agree more!"

"My blood boils because of it," Sara said.

"Mine as well!"

"When I think of the bleary hours I'd sit, bent over shirts and vests, sewing for all I was worth and barely earning enough for a grateful of wood and a mouthful of bread at the end of it all," Sara said.

"Unconscionable!"

"And I was just one of many. You, for instance. And others. Hundreds of other women. Women trying to earn a living wage trimming hats or washing clothes or—"

"I *know*, Sara."

Sara took a breath. "Of course you do," she said. "And the worst of it is how people who wouldn't have batted an eye to sit at your Sunday table with you when you were in good times, and to eat from your larder and drink from your cellar, can't be bothered to say 'Good Morning' to you when you're down on your luck for fear you might ask them for a penny or might embarrass them with your faded neck ribbon or scuffed boots."

Julia sighed. "Or catch what you've got. Poverty or spinsterhood."

Sara shuddered. "Thank Heaven *you* understand," she said.

"You know I do. And you, *Fanny*," Julia said, "will make others understand.

Just then, a little crowd bustled into the café, waiting in a gaggle of groups to be seated. They were holding thick, brand-new books and talking excitedly while waving the books around and pointing out passages from their pages.

Sara narrowed her eyes, focusing. "Why if that isn't . . ." she said, then quickly excused herself momentarily from Julia and hurried to the group of people. Squeezing the elbow of a vibrant small woman, Sara cried, "Harriet Beecher!"

Chapter Twenty-Two

Harriet Beecher Stowe, Boston, Tuesday, February 1st, 1853

"Mrs. Stowe's *Uncle Tom* is too graphic ever to have been written by a woman."—*Exchange.*

"Too graphic to be written by a woman?" D'ye hear that, Mrs. Stowe? or has English thunder stopped your American ears? Oh, I can tell you, Mrs. "Tom Cabin," that you've got to pay "for the bridge that has carried you over." Do you suppose that you can quietly take the wind out of everybody's sails, the way you have, without having harpoons, and lampoons, and all sorts of *miss*—iles thrown after you? No indeed; every distanced scribbler is perfectly frantic; they stoutly protest your book shows no genius, which fact is unfortunately corroborated by the difficulty your publishers find in disposing of it; they are transported with rage in proportion as you are translated. . . . Certainly; what right had you to . . . in short, to raise such a little young tornado to sweep through the four quarters of the globe? You? nothing but a woman—an American woman! and a Beecher at that! . . . you had no "call," Mrs. Tom Cabin, to drop your babies and darning-needle to immortalize your name. . . . I trust you are convinced by this time that "Uncle Tom's Cabin" is a "flash in the pan." I'm sorry you have lost so much money by it, but it will go to show you, that women should have their ambition bounded by a gridiron, and a darning needle. If you had not meddled with your husband's divine inkstand for such a dark purpose, nobody would have said you was "40 years old and looked like an Irish woman;" and between you and me and the vestry door, I don't believe they've done with you yet; for I see that every steamer tosses fresh laurels on your orthodox head, from foreign shores, and foreign powers. Poor unfortunate Mrs. Tom Cabin! Ain't you to be pitied.

—Fanny Fern, *Olive Branch*, May 28th, 1853

Harriet Beecher Stowe clumped, exhausted, down the front hallway of the Boston hotel, key in hand. In her other hand was her supper, a paper sack with three blueberry muffins. In her pocket was Sara Willis' boardinghouse address and a damp handkerchief.

Harriet didn't know how much more stress she could handle. She absolutely craved the loving arms of her Calvin and the cherubic faces of her children, but she was alone in this city, as she was in other cities lately, promoting her book. As was typical in times like these, when she was feeling tired and lonely, she felt more strongly the familiar stab to her heart—the keen pulse of pain that losing a child produces in a loving parent, no matter how much time had passed. Oh, darling babe! It was all so much mental chaos and Harriet's hand shook as she worked the key to her room.

She shut the heavy oak door behind her and locked it; unlaced and pulled off her boots; and hung her cloak, dress, and underskirts up in the armoire. The innkeeper had kindly started a fire in the grate and Harriet stirred it and added coal from the pail near the hearth. She brushed her hands together and held them for a moment over the growing warmth. Harriet unlaced her corset and took several deep breaths the way sister Katy recommended for nervous exhaustion. Harriet took very serious breaths. She wanted to be sure to keep on top of her nervousness and mental strains so as not to end up "indisposed," as Katy called her own periods of recuperation. Harriet and Katy had had several frank discussions about Katy's periods of rehabilitation, periods absolutely insisted upon by their father, Lyman, and brother, Henry Ward. How could Harriet ever forget the last time? Katy's tear-stained face as she begged Harriet to interfere on her behalf, to somehow convince her usually liberal father and brother that Katy needed support, not social banishment, as Katy put it. How could Harriet forget Katy's tight-cheeked words, "You don't know how it is for me there. The treatment gets to be worse than the illness."

Father and Henry kept close watch on Katy, as they did on all the Beecher women, as all men did on all women. Sister Isabelle worked tirelessly on her woman's suffrage issues, Katy on spreading women's educational opportunities, and she, Harriet, on her abolitionist cause. Even Mary did more than the average woman, encouraging her children, especially Frederick, to attend lectures and to write and read and open their minds to new ideas. But even though Father was proud of them, his daughters, he said they were all flirting with the limits of nature, overtiring their delicate constitutions with travel and work and business. Katy and Harriet decided they'd probably be just fine if they were allowed to operate in the world without pinching shoes and corsets—oh, to eat a full meal in public without feeling aftershocks of indigestion, or maybe to stride into a room or up a hill without fretting that a puddle might leave some dingy hemline stain or that after too much tramping, one would lose the feeling in one's toes. Katy and Harriet wanted to embrace committees and town meetings in all weather, without worrying about ruining curled hair and miles of expensive lace. They wished to deliver serious speeches without the prerequisite smiles and ask important questions without male peers feeling the need to feed them obligatory womanly compliments. It was because they were trying to do all they did while engaged in their roles as women that their constitutions were sometimes taxed. It wasn't that they had naturally inferior constitutions.

Father and Henry were unusually understanding, for men, but still they watched. And when one of them, usually Katy, showed signs of anxiety or fatigue—strings of tart words, a too-flushed or too-pale complexion, drumming fingers, twitching eyelids, bitten fingernails—she'd get whisked to the waters for treatment. At first, Katy delighted in her little reprieves. She'd write Harriet about how wonderful it felt to walk around in loose garments and flat slippers, eating all she could without stomach complaint, drinking great quantities of healthful tonics and plunging daily into the warm, swirling waters of the baths. But then the other letters would come, the ones complaining that she was too long forgotten at the end of the world, that she actually needed less solitude and more civilization. The trouble with the water treatments, Katy always said, is that they go on for too long. Although a week or two of recuperation would always be beneficial to the fatigued, nobody needed to be isolated for months. It wasn't healthy. In fact, it was harmful. A funny thing happened with too much social deprivation, Katy said. A person's soul sunk below a relaxed state into stupor and then despondency. Katy fought hard, then, to keep her energy and spirits up, to keep her mind full of ideas and empty of self-pity. If Father or Henry visited Katy and she wasn't perfectly balanced between a state of relaxation and a state of interest, they'd usually decide she needed another fortnight of treatment, and nothing anyone, even Katy, said, could convince them otherwise. It was no wonder Harriet strove to conceal any signs of strain and anxiety from her male relatives, despite being sure that a little venting and a strong embrace would do much to invigorate her. Thank goodness for sisters and women friends, safe places to clear the air.

Harriet pulled a soft beige shawl from her trunk and wrapped it around her shoulders. She unpacked two muffins and reclined on the white top cover of her bed in just her shawl, pantaloons, and loosed corset to eat them. She rolled her ankles in little circles and pulled the pins out of her hair as she chewed.

She'd have to write Katy in the morning about her eventful day in Boston. Isabelle, Mary, and Frederick had met her in town at the ten o'clock book sign-ing. It was one of many such appearances Harriet had made in recent weeks. She still couldn't believe that her little missive from God, *Uncle Tom's Cabin*, was being so well received. Ten thousand copies sold in the first week alone and no lag in sales these months later. Harriet's heart grew full when she thought of the minds her simple words might be opening, the hearts and souls of the enslaved she might be freeing. After working for Katy at the Hartford Female Seminary, Harriet had moved to Cincinnati with her father and had taught in a school there. They were living just across the Kentucky border and Harriet was astonished to see figures crossing the river when she'd go for purple-hued walks at dusk. The Fugitive Slave Act had been in effect some two years by then and the atmosphere of the fair-minded state of Ohio was charged with distrust and secrecy. When Harriet saw a slave mother crossing the half-frozen river one evening, barefoot, and cradling a scantily clad toddler in her arms, she decided she'd have to do *something* to turn this country's thinking around. Thankfully, Calvin encouraged her writing, but it wasn't until after her own darling son died of cholera that Harriet's empathy for that remembered slave mother sparked brightest. That image, of a mother risking her life for her child, was one that even the most conservative slave owners wouldn't be able to argue with. These people were human beings, with all the feelings, the natural joys and sorrows, of human beings. They were not mere possessions, labor to be traded, *animals*. America must rid itself of the sin of slavery. And if it took pricking the hearts of parents to get her message across, then Harriet would do it.

Most everyone Harriet knew had keenly felt the pain of death within their families and the injustices of the world. But few stories could match the severity of what had happened to spry Sara Willis. Harriet wiped her eyes with the back of her hand thinking of the trials Sara had endured. In school, Har-riet had admired Sara's popularity, even as she bristled at Sara's social gaffes. She'd longed for Sara's self-confidence and easy, forthright charm, even as she shuddered at her tactlessness, her brazen materialism, her occasional vulgarity. At dances, every boy wanted to dance with Sara, even if he was soon discarded. At picnics, every girl wished to be counted her friend. Sara seemed infallible then, as if she'd skate across the surface of life's bumps without a care. Harriet supposed it was a good thing Sara had started out so strong. The burdens Sara had had to contend with, since, would have crushed weaker spirits. First, losing so many loved ones—her mother, sister, daughter, and wonderful husband—in so short a period of time. Then, having to give up Grace and scrape by for years, living on pennies and milk-bread. Sara Willis—in a third-rate boardinghouse! Practically disowned by her family! Nearly divorced! Deserted by her husband, in any case. Or had *she* left *him*?

Harriet was so tired she couldn't remember the exact details. All she knew was she had been horrified when Sara had whispered in her ear, "My name is Sara Farrington." *The* Sara Farrington who took multiple lovers to her rooms and flaunted the sacred vows of marriage before her church-going husband, before even her own children? That's what people said anyway. That's what Samuel Farrington said. But one look at Sara's face, drawn and pale as she began to recount her punishing marriage was enough to make Harriet wave her hands in protest. And that he still wrote to her, horrible letters demanding she take her place as his wife, no matter where she moved, no matter what name she used. Harriet finally held both hands firmly in front of her. Stop, Sara, her hands said. I believe you. Harriet couldn't, *wouldn't*, hear any more of the piercing details. She knew pain when she saw it etched on a person's forehead, and pain is exactly what Sara Willis' face was imprinted with. Harriet pulled Sara close and rested her head on Sara's own. Sara quivered in response. Poor thing. To have gone through such unhappiness, such hardships, and then to be accused of lacking womanly virtue. To be so formidably condemned in public, yet obsessively followed by the same man in private. Harriet was sure few women could stand such a trial. That's how women mysteriously ended up drowned in some distant river. That's also how able-bodied women disappeared overnight only to reappear in some distant city as cook, governess, or midwife. That's how convents and insane asylums filled up. Harriet warned Sara to be careful and Sara had solemnly nodded.

But Harriet had great hope. Sara Payson Willis Eldredge Farrington was no ordinary woman. She'd wrapped herself in widow's weeds and had become yet another name. She bowed her head and sweetly whispered it to Harriet— *Fanny Fern*. Her Sara Willis was *the* Fanny Fern. Harriet laughed and clapped her hands. What sweet revenge! Oh, what would Katy say? Sara Willis, Sara Eldredge, Sara Farrington, was Fanny Fern. Who better to take on the injustices of society? Who better to call a blackguard by name and to name a gentleman by his behavior? Who better to throw off her shackles and escape social traps? Who better than Sara Willis? Who better than Fanny Fern?

Chapter Twenty-Three

Fanny Fern, Boston, Tuesday, February 8th, 1853

A little fatherless boy, four years of age, sat upon the floor, surrounded by his toys. . . . Dry your tears, young mother. . . . Cloud not his sunny face with unavailing sadness, lest he "catch the trick of grief," and sigh amid his toys.

—Fanny Fern, *Fern Leaves from Fanny's Portfolio*

Sara carried a tray with a glass of warm milk up from the boardinghouse's dark kitchen to Nelly. It was close to midnight and poor Nelly couldn't sleep again. She wasn't physically ill like she'd been the winter before, but she was heartsick. Nelly missed Grace. The more days and weeks and months and, Sara swallowed hard thinking of it, *years*—it would be almost two years!—went by, the harder it was for Sara to convince Nelly that she'd ever have her sister as her playmate again.

Sara paused on the landing to the second floor, in front of Herbert Winslow's door. Mr. Winslow was an herb doctor. He'd once given Nelly some ground up plant parts that made her lingering cough clear up for good. As if beckoned, Mr. Winslow opened his door at just that moment, nodded to Sara and her tray, muttered something about how somebody couldn't sleep again, eh, and then put a little pouch on the tray next to the glass. "A pinch ought to do it," he said, patting Sara's wrist.

"Thank you, Mr. Winslow. You've no idea how—"

"I can only hazard a guess," Mr. Winslow said. "Anyway, a child needs to sleep."

Sara nodded and continued down the hall to the next door, which was her room.

"Mother!" Nelly shrieked from the bed as Sara entered, nearly causing Sara to spill the tray in surprise. "You're finally back!"

Sara hushed little Nelly as she closed the door behind her. The moon was shining almost-full through the mullioned window and a heap of embers still glowed and cracked in the fireplace. "Of course I'm back. I told you I would be!" She put the tray on the bedside table, sat on the little bed, and gathered Nelly into her arms.

"Oh, Mother," Nelly said, sobbing.

Sara rocked her daughter in her arms. "What is it, dear?"

"Mother." Nelly sobbed again. "I'm so afraid and worried and lonesome."

Sara stroked Nelly's flaxen curls. "I know, my darling."

"I worried you were gone for good. Gone like Grace. Oh, I miss her so!"

"There, there," Sara said. "Calm yourself. I'm lonesome for Grace, too."

"Then why don't you get her? We have enough to share with her, too, now."

Sara sighed. How she *wanted* to retrieve Grace. More than anything, she did want to retrieve Grace. "It's not so simple, my love. Papa and Nana Eldredge need Grace to stay with them for a little while longer. Papa Eldredge is very sick and wants Grace to help care for him."

"But you promised her that as soon as . . . just as soon . . ." Nelly buried her face in her hands. Fresh cries wracked her body.

Sara tasted bile. She was sick about Grace, too, and had even consulted a lawyer the day before in order to better understand her rights. Her rights were solid. She was Grace's mother and had never given that up. She had every right to go and pull Grace away from the Eldredges that instant. But the larger picture was more complicated. Mary's anguished letters in which she was already grieving Hezekiah, long missives begging not to have to lose Grace so quickly, *too*, were almost too much to read. As much as she ached to have Grace with her again, Sara was sympathetic. She of all people knew the cost multiple losses extracted on one's life energy. It'd been over six years since Charly's death, and longer still since mother's and sister Ellen's and little Mary's and Mary Stace's and the children and *still* Sara mourned. It really wasn't punishment for her to wear her widow's weeds as a disguise. She still *felt* newly widowed. Sometimes she had the wispy feeling that maybe Samuel Farrington and her marriage to him had only been a dream. A horrible dream, to be sure, but just a dream. But then, Sara would look around at her boardinghouse room and her small collection of material possessions, and at the oft-filled inkstand sitting on the corner table, and she would know that it was real. All of it. Charly's death, and

Mary's and Mother's and Ellen's—and Samuel, and Mr. Schueller, and leaving Grace, and the writing, and then Sara didn't know whether to laugh or cry.

She hugged Nelly close. "Shhh. Shhh. We'll get Grace very soon."

"Oh, Mother," Nelly said. "When you left I was afraid you were never coming back. I was afraid you were leaving me, too."

"Nelly!"

"Like we did Grace. I remember how we left her. And now we can't get her back, even if we want to."

"Yes, we can," Sara said. "We can and we will! Just you wait another little while and see what Mother does."

Nelly nodded, unconvinced.

"I got us out of that garret, didn't I?"

Nelly nodded.

"And I got you into a nice school and you have new shoes and a dress like the other girls."

"And we eat more than bread and milk now," Nelly offered.

"Yes, darling. You'll see. It won't be long now."

Nelly's chin quivered. "I miss Grace *so*. I feel like the next time I get to see her, she might be all grown."

Sara looked straight into Nelly's eyes. "You will see her before next Christmas comes. I promise."

Nelly smiled a small, wary smile. Her chin dropped to her chest. "Yes, Mother," she said.

"Better yet, she will spend next Christmas with us," Sara said, hugging Nelly tightly. "I promise," she whispered into Nelly's hair.

Nelly pulled away from Sara's embrace and nodded briskly. "May I have my milk now?"

Sara bit her lip. Nelly didn't believe her. She had tried to, like a good little girl, but, still, she didn't. "Of course you may have your milk," Sara said, the line between her eyebrows deepening. She opened the small muslin pouch and put a pinch of the golden-brown powder into the glass of milk. "This is from Mr. Winslow. Remember how his medicine helped your cough? This will help you fall asleep."

Nelly drank her milk and laid her head on her pillow, her features still as stone.

Sara sat on the side of the bed, smoothing Nelly's flaxen curls. She sighed a shaky sigh. How was it that her spunky child was suddenly afraid? Suddenly distrustful? Nelly was a strong little girl, a brave spirit, but she was still a child. Sara might be keeping her together bodily, but what was this kind of life doing to her spirit? It was no wonder Nelly was losing her faith. Despite that many people believed a little hardship was good for children, that firm and hearty punishment kept the devil out of them, Sara didn't believe in those things.

She believed that children needed a childhood. They needed time and space to play and imagine and be loved and spoiled and coddled. There was plenty of time to face the grueling cruelties of living. Why not let the innocent run wild among fields of clover, if even for a little while? When they're older, those sweet memories might help to sustain them through troubles. Sara thought of her own childhood, about her stern father and loving mother, and about how she sometimes felt—even now—that she was still living, still surviving, off her mother's love. Mother's and Charly's.

Sara sighed again. Nelly's breathing was slow and even. Her eyelids fluttered in sleep. Sara tucked the coverlet snuggly around her daughter, quietly left the bedside, then went to the bureau drawer and took out the white satin wedding vest and miniature likeness of her Handsome Charly. She rubbed the vest on her cheek. She had nestled her face against this very vest on the first evening of her marriage. She stared at the miniature. She used to run her hands through that thick dark hair, had buried her cheek into that very neck, had gazed lovingly into those sparkling dark eyes. The love she'd shared with Charly started out young, but Sara soon discovered it went beyond any girlish foolery women seemed to constantly seek. How had she been so fortunate? True, she and Charly had started out adoring each other, babbling their delight at the mere sight of the other, cherishing every moment spent together, no matter what the task. But instead of dying like a hot blaze eventually does, that feeling had grown into a steady warm glow, a deep respect and alliance, a true companionship. Sara could be herself with Charly and always felt loved and accepted as she was. She didn't need to force herself into some ideal womanly mold, didn't need to watch her step, monitor her words, censor her ideas. Since Charly died, Sara better understood the gift she'd had in him, and understood that their marriage was not like most marriages. She thought of Samuel and shivered. Not at all.

And now she was stealing that wonderful safe and happy feeling from Nelly. Not purposely, but it was happening just the same. And who knew if the same or worse was happening to Grace. Sara couldn't allow it. Not as long as she was their mother. She went to the table in the corner, the table that held her old inkstand and a small sheaf of paper. She took a piece of paper from the pile and addressed it. No, she was not writing another column, though the idea had certainly crossed her mind. She was writing a letter. A letter in answer to a question she'd received some three weeks before.

Chapter Twenty-Four

Grace Eldredge, Newton, Tuesday, February 8th, 1853

Thank Heaven, I can stand alone! Can you? Are you yet at the end of your life journey? Have you yet stood over the dead body of wife or child, snatched from you when life was at the flood tide of happiness? . . . If a woman, did you ever face poverty where luxury had been, and vainly look hither and thither for the summer friends that you would never see again till larder and coffer were replenished? Are you sure, when you boast that you can "stand alone," that you have learned also how to fall alone?

—Fanny Fern, *New York Ledger*, August 26th, 1871

Grace was weary. She was weary of waking at dawn, doing her homework, and going to the horrible country school that only had one other girl in it—Francine, who was four years older than Grace, and already engaged to be married, so didn't need anyone's company. She was weary of rushing home from school to help Maggie in the kitchen or Nana with her sewing. She was weary of tea with Nana and Nana's prickly questions about Grace's wickedness and willfulness, the way Nana's tight mouth made Grace feel like an ant. She was weary of breathing through her mouth because of the moth-ball smell that followed Nana around like a poisoned cloud. She was weary of having to take care of Papa Eldredge every evening so Nana could read and relax. She was weary of Papa Eldredge's pickled smell—a smell worse than Nana's, a smell between bad vinegar and old tobacco, a smell Grace was blasted with hour after hour as she wiped his waxy face with the cool cloth, succumbed to the parchy grasp of his clawish palm, slipped grainy broth between his cracked lips. Grace was weary of waiting for her mother.

Grace walked slowly up the stairs to her bedroom. The bird in Grace's chest fluttered with worry and she shook her head. No, she reminded herself, it was not *her* bedroom. It was only the place she slept while she was staying with Papa and Nana Eldredge. It was usually easy to remember that she was just visiting. She must be especially tired.

The bird in her chest stirred again. What if she kept getting so tired that eventually she might wake up some morning and forget she was visiting and would fall in line with Nana's ways of thinking and start hating Mother, and thinking her selfish and spoiled, and distrusting Nelly, and thinking her uncouth and greedy, and, instead, would finally start cherishing this fine opportunity for self-improvement she'd been given by the good Lord and by Papa and Nana themselves? What if she finally listened to her grandparents and finally felt grateful for the sweat and grief she caused them, and remorse for being the innately wicked and corrupt thing she was? Worse, what if her pinned-on smile fell off into the oatmeal as she stirred it, or if the bird in her chest died from old age, and she was left with nothing to remind her of right and wrong?

The bird moved wildly at these thoughts and Grace smiled a genuine smile. Her bird was fine. Her bird would never let her forget. She was thankful for her bird. It kept her grounded. It had come alive within her the moment Grace understood that Mother was truly leaving her, *temporarily*, with Papa and Nana Eldredge. Grace imagined it was a bluebird. Bluebirds could only be helpful. Her bird acted as her barometer. When it fluttered, Grace knew to be careful, suspicious. Sometimes it fluttered when she walked into the parlor and Nana Eldredge was sitting quietly on the horsehair settee with her eyes closed and the Bible open on her lap. Then Grace was reminded to tread as softly and gracefully as possible, lest she disturb Nana's solemn reflection about Jesus Christ. Sometimes it fluttered when Nana told Grace confusing things, like that she was an ugly, unlovable girl, or that her mother was never coming back. Then Grace knew she shouldn't believe those statements. Sometimes it fluttered when Grace, herself, thought certain things, like that she was walking up the stairs to *her* bedroom. The fluttering reminded her to correct her ways of thinking lest she go down some frightening, one-way road.

Mother *was* coming back. She had to. Grace's eyes stung as she climbed the wooden stairs. She just had to. Grace didn't know how much longer she could hold onto her womanly smile, how much longer she could be good. Sometimes, when Grace was walking to school, she fantasized about walking all the way to Boston and finding the boardinghouse on Cambridge Street and waiting on the front stoop for Mother and Nelly to come home from their errands. Oh, how happy Mother would be to see her! She'd sweep her up into her arms and would hug her and kiss her and tell her how she was her own most special lovable girl who had a luxurious place right in the middle of her heart, and always would, forever and ever. Then Mother would be astonished at how grown-up Grace was, and how capable, to walk all the way from Papa and Nana's to their Boston boardinghouse. She'd be thrilled with the little bouquet of flowers Grace would have picked on the way and presented, ta da, with flair, as a glad-to-be-back-together gift. And even though Mother might say she still hadn't enough money to keep Grace, Grace would convince Mother how little money it took to keep her. She'd show her how fine her sewing had gotten these past almost-two years. She'd show Mother how daintily she could eat a piece of bread and how long she could make it last in her mouth without swallowing. Mother would be awed by Grace's new skills, so awed she'd laugh her jolly laugh and would admit that, of course, there was room for Grace, again, in what was left of their family.

Nelly would be so happy to see her beloved big sister. She surely always admired Grace and would jump at the chance to have someone to follow around again and to ask a million questions of. If Mother still had the tiniest shred of doubt left, Nelly would beg Mother to let Grace stay and would offer to split her dinner with her every night. It would be just like old times. She and Nelly would put their heads together and figure out ways to help Mother without Mother noticing. They'd stir the fire when Mother took a little nap. They'd pour just a little more water into the milk bottle to show that it wasn't so low after all. They'd darn the holes in their socks and mittens on the little bench in front of the boardinghouse with their secret needle and the thread they found on the floor under Mother's chair.

When Grace had such daydreams, she almost cried with joy. Walking to school, she pictured the whole scene and how easily everything could be set to rights. But then she'd remember Nana saying how Mother and Nelly had moved from the Cambridge Street place, how they were in a different place now, a place that Grace, try as she might, never could exactly place within her memories of Boston. She would probably walk all the way to Boston and would get lost. She'd never find Mother or Nelly and would wander around until she starved or froze to death or until somebody discovered she'd run away from her grandparents. Then she'd either go to an orphan's house or would be sent back to Newton. Grace shuddered thinking about the reception she'd likely get at either place. She was probably better off waiting patiently, as Mother had told her to do on each of her four visits. Wait, Grace darling, she had said. I will come back for you.

Grace hadn't expected so few visits. And she hadn't expected so few letters. Mother and Nelly visited three times within the first few months alone. Grace had expected such regular visits to continue. It was almost a year before

Mother and Nelly came again and Grace was so startled to see her wonderful mother sitting before her in the flesh that she was dumbstruck. Mother hugged her ferociously and Grace tried to hug back, she did. But she'd gotten so used to living hugless, to living deep within herself. She'd gotten so used to slinking behind her womanly smile that she couldn't make her body feel, couldn't unpin her smile from its funny clothesline and show her real self. So, she'd sat at her usual three-legged chair by the fire and sewed the hem of the skirt she was working on, while Nelly gobbled up Nana's butter cookies (well, not exactly *Nana's*, but the ones Nana had put in her pocket at the O'Mally's Christmas party), and Mother spoke with Nana, yet stared at Grace with that horrible wrinkle between her eyebrows. Grace knew Mother wanted her to speak more, but she had been so overwhelmed that she was afraid she'd break down if she moved her tongue, would shudder apart if she ventured a real sentence. So Grace mostly nodded her head and blushed, which thrilled Nana to no end, as it proved that Grace was becoming a real lady.

Grace entered the room she stayed in while she visited Papa and Nana Eldredge and untied the bow at the back of her dress. She unbuttoned the row of buttons down her back and hung the dress up immediately, instead of letting it lie on the coverlet like slovenly girls sometimes do. She slipped into the threadbare cotton sleeping gown, careful not to glance at her sinful form in the mirror, lest the devil sneak into her soul and blow out her flickering light. It was chilly in her room, as Nana didn't think it prudent to waste coal on a fire that would likely be neglected by an ungrateful child. Grace poured water into the basin and set her teeth before splashing her face and arms with the frigid liquid. Cleanliness is next to Godliness and Lord knew how much dirt Grace managed to accumulate without even trying. Nana saw it in the slop jar, saw it in the chamber pot. Grace would probably never be truly clean.

Grace undid the hair braids looped over her ears and took the pins out of the arrangement she'd made at the nape of her neck. She brushed her hair one hundred times, tensing a different toe each tenth stroke for good measure. Grace took her old wool shawl off the peg behind the door, the one she'd worn when she last left Boston, and, climbing beneath her coverlet, bunched it up in her arms like Nelly used to do with her rag doll. She still smelled Mother on that shawl, bits of Nelly, too. Grace put her face to the fabric and inhaled deeply. No moth-ball Nana smell. No pickled Papa smell. Just bits of Mother's slight ferny smell. Just bits of Nelly's milky-child smell. Grace inhaled and inhaled and inhaled. She wanted to pull Mother and Nelly deep within her lungs so the bird could smell them, too, so the bird could relax and go to sleep. Poor little bird. Sleep little bird. As the bird finally drifted off, Grace did, too, to the lovely smell of ferns and milk. As Grace bumped along in sleepy gray, she eventually smelled Father's hair tonic and sister Mary's dandelion wreath and Nana Hannah's cherry tart, too. She tasted pumpkin pie and raisin cake. She felt the sun warm on her sun bonnet as she sauntered through the meadow at Swissdale. She heard the meadow birds twitter and the heat-buzz of the cicadas. She heard the little lalala songs Mother sang as she kneaded bread and the way the parlor door always used to click shut after the tea tray was taken away and everyone stared lazily into the roaring fire and patted their bellies and said happy things to one another. Grace saw Mother's beautiful face float in front of her. Mother's pretty hair. Her blue eyes. Her merry dimples. Her rosy lips moving and smiling, quietly saying over and over, "Be patient, my Gracie Girl. I'm coming back for you."

"*Mother!*"

Chapter Twenty-Five

Oliver Dyer and Fanny Fern, Boston, Thursday, February 10th, 1853

Walking along the street the other day, my eye fell upon this placard,—
MEN WANTED. Well; they have been "wanted" for some time; but the
article is not in the market, although there are plenty of spurious imitations.

—Fanny Fern, *Musical World and Times*, September 24th, 1853

Fanny Fern opened the door and stood in the boardinghouse doorway wearing a
simple periwinkle muslin with cream netting at the throat and cuffs. Her amber
tresses were carefully done up in a style that showed off her natural curls. Her
cheeks, however, were pale and Oliver Dyer could tell she was upset or maybe
nervous by the way she twisted a handkerchief in her hands.

"You've come," she breathed, darting her eyes up and down the corridor.

"You're here," he said at the same instance.

Fanny rushed into Oliver's arms. "Oh, Oliver! It's so good to finally meet
you. I feel such a brotherly protection, such a friendship—"

"Hush, dear little sister," Oliver said. "I'm your champion. Always. And
it is *my* pleasure to finally meet *you*, Sara Willis." He whispered in excitement,
"*Fanny Fern!*"

Just then Mrs. Dougherty, who had shown Oliver in, happened past the
two standing in Fanny's doorway and gave them both a narrow-eyed nod. "I
see you finally wriggled out of them weeds," she said. "*Mrs. Eldredge.*"

Fanny dropped her eyes to the floor and bit her lip.

Oliver cleared his throat. "Perhaps we should sit in the parlor?"

Fanny shook her head quickly. "No, I don't want to talk here at all. Shall we walk?"

"We could have tea at one of the hotels."

"Perfect," Fanny said. Her hands shook as she pinned a modest feathered cap to her head.

As they walked to the hotel, Oliver Dyer had to keep stealing his eyes sideways to get a look at the woman he'd only dreamed of meeting. He remembered his excitement the day Richard told him they'd received a letter from Fanny Fern herself, accepting his offer to write exclusively for the New York *Musical World and Times*. And to think Fanny Fern had turned out to be his new editor's sister! Oliver felt like he'd found the pot of gold at the end of a very long rainbow. Oliver himself had set the huge type for the front page announcement last September, telling all of his readership that his smallish, prudent, New York periodical had managed to snag the most adored new writer ever, and to gain her new pieces exclusively. And here it was, less than a half a year later, and he was finally, and rightfully, meeting the enigma in the flesh.

"Thank you, again," he said, "for granting me this interview."

Fanny stopped dead in the street, wide-eyed. "It's me who is grateful," she said. "I didn't know where else to turn."

There was something about those deep blue eyes that bore straight into Oliver's heart. In their correspondence these past months, he'd sensed her respectable character, but now he was finally witnessing it. "Shall I call you Sara or Fanny?" he said. "I always think of you as Fanny."

"Call me Fanny, then," she said. "I'm beginning to think of myself that way, too."

They took a seat in the tea room of the Coastal Hotel and ordered. Fanny removed her gloves and laid them on the table next to her cup. "I had to tell them, you know," she said. "They said they wouldn't allow me to sign a contract."

"Understandable," Oliver said. "They should be discreet, though. They've no reason to reveal your identity."

"I don't care a whit except for . . ."

"I know," Oliver said. "Richard told me all about that rascal Farrington."

"He's poisoned my reputation," Fanny said.

"All the more reason to remember that you're Sara Willis. That you're Sara Eldredge. That you're Fanny Fern."

Fanny lowered her eyes. "What will come of all this?"

"Who knows? Who cares?" Oliver said. "You've signed a book contract, and that's the important thing. They're publishing your article collection under Fanny Fern, correct?"

Fanny nodded. "But Moulton has been behaving slyly lately."

"He's a prig," Oliver said, sipping his tea. "No *gentleman* would seek to profit from your misfortunes."

Just then a pair of lace-encrusted twittery women, one tall and one stout, promenaded past Fanny's and Oliver's table, boring their unblinking eyes into Fanny like freshly ground blades. Fanny felt their judgment slice through her. She blinked rapidly.

"What is it?" Oliver said, glancing first at Fanny, then at the two women, then back at Fanny.

Fanny fingered her small feathered cap. "It's this," she said under her breath. "It's me."

Oliver shook his head, bewildered.

"It's my first time out without my widow's drapery," Fanny whispered. "You know, the hat and veil and all."

"And they see you here with a man," Oliver said.

"They see Sara Farrington," Fanny said. "They assume she'd be with a man. They're trying to figure out what sort of man."

Oliver dropped his cup loudly into the saucer, startling the two women. He slowly picked up a butterhorn, brought it to his lips, then bit it savagely. He took another bite, then another, all the while staring wide-eyed at the two women, his jaws working unmercifully on the crumbling pastry, his thick beard shaking as he chewed.

"Well!" the tall woman said. The stout woman pursed her lips in agreement. They shuddered, glanced at one another with a look that portended great gusts of gossip, and bustled out of the tea room, shaking their heads and pulling on their gloves.

Fanny put a hand over her mouth and laughed into it.

Oliver took her hand by the wrist and pulled it away from her face. "What's this?" he said. "Is this delicate smirking any way for Fanny Fern to behave? From Richard's reports I'd expect nothing less than full-blown guffaws."

Fanny smiled. Her deep blue eyes glistened, yet the lines at the corners of her mouth were tight. "I've changed some since I've last seen Richard."

"Society is cruel," Oliver said. "But Fanny Fern overcomes all. That's what her readers say." He smiled gently into Fanny's face. "That's what her editor says."

"You are something," Fanny said. "If it weren't for you and your wonderful paper."

"If it weren't for you, I wouldn't have a wonderful paper. Do you know how much you're copied? Every major city features your work. I've seen it abroad, too. Certainly in England. But all over Europe, as well. Everyone relates to you. Everyone gobbles up your words. In fact, I have swarms of people every publishing day, waiting for that glorious second when I open the doors, so they'll be sure to get the latest wit from Fanny Fern."

Fanny cocked her head.

"You've no idea of your worth, do you?"

Fanny wrinkled her brow. "I know Moulton and Reverend Norris didn't want me to leave their pages."

"*You're* their papers. The whole reason either of them are booming as they are. And how thoughtfully you protected their interests, when any other in your place would leave them and their petty avarice in an instant."

"I felt an obligation. They published my first works. When no one else would look at them. When no one else would give me a penny, would let me *earn* a penny. Especially the Reverend. I'll never forget his aid."

"He helped more than you by taking your work. He helped his pocketbook plenty."

"Oh, I do love him."

Oliver held up his hands. "Don't get me wrong. Reverend Norris is a fine man. An outstanding man. A talented writer and a keen editor. What I'm saying is he's also a business man. And the business man in him saw what you could do for him as surely as he saw what he could do for you."

"He's nothing like Moulton," Fanny said. "Now there's one who would sell me to the wolves."

"No doubt he would. No doubt he might. Have you thought of that possibility?"

Fanny shuddered. "Frankly, I've thought of every possibility. But I can't see how I cannot move forward."

Oliver nodded.

"First, I've simply got to get Grace. I've got to! And not only do I intend to claim her, but I've got to educate her, and Nelly. I've got to provide for their futures. I don't want either of them set adrift like I was, to strive only to become helpless little parlor ornaments leaning with all their might on some man or another."

Oliver stroked his salt-and-pepper beard.

"I've got to expose them to the world. To business and to politics. I've got to show them how to think for themselves and how to fight for themselves. It terrifies me to think of their possible futures. Why just the other day I passed one of those houses."

Oliver raised an eyebrow. "One of what sort of houses?"

Fanny blustered. "One of those . . . one of those . . . Why, I'll just say it. One of those female houses. Where men go and women are paid for lying with them."

Oliver's face colored slightly. "How did you know it was such a house?"

"Oliver," Fanny said. "In our neighborhood? Those women are the only ones with more than one pair of shoes and more than one going-out hat."

Oliver smiled.

"In my mind, I saw the whole thing," Fanny said. "How they ended up there. It could have been me, or anyone, for that matter. It *still could be*. It doesn't take long for the fickle hand of destiny to touch you on the shoulder and melt away everything you take for granted. In a flash, any woman could find herself in my shoes—husbandless, penniless, and without any means of earning a decent wage. It's different for men. They have opportunity. They can knock on doors and ask for a chance and because they're a man and look to be an earnest employee, they'll be given a chance. They'll be trusted to learn a new position. They'll be taught the details they need to know. And it's because this new position won't be much different from their last position that they'll succeed, if they have an ounce of sense and a shred of doggedness. Not so with women! Women have a narrow avenue of employment options, all of which pay poorly! And not a speck of training! Don't you think I wouldn't consider it? Lying on my back for some man in order to eat for the week? In order to buy medicine for my sick babe and coal for our fire? In order to retrieve Grace? It frightens me how quickly I might consider it. And it sickens me that any woman should have to."

Oliver listened to Fanny's speech half-horrified, half-fascinated. That she could talk so freely about brothels and the women who dwelled in them! That she could imagine herself one such woman—under any circumstance! In her periwinkle muslin and dainty feathered cap, she looked like any respectable woman. But the words that flowed without a moment's hesitation from that pretty mouth, the ideas that apparently swam beneath those fetching curls. Oliver realized he was holding his breath. He purposely started breathing again—long, slow, steady pulls. Fanny tipped her chin down but stared unflinchingly into Oliver's eyes. She wasn't the least bit embarrassed, the least bit ashamed. And, really, why should she be? Oliver blinked fast. She was discussing *life*. Society. Problems. She discussed frankly, *brutally* frankly, true, but she was laying bare a well-known issue. A little-discussed issue, but a well-known one. Why was it that some subjects were so cloaked in taboos and others were trotted out and discussed to death? How capricious the kiss of social propriety. How foolish. Oliver stroked his beard and returned Fanny's gaze. What a remarkably brave woman. Either brave or mad! Oliver smiled to himself. He preferred to think her brave.

Oliver Dyer raised his teacup to Fanny Fern in a toast. "That's my Fanny," he said. "That's exactly the spirit I'm talking about. The spirit that will fly you to the stars."

Fanny set her jaw. "I've no more spirit than anyone," she said. "I've just got more anger."

"Call it what you will. It's what our readers want."

Fanny knit her brows. "It's what readers want because they experience it, too. They want someone to make it real for them, to call a spade a spade."

Oliver shook his head slowly. "Yes," he said with a grin. "And you aren't timid about making the call."

Fanny drew a sharp breath.

"So tell me," Oliver said. "Have you signed the contract yet? What have you decided?"

Fanny looked to the ceiling for a moment, then took a sip of tea. "I took your advice, which aligned exactly with my own instincts," she said. "I chose to be paid ten cents for every volume sold."

"Smart woman! You'll reap your just rewards."

Fanny bit her lip. "I hope you're right. To think I turned down a thousand guaranteed!"

"You won't regret it. You've got a smart head for business and the nerve to navigate its world."

"I placed the contract in the post today."

"Without me looking at it?" Oliver said.

"I went over and over it. It was just as you said it would be."

Oliver chuckled. "You're something, Fanny Fern. James Cephas Derby, eh? He's the lucky publisher?"

"There was only one other offer."

"There would have been more in time. Well, good for Derby and Miller. They don't know the enormity of what they've just undertaken. Their presses will be groaning. And as I've already communicated to you in my letters, they'll do a smart job. They've got the power to promote and in this modern world, that will make all the difference in sales."

"Let's hope," Fanny said.

"But you know all that. You really don't need my advice, you know. You already had it all figured out."

"But I paid close attention to your recommendations, Oliver. I really do admire you."

"And I you, my Fanny."

Fanny sipped her tea, put her cup firmly in its saucer, and leveled her eyes at Oliver. "Thank you, dear Oliver, for taking such a keen and generous interest in me and my well-being. It's been so long." She blinked rapidly. "I cannot even tell you . . ."

Oliver patted her hand. "Dear sister. My services are always at your disposal." He smiled. "Not that you needed my counsel much lately. You've a remarkable instinct, I've come to see."

Fanny pulled her handkerchief from her sleeve and twisted it. "I do need your advice, Oliver. About Grace. I've received a heap of papers, all written in gobbly-speak. Wills. Letters. They seem so threatening. I don't want to lose her."

Oliver patted Fanny's arm. "I'll take you this instant to a lawyer I know in town. He's smart and fair and one of my good friends."

Fanny took a shaky breath and squeezed her eyes.

"Don't worry," Oliver said, gently. "We'll get to the bottom of this."

Chapter Twenty-Six

Hezekiah Eldredge, Newton, Monday, March 14th, 1853

Did you never hail the first streak of dawn, as an angel whom you implored to lay a cool hand on your brow, and bring you peace or oblivion? and did you never see that day's sun set in clouds, like its predecessors, and the stars come forth one by one, with searching eyes, staring into the windows of your soul with a free, bold gaze, that irritated and maddened you? You never did? . . . Ask your Maker that it may be a long day before sorrow brings you such knowledge, and if you have a child, and that child a girl, whose heritage is your intense nature, ask Him to take the cup of life from her lips ere she prays to have it done, ere the fair things of earth shrivel away before her eyes like a scroll.

—Fanny Fern, *New York Ledger*, May 8th, 1858

Hezekiah was always thirsty now. He noticed his thirst like he noticed his pain. It did no good to try to placate either. The ravaging beasts would have their way with him whether he fought or tried to make nice. He grimaced. So, he'd come to this point. The point he'd seen in his patients and never could understand. The point of noticing. He almost wanted to smile at the irony. How many times had he scratched his head over some patient or another who suddenly took his medicine or didn't, who slept or didn't, who ate or didn't—and none of it seemed to matter. They still withered at the same rate, still suffered, still, in the end, took that horrible grating breath that Hezekiah sometimes had nightmares about. They were noticing.

Hezekiah wondered if his thirst would go away with some water. He rang for Grace. She'd come racing in with that scared-cat look on her face, and Heaven knew Hezekiah hated that look, and would stretch his last nerve to the point of frazzle with her timidity. Should she sit here or there? Should she look there or here? Should she speak or stare? One would think that after two years the child would have gained a shred of self-composure. And to think of the comforts he and Mary ladled over her head day in and day out—food, fuel, clothing, water, even the slate and texts she needed for school. All gifts, though, were met with the same vapid expression, the same neutrality that made Hezekiah want to slap her. As unconscious and ungrateful as her mother. Hezekiah groaned. Mary will have her hands full with her, no doubt.

Grace tapped on the door instead of entering like Hezekiah assumed she would.

"Come in," Hezekiah tried to say, but his throat was so dry his words sounded gruff and gravelly.

Grace tapped again.

"Come in!" Hezekiah croaked a little louder. The effort made his throat stick together dry and prickly like field burrs. He coughed ferociously in an effort to clear the way, but it was useless, he observed. The more he coughed, the tighter his throat clamped together and the dryer his overall body became. He was coughing out precious moisture. He was coughing out his life.

Grace slowly opened the door. "Papa?" she said. "I think you rang?"

Confound it! Of course he had rang. Who else would be in his room to pull the cord? Perhaps some spirit had tricked the child's ears? Bah! Twelve years old and the sense of an oyster! Hezekiah would have to get Mary to write to that school again to see just *what*, if anything, they were teaching his granddaughter. She didn't seem to know a lick more than she did when she first crossed this threshold. Sometimes Hezekiah wondered if she wasn't addled in the brain. It would be a wonder she wasn't, with that mother of hers. Hezekiah coughed harder the more he fumed. His throat closed tighter with every sputter.

"Papa, would you like some water?"

Miserable wench. Of course, of course! Did she think he called her to watch him cough out his heart? Hezekiah motioned brusquely toward the pitcher, nodding vigorously through his heaving spasms. Water, girl! Yes, bring it. He'd probably die before she managed to pour it and cart it to him. Soggy tortoise!

Grace tripped to the pitcher and lifted it with both hands, pouring the water into the glass Nana left beside the wash basin. As she was ready to put the pitcher down, Papa coughed with such a loud grating blast that Grace jumped and knocked the glass over. Water dripped down the mahogany wash-stand and Grace looked frantically for a towel to sop up her mess. But Nana heard everything and burst into the room before Grace could pour more water or wipe up the spill or stop Papa's coughing fit.

"Hezekiah," she said, rushing to his side. "Such racking!"

Hezekiah continued gasping and hacking while pointing a feeble finger at Grace and the streaming washstand.

"Stupid girl!" Mary said. "What a time to be clumsy. Give me that pitcher."

Grace lifted the pitcher and offered it to her grandmother who snatched it from her with one hand, swiped the glass from the washbasin with the other, and in two shakes had a full glass to her husband's blistered lips.

Hezekiah observed the water trickling down his throat. It had much the same effect as a flash rain on a parched field—it slicked over the surface too quickly for the baked surface to absorb. His throat had hardened like so many of his other body parts. He was solidifying, turning to stone—his breath caught on the burrs in his throat—dying.

The thought hit Hezekiah like an ax. He was dying. He really was. Of course he'd known the fact for nearly a year now, since he'd first observed the specks of blood in his spittle and in his water, and had had numerous frank and brave talks about the fact with Mary, his attorney, his banker, his minister. They had all commented on his courage and dignity and had marveled at his inner strength. In retrospect, Hezekiah thought, as he observed the water skimming the surface of his throat, only to skim the surface of his organs and slosh right back out of him, he knew he hadn't really believed in death before this moment, before he realized he could drink water and that water would only drizzle over his cough, over his disease, without alleviating anything.

Hezekiah broke out in a sweat. He looked down at his arm as he helped Mary guide the glass to his hacking lips and saw the droplets burst through the pores. The water was running right through him. He *was* turning to stone.

Mary put a palm on his forehead. "You're burning up," she said. "Grace, fetch a cool cloth."

Hezekiah shook his head. A cool cloth would do nothing. A bolt of thunder couldn't shake him from this destiny. He was hardening by the minute, would become marble before he had a chance to say everything on his mind or figure out a way to reverse it all.

There would be no reversal. He suddenly knew this as surely as he knew it made no difference if he drank another drop. He pushed the glass away, grateful for the burst of understanding. He had much to do in so little time. He had to instruct Mary about everything—about those Whitakers down the road who had never paid in full for their palsied daughter, about his little account with the apothecary in Boston, about that pony that lost three times now but would win in the end, about the gossip he heard about Sara from the miller's wife, about raising Grace and saving Nelly. So much.

No, Hezekiah had never really believed in death before. Even as a physician, he'd only pretended to understand the chemistry between health and disease, life and death. He had a way of professionally putting forth the absurd, of haphazardly approaching the living and the dying. He and his medical career had profited by his level-eyed way of convincing anyone of anything. Your liver is weak. Your blood is bad. Your heart is nervous. It was all the same for any doctor. Observe and label. Treat and defend. All with a stoic demeanor. They'd received the training with their education. He was sure of it. Hezekiah cocked his head as if listening to a little red bird. Was he genuine? Was he really a doctor? Was he really a man? He suddenly wasn't sure of anything and he frightened Mary by staring, wide-eyed, out the window, considering. Noticing. Such thoughts were amazing. He wanted to go around and around them. They held his attention in much the same way . . . as what? . . . as an ant hill could mesmerize him for hours in his boyhood. He used to be the type to get lost in observing. He'd started as a dreamer, he had! Hezekiah nearly chuckled remembering himself bumping along the lane to fetch water, looking in the treetops for that one bird, the red one that sometimes visited with him. *Told him things.* As he looked at the treetops, sometimes his boy legs would feel like jelly and he'd have to stop and take a little rest, his head nestled deep into a mound of sweet clover, and look further than the treetops, and the red bird, to the clouds themselves. It was there that Hezekiah found all the answers to whatever trivial worries he bore. If one was patient and earnest, the clouds became a sort of crystal ball you could gaze at and understand everything through. Hezekiah had caught it plenty of times for being late from the river and soon the fear of his father's stinging whip outweighed his need for cloud-gazing.

Grace came flying at him with a cool cloth in her shaking hands.

Hezekiah sputtered again and held out a hand. He was thinking something interesting, just now, and didn't want to be jolted back to noticing.

"Put it on his forehead, I say!" Mary said, but Hezekiah didn't want the cloth and blocked it by putting his hand, palm out, over his face.

"What's he doing, now?" Mary said. "He's delirious."

Grace tried to place the cloth tenderly on Papa's face.

"Put that cloth down. Can't you see he doesn't want it?" Mary said.

But Mary's words were too late. Grace had brushed her grandfather's head with her fingers, even as the cloth missed his face.

Something happened to Hezekiah when Grace touched his head, something amazing, surprising. His pain, the pain that clustered like little grapes just behind his eyes, burst and melted. Hezekiah noticed this and marveled. To think he'd had the cure right here all along. The tender touch of Grace. The earnest effort of his granddaughter. This was all he'd ever really needed to stop the hardening, to reverse death. Perhaps . . .

"Go fetch Dr. Wilson!" Mary shrieked. "Hurry. He's fading."

Of course, the doctor could do nothing. Hezekiah shook his head but realized he just imagined he was moving it. The melting Grace's hand had started was seeping down from his forehead, to his eyes, his mouth, his neck.

A wonderful golden honey-like melting—warm and sweet and comforting. His eyes started leaking and his neck was so loose he couldn't nod no to the idea of Grace leaving. Don't go, Grace. Come and melt me back into the living. Come and cure me with your innocent touch.

Mary put a hand squarely in the middle of Grace's back and gave her a push. "Go! And don't come back saying you can't find him!"

Grace flew out of the room and Hezekiah watched as the last bit of her skirt trailed over the threshold. The honey heat flowed down his spine and filled his abdomen, caressed his calcified organs, warmed its way down his legs. Grace! Grace! He leaned toward the door, leaned further, further. Hezekiah was wonderfully loose now, loose and content. He was too loose to move, almost too loose to breathe. Come back, darling girl, and lay your golden hands on me! Show me the little bird. Show me, show me. Hezekiah leaned again. He leaned so far that he soon floated through the door. After Grace. Where was Grace? Behind him, he heard a horrible grating and a sob. Hezekiah grinned. He had melted and saw the difference on the other side.

Grace had turned into Charly.

Chapter Twenty-Seven

N. P. Willis, Idlewild, New York, Monday, April 18th, 1853

"Don't marry a woman *under twenty*. She hasn't *come to her wickedness* before then."

—Kit North, a.k.a. Professor John Wilson (presumably),
Blackwood's Magazine

Well—! If I knew any bad words, I'm awful afraid I should say 'em!! I just wish I had hold of the perpetrator of that with a pair of tongs, I'd bottle him up in sperrits, and keep him for a terror to liars, as sure as his name is "Kit North." "Set a thief to catch a thief!" How came you to know when that crisis in a woman's life occurs? Answer me that! I'll tell you what my opinion is; and won't charge you any fee for it either! A woman "comes to her wickedness" when she comes to her HUSBAND!!—and if she knew anything good before, it all "goes by the board," then; it's no more use to her afterwards, than the fifth wheel of a coach! Don't you know, you wicked calumniator, that thunder don't sour milk more effectually than matrimony does women's tempers? "Come to their wickedness," indeed! Snowflakes and soot! They'd never know the meaning of the word "wicked," if your sex were blotted out of existence! . . . Now you'd better repent of your sins, Mr. What's-your-name; for as sure as preaching, you will go where you'll have nothing to do but think of 'em! and you won't find any women there, either; for they all go to the other place!

—Fanny Fern, *Olive Branch*, June 5th, 1852

Eight months! Nat threw down the copy of the *Home Journal*, upsetting the blue and white china sugar bowl on the breakfast table before him. The sugar bowl tinkled to pieces. Eight months and still living in this *shack*.

"Jacques!" Nat yelled. "Bring a whisk and dust bin. Hurry! I can nearly see the ants climbing the tablecloth."

Nat shielded his eyes from the mid-morning sun and gazed out over his fifty acres—the woods, the meadow, the river. He'd first set eyes on this little Eden along the Hudson's banks two summers before and it had taken him over two months to pry it from the clutches of the French duke who held it. It had cost Nat more than he'd first guessed it would, but he knew, deep in his bones, that once he'd obtain the necessary loans and blueprints, it would be an investment he'd never regret. The only thing about Idlewild he regretted was the slovenly help he'd hired to build his house and construct his gardens. He and Cornelia and the children could have gotten more accomplished on a bright sunny day as this than the whole lot of fork-tongued foreigners he'd entrusted with his estate.

Where were they? If he were at work in the city, he'd have been in his *Home Journal* office for hours already, would have outlined the cover story and would be working to balance the advertisements. He'd certainly paid his dues. He'd worked long and hard in the early years, rewarded himself well, too, as a balance. Lucky thing he had Parton at the helm when he had to be indisposed like this. *Old*. Dotty specialists. First, he had had to travel so much—*doctor's orders!* Relax! Renew! That treatment had chewed up a year and a half and too much money to remember. They had come back to the promise of a decent abode while the main house of Idlewild was being "finished." Funny thing, the crew failed to inform him that finishing meant building from the ground up. Meanwhile they were living in what would eventually be the guest cottage, with Jacques and Hatty in the summer kitchen. Damned primitive. Eight months!

Jacques came to sweep up the glass and sugar. He stacked the hurled newspaper in the basket just inside the door.

"Don't throw those away. I like to keep them."

"I know you like to keep them, sir. I never throw them away."

"You threw one away last week. I counted. One's missing."

Jacques bowed his head. "Sorry, sir."

Nat stood, brushed an invisible crumb from his lap, and headed out the door, toward the construction site. "And see if we can't get the latest issues a little more timely," he said. "If there were any sort of real problem, I wouldn't know about it until the next day."

"The crew isn't here, yet," Jacques called after him. "You know that. *Sir?* No need to go carting down there to wet your shoes. Why don't you sit a while in the shade until somebody's there to talk to?"

Nat kept striding over the spring-mushy ground. "I'm through talking. I'm ready to pick up a hammer myself."

"Now, sir. Remember what the doctors say," Jacques called through cupped hands. "You're not supposed to exert yourself."

Nat flapped his hand over his shoulder. "Tell Cornelia to wear that pretty white silk today. I'm sick of those velvets. It's near enough to summer."

Jacques knew that Cornelia would no sooner wear white silk in April than cut her thumb off, but he just nodded at Nat's back and continued sweeping up the sugared glass. Nat was too far away to hear any reply he might make anyway. Damned mule.

Nat squished through the sodden meadow, down the sticky mud trail and huffed his way up the huge mound of gravel at the base of the carriage path. Why they had to dump these stones right there instead of a little farther up was a mystery to Nat. People didn't use the brains they'd been born with. Nat reached the top of the pile and, gingerly, tested the stones with his feet. Each step loosed a small avalanche. He would have to pick his way slowly down the pile. He began his descent and as soon as he took the first solid step, lost his balance and slid, in a blur of flying stones and dust, down the back side of the pile.

Nat lay, chalky and shaken, at the bottom of the gravel heap. "God-damnit!" he breathed, shaking his head to stop it from spinning. His left ankle throbbed in a way that was all too familiar. He had turned it. He hadn't done that in years. Nat sucked a deep breath and massaged his leg. Not only had he turned his ankle, but his new gray kid shoes were ruined, as Jacques had predicted—soggy at the heels and powdered through with gravel chalk at the toes.

Nat's hand shook as he dabbed at his damp forehead with his handkerchief. Damned hot already for April. He loosened his cravat and unbuttoned a few vest buttons. He'd have to change the whole sweaty outfit before dinner, should hand his laundry bill to these contractors. Mud, slime, dust everywhere. It's a wonder they weren't all sick.

Cornelia was as frustrated as Nat. Frustrated and headachy. Cross and unaffectionate. Nat rolled his eyes at the thought. He could count the times they'd shared a bed this year on one hand. Maybe he should take a lover? Oh, but then the bother of finding so many little gifts, and skirting around in secret, and the coddling and cooing of two finicky women, and paying for all the luxuries they never could live without. Dame Gignette on lower Broadway met his needs without all of those entanglements.

Nat sighed. But what about love? Did it exist? Nat lifted his chin to the cooling breeze, felt the familiar pang in his chest. What a difference it would have made if he'd have married Mary Benjamin. Sweet, petite, little yellow-haired imp. She had a smile that dazzled. Eyes the color of new grass. Skin that gave off the faint smell of apples—not sickly ripe, or raw and new, but perfectly sweet and palatable—fresh, firm apples. Nat wanted to hold her in his arms, in his heart, on his tongue forever—shield her, savor her, consume her. She was the light of his life, the love of his life. Her sweetness would have been the balm his ragged soul needed. With Mary, he could have been a good man. A better man, at least. Then, all of this—ill health, petty nuisances, wobbly fortunes—could have been borne with more grace, more compassion. He'd have been the picture of patience. The model of benevolence. If only her family hadn't broken their engagement. Nat's face still burned with embarrassment. They'd called him a rake, a puppy, a sensualist.

Nat pinched the bridge of his nose. It was true. And he'd probably do it all again, the same way. "Vive l'amour" had been his slogan, since he'd been a shy skinny sixteen. After that first tryst, with Helen in the hayloft, Nat's confidence bloomed and his appetite—for *everything*—grew, too. He remembered his bottle-green coat and how many pretty heads it had turned, not to mention how many of those pretty feet *he* had turned, any which way he wanted. He had liked older women at first. Especially aristocrats. They were rich, usually bored, and always frisky. They praised him, stroked him, made him feel invincible. He could celebrate all evening with his bachelor friends, racking up bills for the best food and drink, then deliver those bills, along with his special rowdy romance, to some plump matron or another and everyone was happy.

Nat rubbed his sore ankle. It had always been punk. Ever since that time he'd had to jump from the second-story balcony of beautiful Marie's bedroom when they heard her husband's unexpected arrival downstairs. Marie had thrown his coat, boots, cravat, and shirt down after him and Nat had run wildly down the street, laughing and dressing in the moonlight. What did it matter that it was January and he stepped stocking-footed into icy puddles? He'd just made love to an appreciative woman.

Marie, yes. She'd been delectable. But so had all the others. There wasn't a lover he regretted and he'd long since given up counting their numbers. But, oh, Mary Benjamin. He'd taken the high road with her. He treated her like the wife she would become and reined himself in with glorious fantasies of their wedding night. And it was because of *that*, he thought bitterly, that her family had broken the engagement. If he'd had just taken her to his bed, as instinct instructed him to do, he never would have sought relief from the others, and never would have been attacked by her father and brothers for his dissipations. True, he'd enjoyed his side amours. Why shouldn't he have? But he had wanted Mary Benjamin for the sacred role of wife.

He was addicted, he long understood, to sensual love. And *variety*! One couldn't say enough about that. Tall, short, blonde, brunette, buxom, slim, hearty, delicate. Nat loved women—all women—as much as he loved delectable food, gorgeous wine, fast horses, and wagering. And now Cornelia froze him out most nights, a fact only made bearable by the reality that her fortune was paying their bills.

Where was love? How could it have eluded *him*? He was a poet, had a sensitive heart. The irony was too bitter. After being jilted by Mary Benjamin, not to mention being excommunicated from Park Street Church and thereby receiving an infinite supply of lectures and pitiful looks from his father, Nat decided to sweep Boston from his memory. He went to New York, where behavior like his wasn't frowned upon in some old-fashioned Puritan way, but was celebrated as evidence of a hearty spirit and an adventuresome artistry.

He enjoyed himself plenty for half a decade, all the while working to establish himself as the nation's preeminent poet and eligible bachelor. The *Home Journal* flourished with his literary touch. Women flourished with his literal touch. Chefs and sommeliers flourished with his recommendation.

Nat stood and brushed off the seat of his pants. The gravel was too dusty. He'd paid for first quality and they were trying to pass *this* pulverized heap onto him. Nat limped to the house's would-be threshold. Here is where he'd finally be happy. Here is where he'd finally find peace and contentment, love and joy. He had the unmistakable feeling that if the workers would just finish this place, he'd be able to move in and feel at ease. It was the same excited feeling he'd had on the ship to England the summer of 1836. In another effort to forget Mary Benjamin, he'd decided upon a little European holiday. Nat remembered standing on deck, leaning almost too brazenly over the rail, unbearably anxious to land abroad and meet with the destiny he could feel was there.

And she had been there—beautiful, innocent twenty-year-old Mary Stace, dancing at that first ball he'd gone to, with a lightness of foot he'd never seen before. She seemed weightless, airborne, ready to fly straight to the heavens. Without his reputation at his heels, Nat wooed her with the tenderness and elegance of royalty. They swooned with love and after her family was convinced of his adequate finances and poetic fame, Nat and Mary married and he brought her and all of her worldly goods (and her significant dowry) home with him. Mary Stace was no Mary Benjamin, but she was close. She had the same yellow hair, the same tiny figure, the same sweet disposition and innocent nature. But, Mary Stace didn't smell like apples, didn't have eyes the color of grass. Still, Nat got used to Mary Stace's warm amber eyes, the musky-milk scent of her skin, especially after birthing dear Imogen. Yes, he'd gotten used to Mary Stace and was comfortable and happy with her and their life together.

Nat walked into the shell of the mansion that would someday house him and his family, ran his hand along the newly installed hand-carved mahogany stair rail. The wood was smooth beneath his fingers, polished and cool, like Mary Stace's forehead the last time he'd touched it, after that screaming last weekend, the weekend she'd tried, unsuccessfully, to deliver him another child. Nat didn't really understand exactly what went wrong, even though the doctors had explained it to him over and over again. He just remembered those hideous shrieks coming from behind her bedroom door and how he wondered what demon had possessed his sweet English bride. He remembered even more clearly the leaden silence that followed and the tight feeling in his throat that something had gone horribly bad, the feeling that he should burst through those doors and box someone's ears. But, of course, he hadn't.

He couldn't cry at the funeral, couldn't cry until he stood, again, six weeks later, on the deck of an England-bound ship. He didn't know how he would tell her family, how he would own that he'd been unable to ultimately protect her, that it was, in fact, his fault she was dead. When he had realized that it was because of him, because of him and his unchecked passions that his wife was dead, Nat vowed to never marry again. Lovers and paid companions were heartier than wives and never seemed to get pregnant. They would keep him sufficient company.

He made his trip, delivered his awful news, and was sailing back to the States when Cornelia Grinnell noticed him. Immensely wealthy and bored, Cornelia sought Nat's company, was actually charmed with his broken-heartedness. Nat smiled. It was the first time he'd been seduced. Cornelia had an eye for him and, as he'd since learned, whatever Cornelia desired, Cornelia acquired. He became her lover, then husband, now puppet. He despised that he'd become so dependent, but couldn't help his appetites for luxury. A newspaper editor and poet did all right for himself, but the Grinnell fortune was unmatched. And they got along reasonably well. Cornelia gave Nat significant leeway and ample allowance to ensure his pleasant demeanor and he gave her uninterrupted sleep unless beckoned.

One maddening point was how her family insisted on slipping her funds on the side. Even though Nat was her husband, her family somehow arranged for her to have investments he wasn't aware of, accounts brimming with undiscovered riches. He simply couldn't locate everything which he legally had a right to, and that caused him undue anxiety and irritation. When he'd fume about it, though, Cornelia would laugh and purr. She'd stroke his arm and entice him to remember a single luxury he'd been deprived of. Of course, Nat couldn't, and then he'd feel foolish to be in search of still more money. But, it was the principle of the situation that bothered him. That his wife could have control of resources he wasn't aware of unsettled him. Something about the arrangement was just not natural.

Nat hobbled up the staircase to the room that would be Cornelia's bedroom. He wondered how often he'd be invited to share it with her. He stood at the open window and looked down at what someday would be one of the area's premier gardens. No, he wouldn't take a lover. That certainly wouldn't endear him to Cornelia. But he would take an apartment in Manhattan, one close to the *Home Journal*'s office. He would take a more active role in the day-to-day business decisions, would give Parton a little extra time off to pursue his own writing, would work to discover and nurture a whole new generation of fresh, young talent. And, weekends, he'd travel back here, to Idlewild, and would enjoy what he was allowed to of his wife and family and expensive estate. He'd find what peace he could. He would.

Chapter Twenty-Eight

James Parton, New York, Monday, June 3rd, 1853

"Courtship and marriage, servants and children, these are the great objects of a woman's thoughts, and they necessarily form the staple topics of their writings and their conversation. We have no right to expect anything else in a woman's book."

—*New York Times*

Is it in feminine novels only that courtship, marriage, servants and children are the staple? Is not this true of all novels?—of Dickens, of Thackeray, of Bulwer and a host of others? Is it peculiar to feminine pens, most astute and liberal of critics? Would a novel be a novel if it did not treat of courtship and marriage? and if it could be so recognized, would it find readers? When I see such a narrow, snarling criticism as the above, I always say to myself, the writer is some unhappy man. . . . I see him writing that paragraph in a fit of spleen—of male spleen—in his small boarding-house upper chamber, by the cheerful light of a solitary candle, flickering alternately on cobwebbed walls, dusty wash-stands, begrimed bowl and pitcher, refuse cigar stumps, boot-jacks, old hats, buttonless coats, muddy trousers, and all the wretched accompaniments of solitary, selfish male existence. . . . But seriously—we have had quite enough of this shallow criticism (?) on lady-books. Whether the book which called for the remark above quoted, was a good book or a bad one, I know not; I should be inclined to think the former from the dispraise of such a pen. Whether ladies can write novels or not, is a question I do not intend to discuss; but that some of them have no difficulty finding either publishers or readers is a matter of history; and that gentlemen often write over feminine signatures would seem also to argue that feminine literature is, after all, in good order with the reading public. Granted that lady-novels are not all that they should be—is such shallow, unfair, wholesale, sneering criticism (?) the way to reform them? Would it not be better and more manly to point out a better way kindly, justly, and above all, respectfully? or—what would be a much harder task for such critics—write a better book!

—Fanny Fern, *New York Ledger*, May 23, 1857

"Fanny Fern is a voice, not an echo," James Parton wrote. What an apt way to finish the book review he'd be sure made it into the next issue of the *Home Journal*. James Derby himself of Derby and Miller had stopped by the office Friday last with a fresh-from-the-presses edition of Fanny Fern's first *book*—a mouth-watering collection of her best articles entitled *Fern Leaves from Fanny's Portfolio*. James literally could not wait to crack the volume, in fact, started reading it as he walked back to his boardinghouse on lower Broadway. It was amazing he'd only passed his domicile by two blocks. If it hadn't started sprinkling out, he'd never have looked up from the copy and would probably have walked straight to Florida.

James loved this writer. He and the rest of the world. There was something about her writing—vivid, fearless, vulnerable—that was captivating. She, and he was assuming Fanny Fern was a she, reminded him of Charlotte Brontë, that sharp British author of *Jane Eyre*. The hoopla over the writer's sex, in both cases! Queer world all around. His own mother was widowed when he was barely five years old and gathered her four young children together to relocate to America. Such courage and strength. Even as a young boy in a strange new country, he'd known his mother was no shrinking violet. She was a pillar, someone to moor him, to strengthen him.

His mother had spoiled him for typical women. He could never gaze admiringly at some pretty bit of fluffery banging out her heart on a pianoforte and trying to win him over with carefully practiced conversation and tosses of a curly head. He wanted the same things from a female companion as he wanted from a male companion—intelligent conversation, stimulating adventure, challenging forays into the world of dreams and emotion. Yes, he knew that custom had it that men should get those needs met in smoky gentlemen's clubs or while duck hunting or wagering together. But, James was not fond of hazy clubs, where one must get inebriated in order to scream loud enough to join the discussion, nor was he particularly fond of hunting, horse racing, or other pursuits thought to be within the masculine realm. James liked to read. He liked to write. He liked to discuss the social topics of the day. He liked a stroll in nature and in museums and among art. He liked to keep up on politics. He liked to cook, when he could, and to coax bright blossoms from plants. And James wanted to share these activities with a life companion. Although he'd found a good number of intellectual foils who could discuss and argue with him in the quiet of someone's study until the wee hours and without more than a few glasses of wine, he couldn't, however, imagine any man wanting to bake a cake with him, wanting to visit a waterfall and write a romantic essay about it later, wanting to lie, mutually, together, exploring the infinity of spiritual and physical bonding.

James sighed. Oh, to meet some like-minded woman. Some woman who wasn't harnessed to her sex like a plow horse, some woman like Charlotte Brontë or Fanny Fern. But, really, what were the chances of that? Such women had scores of admirers, could pick their beaus from a bevy of rich, educated, and prominent men.

James picked up a thick stack of letters, all addressed to Fanny Fern. He'd send them on, as he always did, to Moulton of the *True Flag* or to Norris of the *Olive Branch*, in hopes that Fanny Fern, whoever she may be, would eventually receive them. So many adoring readers. So many people touched by her honest appraisals, by her no-nonsense style, by her feminine strength. She had always written from Boston, but James noticed Fanny Fern was also writing for a New York paper. For at least six months, he'd seen original columns in the *Musical World and Times*. Nat's brother worked there as an editor. James had met him during the holidays at a press party. And Oliver Dyer seemed like a wonderful man, certainly knew which side his bread was buttered. His little paper's circulation had swelled and he had astutely laid the reason at Fanny Fern's doorstep. He told Nat (James had overheard) that the writer was a delight to work with, though he'd never seen her—apparently keeps herself squirreled away in Boston. Nat had snorted and gone back to the punch bowl, leaving James aching with questions.

Oh, that she'd come out into real society. James couldn't fathom why someone of such talent wouldn't want the world to know her identity. Fame and fortune awaited her! Didn't she know it? If he could, he'd meet her, and court her, and nourish whatever it was that was in her that produced such clear-eyed essays. *He'd love her.* James smiled. What foolishness! He laughed out loud. He was already in love with her! In love with a name on paper, with a made-up identity. He shook his head. Too many years a bachelor! He was getting dotty, straying down the path of fantasy. He weighed the packet of Fanny Fern letters in his palm and sighed—he and so many others.

He began to package the bundle up in order to send it to Moulton, but then changed his mind. He'd send it to Oliver Dyer. Why not? As he arranged the bundle, a single page slipped from the sides of a loosely sealed letter. James glanced at it. It was a love poem. A love poem to Fanny Fern practically asking her for her hand. James stuffed the poem as well as he could back into the letter it had fallen out of and before he knew what he was doing, took out his pen.

He'd already written a favorable review of her book, he explained, was really an admiring fellow writer. Should she ever find it within her fancy to visit New York, he'd be delighted to show her around. James wrinkled his forehead. His letter probably sounded like all the others. She'd likely smile at it as she read it, *if* she read it—but James suddenly was sure that someone like Fanny Fern absolutely read all of her letters—and would place his letter on the top of a overflowing pile of other such prattling, happy notes.

He ripped the letter up and dated a new page. Then he wrote boldly, simply:

Dear Unknown: New York is the place for you. You will find subjects here starting up your path wherever you go. Come! Come! come!

Chapter Twenty-Nine

Mary Eldredge, Newton, Monday, June 17th, 1853

"'Tis better to have loved and lost, than never to have loved at all."

Oh no; no!—else you have never passed from the shield of a broad, true breast, where for long years you had been lovingly folded, to a widow's weeds, and the rude jostling, and curious gaze, of the heartless crowd!— never knew long, wretched days, that seemed to have no end— . . . Oh no; no! Better never to have loved!—Ten fold more gloomy, is the murky day, whose sunny morning was ushered in with dazzling, golden brightness! . . . —God pity the desolate, loving heart, the only star of whose sky has gone out in utter darkness!

— Fanny Fern, *Musical World and Times*, October 9th, 1852

Grace would be home from school soon and Mary Eldredge was still in her nightdress. She didn't know what was wrong with her lately. Heaven knew she was no stranger to death, had seen everyone she'd ever loved fall. All five of her children. Hezekiah.

Mary sobbed. She held a fist to her lips to muffle it. How infuriating to behave so cowardly. But Mary couldn't help it. She was frightened. She hadn't realized how heavily she'd leaned on Hezekiah, how she had mistakenly believed that she was *his* rock. And here he was, now, *gone*, and she so unfettered. *Hezekiah!*

· She'd done this more often than she cared to admit—this lingering in bed for most of the day, sobbing and daydreaming and trying to rally enough energy to dress before Grace returned from school. Luckily, Maggie got Grace her breakfast and saw to it she was properly scrubbed and attired before heading out. And then Maggie thoughtfully brought Mary a breakfast tray, followed by a lunch tray, both of which Mary promptly placed outside her door, untouched. She had no appetite. No strength. No reason for living, really, except to see to the proper raising of her granddaughters.

Mary hated her ex-daughter-in-law. Yes, she knew it was a sin to hate, and she felt evil for her feelings, but she hated Sara. Hated her with every fiber of her being. That Sara didn't drop over dead was the cruelest irony. So many noble souls, so many truly lovely people had perished with less trouble than Sara had had. Why wouldn't she submit? When would she buckle and leave Mary, once and for all, with the hope for loving dependents?

Grace's heart was a stone to her, despite Mary's wringing herself out to provide bountiful learning opportunities. She had to push Grace to do everything—her schoolwork, her bible study, her sewing practice. Grace constantly dragged her feet. She was slothful if she wasn't anything else. Slothful and flighty as her mother. The goose walked around with an irritating blankness in her eyes. If Mary wanted anything from her, she had to shout or smack her hands together to stir the child back to life.

It was all Sara's fault. She kept fanning the flame of hope in Grace that she'd be able to take her back, that she'd be able to provide for her. Mary knew it from the gorge of letters she'd sent Grace. Luckily Grace hadn't read the half of that nonsense. It would have probably sent her over the edge. As it was, it had already been two years and Sara's prospects looked as gloomy as ever. She wasn't any closer to being able to care for Grace, in fact, probably wasn't caring for Nelly very well. Mary didn't ask what Sara did to buy her bread and she didn't want to know. She was sure it would embarrass the lowest of the low. Sara didn't have a shred of decency nor the modesty the Lord gave a cat. She had no inner compass, was a ship just ready to wreck. And she was taking her daughters with her.

Mary wanted to hit something. Selfishness! What utter selfishness Sara displayed regarding her children. Couldn't she see how much better off Grace was with a proper education, sturdy clothes, plain food, and a clean bed? And Nelly would benefit from the same. Imagine dragging a child of that age around looking for work, or begging in the streets, or whatever it was they did all day. Sara was doing wrong by that child and by Grace, too. She nurtured false hopes in them both. She played with their natural tendency toward fantasy and let them both live in dream worlds that would never be. Sara would never be able to give them the living they were used to. She would never be able to protect them from harm, in this world or the next, would never be able to deliver them to the Lord.

Oh, Hezekiah! What should she do? Mary would never be able to combat Sara on her own. Hezekiah could always quiet Sara, could freeze her trap shut, with his calm professionalism, but Sara's tongue *flew* at Mary, especially when it was just the two of them. Sara had no respect for her elder. No respect for Charly's faithful mother. No respect for the grandmother of her children. Now that both Charly and Hezekiah were gone, there'd be no controlling Sara. She'd likely storm in here and steal Grace away, despite her promise, despite what was best for the girl, despite what Mary needed—the chance, finally, to nurture and raise someone up her way.

Mary sobbed again, covering her head with the bedclothes so Maggie wouldn't hear. This day-to-day ruminating, this constant crying—frankly, Mary was worried about herself. Sara would run roughshod over her. No doubt about it. Mary would be left utterly alone and loveless. It was only a matter of time. Mary had been able to stave off Sara while Hezekiah was sick. But now? Mary twisted the coverlet. She hated being at Sara's mercy.

A sudden pain shot through Mary's chest. Her hand flew to the spot, just over her heart. It was breaking. She could *feel* it. She, who had never been given credit enough for her love. Mary's hands shook as she awkwardly massaged herself, tried to comfort the flipping organ that had come unmoored yet again. If only Grace would come home and show a pittance of gratitude, a morsel of respect and admiration. If only Grace would reciprocate Mary's love.

Mary wiped her eyes with the back of one hand. She needed so little. Mary never put on airs. Never acquired. Never flashed. All she wanted was a clear path and a little recognition. She wanted to do her work in peace. She wanted to fix up the brokenness all around her. She wanted to teach others correctness in thought, word, and deed. She should have been a schoolteacher, instead of mother to five dead children. She should have been a preacher, herself, instead of one of the loyal listeners. She knew so much, had so much to give. Why were her words always heaved back at her, her advice ignored?

Her chest spasmed again. Mary couldn't tell if she was dying or if it was just some awful indigestion. What did it matter? She was a widow. A *widow!* She was alone.

Mary rubbed her chest as hard as she dared and the pain slowly subsided. She even had to be fierce, sometimes, with herself. Give in, too much, to wild thoughts and the body will weaken with the mind. Mary sat up in bed and dried her eyes on the coverlet. She smoothed the hair back from her face. She'd get up soon. She'd put on that nice gray muslin and would wind her hair up into a topknot. She'd be fresh enough to have tea with Grace and would win that child's love one way or the other.

Meanwhile, Mary needed a little encouragement. She had a battle ahead of her, just around the bend. A battle with the world's fiercest ex-daughter-in-law. She needed to sharpen her wits and her tongue in order to hold her own, in order to protect the futures of her granddaughters. Charly's girls. All that was left of him. Of Hezekiah.

Mary picked up the book her neighbor, Shirley, had dropped off the other day. "Read this," Shirley had said. "It'll cheer you up if anything can."

The book more than cheered Mary, it gave her courage. The world was so full of treachery and dishonesty and hypocrisy. This book named truth and gave Mary ideas. Mary opened the book to a middle page and began to read from the collection of articles. They were all good, all inspiring. They were written by that new writer, Fanny Fern. Everyone liked her. Especially Mary. If Mary could write, *she'd* write like Fanny Fern did. Fanny had a way of knocking the stuffing out of people. Had just the knack Mary needed to study in order to best Sara. Mary read one article. Two. She felt better already. She'd get up now. She'd dress. She'd devote herself to Grace. And when the time came, she'd manage Sara, too—somehow.

Chapter Thirty

Catharine Beecher, Milwaukee, Monday, June 17th, 1853

Never sneer down a sister woman, or pay her a patronizing compliment with the finale of the inevitable—"but." Never run the cool, impertinent eye of calculation over her dress, noting the cost of each article. . . . Never say to a gentleman who praises a lady, what a pity she squints! Never say of an authoress, oh yes—she has talent, but I prefer the domestic virtues; as if a combination of the two were necessarily impossible, or as if the speaker had the personal knowledge which qualified her to pronounce on that individual case. Well-bred, too, are women to sister woman.

—Fanny Fern, *New York Ledger*, March 12th, 1859

Catharine Beecher held her handkerchief to her nose. The smell of death was the worst possible smell. Something about it—that fetid sadness—clung to people more than onions and garlic. People absorbed it. Brought the grief of the newly dead into their own bodies, held it there for a time, then released it in tears. Catharine felt death's smell enter her. Standing at the base of the hill where they were laying the paupers and covering those too-shallow graves with the sticky Midwestern soil, Catharine held her handkerchief to her nose and cried. So many lives. Just like Harriet's little one. Cholera. A horrible disease.

Harriet was the only one who knew Catharine was here, helping to nurse these sick multitudes in a town so far from Boston. Catharine wrote Harriet about it and trusted Harriet to keep her secret from father and Lyman. If they knew Catharine was here trying to set up a woman's college, if they knew she was working in between her educator meetings at makeshift hospitals laying cool cloths on so many burning foreheads, holding hands, listening to delirious confessions, they'd come and get her. They'd march into town and would force her into the nearest stagecoach and make her go to the spa again, for her own protection. They'd sequester her. They'd limit her.

Harriet begged Catharine to stay clear of the epidemic and Catharine had promised she'd be careful. She drank her strengthening tonic every morning and saw to it that she got a full night's rest, most nights. She held her handkerchief to her nose when the death wagons passed. There was so much need here. Catharine's head reeled thinking of everything this city needed to prosper—proper sanitation, better roads, more schools. But it was a young community and Catharine reminded herself to have patience.

Catharine watched the grave diggers straighten up. The graves were apparently deep enough already. They rubbed their backs for a moment, then began the disturbing ritual of flinging bodies, like sacks of flour, one after another, into the holes. She watched one digger grab a pair of ankles and another lift the armpits. One swing and an awful thud. Catharine said a silent prayer for the souls of the deceased, including little Joey who she'd ushered over the threshold just that morning. Poor dear was the last of his strapping family. Farm people. Immigrants. It was likely for the best he succumbed, too, for if he'd have lived, he'd be orphaned. Too many parentless children. Too many childless parents.

Catharine walked up the hill and made her way over the cobblestones to the small hotel where she was staying. She would have a hot supper at the pub across the street and a pint of the dark ale the local people said warded off illness. Then she'd lock her hotel door, don her dressing gown, turn up the lamp, and write her next round of letters pleading for money, permission, and the blessings she needed to build her woman's college. It was a long process, she knew. It sometimes took years. She'd done the same thing in other, less-advanced towns. She could do it here, in Milwaukee, too. And then in other places, other states, like Iowa and Illinois. The need was everywhere—everywhere there were women.

After she wrote her business letters, Catharine would write to Harriet. She'd tell her she was staying well clear of the cholera, that she was healthy and happy and *fine*. She'd ask Harriet how her book was selling and if she was able to see the children and Calvin a little more often. And, of course, Catharine would thank Harriet for her latest gift—the Fanny Fern book. How it brightened Catharine's evening hours! And to think Fanny Fern was their own Sara Willis. Catharine smiled thinking of Sara's bright blue eyes and bobbing curls, of Sara's vivacity and nerve. Of course Sara Willis was Fanny Fern. Hadn't she received just the right training? Hadn't Catharine seen Sara's potential all along? Darling Sara. Fight the good fight. Godspeed!

Chapter Thirty-One

Fanny Fern, Oliver Dyer, and Richard Willis, Boston, Monday, June 17th, 1853

[Why do women write?] Because they can't help it. . . . Why does a bird carol? There is that in such a soul that will not be pent up,—that must find voice and expression; a heaven-kindled spark, that is unquenchable; an earnest, soaring spirit, whose wings cannot be earth-clipped.

—Fanny Fern, *Olive Branch*, February 2nd, 1853

Fanny Fern strolled down Main Street with one hand tucked in her brother Richard's arm and one hand tucked in Oliver Dyer's. Her brown silk skirt, complete with one deep ruffle, swung with each step, showing the shine of freshly polished boots. She wore an off-white fitted muslin blouse and a new black hat, which by itself was plain. But she had trimmed it with cocoa ribbon and a few creamy feathers. At her throat was one of her mother's pins—a simple copper circle. It was the most she'd spent on an outfit in years—twelve dollars.

She'd purchased the skirt fabric at a discount. It was a fall color on sale in the spring. The hat was a looked-over one from the corner of a seconds bin. Luckily, it hadn't been crushed. The blouse fabric was run-of-the-mill, but it was new, and so felt luxuriously crisp. Ribbon and shoe polish were twenty-five cents apiece. All together, Fanny felt presentable enough to meet her brother at the train station, and, of course, to see her good friend Oliver Dyer again.

Fanny embraced Richard. "I'm so glad you came," she said. "I ached to see you."

Richard patted Fanny's hand. "I'm only sorry I didn't know of your troubles. If I'd had known, I'd have sent for you from Germany."

Fanny knew he was lying. Richard had been as poor as she was when he was living in Germany. He could barely afford his fare home, and once in New York, lived much as Fanny had—in a third-rate boardinghouse without meals. He'd only made headway after Oliver hired him, and, of course, after marrying his dear Jessie. "Richard," Fanny breathed.

Richard's face reddened. "You're right. I wouldn't have been able to afford it. But thank God we're both doing better now."

"Amen to that," Oliver said. "It's been three weeks, my Fanny, and your book looks to outsell even *Uncle Tom's Cabin*."

"Harriet's?" Fanny said.

"Harriet Beecher Stowe is Sara's former schoolmate," Richard said to Oliver. "I'm so sorry," he said to his sister. "I can't seem to get the hang of calling you Fanny."

"Call me whatever you'd like," Fanny said. "I've had too many names for anyone to keep track of."

"Though we agreed," Oliver said, "that Fanny would be better, under the circumstances."

Fanny lowered her eyes. "Yes."

"Not that you've done anything wrong. It's just the connotations are difficult, *would be* difficult to explain," Oliver said.

"That worthless Farrington," Richard said, just as they passed two fashionably dressed women walking arm-in-arm. The women glanced at Fanny with her hands tucked into two strange gentlemen's arms and gave each other meaningful looks.

Fanny bit her lip.

"Now don't let them scorch you," Oliver said.

"I don't see how I can help it," Fanny said. "It'll be all over the city tomorrow how Sara Farrington is back to her old tricks, this time two at a time."

"Bother," Richard said. "It's perfectly acceptable to walk with a brother and a married business acquaintance."

"They don't know that," Fanny said.

"They also don't know you're Fanny Fern," Oliver said. "Have you thought what you'll do when that word gets out?"

"I'll see to that if and when it happens."

"Oh, trust me, it'll happen," Oliver said. "It's just a matter of when, not if. And your treatment then will be much the same as this. People will stare, and judge."

"I've handled it this long," Fanny said.

Richard patted her arm. "Yes, you have."

The trio arrived at Nelly's school where they were going to pick her up. They were early, so sat on a bench near the front courtyard to wait for the dismissal bell and the carriage Oliver had arranged. Richard brushed off the bench with his handkerchief. "I think you should move away from Boston once and for all. Come to New York. Nobody there would care a whit that you're Sara Farrington."

"Have you found out if there's been a divorce?" Oliver asked.

Fanny sat on the bench. "Not yet," she said. "But Mr. Derby is looking into it."

"Now there's a smart publisher," Richard said.

"Derby's the best," Oliver said. "And is Farrington still sending you those duplicitous letters?" he asked Fanny.

"Letters?" Richard asked.

"He sends letters proclaiming his love and asking her to join him in whatever city he's staying. It's all a sham, so she can't claim desertion," Oliver said.

Fanny nodded. "They're really rather disgusting and always addressed correctly, no matter how often I move."

"He's still got spies in town, then," Richard said.

"Really, what does he care? You said he doesn't love you," Oliver said.

"No. He has no idea what the word means," Fanny said. "But he thinks I'm his property and Samuel Farrington doesn't relinquish control over an asset without a fight."

"I hope you have good news from Derby," Richard said.

"I hope it's soon officially over," Oliver said. "With your recent earnings, Farrington could resurface and make a claim on them—and you."

Fanny shuddered. "I'd give him whatever he wanted to be rid of him."

"No you wouldn't," Oliver said. "If you gave him a penny, he'd ask for it all. You'd never be rid of him then. Do you realize how much you've earned?"

Fanny inhaled sharply. "According to the accounting statements, almost $1,500. But I won't believe it until I see it. I haven't received a check yet."

Richard whistled.

"You're going to need a good accountant," Oliver said.

"Jessie's family knows a good one," Richard said. "Come to New York—if only to meet a reputable accountant!"

"Oh, I could never leave Boston. What about Grace? How could I possibly leave the state before retrieving her?" Fanny said.

"I know you're set to pick her up the second your check gets to you," Oliver said. "But, frankly, it won't matter where you are when you go to get her. You forget that legally she's all yours. No matter what Mrs. Eldredge says."

"You really should think about moving," Richard said. "I'd feel better having you closer. You could meet Jessie. I'm sure you'd love her and she would love you. Besides, I've already paved your way. All of New York is dying to meet the great Fanny Fern, especially after the glowing review of *Fern Leaves* I just wrote."

"Of course everyone would expect your newspaper to glow about the book," Fanny said. "You carry my column."

"But it's not just the *Musical World and Times*," Oliver said. "Every paper is giving you stellar reviews. Even the *Home Journal*, believe it or not."

"Nat?!" Fanny asked.

"No, not Nat," Oliver said. "We don't think he knows your identity yet."

Richard nodded. "But that other editor there. He adores you."

"Yes," Oliver said. "James Parton. He wrote a great review. In fact, he just sent me a packet of letters for you, complete with one from him. He asked me, personally, to please see that you get it."

Fanny took the packet from Oliver and slipped the letters into her skirt pocket to read later, after their glorious supper with Nelly at the Seafood Garden, after she said good-bye to Oliver and Richard at the boardinghouse door, after she tucked a chattering Nelly into bed, after she figured out, once more, exactly how she would blast in on Mary Eldredge and rescue her Grace forever, after she'd written a little vignette about death or maybe marriage or maybe family, to give to Oliver in the morning. Maybe then, if she wasn't too tired and her eyes didn't burn, she would glance at the packet of letters. They were sometimes dismissive, usually complimentary, always touching. It never ceased to amaze Fanny that some person, somewhere, had been moved enough one way or the other to pick up a pen and write to her. *She* wrote because she *had* to, needed to. She enjoyed it—much more than sewing or millinery work. Yet, she'd never written to a newspaper writer in her life and hadn't ever known anyone who had. It was unusual to get letters from readers. All of her editors said so. Yet, Fanny got them by the score. She liked knowing she sparked something in people. She liked knowing she moved them to action—any action, however small. She liked making a difference.

Chapter Thirty-Two

Fanny Fern, Boston and Newton, Friday, July 1st, 1853

My Dear Old Boston: You know that you are bigoted, and opinionated, and narrow-minded (and like all who revolve in a two-pint measure), given to meddling with what is lawfully none of your business.

—Fanny Fern, *Olive Branch*, June 25th, 1853

It was only five o'clock in the morning and Fanny was already up and dressed. She sat at the boardinghouse's little window desk, the desk where she'd written many an article, and looked out at the trees swaying in the wind. It looked like rain, maybe a thunderstorm. Gritty clouds pushed across the sky. A weak sun tried to rise.

Her desk was empty, as was the bureau and the little alcove near the door. Fanny had packed their meager stock of clothing, Nelly's few toys and books, their little stack of mementos and, of course, Fanny's old inkstand. Everything they'd owned could be stuffed into five trunks. Fanny's sister, Lucy, carried that many trunks on a weekend getaway to the seashore. But Fanny didn't care that she was short of material possessions. Her heart was full. She was going to get her Grace. And they were all moving to New York City.

Fanny had arranged to have their things sent early, on the morning train. Richard promised to pick up her trunks at the train station in New York and to be sure they were properly delivered to the boardinghouse Oliver had found for them. Fanny cringed to think it would cost six dollars a week. She had to keep reminding herself that she'd just received a $1,500 check, and that according to the royalty statement she'd received, she would soon be receiving another $1,200. The amounts didn't seem real. Fanny was so used to counting out pennies, to looking frantically for a lost dime, to rejoicing over every earned dollar that made its way into her little velvet pouch. Now she had a bank account and, according to the balance statement, she had enough money to live for several years. She could afford to get Grace. She could afford to raise her daughters. She could afford life.

Fanny promised herself not to waste a cent. She had no idea how long she'd be able to earn a living as a writer. Heaven knew readership loyalties came and went. But she'd make the best of things while she could and would be sure to save as much as she could toward her daughters' futures. Fanny was grateful. Yes, she'd worked hard, but she was thankful for this stroke of good fortune, this miracle of being able to sell a collection of her articles in a book.

Fanny couldn't wait to see Grace. It'd been over six months since that last stilted visit they'd had. Hezekiah had been ill and Mary had been cross. Again, Fanny remembered the image of a muted Grace, sitting demurely before the fire, stitching at some little cloth and behaving as if some random guests had arrived for tea. Fanny had ached to see a spark of passion in Grace—joy, anger, frustration, *anything*. But Grace had sat strangely unaffected on that little chair by the fire, with a faint smile on her face and dead eyes. Fanny shuddered. Hopefully, it wasn't too late.

Grace was already twelve, on the cusp of womanhood. Fanny remembered the painful amalgam of emotions that ran through her own body at that age. She'd gone through a stretch when she'd refused to attend services, opting instead, as her mother suggested, to sit before the blue-and-white fireplace tiles and gather God, *her* idea of God, into her heart. Fanny liked some of the tiles better than others and could still see Daniel in the lion's den—a calm and authoritative man fending off several snapping lions. The most vicious beast, the one that looked closest to lunging, was an old lioness crouched at Daniel's heel. Daniel's back arm was out, so Fanny felt assured his gesture held the lioness in check. But Fanny worried about that lioness. With Daniel's slightest falter, a cough or a blink, she'd spring and would aim straight for his throat.

Fanny thought of Mary Eldredge. She wouldn't easily relinquish Grace. Even though Fanny was armed with her legal rights, Mary pleaded a strange case lately. She insisted she *loved* Grace. She claimed Grace as her last living relative and clung to the idea of raising her as a daughter. Not only that, Fanny knew Mary coveted Nelly, too. Well, Fanny wouldn't bend. She'd handed over her Grace to Mary for two years now and *would have her back*. It was one thing when Fanny was poor and another thing when Hezekiah was dying. But now Fanny had a fresh start and she would be mother to both her daughters.

Nine-year-old Nelly stirred. She was as excited to get Grace as Fanny was. She begged Fanny to let her buy a hair comb at the apothecary on the corner and wrapped it in brown paper for Grace. Fanny hadn't the heart to tell her that according to Mary's last letter, she'd cut Grace's "foolish curls" because she was spending too much time arranging them in the morning—time she ought to be spending with her bible. Grace's hair would grow back. She'd use Nelly's comb soon enough.

Fanny went to Nelly's side and gently shook her awake.

Nelly's eyes popped open. "Is it time?"

"Almost. The train leaves in an hour."

Nelly scrambled out of bed to dress. Fanny and Nelly packed their two small traveling bags, said their good-byes to Mrs. Dougherty and Mr. Winslow, and walked briskly to the train station. Fanny marveled as she paid fifty cents for two tickets to Newton. Only two years before, she'd had to walk while Nelly rode alone. This time, Fanny rode next to Nelly and they both stared out the window at the misty countryside flying by.

When the train stopped at the little platform in Newton, Oliver was waiting with the rented carriage, as he promised. He looked somber in his black suit and hat. His full beard had a funny way of hiding his expression and, so, made him appear gruff. Fanny wasn't sure what to expect from Mary and had gladly accepted Oliver's offer to accompany them. Fanny respected Oliver's wisdom and calm demeanor and had come to cherish his friendly support. Where she sometimes rose to passion too quickly, Oliver's flame burned slow and steady. Fanny didn't want to offend Mary, or to hurt her. But she was absolutely leaving Newton with her daughter, with both of her daughters.

They traveled the few miles to the Eldredge home in silence. Fanny felt her insides squeeze in upon themselves. Mary's letters had had such a vulnerability to them. Fanny understood that Mary mourned Hezekiah, but Mary had to understand that each day that *Fanny* was without her Grace was just as sad to *her*. Fanny had catered to Mary's wishes long enough. The time had come for Grace to return home.

The carriage approached the house. While they were pulling up to the cottage, a figure ran from the back entrance. It was Mary, dragging a shoeless Grace by the wrist.

"What's happening, there?" Oliver called.

Mary yelled something and nudged Grace down the path that led to the garden.

Fanny didn't know what Mary's intentions were. She didn't think Mary was trying to be deceitful. She only knew that Grace was leaving and that was something she had to stop.

"Grace!" Fanny screamed. "Grace, we've come for you!"

Grace had been scampering down the path with a chattering Mary a few feet behind her when she heard her mother call. Grace stopped so quickly Mary fell against her. Grace turned to look at the carriage and at the familiar faces within it. They weren't robbers after all! It was Mother and Nelly and they had finally come back for her!

"Mother!" Grace screamed.

"Grace!" Fanny yelled.

At that instant Grace lost her womanly smile. She lost her composure and good manners. She lost everything about her that Nana claimed made her bearable and Grace broke down. Right there on the garden path with Nana chiding her and Mother calling and Nelly running and some strange gentleman trying hard to handle the upset horses, Grace collapsed to the ground and cried like a child. "Oh, Mother. Mother," she whimpered.

"Get up," Nana said. "Move. That's not your mother."

But it was. It was Mother. And Nelly. They'd come back. They had.

Fanny leapt from the still-moving carriage after Nelly and ran through the front yard, around the house and down the path. Nelly flew to her sister, and Fanny, just a moment behind Nelly, saw her daughters embrace. Two identical dark-blonde heads, two similar smiles, two sets of blue eyes. Her children. Her daughters. Both of them.

"My girls," Fanny said as she tearfully embraced and kissed them both.

"Mother," Grace said. She sobbed into Fanny's shirtfront. "You've come."

Fanny's eyes spilled over. "Yes, yes, darling. You didn't doubt it for a minute, did you? Of course I came. I said I would."

"Mother can afford us both now," Nelly said. "And we're moving to New York!"

Grace stared, bewildered, into Fanny's face.

"Oh, there's lots to tell," Fanny said. "But the main thing is we've come for you."

"Now?" Grace stuttered.

"Now. Today!" Fanny said. "Run. Go pack your things. Nelly, you help." She turned both girls toward the house. "Hurry now. We've a train to catch."

The girls scampered to the house, clinging to each other. Grace looked stunned but Nelly squealed with excitement.

Mary stood still on the garden path, a rock in her hand. "You'll do no such thing. Grace is my girl. You gave her up."

Fanny turned to face Mary. "I did not give her up, Mary, and you know it. I've got the legal papers to prove it," she said. "I wrote you that I was coming today and here I am. Now put that rock down before somebody gets hurt."

Mary raised the rock higher. "You won't get a penny for them if you take her now."

"I know and I don't care," Fanny said. "You couldn't pay me a million dollars to give up my Grace. It was always only until I could afford to care for her. Now put that rock down and be sensible."

Mary's raised the rock over her head. "You can't take her. You gave her up to me. You did." Mary grimaced and pulled back her arm.

"Mary!" Fanny sprung forward, reaching for Mary's hand.

Mary smashed the rock onto Fanny's shoulder.

Fire blasted through Fanny. She groaned, her arm blazing in pain.

"What's happening?" Oliver called, hurrying up the path.

Fanny grabbed Mary's wrists and held them in front of her.

Mary sputtered and twisted her arms. As Oliver approached, Mary started kicking. "Damn you!" she said to Fanny, kicking wildly at Fanny's shins. "Damn you to hell!"

Just as Fanny didn't think she could hold Mary another second, Oliver was there to help. He pulled Mary's arms firmly back and held them. "Drop that rock now," he said.

Mary's chin quivered. Her eyes brimmed with tears. "She's all I've got left."

"Mary," Fanny said and moved nearer.

Mary narrowed her eyes. "Leave it to you to cause me more misery than you already have. Just leave it to you."

Oliver tightened his grasp on Mary's arms. Mary twisted against his grip.

"Hush now," Fanny said, firmly. "I don't wish you any ill. I never have. But Grace is my daughter and I've come to get her. I can afford to keep her myself and I don't care if there's money in a will from you or not. I won't give her, or Nelly, up to you."

Mary suddenly stopped struggling. She looked at the sky. A tear slid down her cheek. "You've always been heartless. Cold and cruel."

Fanny narrowed her eyes. Her shins pulsed where Mary had kicked her and her shoulder ached where Mary had hit her with the rock. "You've no idea how generous with you I've been," she said.

Oliver released Mary's arms and snatched the rock from her fingers. "You best stop this foolishness," he said.

Just then, the girls broke out of the back door with a few bundles and boxes. They ran across the back yard to the path that wound around the house and led to the front. They ran fast down the path, Nelly out of excitement and Grace out of anxiety, to get to the carriage, to stow Grace's things in it. Fanny looked from her two daughters to Mary's wrenched face. Fanny shook her head as if to clear it and took a deep breath.

"Wait!" Fanny called to the girls. "Come back and say your good-byes to Nana Eldredge. And Grace, you must thank her for taking such good care of you for me."

The girls stopped running, looked at each other, then set their bundles and boxes on the path. They slung their arms around each other and walked toward Fanny, Mary, and Oliver. Nelly came forward first, hugged Mary woodenly around the hips and said good-bye.

Grace stood trembling at Fanny's side. Fanny slid an arm around her. "Go ahead, Grace. Say good-bye, now, to Nana Eldredge and thank her for her care."

Mary's chin quivered and her eyes flooded. She held her arms out to Grace.

Grace's face spasmed. "No, I won't thank her!" she said. "I hate her and I never want to see her again!"

"Grace," Fanny murmured.

Grace turned and ran to the path. She stooped to pick up her belongings and ran to the carriage.

Mary turned to Fanny, "You've poisoned her against me!"

"I've done no such thing," Fanny said.

"Enough of this," Oliver said. He grabbed Fanny and Nelly by the arms. "Come along. We'd best leave immediately."

They hurried down the path, after Grace.

"Grace!" Mary called after them. She crumpled to the dirt and pounded the dry path weakly. "Just like with Charly," Mary yelled. "Just like with Charly!"

Fanny hurried with Nelly and Oliver to where Grace was wringing her hands by the carriage. Fanny pulled Grace to her. "My poor darling," she said. "I'm so very sorry."

"Hurry and get in!" Oliver said.

Fanny helped Nelly, then Grace into the carriage, then climbed in herself and enveloped Grace in her arms, again. "You'll have to tell Mother all about it." Fanny crooned into Grace's ear. "Mother's here now. I've got you."

Oliver glanced at Fanny, then pointed his chin to the road.

Fanny nodded. "Go, go!" she said.

Oliver slapped the reins. The carriage raced away, disappearing over the hill that led to the train platform, leaving a sobbing Mary crouched in the dirt of the garden path.

Chapter Thirty-Three

Fanny Fern, New York City, Friday, July 1st, 1853

Ah, what but this heavenly love, could bridge over the anxious days and nights, of care and sickness, that these twain of one flesh are called to bear? *My* boy! *My* girl! There it is! *Mine*! Something to live for—something to work for—*something to come home to*; and that last is the summing up of the whole matter.

—Fanny Fern, *New York Ledger*, November 18, 1865

It was early evening when they arrived at the train station in New York. Fanny's shoulder had throbbed the whole jostling journey but it was nothing compared to the sick feeling she had in her stomach. She had ruined her daughter. She had tried to save her and had ended up practically killing her, just the same. Oliver purchased a pack of ice from the dining car for Fanny's shoulder, but Fanny didn't use it. Grace wanted to lean silently into her and nothing would ever get between this mother and this child again. Besides, she told Oliver, she didn't think anything was broken, it was just badly bruised. Fanny's eyes welled up thinking that her little injury was nothing compared to Grace's hurts. She stroked Grace's huddled too-quiet head. Hopefully, Grace, too, was only badly bruised, and not broken.

In the carriage on the way to the boardinghouse, Grace still barely spoke. Instead, she clung fiercely to Fanny and wept quietly through her first New

York twilight. Nelly looked helplessly from her sister to her mother while Oliver tried to make small talk. Have you ever seen so many people, he asked Nelly, such tall buildings? It was clear to Fanny that Grace's time with Mary had been more than difficult. Grace still leaned into Fanny's bruised shoulder in a way that frightened Fanny. She had never seen such a shaken child. Just as soon as she thought this, Fanny corrected herself. She suddenly remembered Nettie and Clare—Nettie searching the skies for the answers that would ward off Samuel's blows, Clare's retreating into herself.

The sick feeling in Fanny's stomach grew. So many abused girls. So many hurt people. Why, why, why? She hugged Grace tight, almost grateful that the gesture made her shoulder ache. She would never be able to bear enough pain to make up for having to leave Grace with Mary. If only she had figured out a writing career faster. If only she had made other arrangements for Grace— perhaps with Father and Julia or even Lucy. If only she had *kept* her; Grace probably would have found a way to earn a few dimes here and there and Fanny could have gotten by on less food. Fanny's eyes brimmed remembering the day she left Grace, how Grace had pleaded with her not to go, how Grace had protested, "I'm not big enough to stay here by myself."

Nobody *was* big enough to withstand Mary's harshness. What had Fanny thought would happen? Mary had only enough love for one child—her child, her Charly. Fanny laid her cheek on Grace's soft hair and let the tears slip from her eyes. She would never forgive herself. She, who thought she was doing her children such good by trying to provide for them herself. She should have found a better place, even if it was a permanent one, for such a tenderhearted girl as her sweet Grace.

Nelly tired of Oliver's small talk and stared at her weeping sister and mother. Fanny felt the weight of that stare, too, figuring she was ruining Nelly's disposition just as surely as she had weighted down Grace's. Oh, what would Charly think of her? She was glad he couldn't see what a horrible job of mothering she was doing.

As if he could read her thoughts, Oliver patted Fanny's hand. He gave her a handkerchief. "There now," he said. "Don't be hard on yourself. What's done is done. The child is just overwhelmed to see you again."

Fanny nodded and smiled a bitter smile.

Grace timidly raised her head and said quietly, "Mother, it's true. I'm just, so, so . . . *glad!*"

Fanny held Grace's chin so she could look into her face. "Grace," she said.

Grace wiped her eyes with the back of her hand. "Just please promise you'll never leave me again."

"Never!" Fanny said. "I will never ever leave you again."

Nelly's chin quivered. "Or me?" she asked timidly.

"Oh, darling," Fanny said, reaching over to take her hand. "Never. Neither of you. Never again. No matter if we have to eat grubs."

"We'll eat grubs together," Nelly said.

"I'd rather have eaten grubs," Grace said quietly.

"I know," Fanny said. "I know, my darling."

Oliver cleared his throat. "I believe the restaurants in New York City do not typically serve grubs, young lady. But we can check."

Nelly looked at Oliver and grinned.

Grace looked warily at them both.

"I, myself, prefer a good beefsteak," he said to Grace. "What are you hungry for?"

"Nothing," Grace said. "I couldn't eat a thing."

"Oh, surely there's *something*," Oliver said. "Roast turkey? Apple dumplings? Lamb chops?"

"I like beefsteak, too," Nelly said.

"Strawberry ice cream. Chocolate drops. Potatoes and gravy?"

"Maybe . . . grubs," Grace said with the hint of a smile.

"How should those be prepared?" Oliver asked. "Steamed or battered and fried?"

Grace smiled shyly. "They probably don't do them right here. I guess I'll have beefsteak this time, too."

Fanny bit her lip and glowed at Oliver. "Beefsteak it is then," she said.

Oliver nodded and instructed the driver.

Chapter Thirty-Four

Fanny Fern, New York City, Friday, July 8th, 1853

Such a crowd, such a rush, such confusion I never expect to see again. Equestrians and pedestrians; omnibuses and carriages; soldiers, civilians and *uncivil*—ians; carts and curricles; city exquisites and country nonde-scripts . . . — Well; it's eleven o'clock, and after several abortive attempts we succeeded in arresting an omnibus, labelled "for the Hippodrome and Crystal Palace." Away we go—dashing through the crowd, regardless of limbs, vehicular or human. Broadway is lined, on either side, with a dense throng of questionable looking expectants, waiting "to see the procession." . . . As the eye swept through this magnificent thoroughfare, the rushing vehicles, the swaying motley multitudes, the gaily dressed ladies, the waving flags and banners which floated over the more public and prominent edifices, presented an ever varying panorama, that was far from being the least attractive and impressive feature of the day.

—Fanny Fern, *Musical World and Times*, July 23rd, 1853

Fanny and the girls ate beefsteak with Oliver Dyer that first night, roast chicken with Richard and Jessie the second, and lobster with Oliver, Oliver's wife, Deliah, and Richard and Jessie on the third. New York was good for them, good to them. They ate well and *together*, and began to reclaim themselves as a family.

It didn't take them long to unpack. Jessie had their few clothes hung on pegs and their trunks airing by the time they arrived. They put their personal things away in less than an hour. The last thing Fanny unpacked was her dear inkstand. She held it up to the light, inspecting it for any new scratches, before placing it, with great ceremony, on the writing desk near the window. "Well, old inkstand," she said. "Another place you've managed to get for us."

The boardinghouse unit they rented was actually two adjoining rooms. Fanny could work late in the one with the writing desk and fall asleep on the ample horsehair divan whenever she wanted. The girls could go to bed early in the tightly strung bed in the next room. Both rooms had small fireplaces and their rent allowed them a decent quantity of coal in the cool months, a chamber pot, washing water, towels and soap, and three square meals a day. Six dollars a week still seemed like a fortune to Fanny, but Oliver insisted it was a very reasonable amount for New York City room and board. Besides, he said, her book was selling hundreds of copies a day. Speculators predicted it would become the nation's top-selling book ever.

Fanny decided she'd believe "speculators" when she saw the royalty statements. Meanwhile she made her first week in the city a light writing week, only delivering a column each to Oliver's paper, Moulton's, and Norris'. She dashed off her work between sightseeing and shopping trips with the girls. They walked everywhere—to the market, to the oceanfront, to the fields on the outskirts of the business area. They walked through beautiful residential districts, past the fishing boats and through the many parks among well-dressed ladies and gentlemen. Oliver, Deliah, Richard, and Jessie were faithful escorts, showing Nelly, Grace, and Fanny the city that was growing faster than any other city in the world, the city with more theaters and restaurants than any of them had ever seen.

Grace still clung most times to Fanny's arm, and although Fanny noticed her grip lessening with each day, the chilling leaden look in Grace's eyes remained.

"She's been through a time," Oliver said. "You know how that is."

Fanny nodded bitterly, ill that she'd brought the world's pain to her own offspring at such a tender age. She vowed she would make it up to Grace, would see the light burn in her lovely blue eyes again, would see a hearty smile break out on her face. Time was the great healer. That's what everyone always said. But Fanny knew time could only do so much for some wounds. She still sometimes longingly stroked Charly's wedding vest, still looked around wildly when she smelled a certain shade of green. The pain lessened, the grief abated, and although the wound became a scar, it never quite disappeared. Yet, Fanny knew she was better for her trials—stronger, smarter—and, hopefully, Grace and Nelly would be, too.

They would make up for lost time, Fanny told the girls. They'd be the strongest, most loving family yet, and nothing but death would ever separate them again. The days were long and balmy and all three of them welcomed the bright sunshine. The bustle of the city made everything seem even warmer and Fanny and the girls let the heat of New York's summer melt through their collective fears. Beating down on their bonnets or basking their backs, the sun was like a pair of warm loving hands binding them all together.

It was on one such beautiful, sunny day that they met James Parton. Fanny had promised they'd get an ice cream after she delivered her latest article to Oliver, and the girls were excited to accompany her. Besides, Nelly was curious to see how the newspaper office where Uncle Richard worked differed from all the newspaper offices she'd seen in Boston. When they'd arrived at the *Musical World and Times* office, the girls were drawn to a cache of musical instruments in one corner of the foyer. "These are for sale by one musician to another," Fred, a copyist, told them. "We can look at them if you'd like."

There was an oboe, a bassoon, several violins, three drums of various qualities, a pianoforte, and a banjo. Fred let Grace pluck the banjo and let Nelly blow into the bassoon.

"They should see a concert," Oliver said as he came from his office to greet them. "New York has something playing every night of the week."

"Really!" Fanny said.

"And we've got to get you to the theater," Oliver said to her. "Deliah says you'll love it."

"Oh, I've always loved the theater. I just haven't been in so long," Fanny said. It had been since Charly. He'd taken her to every new production that opened in Boston, back when Fanny had no idea a theater ticket cost as much as a dozen *Olive Branch* articles, back when Fanny had no idea how much she should be treasuring Charly's wonderful company. She sighed.

"Or the opera," another voice said.

"Oh, James," Oliver said to the man who was the presumed owner of the voice. "Meet Fanny Fern and her daughters, Grace and Nelly. Fanny, this is James Parton. The editor I was telling you about."

Fanny offered her hand. "How do you do."

James beamed. "It's a pleasure to meet you. I adore your writing!"

Fanny assessed the glittering dark eyes, the well-groomed dark beard, the sculpted face and delicate hands. She noticed the slight wave to this man's hair—very much like Charly's, though not so thick—and the slightly lopsided warm, warm smile. His suit was perfectly brushed. His shoes shone bright. His nails were smooth. He wore what looked to be an English pocket watch and a cravat of the faintest lavender gray. "You work with Nat," she said, looking him full on.

James was taken aback, not only by the question, but by Fanny's radiance. Her eyes were as bright as a summer sky. She had luxurious dark blonde curls, and a lot of them. Her trim figure fit well into the simple periwinkle day dress she wore. James took her hand and shook it. This slim thing had penned the brilliance he knew. Behind those bright eyes flew the thoughts he admired. Under those curls roared the anger at injustice he adored. He stammered. "Yes, Nat. I just found out he is your brother."

"Or I am his sister, as he'd prefer to think of it," Fanny said. She pulled her hand away. Any friend of Nat's was someone she had better steer clear of.

"The opera," Oliver said. "Now why didn't I think of that?"

"You write as well as Dickens," James said. "Wonderful sketches."

"Thank you," Fanny said.

"Henriette Sontag is singing 'La Sonnambula,'" Oliver said.

"Such pictures you draw—of love, beauty, and suffering," James said.

"If you work for Nat," Fanny said, "I'd guess you'd consider my work vulgar."

"It's bold!" James said. "And no more vulgar than Dickens. Why is it that men and women are judged so differently?"

Fanny cocked her head in amazement and smiled. "Now, there's the question."

"It's at Castle Garden," Oliver said. "If you hurry, you could still get tickets."

"Tickets?" Fanny said, suddenly reddening. "Oh, I don't think . . ."

"Fantastic idea, Oliver!" James said. "Would you and Deliah be available to occupy the girls? They're so smart, yet the opera does get out late. And perhaps I could convince their mother to join me for a late supper."

"Of course we'd be happy to take the girls," Oliver said.

Fanny stared, open-mouthed at Oliver. "Oh, you can't."

"I promised to teach them whist and tonight is the night," he said.

Nelly hopped at his elbow. "Can we stay up late?"

"Whatever your mother thinks," Oliver said.

"Excuse us," Fanny said, pulling Oliver into his office by the elbow.

Oliver shut the door behind him.

"What are you suggesting?" Fanny said. "Don't you remember? I'm Sara Farrington!"

"Probably not any longer," Oliver said. "Derby says he thinks Samuel has filed for divorce."

"*Filed*? Then, I'm still married! I cannot be accompanied . . . to the *opera* . . . by a . . . ," she pointed to the door, ". . . *stranger!*"

"Parton's a jewel. Perfect gentleman," Oliver said. "Trust me."

Fanny's eyes darted around the room. She did trust Oliver, more than anyone she'd met since Charly had died. She trusted him almost *as much* as she had trusted Charly. She thought about Charly and the blind trust she'd placed in him, in his judgment, and about how little she'd really known of his business plans, how little she knew of his financial mistakes. Yet, Oliver had helped her rescue Grace. Oliver had helped her move to New York, was helping her emerge in this great city as a writer and a citizen.

"Fanny," Oliver said quietly. "Trust me."

Fanny breathed quickly.

"It's just the opera," Oliver said. "With a *friend*."

"He's no friend," Fanny said. "I don't even know him."

"But I do," Oliver said. "He's a friend of a friend."

Just then someone tapped on the door. Oliver opened it and saw a distressed James standing outside of it. "It's fine to put it off," he said, biting his lip. "I didn't mean an offense. Really, we could make it another time, after you've gotten to know me better."

He's genuine, Fanny suddenly thought. As genuine as she'd seen. "Don't be silly," Fanny said, amazed at the words coming out of her mouth. "It's just the opera, correct?"

James smiled.

"With a friend?" Fanny said.

"Of course," James said.

And so, they went to the opera.

Fanny dressed carefully for the event. She still only had her two outfits—the periwinkle day dress and the nicer brown silk skirt. She wore the brown silk with a fancy camel-colored silk blouse she borrowed from Deliah.

"We really need to see about getting you a few new things," Deliah said. "Now that you're out of the widow's weeds for good."

Fanny had mixed feelings about retiring her widow's weeds. It was true that she'd hid underneath their shadows for too long. Widows typically only wore them for a year. But, after the fiasco with Samuel and the ensuing social maltreatment she received, Fanny had so happily reclaimed her mourning clothes. In her shabby black attire, nobody questioned her tramping up and down newspaper office stairs, bustling to and from the post office, grocers, and apothecary shops. She could conduct her business in peace, spared the accusatory stares of so many critical eyes. Even though she'd conducted herself to the letter, Samuel's accusations hovered over her like a swarm of gnats.

Of course her black dresses reminded her, too, of Charly. And Mother. And Ellen. And little Mary. And Mary Stace. Fanny sighed. She never wanted to forget any of them. Before putting on the brown skirt and Deliah's blouse—to go to the opera in New York City, with a newspaper editor, some James Parton, who worked for Nat—Fanny sighed again. She took out the miniature of Charly and stroked her finger over his painted lips. She was Sara Farrington, but she still felt like Sara Eldredge. She squeezed her eyes tight. No, she wasn't Sara Farrington. She was Sara Willis. She was Fanny Fern.

And she had written a book. A beautiful green leather book, embossed with gilt fern leaves. A book full of her *articles*. A book Nelly pointed out to Grace every time they passed a bookshop window. A book that was earning her staggering amounts of money. A book that, if it turned out she was still Sara Farrington, rightfully belonged to Samuel.

Fanny put her hair up and fastened it with the ivory comb Charly had given her one birthday. She stared at herself in the mirror, blinked rapidly, then took the comb out and replaced it with several plainer pins. Opera or not, she didn't want to overdo it. Who really knew what James Parton was thinking or whether Samuel still had her followed by his spies? She wore the pins in her hair and the plain black hat. She placed it on her head and found her gloves just as one of the boardinghouse maids tapped on the door announcing that she had a visitor. Until she heard differently, she was still Sara Farrington.

James Parton proved to be a delightful companion. He picked up Fanny and the girls in a rented carriage, a clean one—no soiled cushions or filthy steps to worry about. And the driver was almost elegant with a decent gray coat and combed beard. He didn't blow cigar smoke into anyone's face, curse at other drivers, or drive so recklessly his passengers were busy rewriting their wills in their heads. They dropped Grace and Nelly off at the Dyers' house and proceeded to the opera. Fanny was equally amazed by the hoards of elegantly dressed, fan-waving spectators as she was by the production. So many well-oiled heads and bejeweled throats, so many gator boots and fine kid gloves, so many feathers and beads, satins and silks, so many perfumes and rings, earbobs and pocket watches. "You look lovely," James said to Fanny as she alighted the carriage in her work-a-day polished boots and single-ruffle brown skirt.

Fanny smiled. "Thank you."

Inside, the sumptuous décor titillated. Thick red velvet swags hung from the windows and enveloped the stage. Underfoot, the mossy paisley carpet whispered as viewers padded over it to thick, upholstered seats where they could sit and admire the gilded cornices and the ornate wood and plaster moldings around the stage. When Madame Sontag finally arrived on stage and trilled her way up and down scales as delicately as a princess drinking from her best crystal, Fanny had to dab at the corners of her eyes. So many years since she'd been treated. So many years since she'd relaxed. So many years since she'd been awed by a talented performer.

Fanny was still Sara Farrington. She knew that was likely true. But, still, she was grateful to this James Parton and grateful for this evening. She let the music roll over her frazzled nerves, feasted her eyes on the lush set and the spectacle of the spectators, inhaled the amalgam of perfumes and colognes and finishing oils, fingered the satin tapestry of the chair's arm beneath her hand. She'd never forget this evening—the opera and the good oyster supper James treated her to afterward. It felt so good to be spoiled a little, so fine to take a break from rushing and writing and worrying, so wonderful to talk to this new, intelligent and very attractive New York friend.

Chapter Thirty-Five

Grace Eldredge, Niagara Falls, Sunday, July 10th, 1853

Men's rights! Women's rights! I throw down the gauntlet for children's rights! Yes, my little pets, Fanny Fern's about "takin' notes," and she'll "print 'em," too, if you don't get your dues. She has seen you seated by a pleasant window, in a railroad car, with your bright eyes dancing with delight, at the prospect of all the pretty things you were going to see, forcibly ejected by some overgrown Napoleon, who fancied your place, and thought, in his wisdom, that children had no taste for anything but sugar-candy . . . Yes; and Fanny has seen you sometimes, when you've been muffled up to the tip of your little nose in woollen wrappers, in a close, crowded church, nodding your little drowsy heads, and keeping time to the sixth-lie or the seventh-lie of some pompous theologian. . . . And she has seen you sitting, like little automatons, in a badly-ventilated school-room, with your nervous little toes at just such an angle, for hours; under the tuition of a Miss Nancy Nipper, who didn't care a rush-light whether your spine was as crooked as the letter S or not. . . . And when, by patient labor, you had reared an edifice of tiny blocks,—fairer in its architectural proportions, to your infantile eye, than any palace in ancient Rome,—she has seen it ruthlessly kicked into a shattered ruin, by somebody in the house, whose dinner hadn't digested! Never mind. I wish I was mother to the whole of you! Such glorious times as we'd have! Reading pretty books, that had no big words in 'em; going to school where you could sneeze without getting a rap on the head for not asking leave first; and going to church on the quiet, blessed Sabbath, where the minister—like our dear Saviour—sometimes remembered to "take little children in his arms, and bless them." Then, if you asked me a question, I wouldn't pretend not to hear; or lazily tell you I "didn't know," or turn you off with some fabulous evasion, for your memory to chew for a cud till you were old enough to see how you had been fooled. And I'd never wear such a fashionable gown that you couldn't climb on my lap whenever the fit took you; or refuse to kiss you, for fear you'd ruffle my curls, or my collar, or my temper,—not a bit of it; and then you should pay me with your merry laugh, and your little confiding hand slid ever trustingly in mine. O, I tell you, my little pets, Fanny is sick of din, and strife, and envy, and uncharitableness!—and she'd rather, by ten thousand, live in a little world full of fresh, guileless, loving little children, than in this great museum full of such dry, dusty, withered hearts.

—Fanny Fern, *Olive Branch*, January 29th, 1853

They were on holiday—Grace, Nelly, and Mother. They were visiting Niagara Falls and Grace was trying hard to have fun, as Mother wanted.

Friday night, she and Nelly got to have dinner with the Dyers and learned to play whist while Mother went "out." Grace had always wanted to learn cards and played happily enough, even though Nelly was winning, and even though she had a sick stomach from being left with people she didn't know very well. Mother came to fetch them at nearly midnight and Grace was so happy she was afraid she might vomit. She hung onto her stomach and gladly entered the carriage with her sister, mother, and Mr. Parton. Even though it was so late, the streets were as full as if it were noon on a business day. So many lamps were lit that you couldn't see the stars through the milky haze the city cast upward. Sometimes Grace missed the quiet of Newton, but she never complained. She was finally with Mother and Nelly and she didn't care if they lived in a paper box, as long as she got to live with them.

They rode home in the carriage on Friday and Grace felt the difference. Mother had become light again, lighter anyway. It was closer to the dreams Grace had of how Mother was at Swissdale—smiley and bright, with always time to pluck a pretty posy or give an extra long hug. That wrinkle between Mother's brows was still there, still etched like a deep crack in a plate. But it was softer somehow, was offset by the tiny flickers of light the moon left in her eyes.

Grace was so thankful Mother had finally come and retrieved her from Nana Eldredge. Nana had started acting strangely, petting Grace's head with her damp hoary hand and whispering funny things about dying and living. When Mother finally came, with Mr. Dyer and Nelly, Grace tried to smile and jump for joy. But all she could do was cry and when she wasn't crying, she felt frozen inside and because she couldn't feel anything around the hard cold blocked inside her, she worried that her special bird was dead. She had wished so hard for her mother that she had killed her bird. Froze it, like a giant winter storm. She could never get it all right. She made so many mistakes. And so, Grace tried hard not to wish or think or feel very much at all because of her great power, because she could ruin lives and people, and innocent birds, so easily.

Grace was especially afraid to confide in Nelly. Nelly was still untainted, as far as Grace could tell, had never felt a grandfather's smoky breath on her neck or his rough hands down the front of her apron. She'd never seen her own little sister's frightened stare as she held their mutual mother's hand and *left*. She'd never slept alone and cold in the attic bed with the broken pane whistling death threats all night long. She'd never planned how to run away and realized that all avenues led to the orphan's asylum. Nelly had never had to sew straight with shaking fingers, didn't have to help Maggie peel potatoes nor hide her bottle in the spider-webby cellar after school. Grace was afraid to talk too much to dear Nelly, afraid to poison her with sin. And, so, Grace, worked hard to hold up her womanly smile and to show Mother, over and over, how it hadn't been a mistake to come and get her, and how she'd never have another reason in the world to leave her anywhere ever again.

Mother seemed to be relaxing, seemed to believe in the rightness of Grace's being there. After she'd retrieved them from the Dyers, they rode home, all together, and Grace had even fallen asleep on Mother's soft, fragrant shoulder, lulled by the wispy way Mother's curls brushed Grace's forehead with every bump in the road. Grace went to bed feeling a little warmer inside, as if the ice block within her was succumbing to a long day of sunshine. She was happy and worried at the same time. If she melted the ice block, what would the consequences be? Grace knew, all too well, that you couldn't have it all, that if you got one wish, it was at the expense of something else you held dear.

It didn't take long for Grace to understand what she'd done by allowing her ice block to melt a little. They woke on Saturday and packed their trunks, for they had already made the plans for their weekend trip to see the great falls. They'd boarded the train. Nelly made haste to inspect the tin cup hanging from the water tank. She even took a drink before they left the station. Grace sat obediently by Mother, overwhelmed by the heavy odors of cigars hanging from men's coats and of hay and horse dung dripping from their boots. The train churned slowly away from the platform, then rumbled faster and faster. Grace's melting ice block dripped a cold dread through her heart. Something bad was going to happen, something terrible. And all because she was purposely allowing this melting.

The train gained speed, pumped faster and faster until, right outside of New York, their train *wrecked*. The sundry-selling boy had just visited their car trying to get Mother to buy a copy of her own book. Mother bought them an apple each, instead, and no sooner had Grace taken her first tart bite, than the train seemed to lift off the tracks as it made a turn. Floating, Grace braced herself. She smelled the catastrophe before she felt it. Sure enough, the train crashed back down, not quite on the rails, and their car leaned left, then tipped

tipped tipped all the way over. The window smashed. Nelly's apple went flying. Mother clung to both girls' waists as they slid sideways against the train's wall. Grace thought they bounced a little before the train went into that awful, long, gravelly sounding slide. When they finally stopped moving, many a passenger had a broken hat or cane and one woman, with blood slipping from her lips, complained that her insides hurt. Mother, Grace, and Nelly were all shaking as they crawled out of the compartment and stood alongside the train with the other quivering passengers. It was still not even noon, but the sun beat down on the field they'd wrecked upon, and the people, and the beached beast itself. The good news, Mother said, was that nobody was killed. Grace hoped Mother was right. The bleeding woman didn't look very well. People loosened her corset and laid her under the spotty shade of a dogwood bush.

Grace had gripped her apple as soon as the train bucked up and, later, after they'd retrieved their trunks from the luggage compartment, they sat on the trunks and shared bites. Grace felt good she'd hung onto it. It was the least she could do after conjuring such bad luck. Mother kept hugging Grace and trying to cheer her worries and Grace smiled gamely. She would give Mother no reason to leave her anywhere ever again. The new train came mid-afternoon and they all boarded and soon arrived at Niagara. Mother got them rooms at Falls House and after tea, they took the tourist wagon to see the famous sight. They pulled away from the hotel and that's when Grace first thought she saw the familiar thin lips, the wiry gray head, the hunched shoulders. Samuel Farrington. Grace ducked her head and when she looked back, the man was gone. She might have thought she was dreaming except for what happened later.

She, Mother, and Nelly saw the falls all right. They listened to the roar of all that angry water plummeting over ragged rocks, basked in the misty air that it left behind. Mother breathed slowly, standing holding both Nelly's and Grace's hands. Grace felt love in her mother's touch, felt the promise that Mother said from her lips over and over—the promise that Grace would always live with them from now on. The promise moved from Mother's fingers up Grace's arm and into her heart. There, it melted the ice block just as strongly as if it were the sun beating down that morning on the beached iron horse beside the parched field. Grace felt the liquid drip through her, then gather at the corners of her eyes. They watched the water fall like that, mixing their love, until the last wagon left to go back to the hotels. They'd come back again the next day, Mother said, before taking the train back to New York.

It wasn't until then, after they'd slept in the cool open-windowed room, after they'd drunk chocolate and eaten corn cakes and ham omelets, after they'd climbed aboard another tourist wagon and stood once more, before the beating fury of the falls, that Grace saw Samuel again. Mother saw him at the same time. He had a funny smile on his face and drew close to them as if he were greeting long-lost friends.

"My dear, Sara," he said. "Is it you? I was ready to declare desertion."

Mother jumped when he said this and her eyes darted back and forth. "You've always known exactly where I was," she said.

"And now you're here," Samuel said. He put his hand on Mother's elbow and squeezed it until Mother winced.

The wagon drivers called for passengers and Mother told Samuel we were going now, but he could write whatever it was he had to tell her. Samuel told her that what he had to say couldn't be communicated in words. He licked his thin mustache when he said that and Mother made a funny sound at the back of her throat. She pulled her elbow away from his moving fingers and took Nelly and Grace by the hands. Before Grace knew quite what was happening, they were in the wagon—she, Nelly, Mother, and Samuel. Samuel whispered something to Mother that made her cheeks glow and her lips tight. She clung even tighter to Grace and Nelly.

At Falls House, Samuel got off with them. Grace wasn't surprised. She knew he was going to follow them and make them all queasy like he used to before Grace lived with Nana Eldredge. It was all happening again. Grace tried to think of something she could do to stop it. Mother wouldn't let go of either girl's hand, so Samuel followed behind her, leaning forward to talk into her ear. Finally, Mother huddled close to Grace and Nelly and told them to run, quick, to their rooms. She'd be right along behind them. She gave Grace a little push and Grace grabbed Nelly's hand and scampered up the porch steps. Inside, they couldn't run to their rooms, not without Mother, so stood peering at her and Samuel through the little windows at the sides of the front door.

Samuel talked and talked to Mother, his thin lips barely moving, his tongue sometimes darting out to lick at his mustache. Mother stood with her back very straight, her head leaning a little to one side, and her hands clasped in front of her. Suddenly Samuel looked quickly around him and darted toward Mother. He clasped the front of her dress with one hand and pulled her toward him. Mother's clasped hands went straight up, hard, into his stomach and she kicked him in the shin. Grace screamed and two gentlemen came running from the front parlor, saw the scuffle in the yard, and rushed out the door. As soon as Samuel heard the door open, he released Mother's dress front and ran.

The gentlemen were Uncle Richard and Mr. Dyer! It turns out they came after they heard about the train wreck and because they had to tell Mother the bad news that Uncle Edward was dead. He'd been in a brawl in Ohio, was jailed, then died of nobody knew what while waiting for his trial. They didn't tell her right away after Samuel left (and thank goodness, they all kept saying, that he had *left*), but later that night, after dinner, when they were on the train back to New York and all the grownups thought both Nelly and Grace were asleep. Grace was only half asleep. She had to at least keep her fingers awake. She couldn't completely let go of her mother's sleeve in case there was another train wreck.

"Ellen, Louisa, and now Edward," Mother whispered with tears in her voice. "Who next?"

Grace started saying her prayers. She had a lot of atoning to do.

Chapter Thirty-Six

Nathaniel Willis, Boston, Thursday, September 22nd, 1853

"If your husband looks grave, let him alone; don't disturb or annoy him."

Oh, pshaw! were I married, the soberer my husband looked, the more fun I'd rattle about his ears. Don't disturb him! I guess so! I'd salt his coffee—and pepper his tea—and sugar his beef-steak—and tread on his toes—and hide his newspaper—and sew up his pockets—and put pins in his slippers—and dip his cigars in water.—and I wouldn't stop for the Great Mogul, till I had shortened his long face to my liking. Certainly, he'd "get vexed;" there wouldn't be any fun in teasing him if he didn't; and that would give his melancholy blood a good, healthful start; and his eyes would snap and sparkle, and he'd say, "Fanny, WILL you be quiet or not?" and I should laugh, and pull his whiskers, and say decidedly, "Not!" and then I should tell him he hadn't the slightest idea how handsome he looked when he was vexed, and then he would pretend not to hear the compliment—but would pull up his dickey, and take a sly peep in the glass (for all that!) and then he'd begin to grow amiable, and get off his stilts, and be just as agreeable all the rest of the evening as if he wasn't my husband; and all because I didn't follow that stupid bit of advice "to let him alone." Just as if I didn't know! Just imagine ME, Fanny, sitting down on a cricket in the corner, with my forefinger in my mouth, looking out the sides of my eyes, and waiting till that man got ready to speak to me! You can see at once it would be—be—. Well, the amount of it is, I shouldn't do it!

—Fanny Fern, *Olive Branch*, April 9th, 1853

Deacon Nathaniel Willis sat in his dressing room and smoked his pipe. His beige vest was unbuttoned and his brown braces hung like arcs over the top of his gray trousers. He had on his sheepskin slippers and had stoked the coals in the fire. The fall chill had come early and Nathaniel felt it more than usual in his wrists. Susan was out calling and he had the morning free, since they'd finished this issue of the *Youth's Companion* last night. Nathaniel puffed on his pipe. He blinked his eyes, which watered sometimes, lately, for no apparent reason. He had nine children, three of whom were dead. Of the remaining, he worried most about Julia and Sara. Lucy had married well, Mary and Sara were widows. Nathaniel shivered. Sara was *more* than a widow, of course, but the less he remembered about *that* humiliation, the better. How *was* she getting on? Mary was well provided for. Nat and Richard were doing fine as family men. Julia would never marry.

Nathaniel sighed. Julia had just gotten older and scrawnier. She became queerer by the year. Always reading, scribbling, wringing her hands. The things that made her happy weren't the things that made other women happy. Julia was unconscious of flowers, blasé about fashion, a clod in the kitchen. She sewed reasonably well, considering the years she'd devoted to it, but wrote as clearly and intelligently as many of his correspondents. He'd always relied upon her giving him usable filler, especially after Sara married. And now she wished to make her living by it. Why would any woman *want* to earn her bread? What gross mistakes had he and Hannah made to turn out such an unnatural female as Julia? She hadn't a feminine instinct to her, not a single maternal virtue.

And now Sara had given her a thousand dollars. Nathaniel shook his head, refusing to wonder *how* Sara might have come into so much spare capital. There were some things a father simply didn't want to know. He remembered Sara as a child—how bright she'd been, how difficult. Nathaniel sighed. At any rate, Julia made a case for receiving her own dowry—the five hundred dollars Nathaniel had given each daughter's husband to invest and use as he saw fit. Julia wanted her share and, in turn, wanted to set up her own quarters, pay her own bills, invest and earn her own income. *Why?* Nathaniel and Susan gave her a comfortable room, right under the stairs and away from drafty windows. She had whatever allowance her needle or her pen could earn for discretionary spending and general womanly maintenance. He provided all her meals and linens. He provided heat and a roof. He provided his good name and the company of family.

But Julia didn't want what he offered. She wasn't happy enough with the usual living. She wanted to travel. She spent evenings, lately, studying languages— French, German, Italian, even Hebrew. She read history books and editorials. She collected newspaper articles like other women collected ribbons. Julia had no interest in children, wanted no part in gardening or baking. Nathaniel saw more masculinity in her than in Nat.

Nat was still a puppy, and was becoming an aged one. His jowls hung over his shirt collar now as his belly hung over the top of his trousers. He still dressed like a peacock and encrusted himself with jewels. He put so much oil in his hair he ruined the furniture. Nat was just too fond of luxury—food, wine, and every nicety that Cornelia's money could buy. Nathaniel could live on simple fare like ham and oysters, could eat unbuttered bread and drink spring water, but not Nat. He had to drown every meal in cream sauces and alcohol, smoked, sucked, and licked victuals all day long, doused everything with sugar or butter or gravy. What Nat needed was an honest day's work and to feel the rumble of his stomach before stuffing it.

Then there was Sara, still unpredictable, unfathomable. Nathaniel thought she'd landed hard after Charly, harder after Samuel. But no matter Sara's crashes, she rose up again, angrier and more uncontrollable than ever. Mary Eldredge had given her up for good. She'd tried to salvage Sara's girls, to provide the structure and discipline every child needs, to steer them down the path to providence and salvation. But Sara's headstrong temper thwarted every good intention. *She* knew everything about mothering. *She* would do everything herself. *She* wouldn't marry without rainbows and leprechauns, wouldn't roughen her hands with honest work, wouldn't listen to the wise counsel of her elders. Mary Eldredge had visited and told how Sara had stolen Grace, how she'd come, unannounced, and frightened them to death by swooping down and whisking Grace away without good-byes or displays of gratitude of any kind.

Nathaniel shuddered. Sara had had some gentleman with her. No surprise. Mary said he'd threatened her with his riding whip and Mary was left cowering on the garden path, afraid to even venture into her own front yard for fear the brutal creature lay in wait for her. How cruel of Sara to treat her own mother-in-law so fiercely. And after the Eldredges saved her skin by taking in Grace. Hadn't he taught her differently? Where had he gone so wrong with her? Nathaniel puffed his pipe. He was tired of battling Sara. The Eldredges probably should have gotten Nelly, too, should have insisted upon adoption.

Mary wanted Nathaniel's help again. Nathaniel sighed. He didn't know. Mary wanted Nathaniel to write Sara and insist that Mary was dying, that she called and called for her dear Grace, that she was alone and frightened and without any relative to nurse her in her infirmity. Nathaniel had asked why Mary didn't write the letter herself. She said that she had to be too sick to even hold a pen. That's how sick a grandmother had to be to earn any warm feelings from the likes of Sara. Besides, the letter would carry more weight coming from her father. Perhaps he could be sure to include biblical references regarding the need to respect, revere, and caretake one's elders?

Nathaniel puffed on his pipe but got no smoke. Infernal thing had gone out again. He had no patience to fiddle with it any more this morning, in fact, had no patience to sit lollying the day away in his dressing room. He kicked off his slippers and wriggled his feet into his shoes. He buttoned his vest and donned his rust-colored jacket. Ah, there was his trusty black hat and dark gloves. A ride was what he needed. A good swift jaunt on one of the grays to clear his mind, to get rid of all these incessant ruminations.

Sara would do what Sara would do. Julia would do what Julia would do. Nat would do what Nat would do. Lucy, Richard, Mary would all survive, until they didn't, despite what he or Susan or Mary Eldredge or anyone said or did or thought. Nathaniel was tired of worrying. He was tired of fighting. He just wanted to ride. He wanted to ride and come home to some hot tea and a piece of pie. He wanted to clear his head of children and words for an hour and let them all take care of themselves.

Nathaniel clomped down the stairs and rang to have Moses saddled. He'd ride and would have some simple dinner in a pub somewhere. He was happy with a little ham and some spring water. He'd ride and he'd be back for tea. He'd warm himself and would have a slice of pie. He wouldn't worry about his children for the rest of the day. He'd give Julia her dowry. He'd refrain from haranguing Nat. He'd let Mary write her own damn letter to Sara.

Chapter Thirty-Seven

Ellen (Nelly) Eldredge, New York, Thursday, September 22nd, 1853

God shield the motherless! . . . Childhood passes; blooming maidenhood comes on; lovers woo; the mother's quick instinct, timely word of caution, and omnipresent watchfulness, are not there. . . . Thank God!—not unheard by Him, who "wipeth all tears away," goeth up that troubled heart-plaint from the despairing lips of the motherless!

—Fanny Fern, *Olive Branch*, August 21st, 1852

Ellen was nine now, too old to be called Nelly. When she and Grace marched off to school this year, she made sure her teachers called her Ellen straight off. Mother was being called Fanny in New York and she would be called Ellen. Grace, though, would still, and probably always, be called Grace. There was no way to change it.

Ellen liked making jokes and fun. Once, when she was out to supper with Grace and Mother and Mr. Parton, Mr. Parton asked her if she wanted soup and Ellen said, "You'd better ask my Mother if I may. She's my soup-erintendent!" Everybody laughed. Things were different now that they were in New York. There was food (Ellen even came back to liking pudding!) and there were friends and, of course, there was Grace again.

Grace sometimes slipped and still called her Nelly. Ellen excused her when that happened. Grace couldn't know everything right away, Mother said. Grace had spent the last two years being afraid at Nana and Papa Eldredge's house. Nobody really said she was being afraid, but that's what Ellen decided. The way Grace's eyes skittered over someone's face, the way she wrung her hands, the way she walked with her head thrust forward, Grace looked like she was still afraid. Most of the time Ellen felt sorry for Grace. But she wanted to jump up and shout that she'd been afraid sometimes, too. She had had to play alone and go to the grocer's alone and beg Papa Willis for a dollar alone and face strange faces along boardinghouse steps alone. She, Ellen, had been alone and afraid *herself* and nobody made a fuss about it. Sometimes Ellen wanted to shake Grace. She wanted to stomp her foot or bang a pot and jar her sister out of the fearful dream place she so often lived in. Ellen wanted her sister back, her big sister. She wanted Grace to start offering protection and comfort, to start doting on her affectionate, whimsical little sibling and to *stop worrying*. She was *away* from Nana's house. She was *with them* again, just as Mother promised. They were in New York and had *plenty of money*. Grace didn't even have to eat bread and milk. She'd never had to eat bread and milk so many nights like Ellen and Mother had.

Ellen liked Mr. Parton. She liked his smooth, dark whiskers and his glossy hair. She liked his cinnamon-colored eyes and the way his mouth smiled sideways. She liked how gentle his voice sounded and how long he waited for her answer whenever he asked her a question. Mr. Parton liked them, too, Ellen could tell. He liked Mother and he liked Grace and he liked Ellen. Mr. Parton liked Mother so much he sometimes forgot to talk and would just stare, dazzled, at her for a few seconds as she nibbled a biscuit or brushed a loose curl out of her eyes. He liked Ellen, too, but would never look dazzled at her. He mostly smiled at Ellen. Smiled and patted her head. Sometimes when he patted, he would rest his warm hand on the top of Ellen's head and Ellen could feel kindness streaming from that hand down into her head and through her body. Mr. Parton was less demonstrative with Grace. He didn't pat her head or shake her ringlets in fun. He talked to her more like she was a grownup, even though everybody knew she was only just turned twelve.

Mother treated Grace like this, too, as if she were a new creature that they had to study and dress beautifully and blow on once in a while to make sure it didn't get dusty. Mother bought Grace a new pair of mustard-colored gloves. They matched the tiny golden tones in her blue eyes perfectly and she wore them every day. Ellen thought Grace should sometimes still wear the black ones from Nana Eldredge's, but, of course, Ellen would never make such a suggestion. She, in fact, took every opportunity to gush over the gloves, not because she'd want a nice pair like that herself, but because Grace seemed to need them, seemed to need the yellowness of them, the sunshine they seemed to capture, the warmth they provided, both on her hands and in her head.

Ellen understood about the gloves, how they were helping to draw Grace back from that fearful dream world, back to their family. They were magic in a way *people* simply couldn't be for Grace, at least just yet. Those gloves would be able to restore tranquility to Grace, to straighten her shoulders and quiet her hands. So Ellen didn't begrudge Grace the gloves. Not at all. Not even a little bit. She only wished they'd do their magic a little quicker.

Chapter Thirty-Eight

James Parton, New York, Thursday, September 22nd, 1853

"A crust of bread, a pitcher of wine, a thatched roof, and love,—there's happiness for you."

Girls! that's a humbug! The very thought of it makes me groan. It's all moonshine. In fact, men and moonshine in my dictionary are synonymous. Water and a crust! RATHER spare diet! May do for the honey-moon. Don't make much difference then whether you eat shavings or sardines— but when you return to substantials, and your wedding dress is put away in a trunk for the benefit of posterity, if you can get your husband to smile on anything short of a "sirloin" or a roast turkey, you are a lucky woman. . . . We know these little accidents never happen in novels—where the heroine is always "dressed in white, with a rose-bud in her hair," and lives on blossoms and May dew! There are no wash-tubs or gridirons in her cottage, her children are born cherubim, with a seraphic contempt for dirt pies and molasses. . . . But this humdrum life, girls, is another affair, with its washing and ironing and cleaning days, when children expect boxed ears, and visitors picked-up dinners. All the "romance" there is in it, you can put under a three-cent piece!

—*Fanny Fern, True Flag, June 12th, 1852*

James Parton was giddy as he walked to his neglected desk at the *Home Journal.* Ignoring the sun's dazzle, mindless of the cool breeze that bathed his forehead,

James would bump into passersby, then would apologize profusely. He found himself whistling and swinging his arms like a schoolboy. He stepped, not once, but three times, into unsavory and undeterminable mushy messes on the cobblestones and, each time, found a stick and cleaned his boots with enormous patience. What's a little squashed apple, a little horse dung?

James laughed at himself. It was true. He was staring-at-the-moon, losing-weight, can't-find-his-shoes in love with Fanny Fern, famous writer, wonderful woman, charming companion. He'd pour a cup of tea, then forget he'd done it, and make another pot—never getting around to drinking any of it. He was getting frighteningly fond of flowers and gingersnaps and all sorts of sentimental luxuries. His head seemed to float two feet over his body and from that vantage he could look down upon his own contented face, grinning like a Cheshire who'd just had free play in the dairy pantry.

James kept a keen eye out for a certain pretty foot, a certain pile of gorgeous straw-colored curls, a certain pair of flashing oceanic eyes. Every woman he saw reminded him of Fanny, but, of course, was a disappointing copy. One trim beauty might have the jaunty step, but wouldn't have the requisite smile. Another might have the same colored skirt, but the wrong colored hair. And then, when, glory of glories, Fanny herself might turn an actual New York City corner, like she'd done just at lunchtime Tuesday, James' heart raced so violently he tried not to make any sudden movement to avoid further stressing it.

Tuesday had been wonderful. He'd gotten to spend seventy minutes alone with the most impressive woman he'd ever known. Not that he didn't enjoy Fanny's daughters. Quite the contrary. Ellen was a lovely little thing—sunny, smart, an adorable replica of her mother. Grace, though still recovering from the abrupt reintegration with her family, was pleasant and polite and displayed daily social improvements. But to have had a tête-à-tête with Fanny, to have been allowed, without a morsel of preplanning, to share a sandwich and watch those luscious lips move in skillful conversation, to brush an ink-stained finger of hers, as he'd done twice, was the happiest of surprises.

A flood of memories was at James' disposal, memories he could conjure at will and revel in limitlessly. Their first evening together at the opera—Fanny elegantly resplendent herself, but surprisingly interested in the gaudy brightness of the theater and the many fashion slaves who regularly attended it. James had since learned that Fanny didn't covet with her frank stares, but was simply observing, was, as she always was, writing columns in her head. She had a marvelous way of seeing through things—events, societal rules, personalities—that uncovered a topic's essence, and then Fanny would comment, with the wisdom of Solomon and the frankness of a child, about the rightness or wrongness of that essence.

He remembered how, at the opera, he could barely listen to Madame Sontag's magnificence for fear of missing out on some small exclamation his companion might make, or some smile she might unknowingly display. James knew Fanny would grimace if he knew he elevated her so, if she knew he cherished her for more than her witty pen strokes. She was a woman who had moved romance to the bottom shelf, who had tasted poverty and fear and had developed a ruthless practicality because of it. She would not be caught leaning on anyone or anything again, would not be left unprepared to provide life's necessities and comforts for her daughters, would never allow herself to wallow in dreams and wishes and rapture.

But that didn't mean she didn't enjoy life. She did! He never knew anyone who paid such careful attention to children and stray cats and blossoms, whose tongue savored the sweet and savory alike, whose eyes feasted on changing light and hues, whose fingers sought comfort in velvet pillows and silk tassels. James pondered the puzzle of Fanny Fern, the duality of her zest for living and determination to do so with scrutiny, her generous gifting of time, energy, and funds and her careful appropriation of each, her sentimental leanings and her self-trained productivity. Fanny Fern was so complex, so mysterious, so fascinating that James often felt woozily deflated as he stood near her edges, basking in her glow and throwing that glow crazily back to her like a bent mirror.

Happily, there'd been more times like they'd had at the opera—many more times. Fanny wanted to drink up this city like it was a strawberry soda. She thirsted to experience everything it had to offer—culture, social variety, enterprise. James made an affable companion and thoroughly enjoyed introducing Fanny to museums, Broadway, shops full of Indian and Chinese wares. He loved seeing her reaction to cathedrals and parks, to street singers and gold rushers. He loved offering her Italian ices and French truffles, German sausage and Irish soup. Fanny rushed to meet each new experience like it might be her last chance, and often, James noted, her impressions made their way into her columns.

James opened the door of the *Home Journal* and sprung up the stairs. He was taking Fanny to the theater tonight, to the opening of a new play. Fanny had heard that it involved a hurricane and a shipwreck and said she wanted to compare a watery tossing with the land one she'd experienced. She'd said it offhandedly and with her ringing laugh, but James sensed an urgency in Fanny's request, a barely contained need to understand tragedy and its effects on the human spirit.

She was like his own Mum that way—a real fighter, an independent woman. James had only been five years old when they'd moved to America, but had splotchy memories of the trip over—feeling queasy for days on end, the frightening blue expanse of sky and water, being scolded for harboring his favorite playmate—a little mouse—in his coat pocket. But even at so young an age, James's chest expanded with pride whenever he thought of Mum. Pragmatic, energetic, and brave enough to try anything. She didn't smile as much as James wanted, nor sing lulling tunes or dole out fragrant comfort. Yet, he felt safe with her. If she could manage to ferry him across that giant wash of water; feed, clothe, house, and educate him, then certainly no real harm could ever befall him. Fanny gave James the same feeling, the feeling that no matter the difficulty, *she* would never bow to it, *she* would find a safe way through. And she combined that rock-solid security with the sweetest warmth James had ever seen.

James pulled out his key and unlocked the office door with a sigh. Not that he wasn't a risk-taker himself. Hardly. His career proved that. But he appreciated Fanny's unabashed strength, her granite presence beside him in carriages, porch swings, theater rows. It made his own strength stronger. When James was near Fanny, a protective bubble enveloped them and anyone else they were with. *This* was love. This was the magic so often written about, sung about, searched for. James had never really *looked* for it, but he had surely ached. It was an ache he always knew was there, just below his skin, but one he never allowed himself to notice. Well, here it was—the ache and, thankfully, the means to alleviate it, all at once. Wonderful Fanny. Beautiful Fanny. Glorious love.

James hung his hat on one of the hooks near the door and pulled off his jacket to hang over the back of his chair. He had piles of articles to edit today—some that just needed proofing, some that would need major revision. He pulled Fanny's latest article he'd clipped from the *Musical World and Times* out of his pocket and placed it on the stack of items to include in this edition. He always had room in the *Home Journal* for Fanny's pieces, not only because he knew her, but because the public did. If there was any sought-after column, in all of New York, in all of the world, really, it was Fanny's, and James wouldn't think about disappointing their readership. He had to admit, though, that he despised pirating articles. Never mind that it was *modus operandi*, not to mention an expected duty of his, he felt squeamish picking writing from one source to use in another. It seemed worse than rude, it seemed like it should be criminal. Still, there never seemed to be enough time, talent, and copy to fill the pages the voracious reading public demanded. Almost more than their daily bread, Americans craved reading material.

Through the gap between his desk and the adjoining room, James could see that Nat was in. He'd been in more often this year, seemingly too frustrated with something—the pace, the style, the temperament—of life at his newly finished estate on the Hudson. Idlewild. James thought of his rented place on Waverly and wondered if it was proper to name one's boardinghouse room. Perhaps he could call it Shipshape. Or maybe The Den. Or perhaps simply Room with Bed. Nat coughed wetly. James supposed Nat's health was still an issue. Nat spat into an ornately decorated handkerchief. Must've cost at least fifty dollars, that handkerchief, and now awash in who knew what. James shuddered. Nat had on the claret trousers and the emerald vest outfit James hated. The colors were too gaudy for someone as fair-complexioned as Nat. He'd looked better, more tolerable, to be precise, in soft mustards, honey shades, even charcoal. James couldn't imagine strutting around looking like stained glass and didn't Fanny just compliment him the other day on his smart black tweed with the smattering of blue flecks? His black trousers and charcoal vest did just fine with a crisp white shirt. James had stretched his limited fashion knowledge by adding a pocket handkerchief—cream linen with a subtle blue border.

Nat coughed again and James winced at the sickly rattle. Boring or not, Nat had probably better schedule more time at home this winter.

"Parton, come in here," Nat said after his coughing spasm quieted.

James grabbed his customary notebook and hurried to sit in one of the two caramel-colored Italian leather chairs opposite Nat's large mahogany desk. He enjoyed sitting in those chairs, especially in the morning, like this, when the early sun cast a warm glow on the desk and made the garish Turkish carpet almost disappear under white light.

Nat sat opposite James and threw down the latest copy of the *Home Journal*. "This is not what it used to be," he said. "The *Home Journal* sets the standard, *is* the standard of good taste and fine living."

James wrinkled his forehead. "Of course."

"We're using too many copied pieces," Nat said. "Especially since I personally know hundreds, no, make that thousands, of writers willing to write for nothing but the personal gratification of seeing their name in our pages. Surely we can find enough copy?"

James smiled. Wonder of wonders, Nat felt as *he* did about pirating. "I'm so glad you feel that way, too. I was just thinking how I hated stealing works from other publications. It seems dishonest somehow."

Nat stiffened. "*Stealing?* Is that what you call it? Dishonest? Are you saying I run a dishonest business?"

"Well . . . you . . . just," James said.

"I'm talking specifically about copying vulgar, plebian pieces, pieces everyone could read anywhere anytime, pieces too ubiquitous to soil our pages."

James furrowed his brow. He didn't like this tone of Nat's. He'd seen it on other occasions, of course, but never directed at him. "I don't believe we run anything like that, and if we have, it was by sheer accident." James pointed to the latest edition on the grand desk between them. "Which pieces are you worried about?"

"Fanny Fern," Nat said. "I don't want a single article from her ever again. Her writing is coarse and offensive and her little star will soon burn out and we'll be seen as superior for knowing it."

James leaned back in his chair. "But she's your sister, sir. I know things haven't been the best between you lately, but—"

"And you're quite her regular companion," Nat said. "Smacks of nepotism to my eye. Publisher brother. Editor beau."

James' face reddened. "What are you suggesting?"

"Do you know my sister? I mean do you know *about* her?"

"What, exactly, do you mean?"

"I mean she can do nothing but pull you into the gutter with her. Once her history is disclosed to the public—"

"She's been maligned!" James said. "A victim of false accusations and circumstance. A situation, might I add, that could have been greatly relieved if certain relatives would have found it in their hearts to defend her virtue!"

"You obviously don't know a whit about Sara," Nat said. "She's never needed defending a day in her life. Defending *against*, maybe," he said with a chuckle, "but definitely not defending."

"What are you saying?" James said. "Though strong, true, and opinionated, Fanny's still a woman and, therefore, vulnerable to social ostracizing. You should *celebrate* her spirit, not try to snuff it. This country *needs* hearty *women* as well as men."

"And 'hearty' women, in my mind, are not 'ladies,'" Nat said. "Ladies and gentlemen read the *Home Journal*. They are not looking for the vulgar rantings of someone like Sara. Sara has always had this problem, you see. She has never quite figured out how to maintain that womanly self-control essential to good manners."

"She has beautiful manners, to my mind," James said peevishly.

"Your personal opinion about my sister is of no consequence. What I'm saying is that as a writer, Sara, or shall we say *Fanny Fern*, is not acceptable for our type of readership. We will no longer stoop so low as to include her work, especially clipped columns from two-bit rags struggling to meet their mortgages."

James pressed his lips together, squeezed his eyes, then took a sure breath. "Well, if that's how you feel," he said.

Nat pounded a fist on his desk. "That's exactly how I feel." The noise echoed from that rich wood throughout the compartment of rooms occupied by the *Home Journal*.

James' face reddened. "I believe that by not including the latest from Fanny Fern, you will be sorely disappointing our readership. Fanny writes what is already in the hearts and on the minds of her fellow citizens. She's brave enough to put such thoughts and feelings into words, sharp enough to understand the social issues at stake."

"Bah!" Nat said. "She's no great talent, believe me. She's got you twisted 'round her finger like packaging string."

"As I said," James said, standing, "I believe that by not including the latest from Fanny Fern, you will be sorely disappointing our readership."

Nat smiled. "You already said that."

"In fact, I believe it so strongly that I simply cannot work for any publication that would not only so severely miscalculate readership and talent, but one that is so poorly managed as to rely upon the leadership of someone so petty and insecure, so threatened by a *woman*—"

"What are you saying?" Nat spat.

"So unfaithful to his own sister!" James said, his hands clenched upon the notebook and pen.

Nat assessed James with a look so cold it made James long to look away. After a moment, Nat smiled. "Unfaithful you say. You have no idea."

"I have idea enough," James said quietly.

"And faith enough, apparently," Nat said, "for the both of us."

James spun and strode to his desk.

"You'll not get paid for this week, you know," Nat called after him.

James pocketed the article of Fanny's from the top of his pile of work. He opened a satchel and stuffed his personal things into it.

"And I'll be sure no worthy place will hire you!" Nat called again.

"I've no doubt you'll try your best," James said under his breath. He tied the satchel briskly, plucked his jacket from the back of his chair and his hat from the hook, and strode through the doorway of the *Home Journal* without a backward glance.

Chapter Thirty-Nine

Fanny Fern, New York, Tuesday, January 17th, 1854

"I *can* do it, I *feel* it, I *will* do it," and she closed her lips firmly; "but there will be a desperate struggle first." . . . And still "Floy" scribbled on, thinking only of bread for her children, laughing and crying behind her mask,—laughing all the more when her heart was heaviest; but of this her readers knew little and would have cared less. Still her little bark breasted the billows, now rising high on the topmost wave, now merged in the shadows, but still steering with straining sides, and a heart of oak, for the nearing port of Independence.

—Fanny Fern, *Ruth Hall*

Fanny clenched both hands into fists and pressed them against her forehead. It was only half past nine and she could already feel one of her bad headaches beginning. She wanted to scream. There was no worse time than now for this headache. She had so much to do, so many decisions to make, so much to think over. She picked up her pen in a feigned attempt to write and was seized with the overwhelming urge to hurl it as hard as possible across the room.

Fanny checked her impulse, laid the pen, unmolested, back on her butternut desk. The last time she'd had such an impulse to throw something was a little over five years ago when she had sat in her boardinghouse room on Cambridge Street, desperately sewing and trying to avoid having to marry Samuel. She'd flung her good Hemmings drill-eyed needle across that attic room and had regretted her rashness the minute it left her hand. She chased the flying needle before it had even landed and, thankfully, had found it after not too long a time on her hands and knees. To throw away her only means of support in a fit of temper! Fanny had chastised herself severely. Luckily, the needle hadn't landed between the cracks of the wood floor.

Fanny sighed. She'd had to marry Samuel anyway. Five years ago on this very day. Fanny looked out the window next to her desk. The day was overcast and cool, but not frosty cold and snowy like that day she'd been tricked into her second marriage. True, she'd been sidling up to the idea under the constant encouragement of Julia and Father and Samuel himself. True, she had been beyond desperate after not getting the teaching position. Looking back, she probably had had no choice, especially since she hadn't yet imagined earning a living by her pen. A woman could sew twenty-four hours a day and still not make enough to comfortably support three people. It was a crime. An able body ought to be able to earn a living. Not to mention those who were disabled. How did *they* survive? Fanny had seen many sad sights on the streets of New York—dirty, shriveled children; toothless, stooped widows; addle-brained, whiskey-infested men. They *didn't* survive, that's the story. Not for long anyway.

Suddenly it dawned on her—it had been Samuel all along. *He* had been behind that newspaper announcement, the one that proclaimed them already married. Samuel, the master of newspaper manipulation. He'd come to her room early that morning, all a lather about the *duplicity* of some unknown villain to report on their marriage as if it had already occurred. The day before! There was nothing left to do but make haste to the justice of the peace. Save both of their good names. Make an honest union. He'd had Nettie and Clare with him, all dressed up and freezing in last year's Easter outfits. Fanny felt as she had at Charly's funeral—disconnected. Samuel and his girls waited in the boardinghouse parlor as she woke and readied Grace and Nelly for their day. It was as if Fanny had told them to up and ready for a day at the park. Neither girl protested, nor asked a single question. The three of them accepted their fate like lambs.

As she craned her head toward the window, Fanny's neck was so tight she could barely turn it. If she didn't relax it soon, she'd have a king of a headache. She went to her dressing table, found her bottle of lavender water, and bathed her temples. Blasted Samuel! What a sniveling, pusillanimous excuse for a man. Just as Fanny thought this she felt an instantaneous wave of relief wash over her. But for the grace of God. She'd escaped an eternity with him. That confrontation at Niagara had terrified her. He'd claimed they were still married, and for all Fanny knew, he was right. He wanted her to come to his rooms, was quizzing her about her earnings, threatening her about the girls.

Thank Heaven for Richard and Oliver. To think she might have succumbed to his rancid appetite, to think she might have endured his caresses yet again. Fanny felt bile at the back of her throat. And the girls—so frightened! When they'd returned to New York, she learned that James Derby had finally discovered the divorce papers—written in Chicago, signed and witnessed. Samuel had proclaimed desertion and had cut her loose, probably before realizing her earning potential. Her nom de plume had saved her again. Fanny Fern. She liked the name, liked the woman it connoted, was becoming that woman.

Fanny blew out an exasperated breath. She would get no work done at the moment, what with her head swimming with so many thoughts. She donned her bonnet—the new one with the sky-blue ribbon—wrapped herself in her warmest shawl, pulled on the nice, thick dun kid gloves, and headed out for a stroll. The cool air might calm her nerves, might clear her head. Fanny stepped down the stairs and out onto the bustling street in search of a park or at least a lightly traversed avenue.

Five years ago, she'd married Samuel. Four years ago, he'd raped her in their kitchen. Fanny's eyes brimmed. She hated that she could still remember it, even though she'd been about as dazed as she could be when it happened. There had been other times just like it, of course, but that time, in the kitchen, had affected Fanny most severely. It must have been the surprise of it. She'd had time to prepare, all the other times, time to dampen her senses and muddy her sensibilities. But to take her, like he did, so brutally, in broad daylight, and *almost* in front of the children, had proved the most shocking. Fanny simply couldn't forget it, not completely. And for that, she'd never forgive him.

Fanny turned a corner and the winter wind slapped her cheeks, just like it had on the day she escaped Mr. Schueller's lewd clutches. She dabbed at the corners of her eyes with her gloved finger. Things were different now. She'd never again be at the mercy of another. She'd never again put herself in the position to be so disgustingly dependent on the fancies of anyone else. Never!

A woman in a well-made sea-green cape brushed past Fanny. She smelled deliciously green, looked as fresh as the countryside at Swissdale. Fanny thought of her mother, clad on special occasions in her drapey sea-green turban, the one with the bright copper ornament that tucked the turban's folds together at her crown. Mother's blue-green eyes were brilliant when she wore that turban. Fanny sucked in a deep breath. The woman in the cape had left her scent behind. Despite the gray branches of the trees and the withered stems still poking out of the occasional flower box on some stoop, Fanny swore she smelled a forest. That lovely green scent. Ferny, damp, earthy.

Fanny turned to see if she could glimpse the woman in the cape again, but the woman was already gone into some shop or up some staircase. Oh, Mother! How she loved to visit them at Swissdale. Fanny remembered one such visit—it was the height of summer, one of those steady rainy days you hold your breath for. Mother had been scheduled to leave, but because of the weather, they'd stolen an extra day with her. It was a day where nothing was scheduled but bread-making. There was nobody to visit and nobody coming to call. No fancy dinner to worry about and no outdoor adventures queued up. No picnic to pack. No flowers to cut. No carriage to order. No market to visit.

Fanny rose early and, seeing the weather, made a special breakfast in bed for Mother—corn cakes with molasses, bacon, and hot coffee. Mother relished it, snuggled under Fanny's hand-embroidered coverlet in the guest room. The guest room! How long it had been since Fanny had entertained guests in her own home. Those days with Charly seemed far away. The riding parties they'd host at apple-picking time, the ice-skating Sundays, that middle weekend in June when everyone would gorge themselves on wild strawberries. Fanny and Jemisee would laugh together, slicing, chopping, and trussing in anticipation of their guests. Then they'd scrub up the dishes and while Jemisee rested her swollen ankles, Fanny would take the dish towels out the back door to hang along the fence. Outside, Fanny usually couldn't resist grabbing her cutting shears from the hook and snipping together a bouquet. She kept that house bursting with posies. The girls could name them all. And Charly's happy smile, when he'd come home from the trials of the banking business (not to mention his kisses), made Fanny's efforts seem trivial.

They *were* trivial, Fanny thought. Although making a home for her husband and children was satisfying and wonderful, Fanny found the ability to *pay* for the making of her home even more satisfying. What a mystery! She'd gotten as much, if not more, satisfaction from being forced into the man's world than she ever got stuffed into the woman's. Mother understood it, though. Even when Fanny was a young woman boarding with Catharine Beecher at her seminary in Hartford, Mother made it known to Fanny that her education was as important, despite what Father might think, as Nat's, Richard's, and Edward's. And Mother constantly tried to get Fanny to look at the bills from the dressmaker's and the butcher's, to understand about payment and credit and discount. True, Mother had said, Fanny wasn't allowed to go to Yale, like Nat, but that didn't mean she shouldn't understand the world of business and law, the ways of commerce and politics. Fanny wished she remembered more about such talks with her mother, but truthfully, despite always showing a quick wit and robust personality, Fanny's character had been too naive, her troubles too few, to imagine needing to know about anything but how to hide novels under her bedclothes and how to make the best lace undersleeves.

That rainy extra day when Mother stayed held no business lecture, though, was lapped up by them both as pure enjoyment. Jemisee had the day off after the fortnight of wonder she'd produced for them. Grace was an infant and Mary (God, Mary!) was but three. After Fanny had done up the breakfast dishes and nursed baby Grace, Mother sat with little Mary and a picture book by the glowing fire while Fanny mixed the dough. Next, Fanny and Mother sat at the lightly floured oak table and worked the dough, setting each smooth loaf to rise in pans at the end of the table. Grace slept at Mother's foot in the pretty walnut rocker Charly had made. Sweet Mary was her quiet smart self sitting at Fanny's elbow working a scrape of dough into alphabet letters, as Fanny had taught her.

"L, Mother. I make L."

"Yes, darling, you have."

"And what L is for?"

"L, you silly, is for love."

Fanny looked up and down the streets of New York City and felt a little dizzy. How far she had come from Swissdale! She staggered her way to a little bench, sat down hard upon it, and buried her face in her dun gloves. Oh, little Mary. Oh, Mother. Oh, Charly. Where, where, where had all of her love gone? Then sister Ellen and Mary Stace, Louisa and Edward. Fanny's shoulders heaved. Love—what a frightening investment! She had given it out, so willingly in her youth, only to be surprised with death over and over again. Was she afraid to love so openly again? Would she? Could she? Fanny wiped her nose with her handkerchief, a lovely lace-trimmed thing James had given her. No, she *did* love, still. Of course she did. She loved Grace and Nelly (*Ellen*, she reminded herself!). And James.

Fanny sat upright on the bench. *James?* Was it true? Could it be? No, no, no, she told herself. He was so young—ten, eleven years her junior, at least. He certainly must be looking for some pretty spry thing to make a home with, to start a family with. *That* was no longer Fanny. With Grace nearly grown and Ellen solidly in school, Fanny honestly didn't think she could pull herself from the thrill of her writing life, the ease of this advanced state of mothering, to venture into the world of patty-cake and teething again. *James Parton?* Fanny sighed. She raised her head and watched a little smattering of clouds float gently above her. Maybe it was true. Maybe she did love him. But, perhaps it was in a different way than with Charly. Maybe she and James were meant to be like brother and sister and share a deep affection along with their love of adventure, conversation, and culture. Yes, Fanny supposed, she'd probably had had enough of marriage by now. An excellent companion, really a wonderful friend, as she had in James, was certainly enough. And she'd welcome *his* future lover with open arms like some great auntie, and she'd nestle his children like a grandmother, and she'd always always always cherish these days when he was, for a little while, her very own.

Fanny's eyes glistened again. She was grateful for James, for his friendship, and for the support he unfailingly showed her. Oh, that he quit his job defending her! And against the likes of Nat! Fanny still boiled when she thought of Nat's blindness, his stubborn selfishness. How could a brother she'd once absolutely idolized despise her so? James Derby hinted that Nat was jealous of Fanny's success—but why? Nat was *enormously* successful. He was a tender poet, a flourishing editor, a well-heeled citizen. He had a lovely wife (who Fanny had never met!) and apparently some children besides little Imogen. According to Richard, he had a glorious estate not far from James Derby's on the Hudson.

Fanny had visited the Derby estate several times since *Fern Leaves* had come out. A hundred thousand copies sold! Fanny shook her head. And then the other two collections, both selling wildly as well. She laughed. Her books probably paid a lot of bills at the Derby estate. And what a place! The languid, starlit excursions on Derby's boat, the sumptuous meals with his very own hothouse oranges, strawberries, and tomatoes, the magnificent guestroom with linens finer than the finest silk undergarments Fanny had ever seen. James Derby was doing well, and from what Fanny knew, Nat was in his class.

She shook her head again. No tears for him. She'd long since mourned the loss of her favorite brother, relegating him to the tombs with her other fond memories. She'd even written a column about him, one that generated scads of letters, all recognizing her little sketch of some "Apollo Hyacinth" as none other than N. P. Willis himself. Talented as he was, he was a social climber. Nat certainly had his admirers in this town. But he'd also climbed over more than a few stricken bodies, and those people, those flesh-and-blood human beings, understood what it was like to be used by Nat. Fanny's column about Nat had been a raging success, had been all anyone could talk about for a fortnight.

Of her male relatives, Richard was the only one left to her. Sweet Richard and sweeter Jessie. Sad, though, that it had come to that. Sometimes her filial loyalty kicked up and Fanny regretted writing about Nat, wondered what Father would have to say. But she only had to reread Nat's dismissive last letter, only had to see darling James, struggling, unemployed, to boil up again. Why shouldn't a woman say what was really on her mind? Proper breeding aside, sometimes a man's character needed airing, especially considering the social interest and criticism of too many a female's character. It should work both ways, this social judgment. If women could be held so close to every light, then so should men. Men's grievous deeds should be uncovered for wagging tongues as often as women's, so long as doing so didn't bend the truth.

Fanny was not one to gossip, nor was she one to slice down a person's good name, sliver by sliver, as if carving hot ham. That's why she still worried at times that she'd wounded Nat with her column. But then she thought of all of Nat's self-absorbed words and actions over the years, his collusion with Father about hemming her in, and she felt ready to spit. She'd had her say. She'd write no more about him, would try to think no more about him.

But what about James? Fanny knew he struggled, writing stray articles here and there for as many stray dollars. She knew all too well the fickle world of periodicals. It shouldn't be so. James was one of the most talented minds, and pens, she'd ever witnessed. He carefully crafted every article as if he were writing a masterpiece, which, come to think, was exactly what he should be doing—writing that splendid idea of a book about Horace Greeley he always talked about. How could it be arranged? James hadn't a moment to spare lately, using up every minute writing for his daily bread and the theater tickets he always insisted on paying for. Surely he could get along nicely on fifteen a week. Fanny would speak to her new publisher, Mason Brothers, about it. If they could manage an advance, Fanny was more than sure they'd have another best-seller on their hands. Surely Oliver could help her arrange it. He'd introduced her to the Masons just recently and she trusted him completely. Let Derby handle your collections, Oliver had said, but work with Mason Brothers on something *new*.

Fanny thought about the Masons' latest *new* proposal—for her to write a novel. Fanny just didn't know. She'd willingly given her name over to collections of her articles, and would continue to do that as long as Derby and the reading public were interested. But a novel? Fanny had no idea how to begin such a project. Fanny had no idea what to write about. She was no novelist. She sometimes doubted she was a newspaper columnist, those memories of the boardinghouse's attic room ever too clear—the three flights down to retrieve her little bottle of milk from the swing shelf in the cellar, scrubbing those very stairs more times than she could remember, sewing and then scribbling before the broken pane—the cold draft chilling the already fireless room. She remembered Nelly coming in bruised around the eye from a scrape with a street urchin, Nelly's horrible months-long cough, cutting the tips off of her darling's shoes so she could walk without pain for a few more weeks until Fanny could afford a pair of those cheap shoes from that thief at the end of the block. It was a wonder Fanny could write a word, as soaked through with worry and hunger as she was, more wondrous that she'd finally gotten something published and that her work resonated with the public. But to write a novel? Was it within her reach?

Yet, Hatty was doing it! Slowly but surely. Dear Hatty was a braver writer than Fanny. Hatty still worked for Nat, but was allowed occasional days off. Twice since Fanny had moved to the city, she'd met Hatty halfway between their residences for a catch-up tea. This last time, Hatty had brought along her new friend, a writer, too—Lydia Maria Child. This Maria had abolition fever! And she wrote scores for all sorts of publishers. Fanny sat in awe as Maria and Hatty told her about the rallies they'd been to, about the incredible speeches touting *equality*. Equality! Imagine men and women of every race and creed commingling without fear, without judgment.

Maria said she was tutoring Hatty, getting her writing skills honed in preparation for her book. "I am going to write it," Hatty said, "if it's the last thing I do."

And it looked like it might be the last thing Hatty did. She was as consumed with earning enough to survive as anyone, and such undertakings left precious little leisure time. Fanny admired Hatty's determination, but was most impressed that Hatty was willing to write it *all*, even the most embarrassing, even the most painful parts. Hatty was willing to use her life tortures to educate. "If someone gets a truer idea of the hell of slavery," she said, "even just one person, then my trouble to write this book will be worthwhile."

Fanny wondered how she could help Hatty. Nothing pleased her more than giving other women a leg up. It made Fanny so happy, for instance, to send Julia a little something to keep her whole, body and soul, and to allow her the *freedom* to live her life. If Julia had been a man, a bachelor in his forties, she'd be wealthy and feted and the apple of many a gorgeous eye. But to be an unmarried woman of the same age meant only ridicule and want, embarrassment and sacrifice. It made Fanny ill to think of her sister laboring under such restrictions and sent her what she prayed would be enough to buy Julia her independence, to give her the thing Fanny herself cherished—self-sufficiency.

Julia had written recently from Paris where she was visiting and writing and meeting a circle of interesting, well-educated people. Fanny silently blessed her sister. Julia had written that she'd met Harriet Beecher Stowe in London, and Harriet was, as usual, under siege for signatures to accompany her wonderful *Uncle Tom's Cabin.* "Harriet sends her love," Julia wrote. "She says she will call on you when she is next in New York."

Fanny remembered the last time she'd seen Harriet, in Boston. That seemed like ages ago. She shuddered, half from the chill of a stiff breeze, half from remembering her old city. How she had suffered there. Oh, the indignity of having to sell her possessions, one by one, for necessities. Her coral pin went for some ham and cheese. Her garnet earbobs bought one week's room and board. The tortoise comb, the silver buttons, her silk shawl—all gave their lives for food and shelter. Fanny remembered the two dresses she'd allowed herself to keep—the brown calico with the little white dots and the blue deLaine with the white bishop's sleeves. She had two three-shilling collars, a few ribbons, a pair of undersleeves, a smattering of pantaloons, corsets, stockings, and the like. She smiled. She'd worn both of those dresses, over the next near decade, into shreds. When she wasn't in her mourning clothes, that is. Those widow's weeds—the two well-made black dresses, the hat, parasol, shawl, gloves, stockings, and nice gator shoes—were the last articles she'd purchased under the name of Sara Eldredge. No wonder she held onto them. They were sentimental favorites as well as a prudent alternative to her worn-out day dresses.

She'd gotten several new dresses when she'd first married Samuel, but he'd taken them away after that first year, when he banished them from his house and put her and the girls up, instead, in the boardinghouse. Fanny had never cared that she had to give up the clothes, despite how Samuel played that trick like a trump card. She only cared about the welfare of her daughters, and the welfare, believe it or not, of *Samuel's* daughters. She could not have conjured a sweeter revenge than when they both ran to her, as they were settling into the carriage to leave for the boardinghouse, insisting, tearfully, on one last kiss, one last hug. Fanny whispered, "God Bless you," and was never allowed to see them again. She sighed. More casualties of the heart. What ever became of those two doomed children?

Samuel hadn't cared that she took her widow's weeds with her. Those clothes, along with the ivory hair comb, the miniature, and the white satin wedding vest, were all she had left of Charly. What comfort when she'd decided, before heading off to that cheaper boardinghouse, to don them again. Fanny remembered the blistering looks she'd endured standing in line for bread or thread, the wilting glares, the whispers, when she was on display as Sara Farrington. But what relief under her black bubble! The world moved aside for widows, ignored them, and Fanny gratefully embraced that social anonymity.

She'd first met Norris and Moulton in those weeds. Ah, the Reverend! Fanny would never forget the break he'd given her. He was stern, at first, but became almost fatherly to her. He certainly behaved more fatherly than her own father had. Fanny rested her face in her hands again. Reverend Norris died last month. She'd read about it but, of course, couldn't attend the funeral. How she wanted to say good-bye to that wizened face. He'd been disappointed to see her go to New York, but had wished her well. The only thing certain about life is that it always changes, he said with a smile. Other than Julia, Norris was perhaps the only Bostonian she missed. Fanny certainly didn't miss William Moulton.

She remembered their last meeting with a shudder. He always caused something cold and clammy to crawl up her spine. Whether she spoke to him about upcoming articles, was arranging for payment, or collecting copies, Fanny never felt anything but revulsion for Moulton, despite his steady grin and constant banter. Moulton was stunned into silence when Fanny told him she was moving to New York and planned to write nearly exclusively for New York papers. She was still under contract with Oliver at the *Musical World and Times*, James Derby had her busy compiling the collection (the one collection that quickly turned into two more that year), and she was being courted by Philadelphia's the *Saturday Evening Post*, a publication she respected and longed to be a part of (and one for which she had an article due right now!). Fanny promised to send a few pieces when she could, but since there was no exclusive contract between them, she could no longer promise weekly work.

At first Moulton couldn't believe Fanny was serious. He laughingly assumed she just wanted another slight raise, or to write fewer columns.

"Not at all, Mr. Moulton," Fanny said. "I'm serious when I say I am moving and can no longer be your reliable correspondent."

Moulton's grin straightened into a thin line and his eyes went flat. "How ungrateful you are," he said. "After I've put so much effort into promoting your career."

Fanny gasped. She was well aware that the *True Flag*'s circulation had risen since her articles started appearing in it and that Moulton kept most of those profits himself. It had only been recently that he'd agreed to match the raise Norris offered, in order to keep her writing for Boston papers as well as Oliver's. "I believe it is my articles that have promoted your paper," she said. "But so as not to part on a sour note, let's shake and be friends and agree that we both helped each other along as best we could."

Fanny offered her hand and Moulton spun away. "Shake hands? I'd as soon be bitten by a rattler."

"What?" Fanny said.

Moulton narrowed his eyes. "You think you can just walk out on me and leave me with nothing flat? You think you can just turn my business upside down and I'll smile while you do it? You want to play in a man's world, then let's have at it."

"What do you mean?" Fanny said. "I've never had any intention of hurting your business. If you wanted to ensure I wrote especially for you, then you should have offered me a contract . . . with a living wage."

"Dear Mrs. Farrington," Mouton said.

Fanny winced.

"Of course I know who you are. And I've kept your secret despite many lucrative offers to disclose it all out of respect and consideration for you and your reputation."

Fanny's cheeks burned. He didn't respect her. He knew that if her reputation was compromised, his circulation might dip.

"My editors in New York know all about my slandered name," Fanny said. "Thankfully, New York is a much more forgiving and liberal city. New Yorkers judge people on what they see of them, not what they hear of them."

"You think so?" Moulton said. "We'll have to put your theory to the test."

Fanny turned and rushed to the door. She opened it as quickly as she could but not before she heard Moulton add, "You haven't heard the last of me, *Sara Farrington*."

A few flurries floated down from the sky. Fanny decided to continue her walk, before she got too chilled. She blew her nose and sucked a lungful of crisp, snow-scented air. It was good to be in New York this winter. She loved this place and sometimes hated it. It was as gaudy and carefree as a birthday party, as cruel as an apple press. So much squalor set right beside so much plenty. Fanny had savored the best meals, had seen the most winning productions of her life these past six months—and had seen poverty and disease ten times as bad as anything she'd ever witnessed in Boston. Whole families shivering in newspaper-lined packing crates, maimed and crippled children begging on street corners, dead-eyed drunks—men and women—staggering the streets at every hour.

Well-heeled ladies and gentlemen passed these sights without a glance. The enormous sums they paid for their attire! Fanny had passed by shops where a single handkerchief went for seventy-five dollars, collars for a hundred, and shawls for a thousand. Fancy gator boots could be had for two hundred, linen bedclothes went for hundreds a set. This was besides the jewelry, perfumes, hair oils, and youth creams hawked for both sexes. New York City teemed with the ultra rich as it was packed with the ultra poor.

Fanny turned down a busier street. Carriages, gigs, and carts whizzed by from every direction. Passersby scurried to keep out of their way and Fanny had witnessed more than one failed attempt. "Something has to be done about this traffic," she'd said to James, after they'd once seen a speeding carriage collide with a hunkered-down old man, leaving the man unmoving, thrown ten feet from the road. "The public safety is at risk."

She passed a Magdalene house, an eerily quiet building that housed unwed expecting women amid the hubbub of New York commerce. Fanny paused to look through the front gate. Not a creature could be seen. Nothing stirred behind the drawn curtains. She must write about this place, about the need to avoid judging others. But for luck and good timing, Fanny knew all too well how quickly those leading a rosy life could be surprised.

Fanny rolled her eyes and pursed her lips. How could she forget? "Fanny Fern" had already written a column about this place—or more truthfully, another one of her impostors had attempted the feat. It irritated her when her works were kidnapped and baptized by hundreds of periodicals without a penny sent her way. But, there was nothing she could do about that. Once her work made its way into print, it was a scramble to see who could get it and where and when it'd be printed somewhere else. But what made her furious was when someone blatantly tried to write using her own signature, when someone wrote in the *style of Fanny Fern* and tried to pass it off as her work. That's what happened with the Magdalene house article. True, the sentiment portrayed in the piece mimicked her own—it called for charity without censure of the often-abused young women who found their ways to the asylums—but the writing was so awkwardly constructed, so obvious a mockery of Fanny's style. Fanny dashed off a scathing reply to the paper that first ran the piece and Oliver made sure the editor in question ran the letter prominently in the next publication. Fanny had blasted her imitator and dryly suggested that he or she discover his or her own pseudonym and writing style and leave off pretending to be her twin.

Well, she would write about Magdalene houses anyway. Her way. Fanny Fern's way. Oliver had once asked her to explain her writing style to him, how she managed to combine the rash with the sentimental, the logical with the humorous. Fanny didn't know what to tell him. She wrote from the heart. She wrote what she felt. She'd think about a piece for hours, sometimes for days, and then suddenly, the whole thing would materialize in her head and she'd have to fly to paper to get it all down. No editor had, as of yet, actually edited one of her pieces. She knew she used colloquial grammar at times, knew she was free and sometimes incorrect with her punctuation, but that was her way. It allowed her to creep closer to her readers' minds and hearts, to connect with them. Her piles of reader mail told her that. Fanny dedicated hours each week to answering the many letters she received.

Fanny passed a confectionery advertising plum cake, brandy-drops, Roman punch, Charlotte Russe, and four flavors of ices. Fashionably dressed men and women streamed in and out the doors. She passed a shop selling elaborately crafted pewter goblets, another selling inkstands inlaid with mother of pearl and alabaster. Fanny would keep her old cast-iron inkstand and the little wooden sandbox beside it, thank you. The next shop specialized in tin ware—cups, plates, platters, candlestick holders. It abutted a lamp store and Fanny paused to admire the etched glass designs displayed in the front windows. She recalled the lamps she had been lucky to have instead of candles at some of the Boston boardinghouses. Not surprisingly, she'd only been able to afford the cheapest oil and so they sputtered, crusted quickly on the wick, and created such a dim light that candles often proved better.

Fanny turned the corner and came upon a lovely, quiet street. How had she never seen such a little tucked-away beauty? It had a row of mature trees down both sides and lovely gardens behind pretty fences. Birds chirped as if in a much smaller town and a few squirrels scampered up and down the faces of the beeches and oaks. Fanny stopped before one of the fences and read the signpost, Delancy House. Oh, how quiet a lodging! On a whim, she walked up the front path and through the tall, heavy outer door. The vestibule was bathed in a buttery light cast from the polished chandelier. The wallpaper was a sedate moss green, the parquet floors polished and gleaming.

The young man behind the desk greeted her. "We don't rent overnight," he said. "Strictly by the month. We're a residence for those who prefer the quiet, who'd like to escape the frenzy of the city."

Fanny raised her eyebrows. "Really?"

"We have one set of apartments vacant. Would you like to have a look? They're not the most elaborate, but they're clean, include meals prepared by our restaurant chef, and offer use of the back walking garden."

Fanny swallowed hard. She supposed a place like this would be out of her reach. She thought of the drafty attic boardinghouse she'd shared with sick little Nelly, its broken pane, the cot with the lumpy straw mattress, the narrow, coarse sheets and the torn coverlet. She and Nelly had huddled together under all of their shawls to keep warm. Their little fireplace smoked more than it roared, that was, when and if Fanny had coal or wood for it.

The young man led Fanny up four flights of stairs to a corner door. There were three adjoining rooms, a single central parlor furnished with rocking chairs, a plump horsehair sofa, tables, lamps, and even a bookcase. At the far end of the parlor, in a little alcove, with its own privacy door, stood a beautiful walnut writing desk and a balloon-backed chair. Fanny went immediately to the desk and sat at it. The light from the nearby window streamed in and if she peeked through the pane, she could see the walking garden.

Bedrooms stood on either side of the parlor, one with two beds and the other with one larger one. Chamber pots, armoires, and a thick patterned carpet completed each room.

"You can have these apartments for eighteen dollars a week."

Fanny caught her breath on the inhale. Eighteen a week? She'd expected them to go for at least forty. Her cramped, clean rooms in the heart of the city went for twelve.

"We're off the beaten track," the man offered. "Some find that a problem."

"I see," Fanny said with a smile that said it was no problem with *her*. "May I look at the garden?"

An hour later, Fanny headed back the way she came, lighter of foot and of spirit. In her pocket was her newly signed lease. She would move to this lovely hotel March 1st! She imagined writing at the beautiful walnut desk overlooking the garden or walking in the garden itself. Fanny had taken a tour and had admired the brick walkways, the raised brick benches with the wooden planters on their ends, the white arbor heavy with some dormant vine. The young man had assured her there were rhododendrons, irises, peonies, lavender, delphiniums, and phlox. A garden! It had been so long since she'd had access to one. She would surely be able to write overlooking such a wonder or walking through it to clear her head and soothe her nerves. Fanny stopped in her tracks. Suddenly, she knew what she could write about.

Fanny glanced at a clock set atop a bank building she passed. Time enough left in the day to pay a visit to James Derby, who was in town from Auburn, conferring with Oliver about publishing projects. Time enough to tell him her good news—that she *would* write a novel for his friends the Mason Brothers, would start on it as soon as possible. It would be about facing injustice, about how women's schooling left them unprepared to make their ways in the world, should they have to—and Fanny knew that more than a few of them would have to. The story would be about an average woman in a happy marriage who finds herself widowed. She struggles to support her two children, in fact has to relinquish one of them to a set of stern in-laws. Eventually the heroine, perhaps she'd be named Sally or Betty—no, *Ruth!*—would take her pen in her hand and would commence to earn her own living by writing articles. She'd take the country by storm with her frank assessments, would warm hearts while chastising unexamined belief systems.

This story, Fanny knew. She could write it all out—about Father and Nat and Moulton, about Charly and Ellen and Mother. She could write about giving up Grace, about being a woman, a mother, and a writer. In a novel like this, she could continue where her articles left off. Continue to shine a light on society—both the pleasant and the vicious.

Fanny quickened her pace. She couldn't wait to discuss the idea with James Derby. He had told her over and over that he would support any idea for a novel she'd want to write, but, still, she wanted his blessing for this one. It would be a truthful picture, would likely taste of criticism and anger. *Her* anger—at so many injustices. Feminine anger. It would be piercing. It would probably be judged vulgar. It would certainly ruffle feathers. It might not sell well. Fanny bounced up the stairs of the *Musical World and Times*, where she was sure to find Oliver and James Derby, both. She didn't care if it sold or not. Suddenly, she didn't even care very much if James Derby approved it or not. With every passing second, though, she was surer that this was the novel she would write, these were the issues she would unearth, no matter the outcome.

Chapter Forty

Walt Whitman, Brooklyn, Thursday, February 8th, 1855

And speaking of books, here comes Walt Whitman, author of *Leaves of Grass*, which, by the way, I have not yet read. His shirt collar is turned off from his muscular throat, and his shoulders are thrown back as if even in that fine, ample chest of his, his lungs had not sufficient play-room. Mark his voice! rich—deep—and clear, as a clarion note. In the most crowded thoroughfare, one would turn instinctively on hearing it, to seek out its owner.

—Fanny Fern, *New York Ledger*, April 12th, 1856

Walt Whitman lay in his bed in the drafty third-floor Brooklyn boardinghouse room, gazing at his little collection of books lined up on the dressing table. Three of those books, in particular, stood out to him. They were green with gilded titles. It was suddenly all very clear. Like so much that had been made clear to him these past six, seven years. He sought silence and the answers came, over and over, whenever he needed them. His volume would be called *Leaves*. But what kind of leaves? Certainly not fern leaves. Oak leaves? Willow leaves? *What is the Grass?* (He loved that line.) Grass leaves? But they're grass blades, not leaves. Sheaves of grass. No, not close enough. *Leaves of Grass*. Short, succinct, like the central throbbing spirit that beat through everyone at the same time, even if not at the same intensity. And he wouldn't promote his name, not in the sense that it mattered, but would *illustrate* the *presence of* himself (instead of merely naming himself), as author, as a conduit of this collection of ideas, borrowed from the larger source.

Walt scratched his chest through the red flannel undershirt he had slept in. He ran his fingers through his beard. The sun was already higher than he had hoped. It had to be mid-morning already. Too many late nights. He would call on some of the area printers and see if he could use their presses. He would set the type himself if he had to, but this little book of poems must get published. His voice must be heard, those conducted ideas must be spread over humanity like soft sweet butter. It had nothing at all to do with him. *He* would be content hidden in anonymity forever. But the larger forces had baptized him (Walt shuddered at the religious connotations the word implied), or rather, had invested their wisdom in him. He felt the grand plan, the larger ideas, rush through him.

There were others, he knew. It would be foolish to think himself the only one anointed (again, the religious connotation, followed, again, by a shudder), the only person blessed. Walt sucked a sharp breath, his hand in frozen midstroke while finger-combing his beard. Why these religious words? What was the muse trying to tell him? Not the muse, the force of creation, the greater power. The universal energy. Walt took a deep breath and allowed the answers to come to him. It isn't about *religion*, as he naively judged, but about spirit (like Emerson wrote). Spirit was the inspiration to religion and, so, this inspiration, like all inspiration, also being spirit, felt like religion to his unexamined musings. It wasn't dogmatic, though, and never hoped to be. He must be careful to make that point very clear. He must be careful to keep the pure spirit quite separate from all things crammed under the umbrella of religion. He must be careful to relay only the essence and not the packaging his untrained essence longed to wrap that essence in. Tricky.

Others had similar charges. Fanny Fern. Obviously inspired by the benevolent source Walt knew too well. Four books in two years, three of them collections. Ah, the pebbly forest-green leather, contrasted with the gold tendrils, winding, lacing, swirling over the cover and spine and around to the back of each volume. Walt had *Fern Leaves*, *Fern Leaves Second Series*, and this new one, a novel, *Ruth Hall* (he didn't, as yet, own the collection meant for children, though he meant to acquire it, just as soon as he had the funds—had a copy on hold in his name at Burnton's Books). Had the author chosen the name Ruth as an ironic statement? It meant "compassion," or something close to that. Walt chuckled. This book showed the antithesis of compassion (not by the author as confused readers may think, but by society), which was, of course, the point.

Her real name had come out. Sara Willis, sister of that poet. She'd gotten herself maligned somehow, Walt wasn't sure about all the details, and she ran away from her Boston in hopes of getting lost in the city. Petty somebody who decided to uncover her. Had listed a string of aliases she'd gone by and marriages or liaisons or some such details. Walt didn't care. What did it matter? Unnecessary social judgment. But the public gobbled up the news, worked it into their assessment of her work, slanted their rude light on her character, whatever *that* word meant, while inhaling her artistry.

Walt frowned. *Ruth Hall* wasn't being well received, not the way her collections were, but was still flying off the shelves. The novel was tart and exacting, shone its own light on certain types of people, namely, those most modern sheep aspire to be. It told the story of a widowed woman and her two children, how they struggled to survive. It told the story of how she earned her own way and wasn't ashamed to admit it, how the heroine felt proud (boasted!) of her accomplishments and insisted that others respect them, too. It was Fanny's own story, rumor had it, complete with a slippery brother and other family members whose eyesight seemed too dim to see her want, whose pocketbooks were sealed to her needs, whose hearts, though softened toward any number of church-sponsored charities and high-profile victims, were stone regarding this sister with the slicing tongue. Well, Fanny would have the last laugh, as they say.

After he visited the printers, Walt would put the finishing touches on the reviews of his book he was working on. It was amazing how a little pre-release advertising had profited Fanny Fern. The papers were singing the arrival of *Ruth Hall* before anyone had had a chance to read it. Singing the praises of a book because they thought they knew the author. Nobody knows the author. Not even an author knows the author. Know yourself and you're a leg up. Know thyself. Oh, try, oh, try. Sing of yourself. Songs of Walt. Sing of yourself. Songs of Ruth. Sing, Ruth, sing, and don't let the crows stop you.

Walt got out of bed and made a note to himself to send a copy of his poetry collection, once printed, to Mr. Ralph Waldo Emerson. He opened his window, rested his chin in his hands, and stared directly at the sun. Black spots swam, arc-like, over his vision. The deed was as sure as done. *Oh, Fanny, Sara, Ruth, forgive me my trespasses.* Walt's eyes watered and he closed them. *You understand.* Walt breathed in and out. His cheeks warmed. His jaw relaxed. The inside of his eyelids swirled orange and red. His heart pumped steady and slow. *I know. You know.* Already, he was forgiven.

Chapter Forty-One

Fanny Fern and Catharine Beecher, New York, Friday, March 30th, 1855

Our insane asylums are full of women, who, leaning on some human heart for love and sympathy, and meeting only misappreciation have gone there, past the Cross, where alone they could have laid down burdens too heavy to bear unshared. A great book is unwritten on this theme. When men become less gross and unspiritual than they now are, they will see the wrong of which they are guilty, in their impatience of women's keenest sufferings because they "are only mental." The only "day of rest" to many of them is the day of their death.

—Fanny Fern, *New York Ledger*, March 11th, 1865

It was an overcast, drizzly day and Fanny Fern plodded along the slush-covered street to the Greenbriar Inn where she was to have tea with her old schoolmistress, Catharine Beecher. It was the last thing Fanny wanted to do. Not that she didn't want to see Catharine; Harriet Beecher Stowe had always provided exciting details about all of sister Katy's latest adventures and Fanny couldn't wait to hear more about them. But, Fanny was worn out. Body and spirit, she felt wrung of strength, hope, and gratitude.

Fanny admonished herself. She'd just locked the door of her beautifully appointed apartments in Delancy House, had shown her healthy, happy girls off to their wonderful school, had dined on lobster and broiled potatoes the evening before with darling James. It was this work of writing that served both to energize and deflate her. Oliver told her she simply mustn't listen to the steady hiss of public opinion, lest those constant elevating and plummeting words destroy her. She must only write, as she's always done, from her heart, with no thought to her audience.

But that wasn't easy. Fanny hated that anyone found fault with her, especially when they directed that fault, not at her work, but at her personally. Somehow judgments of her work became enmeshed with judgments of her, and both became one tangled, gossipy, sought-after elixir to which the vast majority of the public showed signs of addiction. She passed a women's clothing boutique and paused at the front window. A sign next to a smart black gauze-trimmed hat advertised it as "The Ruth Hall Bonnet." Across the street, people lined up to buy sheet music to "The Ruth Hall Schottische." The other day, Fanny saw a train car apparently christened "Ruth Hall" and elegantly painted to advertise the fact. Copies of her books were stacked each morning in tall piles at all the bookstores, only to be regularly depleted by day's end. The few times she'd ventured into such a shop, she'd soon been made busy inscribing title pages until her hand shook.

And yet, the scathing reviews. The biting personal attacks. She was unwomanly because she wrote about tough issues. She was unfeminine because she wrote about those issues plainly. She was ungodly because her frank writing often veered toward sarcasm and her wit, more often than not, left a stinging aftertaste. Her writing was the bracing slap society needed. After feeling the effects of a metaphorical cold bucket of water in the face, people first were exuberant to be so awake, but next were angry to have been so roughly roused. It was a sensation they craved, though, because they always came back for more and more and more of Fanny's words.

And now Moulton's book! Fanny's stomach twisted. Of course the book was written anonymously, but she knew Moulton was the author. Coward! How he twisted her words! He used what little intimate knowledge he had of her for his own advancement. *The Life and Beauties of Fanny Fern*, was selling as well as James' stellar biography of Horace Greeley. According to Moulton's book, Fanny was everything Samuel had advertised her to be, and then some. She was a shameless adulterer, a heartless racketeer, a spiritless manipulator of people and her pen. She pined for the material, loathed babies, and in all of her rough vulgarity, made plain her cravings to be a man.

From her carefully chosen table by the window, but far from most of the other patrons, Catharine Beecher watched Sara Willis (*Fanny Fern!*) approach the tearoom. Sara was as impeccably dressed as Catharine remembered. Flowing, gray skirt; smart, fitted jacket; polished boots and a crisp collar. Even from a distance, Sara's kid gloves looked perfectly brushed, her bonnet artistically tied. Not a loose curl, not a chipped button, or a snagged thread. Yet Sara's step was different—more somber—and her face, though full and healthy, looked astonishingly pale. The doorman opened the door for Sara, who kept her head low and her eyes down. A flood of realization washed over Catharine. How difficult it must be to *be* Fanny Fern! Even for someone as bright and strong as Sara Willis.

Catharine had read all she could of Fanny Fern's writing, especially after Harriet had told her that Fanny was, indeed, *their Sara*. Catharine had also read a great deal of writing *about* Fanny Fern. Cutting words! Cruel admonishments! The reviews of *Ruth Hall* were, for the most part, scathing, but Catharine noticed those reviews worked to make people hungrier to read the novel. And it wasn't just a morbid desire for depravity that drew readers; they couldn't help but align themselves with heroine Ruth and to cheer her on through her struggles. The book's ending, that Ruth should be financially solvent and *not* be saved by romance and marriage, *was* unconventional. But, how refreshing to think that women, at least some women, might have such a choice. Catharine felt the same conflicted feelings she supposed other readers felt. She loved Fanny Fern's vision but cringed, to be so callously shown it. Theirs was a society that prided itself on the gentle suggestion. A collective shudder went through the body of the world after reading *Ruth Hall*. Fanny's words cut through all the expected swags of propriety and allowed the bright sunlight to beam, unfiltered, onto the delicate tufts and fringes of society's inner chambers. In the dazzling rays of Fanny's words, all of society's shameful dust was exposed.

Sara scanned the tea tables until she saw Catharine. Her blue eyes lit up with the zest Catharine remembered. Catharine smiled a welcome. Sara Willis was alive and well after all, entombed or not in the persona of Fanny Fern. Catharine rose to greet her friend. "Sara Willis!" she exclaimed, kissing her cheek.

A flutter flew through the patrons at the nearby tables and Sara's face colored.

"Oh, I'm sorry," Catharine said.

Fanny flapped her hand. "Oh, never mind. Everyone knows all about me, *now*. Especially after some *dear, close friend* of mine decided to write that book about me. Have you read it, dear Catharine?" Fanny raised her voice for the little crowd of tea-takers to hear, "*The Life and Beauties of Fanny Fern?*"

Catharine winced. Sara was hurt. As if Catharine had any doubt, the book must surely be a lie. "I have read it. Of course," Catharine said quietly. "Who hasn't, really?"

Fanny blew an exasperated breath and sat opposite Catharine. The waiter brought her a pot and a cup.

Catharine placed her hand over Fanny's. "I wanted to hear *your* side of the story."

Fanny squeezed her eyes in gratitude. "You always were good to me."

"Even when you didn't deserve it!" Catharine said with a smile. "Stealing pies from the larder. Sneaking out at midnight to go riding with, with—"

"*Your* brother. Henry Ward."

"No!"

"Yes. He was, and is, delightful."

Catharine patted Fanny's hand. "And so, dear Sara, are you."

Fanny's chin quivered. "Oh, Catharine." She ventured a smile. "I almost, just now, called you Miss Catharine."

"Oh, I'm still a *Miss*! And happily," Catharine said. She poured Fanny her tea and held out the plate of biscuits and tarts. "Tell me your story, Sara, and then I will tell you mine. We're two old friends catching up, you know."

Fanny took a raspberry tart and placed it on her tea plate.

"That's all. No conspiracy," Catharine said, holding Fanny's eyes in her own. "You can trust me."

Fanny nodded. "I always could. You always chose to see the best in me."

Catharine smiled. "You were my favorite student. Though a challenging one!"

Fanny blew out the breath she was unknowingly holding, sipped her tea, and took a hearty bite of her tart. Then she told Catharine everything—about Charles and Samuel, Nat and Father, about Reverend Norris and Moulton, Oliver Dyer and James Parton. She told about losing Grace and finally getting her back. She told about her darkest days in her Boston garret and her brightest in her New York hotel apartments. She even told Catharine what she hadn't had the nerve to tell anybody yet—that another paper, the *New York Ledger*, had offered her one hundred dollars a column to write a sequenced story for their pages. A hundred a week. Catharine had gasped. It was more than many make a year. "You're rich, Sara Willis," she said. "Rich and wise and beautiful."

"Wise or despised," Fanny said.

"Tut," Catharine said. "People will see that book for what it is—a jealous man's attempt to cut a worthy opponent. That you are a woman just makes it easier for him. All a man has to do is to breathe the slightest taint over a woman's reputation to color her."

"And yet a man's reputation can be earned merely by a good birth, and can scarcely ever truly be destroyed."

"It's a strange society," Catharine said. "Though, arguably, it has not been a conscious conspiracy on the part of most men. They're more than happy, though, to participate in a method that privileges them."

Fanny huffed. "And all the while denying that privilege."

"Don't you worry about the ravings of some little man," Catharine said. "He is editor of a floundering Boston paper and you are sought after around the world. Your readers will see the petty envy, the wounded ego, of that writer. You just have to display that which is *you*, that which is Fanny Fern, in order to keep your character clear."

Fanny bit her lip and nodded. She was trying to move ahead. In fact, she admitted to having accepted the *Ledger*'s offer and was already hard at work on her story, "Fanny Ford." The editor, Robert Bonner, seemed made of steel, wouldn't take no for an answer. And Oliver was happy to release her from her contract if it helped her career. His paper had already received ample Fanny Fern rewards; he didn't mind sharing the wealth.

Catharine scratched her chin. "Bonner publishes all sorts of prominent writers. Emerson, right?"

Fanny nodded. "And Margaret Fuller. Charles Dickens. Grace Greenwood," she said. "How nice it might be to talk, really talk, with other women writers—Grace Greenwood, or even Hatty's friend, Maria Child."

Catharine chuckled. "I predict you'll soon be running a women writer's group, just to talk with Grace Greenwood."

"Now there's an idea," Fanny said. "But one for a little later, I'm sure. My time in New York had been the fastest year and a half of my life. Always writing, always flying about."

"And this escort you keep mentioning," Catharine said. "What are you planning to do about James?"

Fanny's face became blank. "*Do* about him?"

"Surely you realize his intentions," Catharine said. "I don't even know him and I'd say it sounds as if he's in love with you."

"Love? James? Oh, I don't know. We get along nicely," Fanny sputtered.

Catharine raised an eyebrow.

The truth was, Fanny rambled, that she hadn't thought much about James in connection with love, certainly not in connection with marriage, didn't think she trusted the institution of marriage anymore, simply couldn't even fathom the idea. With Charly, she'd been happy to be married, but hopelessly naive, had bumbled along like a daft dreamer in the misty world women were encouraged to occupy. With Samuel, she couldn't enter that world for anything. Her blinders had been removed and nothing short of surgery could replace them—precisely what probably angered Samuel more than anything. True, she'd been materially provided for by Samuel, but she'd also been mistreated. Fanny shuddered, thinking about it, again. She was grateful Samuel had pushed through with the Chicago divorce before he understood the enormity of her writing success.

"Have you *really* lost faith in the institution of marriage?" Catharine asked. "Listening to you, I'm not so sure."

"What do you mean?" Fanny replied. She sipped her tea and listened as Catharine waxed on about what she supposed a perfect union between woman and man could be—Catharine, who, to Fanny's knowledge, hadn't had a serious beau in her life. Fanny smiled. Women's illusions were so far from the realities of married life. Being married was really the hardest way to get a living. How much better to work her own fingers, ply her own brain for her daily bread. How much sweeter, how much stronger, it made her feel. It was only now, recently, that Fanny'd finally felt whole. And she felt that way all by herself. Not as a part of a couple, certainly not as an appendage to some man, not married or cared for by brother, father, or institution. Fanny felt whole because she led her entire life herself. She made her decisions, sheltered herself, nurtured herself, fed herself. Fanny expressed herself and wrote her own checks. She collected her earnings and made investment choices. That didn't mean she didn't enjoy James' good company at the theater or the table. It didn't mean she didn't enjoy a new lace collar, like any other woman, or didn't delight in tying the ribbons of spring's prettiest bonnet under her chin. She wanted it all—to be independent and part of a couple, to provide for herself and to care for and be cared for by another. Fanny didn't think she'd given James much thought, but the truth was, she really had. She'd been thinking about him, and about men, and about relationships, ever since he first took her to the opera. But James was eleven years her junior! And, liberal as he was, what man could really accept marriage the way Fanny envisioned it, the way she knew she would *need* it to be?

"I really do *not* know what to do about James," Fanny finally said.

"Before you decide," Catharine said. "Listen more to my story. You might think me an old maid. You might think me the last to be able to speak intelligently on the subject of marriage. But, I've gathered my own information, Sara, I have. And I've made my secret little decisions of survival based upon that research."

Both women had finished their tea and Catharine suggested a little walk. "I want to show you something," she told Fanny.

Once outside, the weather was still dreary, but the drizzling had stopped. A frigid draft occasionally blew hard down the street and caused Catharine and Fanny to huddle together a little closer, for warmth, and because Catharine was speaking so low and quietly that Fanny didn't want to lose a single word to the wind.

Fanny had too-quickly judged Catharine. As someone who hated being judged, that realization stung. Catharine hadn't married, *by choice*! Yes, she'd been engaged once, but after her fiancée, Alexander, had died, she couldn't think about another man, especially once she realized the control he'd legally have over her.

"I didn't decide not to get married, at first," Catharine said. "But as time went by, and I ran as fast as I could from every possible chance at the union that came my way, I quickly realized that my lack of choice regarding a husband, was in itself, my choice."

Of course she'd had admirers! Catharine grinned at the idea that an unmarried woman was an *undesired* woman. What quicker way to appease male egos than to assume a single woman is single because no man would have her, instead of because she would have no man? We're alike that way, Catharine said to Fanny. Any men they accepted must allow them control over their own lives. And that freedom was something Catharine knew she'd die without. Fanny nodded agreement, thinking hard about James. As it was, Catharine said she was loosely under the thumbs of her father and even her brother, Henry Ward. Yes, she did her work, usually under the shadow of *Christian* duty, for what better way for a woman to be allowed to labor in public than by dedicating that service to the church? *You know better, Sara,* Catharine said. Catharine gently encouraged, though didn't push, religion at the seminary—though everyone thought she did. Even as she winked at student exploits, she painstakingly assured worried fathers that she was drilling the love of God into her pupils' stubborn heads. Naturally, religion was taught. It had to be. It was important. But so was everything else. And *that* was the beauty of the school. To teach women mathematics and geography. To expose them to art and literature, to science and law. To teach them to read and think and write.

The education of women had become Catharine's mission. She traveled to many an established or rustic city and convinced as many boards of skeptical men that she meant to enlighten their women, all within the safe bubble of the spiritual, of course. Lately, many of the more progressive towns allowed her to drop the seminary plan and just call her proposed institution what it would be—a school for women, a real school, akin to (but, unfortunately, not yet completely equal to) men's schools. Education was the key to the liberation of women. Just as it was for slaves. If slaves knew how to read, they would better be able to understand the powers that enslaved them. If women were as educated as men, *they* would better be able to understand the powers that enslaved *them.* So, Catharine worked herself ragged, on her own time, without much interference.

Except when she was discovered in a frazzled state. Then, she'd be as caught in men's power traps as a rabbit in a string snare. It had happened a half dozen times or so, and each time, Catharine had secretly feared she'd never be able to spring herself. Catharine's days were long and usually hard, especially when she traveled to the edge of the frontier and sought to help establish education in the scads of mushrooming Midwestern towns. Catharine understood that she had to work within the system in order to facilitate any change of that system. That meant, simply, convincing men of the value of women's education. Catharine had to command her most logical reasoning abilities—any displayed emotion was immediately suspect—and her most proper decorum. She couldn't have a hair out of place, nor a syllable. She sat, hour after hour, patiently convincing man after man that her ideas would help *them,* that her ideas would benefit all of society.

At the end of such days, Catharine usually took measured steps to whatever lodging the new city might offer, and didn't tremble or weep until she'd locked the door behind her, yanked off her shoes, hat, and gloves, and ripped off her corset. Then, if the day had gone well, she might write until the wee hours—articles for the local papers, contracts, business plans. If the day had been frustrating, if she'd taken in too many leers or heard too many patronizing comments, Catharine would get on the bed and kick her feet, pound her fists into her mattress, all while screaming her anger into her pillow. The first time Lyman Beecher had sent her away had been one such day. She'd let herself into her room and had been surprised to see her father sitting in the dressing chair. Of course the hotel staff had let him into her room. He was her father. He had that right. Catharine had been startled to see him and found it hard to rein in the frustration she'd just assured herself she'd be able to release.

Lyman Beecher pronounced her "nervous" and "exhausted," and made haste to whisk her off to seclusion for some water therapy. Nothing Catharine said made a hair of difference. Lyman decided she'd been working far too hard, for a woman, and was so tilted away from all that was feminine that she couldn't be trusted to judge her condition herself. The school plans Catharine had been inches from establishing were never realized. Catharine sent a scribbled note of apology from the door of their late-night carriage, but when she came back to the town six months later, she was greeted with more than a few arched eyebrows and wasn't seriously listened to again.

At the rest asylum, Catharine *was* happy to have whole days floating along without a corset. At first, the physical freedom from the clenching whalebones consumed her. She was grateful for each deep breath, for each heartily enjoyed meal, for each long soak in the hot bubble of mineral water. But after a few days, Catharine was ready to squeeze herself back into her clothing (and her woman's position) and to continue her rally. She couldn't leave, though, until her *father* deemed her well enough. Each fortnight he'd visit and would assess her color, her spirit, her frame. If he detected a single rapid blink, the slightest cheek-coloring of frustration, a chance bitten nail or shaky breath, he decided she needed more recuperation to ease her back into the naturally peaceful womanly state.

Each time he left, Catharine would almost scream. She nearly choked with each mineral-laden draught she was expected to guzzle, felt ready to explode each time she was serenely led to her bath, almost tore her hair out with boredom sitting in her resting room. She knew three possible fates awaited her. Quite possibly, she'd never be considered "well," and would have to live out her days at the baths or, more likely, at one of the many sparsely appointed asylums filled with madwomen—women whose passion, anger, or vision made them incongruous with civilized society. If she was very unlucky, that would be Catharine's fate. If she was lucky, though, she'd check her rage and excitement, would bury them deep within the facade of quiet good grace and would be released, albeit with a stern paternal warning about knowing her workable place, to begin her educational crusade again. This had only happened twice, of the six times she'd been committed, but it was still the best Catharine could hope for. The other four times, she'd succumbed to the treatments and had sunk to such depths of lethargy that it was often difficult to rouse herself and dress for the day. Catharine shuddered when she told Fanny of those times.

They happened out of intense pressure to *relax*, as the staff put it. There were agonizingly long spells where she'd be left alone in her resting room, with nothing—not a book, nor needle, nor candlestick, to help pass the hours. These droughts were followed by placid dips in the mineral baths and regular flushing of her system with the medicinal tonics. Catharine tried to resist sinking. She tried to keep her mind busy reciting poetry and planning her schools. But, in time, the rest cure would deaden her, as it was intended to. She'd slowly, day by day, week by week, forget about educating women. She'd forget how energized she felt signing building contracts and hiring teachers, convincing governance boards and overseeing curricula. Catharine would lose herself. She valued nothing but sleep and quiet. She wished for no stimulation, but craved longer and longer languid moments lying still, sitting still, thinking of nothing. And that was the water treatment's goal. She would be considered well when she was womanly weak and passive, when she did what was expected of her by others, instead of what she selfishly wanted to do for herself.

Catharine wasn't alone. She'd pass other institutionalized women on her way to treatments and would see varying degrees of fire in their cheeks and eyes. As the months wore on, almost every woman lost that spark. Catharine always swore she wouldn't let it happen, but it had, more times than not. Yes, those two times, those two wonderful times when it *didn't*, she'd been able to hide her passion beneath a studied cool demeanor. She had learned to look vacantly toward her father and ask *him* if he thought her improved. She couldn't know, certainly didn't trust herself to guess. If he was in the right mood, not too suspicious or cross, Lyman would chuckle and kiss her and tell her that yes, indeed, she was much improved and if she felt strong enough, he'd take her on a carriage ride to a nice hotel. If Catharine mastered her exuberance and, instead, listlessly shrugged her shoulders or said *perhaps that'd be all right*, her trunk would be packed for her and she would be sitting with her head resting against the carriage door and her eyes closed for fear she'd explode with joy.

Once, she'd gotten all the way to the carriage, and was nearly a mile away from the spa, when tears of gratitude seeped down her cheeks. Catharine had mistakenly begun to think of all she could do, now that she was again free, and was overwhelmed with excitement. Naturally, though, Lyman assessed her with a deep crinkle between his brows. "You're not at all better," he decided and ordered the carriage to turn around before his sweet Katy melted before his very eyes. Of course, Catharine sobbed all the way back to the spa, which earned her another two months of treatment.

She'd managed not to lose her spirit the first and last times she'd been committed. After the first time, when she was allowed access to her personal belongings again, she went straight to her trunks of papers and wrote herself a manifesto, listing who she was and what she wanted out of her life. Each of the other times, when she'd finally become subdued enough to be released from the water and rest treatments, she'd eventually stumble upon this work of hers and it would remind her of herself, and, with it, she would begin the secret climb back into her personality.

But, she told Fanny, that climb was a very difficult one to make. The goal of the baths was to numb a woman's spirit. Catharine sometimes wondered if the draughts she drank and the baths she was made to soak in weren't laced with ether or maybe camphor. She smelled nothing but the yellow smell of sulfur, of course, but that didn't stop her from wondering how the treatments succeeded, most of the time, to stupefy the patients.

Fanny listened, stunned, to Catharine's accounts. *She* had nearly broken down simply because Samuel had *threatened* her with the asylum. But Catharine! Committed six times! True, the baths were a gentler version of seclusion, but they dulled the spirit all the same. Fanny squeezed her eyes and clutched her former schoolmistress's arm. "Catharine," she whispered. "I'm so sorry."

"Thank you," Catharine said. "But, I'm here, now, aren't I? And I have learned a few tricks in the process."

Fanny shook her head in amazement.

Catharine tapped her forehead. "Knowledge," she said. "It's our secret weapon. We can't be afraid to tell the truth about what we know. I hope to instill that power in my students. And *you* do the same. You show the truth with your writing."

Fanny nodded. Of course Catharine was right. She and Catharine had each gone through painful experiences and had come out on the other side of them. Who was to say which circumstance was worse? Who could compare injuries, judge suffering? It all needed exposure—each and every social, intellectual, physical, and spiritual injustice.

Fanny and Catharine walked into a dingy part of the city. The wind swept through their clothes and they shivered against it. An occasional rat scurried across the street to forage scraps left outside the door to some eatery. The buildings displayed less colorful signs, sometimes had broken panes or crumbling stoops. All New York streets harbored a small village of ragged orphans, but this section swarmed with more than the usual number. They stood solemnly at one corner or another, holding little tin cups (staying there for hours, especially if they were ill or maimed) or, the healthier ones, frustrated with continually behaving downheartedly, eventually took to the alleyways to play stick ball or run races. "They'd do better in an orphanage," Fanny said. "It breaks my heart to see them so neglected."

"Perhaps they'd do better. Probably they'd do worse," Catharine said. She stopped in front of a three-story wooden building set far from the street and circled with an iron fence. A small wooden sign near the front gate read Bower Street Woman's Insane Asylum. "We're here," Catharine said.

They stood on the slush-covered lannon stone slab under a stone archway. The cold from the stone inched its way through the soles of Fanny's feet, up her ankles and legs, and grasped her firmly around the knees. "But for the grace of God, this could be any woman's fate," Catharine whispered.

Fanny gasped. "Is this where you were?"

"Heavens, no. It's much worse." She held Fanny by the elbow. "Come along. I'll show you."

Catharine led Fanny a half mile down the road to a vacant lot. "We'll walk through here and cross round to the back."

They stepped through matted clumps of grass and weeds poking through dirty piles of snow, then trudged down a muddy hill past a rude gardening shed and a pasture where three horses huddled together. There, at the back of the asylum, was the same iron fence surrounding a simple garden. The garden had benches, pebbled walkways, patches of shrubbery, a scanty assortment of trees and a half dozen of the most disheveled women Fanny had ever seen.

"These are the most-promising cases," Catharine said as they approached the fence from beneath a canopy of willow branches. "Some never come out."

"How do you know?"

"I've come here before."

Catharine pointed to a slight woman with dingy blonde hair sitting statue-like on a near bench. "There," she said. "I call her Charlotte. She doesn't move. They walk her out to the bench and after a few hours, they walk her back inside."

Fanny stood, wide-eyed, behind the fence as Catharine pointed out other inmates. Beatrice, chained hand and foot to the giant metal ring bolted to the asylum's back wall, sat quivering in scant clothing. She soils her clothing, Catharine explained, so they send her out with less and less of it. Fanny tasted bile. Gertrude, a similarly confined, elderly woman, rattled her chains and muttered under her breath. Catharine whispered that she once saw her claw at the face of an attendant. The next day, while she was out in the freezing air, buckets of water from an attic window were dumped over her head.

Fanny wiped her damp forehead with a handkerchief. "How awful."

"It's nothing compared to the whippings."

"Don't say you've witnessed that?"

"No," Catharine said. "But I've seen them file out here after the fact with stripes of red still seeping through their dress backs."

Fanny's stomach churned and her face felt tight. Samuel's face swam before her. Rulesandtwoandonethreefour.

Catharine pointed out a woman in the exact center of the garden, her feet manacled, her hands tied behind her, a stained leather muzzle over her face. "She used to scream," Catharine said. "Even now, she moans. Listen."

Fanny took great gulps of air. She could, indeed, hear the creature droning a low, sour note.

"I call her Nettie," Catharine said. "She sometimes notices me." She waved her handkerchief at the woman.

Fanny's mouth dropped. "Nettie?" she whispered. A spasm clenched her abdomen and she leaned forward, panting. *In front of the children.*

"Sara, are you all right?"

Fanny clutched her middle and squinted in the gray light. Her throat squeezed so small she could only take the smallest gasps of air. Was it Nettie Farrington? It was hard to tell. This was a grown woman and Fanny had last seen Nettie when she wasn't even of age. Fanny's hands shook. Her arms shook.

"Sara?"

Fanny gasped. "I know her," she said. "It's Nettie Farrington."

"No, Sara," Catharine said. "It couldn't be. I just call her Nettie. That's not her real name." She pulled Fanny away from the fence.

"Nettie?" Fanny called as Catharine started to lead her away.

The woman's eyes blinked rapidly and she thrashed against the restraints, moaned into the muzzle.

Fanny froze. "It *is* Nettie!"

"Sara, no," Catharine whispered. "We've agitated her is all."

The asylum's back door banged open. The woman thrashed harder. Her low moan grew more strangled.

"Nettie!" Fanny called through the fence.

Catharine grasped Fanny by the arm. "Sara, please," she said. "Come! *Now!*" She pulled Fanny under the willow boughs and back up the muddy hill toward the pasture and gardening shed.

The rain started then. A cold, steady patter. Catharine pulled Fanny along. Thunder rumbled in the distance and flashes streaked across the gray sky. Fanny could barely listen to Catharine's steady tone, whispering, explaining in her ear. Instead, she strained against the storm's swoosh and crackle to hear the faint and disappearing timbre of the muzzled woman's moans. It *was* Nettie. Wasn't it? It had to be. Fanny had been her stepmother and would-be protector for almost two years, had braided Nettie's hair, tied her bonnet strings, served her cocoa. Fanny had read to Nettie when she had a cold and taught her to tat. She had told her stories and wiped her tears. Fanny stopped marching, covered her mouth with her hands, and sucked air between her rigid fingers.

"Dear Sara," Catharine whispered. "Take deep breaths."

Fanny panted against her corset and against a tongue that seemed like it would choke her. How selfish she had behaved! She could have saved them, both Nettie and Clare, if she had only been able to swallow her self-righteousness and taken on her womanly yoke. Fanny's stomach spasmed. Oh, Nettie. What had she done to poor, sweet Nettie? Not to mention Grace! Damaged, as well! They had the same darting eyes, Grace and Nettie, the same desperate gaze, aimed at Fanny. Asking for Fanny's help. Leaning on her as their mother, a mother who had abandoned them both. Fanny's heart pounded, whimpers escaped her attempts to breathe and she blinked against the flood in her eyes.

Catharine pulled Fanny's arm again, roughly. She pulled her uphill, over the slippery mud, through the brittle of dried grass and leaves and back to the shiny wet of the street. Fanny shook her head from side to side. Nettie Nettie Nettie. What a horrible mother she had been. How she'd ruined so many dear lives. *She*, Sara, Fanny, had done it herself. "Hush, now," Catharine whispered. "You've done no such thing. One woman can't overcome every natural obstacle." They were back in front of the asylum's entryway, now. Fanny flung herself against the iron fence posts, wrapping her arms around them and groaning in a way that frightened both women. Catharine's fingers pried at Fanny's arms. She talked steady into Fanny's ear. But Fanny wasn't listening to Catharine. She hugged the fence posts, the cold metal hard against her chest. Her heart beat against the iron, against her lungs. Rain poured from the rim of her bonnet in a thin clear stream. Fanny watched the stream. How cool it looked. How clean.

Catharine continued to pull Fanny's arms from the fence, talking rapidly all the while.

Fanny moaned. "I can't leave her!"

Catharine shook Fanny until she loosed her grip. Rain spattered off the cobblestones around their feet. She grasped Fanny's wrists and pulled her down the street. Fanny looked over her shoulder at the three-story structure. Tall, wooden, dark. How could she leave Nettie there? She wanted to go back and rescue her. She couldn't leave her, not after seeing her muzzled like an unruly horse, not after Grace. Fanny leaned away from Catharine, pulled toward the building.

Don't look back, Catharine said, her voice distant and tinny, like an echo over a wide river. The asylum's front door suddenly sprung open. People hurried down the walk.

Fanny heard the iron fence gate creak open. She heard shouts. Catharine yanked her arm, hard, and soon they were running. Fanny heard her heart pounding. She heard the rhythmic tap, tap, tap, tap that she and Catharine made racing down the cobblestones, panting in unison. The cobblestones shined wet and slippery under their moving boots. Blocks away, they finally stopped, clutching their middles, aching for breath. The rain had quieted to a cool mist that leaked silently down from the dark sky. At the end of the street, a cab horse stamped in place, his breath steaming.

An awful clenching pulled Fanny's insides. She leaned forward toward the rainbow rings dancing over the wet cobblestones and vomited.

Catharine patted Fanny's back and held out a damp handkerchief. "There, there."

"Oh, Catharine."

"I forget how shocking the place is at first. Forgive me for not better preparing you."

Fanny's panting lessened. "Do you think it was . . ."

"Not at all," Catharine said. "Listen to me. That woman was at least fifty years old if she was twenty. Do you hear me? It was absolutely *not* your Nettie."

"But she looked . . ."

"She looked awful. It's true."

Fanny stood upright and blew a giant breath. It caught the wind and whisked across the city. "I failed her, Catharine," Fanny said. "I failed them all."

Catharine shook Fanny's arm. "Don't you take responsibility for Samuel's actions. You did the best you could. The best anyone could expect."

"But *Grace*," Fanny whispered.

"Will be fine. She's got her mother's blood. Her mother's resiliency. You said yourself you saw improvements."

Fanny bit her lip. "But they're so slow in coming."

"Slow and sure," Catharine said. She locked eyes with Fanny. "I'm sorry I brought you there. It has upset you so. Let's sit on that bench and steady ourselves."

Fanny's stockings were wet from splashing through puddles and her hair was coming unpinned in the back. She sat, trembling, with her former school-mistress, and relived the past hour's events. Eventually, her breathing slowed and her heart beat a solid regular rhythm. But her hands still shook as she struggled to brush a wisp of hair from her eyes. No, it wasn't Nettie, Fanny finally agreed, but it could be. And so what if it wasn't someone they knew, a woman was held, tied, and muzzled! Other women chained! Whipped!

Catharine nodded her sympathy. Education. This was the answer. Catharine would educate with her schools and Fanny would educate with her writing. Fanny took a steadying breath and nodded. She had already started her series for the *New York Ledger*, but she guessed the paper's editor, the progressive Robert Bonner, would retain her column after her story-in-chapters was played out. Fanny would make sure of it, especially now, and would have some pieces ready to print. The *New York Ledger*! Its circulation was approaching four hundred thousand! Fanny would get her ideas out. She would. She'd use her words to help the disadvantaged, to free this Nettie, to free all of the women at Bower Street Woman's Insane Asylum. And above, all, she'd keep herself free. Never never never would Fanny bend to a man's will. She'd worked hard for her independence and she saw how vital such independence worked to ensure her sanity. Fanny ate what she liked, dressed how she liked, bought what she liked, lived where she liked. Fanny decided how her daughters would be educated and Fanny decided how they'd be brought up, even if she made mistakes in the process. Most of all, she wrote what she liked. Fanny earned and saved and spent her own money and didn't have to beg it from any man nor account for it to anyone. Right or wrong, she was herself.

Fanny and Catharine finally parted ways when the dreary day turned even colder. They gave each other a giant shivering hug and promised to write often. Fanny tramped in her wet clothes down New York's streets. Her fingers and toes ached with cold. Her head pounded. Finally, she entered the warm foyer of Delancy House, gathered her mail from the desk clerk and was soon shakily unlocking the door to her fourth-floor apartments. She unbuttoned her boots and kicked them off, letting them fall where they would in the entryway, dashed off her bonnet, peeled off her gloves, wrapped a thick shawl around her shoulders, and slumped onto her new buff-colored settee in front of the fire. Her wet clothes clung to her chilled limbs but Fanny was too spent to change. She huddled close to the fire and rubbed her aching temples. She took slow calming breaths. She admired the two large portraits of Grace and Ellen she'd just had hung in the parlor, nestled in the radiant warmth of the large fireplace that never wanted for fuel, and marveled at the plethora of gas lights ringing her with soft, warm light. Oh, those days in the garret, those days with Samuel, were not so long passed! Fanny shuddered, both proud and ashamed at her level of living, especially juxtaposed with the conditions so many less-fortunate people were forced to survive in.

The bell rang.

Fanny wasn't expecting anyone. She called for Molly, but when the maid didn't come, Fanny struggled to her feet and opened the door herself. It was only Jemmy, beaming his bright, crooked smile, and cradling an enormous bouquet of white lilies.

Fanny tensed when he got down on one knee, right then and there, in the entryway. Her heart stuttered. Her hands shook with dread. "James—"

"I couldn't wait another day. I adore you, Fanny, as you must know by now."

"No, James—" Fanny tried to stop what she could see unfolding, tried to halt James's tongue in mid-sentence, but before she could spring on James and clasp her hand over his mouth, his marriage proposal had already been uttered.

Chapter Forty-Two

✲

Fanny Fern, Hoboken, New Jersey, Saturday, January 5th, 1856

And there is Mr. James Parton, author of the *Life of Horace Greeley*, whom I occasionally meet. Jim is five feet ten inches, and modest—wears his hair long, and don't believe in a devil—has written more good anonymous articles now floating unbaptized through newspaperdom, (on both sides of the water) than any other man, save himself, would suffer to go unclaimed. Jim believes in Carlyle and lager bier—can write a book better than he can tie a cravat; though since his late marriage I am pleased to observe a wonderful improvement in this respect. It is my belief, that Jim is destined by steady progress, to eclipse many a man who has shot up like a rocket, and who will fizzle out and come down like a stick . . .

—Fanny Fern, *New York Ledger*, March 29th, 1856

James Parton took Fanny Fern's gloved hand and gave it a squeeze. First, they had taken the ferry from New York to New Jersey. Now, at last, they were riding in a carriage, a fine, rented black one with gold trim. The day was gray and overcast, but not cold. A mild dampness blew occasionally, stirring the dried flower stalks and bare branches of the January landscape. Bits of old, gray snow clung icily to patches of gravel here and there and the roads were passable—neither sloppy with mud nor slick with ice. Seasonal bells jingled on the necks of the two mahogany bays that pulled the carriage and the driver was handsomely done up in black velvet, gray wool, and hints of red satin. Oliver

Dyer, serious in his heavy gray coat and tweed muffler, sat opposite them going over the contract they would soon sign. "I can't wait," James whispered to Fanny.

Fanny bit her lip.

"You're not changing your mind on me, are you?" James asked.

Fanny had refused James Parton's marriage proposals for nine months. Each time he asked her for her hand, she'd just witnessed some marital atrocity or had just relished some new independence. Marriage, Fanny declared, wasn't for her. Why did she need to be legally bound to someone? She didn't want any more children. She made her own money and wanted to keep it, thank you very much. The minute she got married, everything she'd worked so hard to establish for herself would no longer belong to her. Legally, she wouldn't be in control of her children, her finances, her writing, or even her own behavior. She would have to change her name, give up her earnings to her husband, and abide by his wishes. If he wanted onions every night, he would have them. If he wanted to gamble away her daughters' inheritance, he could. If he wanted her to quit writing, he could order it. If he wanted to commit his wife to an insane asylum . . .

No thank you, Fanny repeated, whenever James presented the idea. Yes, she enjoyed his company. Certainly, she respected and admired him. She very likely loved him. But how could she be sure that the egalitarian relationship they enjoyed in courtship would continue if they married? Every woman in the Bower Street Woman's Insane Asylum was sent there by a husband who wanted to be rid of her. Perhaps he was tired of a sharp tongue or cold caresses. Perhaps she didn't produce enough or the right sorts of heirs. Perhaps he was more attracted to some sweet young daughter of a neighbor or relative or friend. Divorce was so vulgar. Only the truly desperate, or maligned, conceived of it as an option. Even outspoken Fanny never mentioned Samuel, if it could be helped, preferring that everyone assume her to be Charly's widow and nothing more.

Let's get to the bottom of that place, James had suggested, after Fanny had talked, again, of the frights she saw at the asylum. He convinced Fanny to allow him to visit the asylum without her, as a journalist, to see what sort of story he could discover. But when he returned, he reported that there was no response to his repeated knocks on the door.

"Did you go round to the back?"

The garden was as Fanny had described it, but there was nobody in it, James said. "I wonder if the women were moved somewhere else?"

"Or dead," Fanny said.

They sent others to the building—Oliver Dyer, Robert Bonner, Fanny's brother Richard—but each man saw nothing, met nobody at the house.

"Do you think I'm mad?" Fanny asked James.

"Of course not. You and Catharine both saw what you did."

Three weeks later, Catharine sent Fanny a missive, "Don't forget them!"

How could Fanny forget? It boiled her blood to think of those women, to think of Catharine's misery, and what could have been her own. "I could write flaming words," she said and she did.

Fanny's hundred-dollar-a-column story, "Fanny Ford," a tale about women getting trampled—as seamstresses, mothers, wives—did spectacularly well for Robert Bonner and the *New York Ledger*. When that story ended, some ten weeks later, Fanny continued writing strictly for Robert for the solid fee of twenty-five dollars a column. Robert Bonner, an Irish immigrant with stunning blue eyes and the loveliest lilt, ran a paper that was free of the excessive gore and drama that was popular, and contained what he hoped were thought-provoking articles of social criticism, news, and political, historical, and literary essays. He frequently ran works of fiction and poetry from well-known authors and fought hard against a blandness he said infiltrated many a periodical. He appreciated Fanny's forthright style and wit, and Fanny appreciated the free hand and genuine respect Robert gave her.

Fanny's columns were eagerly anticipated, with hundreds of people often waiting at dawn for the office's warehouse door to open in order to hurriedly buy the latest copy of the *Ledger*, too impatient to read Fanny's latest words an hour later, when the newsstands and vendors would have their allotment. And she'd written *another* novel, out just last month—*Rose Clark*—which was selling magnificently. It'd been about Samuel, mostly, and about how marital power could so easily be abused and, yet, it was also about how single women were not exempt from danger either. That great slap of innuendo, that Fanny knew all too keenly, could brand the most-innocent woman and strip her life of respect and care.

It still pained Fanny—to be maligned, socially insulted. She had enough money to last her and Grace and Ellen several lifetimes each. Fanny had a fine circle of truly good friends now—Oliver, Robert, brother Richard and Jessie, Catharine, Harriet, Hatty, and of course, James. Fanny still worried about Grace, even though Grace seemed to be almost cured of her skittishness. Grace sometimes still had horrible nightmares when she would scream "Mother!" in such a high-pitched frenzy that Fanny thought she was being murdered, and she sometimes still followed Fanny like a shadow and needed to sit *that close* during dinner or tea, especially when more than a few other people joined them. But Fanny could admit to being less worried about Grace than she had been only a few years before. To have her there, at her own table, under her own roof, was like lounging in a fragrant bath on a rainy day. And Fanny swore that no real harm would ever again befall Grace. She was now, decidedly, under Fanny's protection and this mother would never again allow anything of consequence to happen to her daughter—surely nothing warm soup, loving hugs, and frank conversation couldn't erase. Fanny's eyes grew moist when she saw her almost fourteen-year-old darling sometimes burst into a room, instead of creeping, bent-headed, as she did when they were first reunited. Slow and sure improvement. Fanny was grateful for it.

And Ellen! Always a delight, and certainly less cause for worry. Fanny's ten-year-old bundle of happiness didn't seem a bit altered by their years of poverty and fear. Perhaps Fanny had done an adequate job of shielding Ellen's childhood after all. Oh the pains Fanny had taken to *pretend* sometimes—that she wasn't hungry, that she wasn't afraid or lonely or depressed. But there had been plenty of other times when Fanny simply *couldn't* pretend. Her velvet pouch would stand so empty and the landlords and editors seemed to hold such advantage, that often, Fanny had to admit, she would give in to the misery of their sad little world and wouldn't have the energy to conjure a bedtime story or stroke Ellen's curls. Fanny hoped Ellen would soon forget those times and would better remember, instead, *these times* of plenty and gratitude and freedom and love.

"You're not changing your mind, are you?" James repeated, as the carriage bounced over a rough part of the road.

"Not a whit," Fanny said, and meant it. In the last nine months she and James had had numerous frank discussions about marriage and commit-ment. Fanny confided her fears about the institution's inequality and eventually James proposed a solution. He agreed with Fanny that married women were legal nonentities, so suggested they sign a contract asserting that Fanny would continue to have full discretion over her own work, earnings, daughters, and property. "I fell in love with you exactly as you are," he said. "Why would I want to shackle you in the least?"

Even after James first suggested the prenuptial agreement, Fanny hesitated. Finally, last week, circumstances came together in a way that changed Fanny's mind. She had been basking in the swift sales of *Rose Clark*. After her "Fanny Ford" series and a whole year of solid columns for the *Ledger*, Fanny had hoped the dust that had billowed from Moulton's vindictive "biography" of her was quite settled. She still walked the streets and saw her name everywhere—on the sides of hand-carts and mud-scows, on perfume bottles and tobacco sacks. Scores of babies were named Fanny and a steamboat and hotel and who knows what else were christened after her, too. People routinely pointed her out as she did her errands, sometimes abusing her for what they considered vulgar writing, but often simply staring, glazed-eyed, as if she weren't real flesh and blood after all, but some automaton in human likeness. These events were sometimes annoying, but Fanny was patient. She tried to imagine how she would have reacted even five years before, to, say, seeing the wondrous Charlotte Brontë (rest her soul) on this side of the water. It was the gossipers she couldn't abide. Moulton's vile accusations—that she was cold, heartless, promiscuous, and manipulative—still found willing ears and, more than once, Fanny had been publicly stung by some heartless comment or blatantly false accusation. How *could* she tout her writing wares like a market hawker, more manipulative and cunning with her feminine charms than the shrewdest businessman could dream to be? How *dare* she entertain such a steady stream of gentlemen callers, and at all hours, with her one young child as witness and the other abandoned? How *could* she lash out so callously at her own *family*, show such disrespect for those who had lovingly reared her?

Last week, in a glow of post-Christmas cheer, Fanny had consented to sit for an hour at a prominent bookstore's front table to sign copies of *Rose Clark* for customers. She laughed heartily as she inscribed the title pages to one after another of the bookstore's patrons, bantering with them. *Yes, ma'am, I do all my writing myself. No, sir, I don't have any fear of eternal retribution. Yes, little miss, I have* two *daughters*. A gentleman approached the table with a look of contempt on his face. He glared down at Fanny with hard gray eyes and cleared his throat. Fanny blinked in shock as the man rapidly told her she was a weasel, a jackal, a common mongrel posing as a pureblood. Fanny felt her blood drain from her vital organs and pool somewhere near her ankles. Spit formed at the corners of the man's working mouth. She was an abomination of womanhood, some devilish blend of ghoul and sensuality sent by Satan to try men's souls! Momentarily paralyzed, Fanny stared wide-eyed and open-mouthed at the stranger. His voice rose. She would twist and scream in the flames of hell, guilt-stricken with the fellow souls she snared for her cloven-hoofed master! Exclamations of shock and wonder reverberated through the bookstore's little crowd. Women hurried their children to the door. Men pulled their necks in like turtles. Fanny pushed her chair back from the table and the man who leaned over it, gesturing wildly with his bible, his voice now louder than any preacher's Fanny had ever heard. She was vain and gluttonous, he shouted, sitting there parading her wares. She was disrespectful and obscene, questioning authority—family, society, and church!

The man threw his bible down and pulled Moulton's book from his pocket. He opened it to some page Fanny assumed he meant to read out loud. Fanny knew she wasn't guilty of anything but trying to express herself, make a living, and raise her two daughters. She knew Moulton's book was a jealous rage from a bitter peer. But to be so publicly blasted stunned her speechless. She blinked at the once-pleasant crowd slowly backing away from her, as if her skin crawled with some unnamed disease, and suddenly felt her blood pumping furiously again. It pounded in her ears and her chest swelled with indignation. To be so accused was horrible. But to see more than doubt, but *belief*, fill the eyes of once-giddy supporters was worse. Fanny sucked a shaky breath, quietly rose and gathered her pen, pocketbook, shawl, and bonnet. She tied her bonnet as she walked away from the table and flung her shawl over her shoulders as she strode through the gasping crowd, past the spitting maniac, and through the heavy glass front door. She could hear Stanley, the bookstore owner calling after her, apologizing, promising something, but then she heard the door close behind her. On the street, Fanny walked as fast as she could, not muttering a syllable or allowing a single tear until she was safely up the four flights and through her own door, into her parlor's alcove and behind its closed door and solid desk. Sitting with her expanse of walnut between her and the world, with her courageous inkstand at her side, always at the ready, Fanny laid her head in her arms and sobbed.

She hadn't lit a lamp, nor even a candle. The fire, stoked by Molly expecting her mid-afternoon return, eventually settled from a merry blaze to a faint glow. Fanny's head ached from her eyelids straight back to the base of her neck, yet she didn't move it from the desk. Her chest was heavy and her fingers and toes were numb. She could try and try and try and somehow, somebody always thought the worst of her. Why was her nature so suspicious? Why did she appear so threatening? All she wanted was to be allowed to live her life as she saw fit without public scorn and judgment. She didn't even want support. She just wanted respect. And tolerance. And the permission to be who she was—a woman, a mother, a writer. *All three.*

Someone knocked and she called out that she didn't want any tea today, or likely any supper later. The knob turned and Fanny sprung her head up and tried to smooth her hair and cheer her features, sure that one of her daughters would soon be standing near her, worried because she'd shut herself up for the last few hours.

It was Ellen, a wrinkle between her eyebrows, but still wearing her usual elfish grin. "Mother, it's been so quiet. Are you all right?"

Fanny smiled weakly. "Fine, my dear."

Ellen's face grew serious. "I know that smile. You're not fine." She rushed to her mother and put her arms around her. "Oh, Mother. Are we poor again?"

Fanny snorted and nestled her cheek against Ellen's soft hair. If only that were the worst thing! "No, my love, we've got money galore," she said. "Don't you worry."

"But it's something else, then?"

James was suddenly in the doorway. "Indeed it is," he said.

"Mr. Parton is here," Ellen whispered.

"I see that," Fanny answered. She returned Ellen's hug and patted her back. "Mother's all right. Just a bad day, is all. I'll have a little word with James, now."

Ellen pulled away from Fanny. Despite the small smile she attempted, a tear rolled down the side of one cheek.

"Darling," Fanny said, wiping the tear.

"Please don't be sad, Mother," Ellen said. "We've got plenty of money now. And we're together, all of us."

"Yes, and having us together, money or not, is the most important thing."

"And you have good, good friends who really know and adore you," James added from his position in the doorway.

Fanny looked up. "That is certainly true." She smoothed Ellen's hair off of her forehead. "Mother's good friend, Jemmy, will probably chase these clouds away."

A tiny smile flitted across James' face.

Ellen kissed Fanny and left her mother in the care of good Mr. Parton.

James ordered tea from Molly as he entered the alcove, went to the fire and stirred the embers. "I heard about this afternoon," he said, as he added wood to the grate. "Stanley Hazelton sent me a note."

James straightened and went to Fanny, still sitting behind her desk. He took her by the hands and pulled her upright. "Your hands are like ice," he said, pulling her toward the fire. "Come." He sat her in the high-backed chair and settled her shawl around her shoulders. "Poor thing." He pulled the low stool close to her and sat across from her on the cricket. "How much more will you suffer?" he asked.

Fanny reached for his hand. "Jemmy."

James held Fanny's hands in his. "Marry me, Fanny," he said. "Let me shelter you."

"I don't need—"

"Of course you don't, but I am offering it anyway. *Again,*" James said.

Fanny smiled a small smile.

"People, like that man," James said. "They don't know you, don't understand what you're doing, how you are, *who* you are."

Fanny looked at the fire, spitting and popping as it devoured the cut logs. She blinked back tears.

James squeezed her hand. "Let them fall and I shall dry them," he said. "I want to support you, not rule you. I want to make your life a little easier, if I can. I want to love you and care for you—"

Fanny's head snapped up.

"*Not* because you're my delicate subordinate and you can't carry on by yourself." He cupped her chin. "Look at you." He swept his arm across the room. "Look at this. You obviously can take care of yourself and your children."

Fanny turned toward the fire again.

"I know you don't need a man's protection. And you know that. But the world doesn't."

"Why is it considered a threat for a successful woman to be single?"

"Why is it a threat for a woman to be successful?" James said. "It's all the same. You're a threat. In so many ways. To our ways of thinking and living."

"How will marrying you change that?"

"It won't, of course. But it might make it a little easier. The next time some rake wants to blast at you for not valuing families or womanhood, you could smile sweetly and say your husband disagrees."

"As if that were the final authority."

James laughed. "You know I have my selfish motives, too. It wouldn't be so terrible to wake up every morning with someone who finds you a delight, who wishes to watch you make your wondrous way along your singular path, who wants to share your joy and pain and dessert."

Fanny smiled. "You don't have to marry me to share my dessert."

"I don't *have* to marry you for any reason," he said. "Except that I love you and want to shelter you, if and when I can—"

Fanny's eyes popped.

"*You'll* shelter me, *too!*" James said. "And we'll hear about each others' triumphs and knocks and will provide a safe, lovely haven for each other."

Fanny searched James' face.

"We love each other, Fanny. You know we do. I never have so much fun as when I'm with you."

Fanny looked deep into James' earnest eyes. He was serious.

"Jem."

"The question is, will you have me? As I am, with all of my foibles?"

"Foibles," Fanny said with a smile.

"I'm eleven years your junior," James said.

"And therefore should have a young wife and children."

"*Should?* I don't want that. I want you. If I ever have children, I hope they will be with you."

"James, I'm forty-four."

"And if we don't have any, then we don't."

"Would you be disappointed?"

"Not a whit. As long as you let me be father to Grace and Ellen."

"They treasure you."

"And you?"

Fanny took a deep breath and smiled. It wasn't like with Charly, when she felt like she'd jump out of her skin whenever he walked into the room. It was different, though still very nice. There was a warmth between them, between Jemmy and her, a steady low-burning fire. Not the roaring blaze of Charly, and, thankfully, not at all the ice box of Samuel. And really, what *was* that roaring Charly flame if it wasn't dependence and ignorance and a certain amount of blind trust in him as a man, in him as her head. She adored Charly, but was it because he was a perfect husband for her or because she told herself he was the perfect husband for her? She really didn't know him half so well as she knew James. She had never asked about his work and hadn't shared in his worries and fears. She hadn't dreamed he would have any—thought him the pillar of strength he made himself out to be in her presence. If she had only known about the financial blows, about his business problems, they might have fixed the troubles together. She could have at least offered her warm arms and loving encouragement. Fanny had loved Charly, she had. But she hadn't known him. She wasn't allowed, or didn't allow herself, to understand him beyond her vision of him. And it was probably the same way with him. She was the ideal wife, then. A little outspoken and jaunty, certainly, but always attentive and nurturing, sweet and tender, with her Charly. They nicely acted their parts, not without feeling, but often without thought.

What sort of marriage could this be, then, if James didn't seek to rule her? This was something Fanny could scarcely imagine. Suddenly, her heart swelled at the mere thought that Jemmy would consider, *had considered* such a new vision. *She* had all of the marital experience between them, and yet it was *he* who was suggesting a new way, an equal, loving way, of being together. "Companions," Fanny said. "Is that what you suggest?"

"Companions is a good way of putting it. I might call us loving companions. Willing companions. Conscious companions."

Fanny smiled. "I do love you, Jemmy. What a plan you have."

"I never would have conceived of it without the best inspiration," he said, smiling. "We'll sign papers guaranteeing everything. Legal contracts. You will always be yourself. You'll run your career, will be in charge of your finances and your daughters. I'll be but a bit player, if I'm allowed . . ."

"Bit player! We shall all be equal."

James' eyes lit up. "Are you agreeing then? Will you consent?"

Fanny smiled.

"Fanny, will you marry me?"

A spasm clutched Fanny's heart. Fear, again. The old demon that would choke the trust out of her. She shook it away. She'd have her freedom. She would never be under his heel. He'd promised that, had promised to put it in writing, to make a legal contract between them. She would never be mastered by anyone ever again. She would always be free to make her own decisions and live her life as she saw fit. And with something new, something she never could have wished for—a support, a love, standing equally beside her. Like Mother and Charly together, only better. Like James. Her Jemmy.

Fanny nodded.

"What's that?" James asked. "Is that finally a yes?"

Fanny smiled. "Yes."

"Yes?"

"Yes, it's a yes! Yes, Jemmy, I'll marry you, exactly on the terms you described."

"That and more," he said. "We will chart our own course. One that is equally wonderful for both of us. We'll make a marriage *our* way, with our personalities and needs and desires." He paused. "And fears."

"Fears?"

"I know you're afraid of getting trapped again."

"And I know that won't happen," Fanny said. "I'll always have my freedom. Freedom within the commitment of marriage *to you*."

James took a breath. "I'm afraid, too, you know."

Fanny wrinkled her brow. "Of being trapped?"

James smiled. "No. Never."

"Then, of what?"

"I'm afraid . . . oh, this will sound silly."

"Go on," Fanny said.

"I'm afraid of losing you."

Fanny raised her eyebrows.

"Some smart writer could come along and impress you—"

"Some smart writer *has* come along and has impressed me a great deal. *You*."

"I mean like, say, Charles Dickens. Now *he's* impressive."

"Charles Dickens is married, in England, and of no interest to me. If anyone should be worried, it should be me. I'm eleven years your senior." Fanny looked down at her still trim figure. "With almost-grown children."

"I adore Grace and Ellen."

"I know you do," Fanny said.

"And I adore you."

Fanny smiled. "No worries, then, about Charles Dickens—"

"Or age," he added.

"We will make our own marriage, then," Fanny said.

"One equally wonderful for both of us," James said.

"That suits our personalities."

"And takes into account our unique needs, desires—"

"And fears," Fanny said.

James kissed Fanny's fingers. "With mutual love and respect."

Fanny smiled. "Until we die. Oh, Jem."

Fanny really considered them married from that moment on. They'd spontaneously spoken their vows and sealed their agreement with a kiss. Still, they must make it legal. No hysteria or hoopla. Just the two of them and a witness. Something simple. Someplace close, but not New York.

"Soon," James had whispered.

In the smart black carriage, Oliver Dyer folded the contract and placed it back in the envelope, then into his inside breast pocket, before pronouncing it legally sound. Oliver, Fanny, and James watched fat, soppy snowflakes drift from the lead clouds and begin to pile up on the tops of bushes and dried perennial stalks. Five minutes later, the carriage stopped in front of a little green church with an enormous bell set in a rusted stand by its front stoop. James alighted first from the carriage, and, as he held his hand out for Fanny, his dark coat was quickly covered with fluffy white stars and his eyelashes blinked away the crystal shapes falling into his face.

"First Presbyterian Church," James said. "Reverend Isaac Stryker, presiding."

"The only person within fifty miles who hasn't heard of Fanny Fern," Oliver said.

"Thank God for some privacy," Fanny said. She swept up her pale-gold satin skirt with one arm and clutched her cream beaded bag in her other silk-gloved hand. She'd had her hair professionally arranged in a series of curls designed to take full advantage of her wedding hat—a dainty, cream-colored satin model embellished with pearls, crystals, and pale gold ribbon. A wisp of a lacey veil hung from the hat's back, the lace matching that at her throat and cuffs.

"You are beautiful," James said, taking her hand.

Fanny stepped down and stood for a moment, the giant puffs of snow falling fast on her head and shoulders. "Thank you, my handsome Jemmy."

They were an hour early for the five o'clock appointment. The Reverend was busy in his parsonage and so Fanny and James went over the prenuptial agreement with Oliver Dyer. They signed it, he witnessed it, and, then, together, they watched, with a little trepidation, the once-dainty snow, suddenly pour down from the sky. The air was so white with flakes, they could no longer make out the parsonage, just fifty yards down the back lane. Tree branches were being meticulously covered, each twig fattened with the white coating. Thank Heaven for the driver's red satin cravat and hat band; they could make him out, standing near the feeding horses under a large oak.

"Should we call him in?" Fanny asked.

"Here's the Reverend now," James said. "We'll soon be back in the carriage."

Fanny Fern and James Parton walked each other down the church's short aisle and stood together before the preacher. They'd already informed him that they didn't want, or need, lectures or bible readings. They recited their vows, vows very like the first ones they'd said to each other the week before in front of Fanny's fireplace. They said them together, slowly, thoughtfully, holding hands. A tear slid down James' nose and Fanny wiped it away with a loving fingertip. Oliver Dyer blinked rapidly. The minister pronounced them married and they fell into a rapturous kiss, a kiss Fanny never wanted to leave.

"The snow is falling fast," the minister finally said.

James pulled a little back from Fanny's embrace. "I love you," he whispered in her ear.

The snow was indeed swirling now. They could no longer see the carriage amid the white blur. The three bundled themselves back into their cloaks and gloves and slogged through the already ankle-deep cover. They buried themselves in the fur robes and blankets the coachman provided and told him to make haste back to the ferry dock. They boarded the ferry and it maneuvered through the fog back to Manhattan, where the snow fell as heavily as it had in Hoboken. They hurried to another waiting carriage, and tucked themselves in. The driver stopped every twenty minutes or so to brush the snow from the wheels, to walk the team through a particularly deep drift, or to give the horses a few handfuls of oats. Eight hours and a mere twelve miles later, the carriage dropped Oliver at Fanny's apartments at Delancy House, where he and his wife were spending the night in charge of Grace and Ellen. Fanny and James continued on to their honeymoon suite at the Waldorf Astoria. The wedding ceremony had only taken five minutes. They'd said their vows, kissed, and smiled at Oliver. But during the eight-hour carriage ride, between snacking on the ham and biscuits Molly had thankfully packed for them and continually marveling at the abundance and wetness of the snow, Fanny looked out the snow-framed carriage window—at the deep drifts, at the rapidly disappearing rooftops—and relived that sweetly brief ceremony over and over again in her head. That little dip of James' head, the rapid blink before he cried.

When they finally sprung, achy and chilled from the cold confines of the carriage and made their way up the snow-packed steps of the hotel, Fanny felt like she'd married James a thousand times. A thousand times married and, yet, no wedding night memories. She grinned at James as he held the door for her. "Time to make you my husband," she said.

Chapter Forty-Three

Fanny Fern and Walt Whitman, New York, Friday, March 14th, 1856

Because a man is a "genius," must one endorse [unspeakable] things and write them down as "eccentricities" inseparable from it and to be lightly passed over? Must intellect necessarily be at variance with principle? . . . I do hold that he is to be held as accountable for his errors as the most ordinary farmer's boy who is unable to spell the name of the plow which he guides.

—Fanny Fern, *New York Ledger*, June 4th, 1864

"I have a confession to make," Walt Whitman said to Fanny Fern as they strolled over the cobblestones of Manhattan's Stuyvesant Square. It was pleasantly warm for March; the thermometer outside James Parton's study window had registered nearly fifty degrees. The brilliant sunshine glistened off the crispy mounds of rapidly melting snow as Walt steered Fanny clear of stray remnants of ice still clinging stubbornly to the cobblestones in some places. He squeezed her elbow and turned to face her, a tall, almost-gangly figure in contrast to her small, round frame. "Do you want to hear it?"

"I will hear anything you've a mind to say, Walt. These last luscious weeks with you have brightened Jemmy's and my days. We like the way you think," Fanny tapped the brim of her bonnet.

"This is serious," Walt said, his deep voice gravelly as he tried to whisper.

"Well, what is it?"

"I've always loved you."

Fanny cocked her head. She knew Walt Whitman wasn't making love to her. She'd never felt his eyes linger on her when he thought she wasn't aware, had never seen a faraway glint in his eyes or a too-hardy smile when she entered the room. Jemmy would never have introduced her to him if he'd suspected Walt had any sort of romantic interest nor would she have consented to his constant society this past month. They were fellow writers. Pioneers in the wilderness of words. They were each dedicated to forging new understandings among their peers and were using their writing to stretch as many minds as possible. "How long is always?" Fanny said to Walt with a smile.

"Since 1853 at least," Walt said.

"Since sometime in June of that year?"

"June 18th," Walt said. "The first time I saw *Fern Leaves from Fanny's Portfolio*."

"Well, I would expect nothing less than your utter devotion," Fanny said. "I wrung my heart dry into those pieces."

"I can see you did. Everyone could." Walt gave a long, slow whistle. "Seventy thousand sold. I cannot imagine."

Fanny tapped his arm. "One hundred thousand, if you count England. And the delicious part is that I chose to take a percentage per book sold rather than a flat rate. You'd best do that with your *Leaves*."

"Really? Considering I've sold a grand total of ten copies, I don't think it much matters."

"Oh, Walt!"

"You, though, will be immortalized! You will be remembered until the end of time as the brave, straight-writing wit that made a difference. How I'd love to do that."

"Bah!" Fanny said. "Everyone makes a difference. Everyone counts the same."

Walt looked skeptical.

"You make as much of a difference as I do," Fanny said. She pointed to a young mother walking an infant in a buggy. "As that woman does." She indicated a sharply dressed businessman eating a sandwich on one of the ironwork and wood benches. "As that man. In fact, you're making a difference right now, at least to me, by providing me with lively conversation and keeping my brain from going to mush. And no doubt your own mind is whirling, conjuring up a new poem or two. We make a difference to each other, in small, wonderful ways."

Walt gave her a charming smile. "Wonderful ways, indeed! Your brain will never falter. How quickly it works! And mine, yes, it spins almost constantly, as well." He laughed and tipped his broad-brimmed hat back just a little. "We're alike that way, I think. Anyway, you interrupted me."

"Oh, forgive me my unfeminine ways."

"Always, though they are more genuinely pleasant than any I've ever seen. But I was speaking of being in love with you . . . and your book, your first book, I mean, though the others are just as stunning."

"Thank you, Walt."

"Do you know what I did? Out of my extreme love?"

"Ate nothing but bread and butter for a week?" Fanny guessed.

Walt shook his head.

"Picked petals off daisy heads?"

"No, Fanny," Walt said quietly. "I imitated your cover."

Fanny stopped walking and turned to look at him. "Well, I could see that."

"And you don't mind?"

"I must say I wondered about it. With your infinite imagination—"

"But they aren't *exactly* the same," Walt said. "*Fern* Leaves, Leaves of *Grass*."

Fanny grew serious. "*Leaves*, Walt. *Tendrils*. Gold Engraving. Even the triple border!"

"But mine is . . ."

"Bigger?" Fanny said, locking eyes with him.

Walt gulped and lowered his head. "To allow for my extra long lines. To be printed as I envisioned them," he stammered. "Oh, Fanny. Are you cross?"

Fanny inhaled slowly and looked at something far away over Walt's shoulder. "Not anymore."

"But you were?"

"Of course. Who wouldn't cherish such a unique offspring? You, of everyone, must know my attachment to my work."

"It won't happen again, I can assure you, and I also assure you that I only did it out of extreme appreciation. I somehow knew we were kindred souls. But I never dreamed we'd actually meet, that one day I'd be talking just like this to you as a friend and fellow artist."

"I'm not so far from humanity, am I?"

"Happily, no. Not at all. Despite your fame."

Fanny rolled her eyes.

"You are everything your column hints you are. There's no cloaking, no pretense. Oh, Fanny, you're a jewel!"

"Walt, you must calm down. People will think you really *are* in love with me! I suppose you never thought, either, that you'd have to actually admit to riding my coattails."

"No, of course not. But, I admit it, I do."

Fanny sucked a sharp breath. "There. What's done is done. And, frankly, I wish you all the best. I know as well as anyone how hard it is to make a living with one's pen."

Walt smiled broadly. "Thank you, my dear."

Fanny turned her cheek to him and allowed him to kiss it. "I must head back now," she said, "and get some things done so I can rest easy tonight knowing I've 'made a difference,' as you say—even though I only plan on straightening up my desk and refilling my inkwell." She pressed his hand. "But do come by this evening, if you can."

"I'm always free to see you. And James."

"Come for dinner, if you like. I know how bachelors dine!" Fanny couldn't miss the thin frame, nor the gusto with which she'd frequently seen Walt partake at their table. She remembered her own lean times, when she and little Ellen routinely shared a meager bowl of milk floated with a few scraps of bread. She'd feign indigestion so her darling would feel no remorse in eating most of the supper.

"I'll see you at seven then!" Walt cried.

As Fanny left to walk the three blocks back to her house, Walt turned and walked in the other direction, south, to the ferry, which would take him across the East River to the small room he rented in Brooklyn. It was a long walk, but Walt never minded it. He had sturdy boots, a loose-fitting coat, and didn't tie his breath off with cravats if he could help it. To think he'd become friends with Fanny Fern! And to think he not only tolerated her, but deeply liked her. That was the real miracle. Walt was fickle in his friendships, especially friendships with those of the weaker sex. Too often, their simpering and moon-ing made him ill. The married ones were usually better, probably because they weren't looking at every man as a meal ticket, but Walt had to move carefully among the wives for fear of arousing jealousy in husbands. Thank God James Parton had more sense than most. He loved his wife, true, but he also respected her, and with that respect came trust.

Sara Payson Willis Eldredge Farrington Parton (yes, she'd told Walt her whole story) was in his circle. Or he was in hers. What mattered was what that meant. Walt clumped along in his sturdy boots, squishing through the mushy piles of mud and snow, and could see the future. He could see his book, *books*, taking up whole shelves in libraries and bookshops, outselling even Fanny Fern's volumes, outselling everyone's. Fanny was right. He'd make a difference. The world would respect his vision, his method, and would profit from it. It was only a matter of time and persistence.

Walt just made the ferry and rested his limbs, leaning against the rail. The splash refreshed him, cold as it was. Once on shore, he traveled the well-loved streets to his street, climbed the three flights to his Brooklyn boardinghouse room, tucked a stack of books under his arm, and soon stood hawking them on the corner of Hicks and Orange. "*Leaves*," he cried. "Just out!"

A young woman and her mother, laden with shopping bags, approached Walt Whitman. "Look, Mother," the young woman said. "A new *Leaves*. I hadn't heard to expect one. May we get it?"

"Of course!" her mother said, opening her purse. "I expect the pieces will be just as wonderful as they always are."

She paid Walt a dollar and he gave the young woman the book. "Eleven," he said under his breath.

"Pardon me?" the mother said, but Walt just shook his head in reply.

As the two women walked away, the young one couldn't wait to peruse the fresh pages. She handed some of her packages to her mother, oh please, oh please, she'd only read *one*. Her mother smiled indulgently as the daughter, still walking, held the thin volume open with one hand. The daughter suddenly stopped. "Why it's different!" she said, dumping the rest of her packages onto the street and gaping at the page before her. "These are poems . . . oh, my. And they're not by Fanny Fern, at all!"

"Let me see that," her mother said, seizing the book. Opening it to a random page, her face reddened as she read. "Why the scoundrel," she said. "Duping us like that! We'll go right back and have a word with him."

They turned to confront the bookseller, but he had vanished. Two children scampered after a squirrel, holding out some sort of treat for it. An elderly man wearing an old-fashioned tweedy coat and carrying a heavy walking stick hobbled just ahead of the children. The cool late-winter sunlight sparkled on the small mounds of messy, melting snow surrounding the man, the women, and the children. The women's heads swung from the street to each other and back again. They set their jaws.

When they returned home, the mother walked straight to the hearth in her boots and gloves and threw the book into the fire. "I've never seen such trash in all my life," she said, turning her back to the smoldering pages. "Leaves?" she sputtered. "More like weeds."

Chapter Forty-Four

Grace Eldredge, New York, Sunday, June 8th, 1856

Climb, man! climb! Get to the top of the ladder, though adverse circumstances and false friends break every round in it! and see what a glorious and extensive prospect of human nature you'll get when you arrive at the summit! Your gloves will be worn out shaking hands with the very people who didn't recognize your existence two months ago. "You must come and make me a long visit;" "you must stop in at any time;" "you'll always be welcome;" it is such a long time since they had the pleasure of a visit from you, that they begin to fear you never intended to come; and they'll cap the climax by inquiring with an injured air, "if you are nearsighted, or why you have so often passed them in the street without speaking." Of course, you will feel very much like laughing in their faces, and so you can. You can't do anything wrong, now that your "pocket is full." At the most, it will only be "an eccentricity." You can use anybody's neck for a footstool, bridle anybody's mouth with a silver bit, and have as many "golden opinions" as you like. You won't see a frown again between this and your tombstone!

—Fanny Fern, *Olive Branch*, June 18th, 1853

Grace shuffled into her bedroom at Delancy House and dropped her armload of boxes in the middle of the floor. She hated packing. She hated moving. Just when she'd gotten comfortable putting her full weight onto the squeaky spots of the hardwood floor, just when she could fall right to sleep and sleep all the way through the night in the snug little room she shared with Ellen, just when she could swallow just about anything without fear that it might get stuck—mother announced she'd bought a house.

A house in Brooklyn, no less. Granted it was pretty with a real staircase and a back garden and a front gate. She and Ellen would get the beautiful front bedroom with the yellow wallpaper, the better to watch for visitors, Ellen said, while Mother and James, of course, would have their own quarters. James' room was in the middle, with an enormous fireplace and one peep of a side window and Mother's was at the rear, so she could better look over the garden when thinking about her column. And even though Grace's and Ellen's room was perfect—it already had ample hooks for dresses and the fireplace screen had two silhouettes, a lady and a gentleman, who both looked to Grace as if they were about ready to dance or speak—dance, mostly—they were still moving to the white house on Oxford Street and Grace hated the wrapping and packing and boxing and carting and unwrapping and sorting and settling.

Grace unfolded a stack of newsprint. There was Mother's column. It appeared everywhere, all the time. People loved Mother. She was witty and smart and the bravest woman Grace had ever seen. Even when they criticized her, people still loved Mother. Grace wrapped her treasures in the newsprint—the tiny glass ballerina James had given her for her birthday, the music box Mother had bought her when they went to Niagara Falls (before they saw Samuel), the ivory comb from Ellen.

Grace had to admit she liked the silhouetted couple on the fireplace screen in the Oxford Street house. That was one good thing about moving there. She imagined it would be pleasant to fall asleep watching the talking, dancing, quarreling, flirting going on between the pair. The gentleman on the screen reminded her a little of Mr. Whitman, who had started coming around all the time. She wouldn't have to think hard to imagine him talking. From the moment he took off his hat to the moment he donned it again, his mouth, whether chewing or speaking, was in constant motion.

Mr. Whitman was an acquaintance of James, Mother said. We must welcome him. We must sit politely through his poetry readings. We must listen to his opinions, which were many and long. Grace wondered that Mother and James could tolerate him. But they more than tolerated him, they adored him. Mother was forever pushing plates of food toward him—ham, beef, vegetables and don't forget the potatoes. Mr. Whitman's quick eyes would spy the choicest slice of meat, the biggest beet, the most perfectly roasted potato and, quick as a snake, his fork would dash out and stab his intended and harbor it to his plate. He'd then make short work of transporting the victuals to his chomping teeth and ingesting them vigorously, all the while telling of his latest coup—how he might have sold *one* more copy of his book.

Mother and James would cheer and whoop with delight. Good for you, Walt, they'd say. You must persevere. You must be patient. The world will know you if it kills us. Mother, especially, has turned herself inside out for him. Grace heard Mr. Bonner asking Mother if she'd like to write reviews, now that she'd so gushed about Mr. Whitman's *Leaves* in her column. But he's sympathetic to my causes, Mother said. Walt understands about real living, about equality, about soul. Mr. Bonner chewed a peppermint from the bowl near the door and told Mother to be careful, that Mr. Whitman cared mostly about Mr. Whitman and like any good chameleon, he'd appear to her exactly how she wanted him to appear. Mother so respected Mr. Bonner that she was speechless. She said she'd be on her watch, but that for now, she saw nothing but fresh air in Mr. Whitman and his works.

Grace agreed with Mr. Bonner. She didn't like the way Mr. Whitman sucked up all the attention, especially if any of Mother's other writer friends were around. Grace didn't like the way Mr. Whitman's smile dropped the minute Mother left the room or as soon as James' back was turned. Grace didn't like the way Mr. Whitman put his big, cloddy boots on the newly polished table or the way he let his cravat hang limply at his throat like a dying bird.

Mr. Whitman never spoke to Grace or Ellen. He had no use for children, though he read plenty a piece about robust boys and bustling girls. He didn't seem to have any real use for women, either, outside of Mother. He ignored wives and servants alike and when they'd arrive, would call them blubbering belles under his breath to Mother. Mother fancied they had a connection, in their abhorrence of the superficial. Mother hated spectacle and anything that smacked of dandyism. She liked genuine human beings, she always said, people who ate and thought and felt. She had no use for prim women who lived on sugar drops or nervous well-dressed men who lived on liquor. She was always telling Grace to eat her beefsteak and loosen her shoes, to take a deep breath and enjoy a joke.

Mr. Whitman looked like Mother's type of person, from the outside. But if you could see him from the inside, like Grace could, you'd see two people—the Mr. Whitman who thought he really believed in all of the egalitarian things Mother did, because of the lusty way he could let himself write about those ideas; and the Mr. Whitman who believed most of all that he alone understood the world and should be afforded the recognition and respect of a king. Everyone was equal but him. He, alone, was better than anyone else, and would take every and any means to make sure others saw the truth.

Grace didn't think that was equal at all.

Grace imagined that the gentleman on the screen would whisper some derogatory comment to the woman on the screen, perhaps about Hatty Jacobs or Oliver Dyer or some other true friend of Mother's, and the woman on the screen would realize she'd been duped and would point her finger at the man on the screen and order him away from her table, away from her home, away from the vicinity of her beloved children, and out into the cold streets that rebuke him, and out into the crowds who would see him as the blowhard he is, and out, far away from the safety of their little family, to feed himself, to applaud himself, to glory in his poetry all by himself.

Chapter Forty-Five

James Parton, Brooklyn, Saturday, October 4th, 1856

Well, old Ink-stand, what do you think of this? Haven't we got well through the woods, hey? A few scratches and bruises we have had, to be sure, but what of that? Didn't you whisper where we should come out, the first morning I dipped my pen in your sable depths, in the sky-parlor of that hyena-like Mrs. Griffin? With what an eagle glance she discovered that my bonnet-ribbon was undeniably guilty of two distinct washings, and, emboldened by my shilling de laine, and the shabby shoes of little Nell, inquired "if I intended taking in slop-work into her apartments?" . . . Do you remember that, old Ink-stand? . . . And don't you wish old Griffin, and all the little Griffins, and their likes, both big and little, here and elsewhere, could see this bran-new pretty house that you have helped me into, and the dainty little table upon which I have installed you, untempted by any new papier-mache modern marvel? Turn my back on you, old Ink-stand! Not I. Throw you aside, for your shabby exterior, as we were thrown aside, when it was like drawing teeth to get a solitary shilling to buy you at the second-hand shop? Perish the thought!

—Fanny Fern, *New York Ledger*, July 19th, 1856

James Parton was the happiest he'd ever been. Strolling down Oxford Street, he nodded hello to that wonderful Mort, "Doesticks," and his future wife, Grace's new friend, Nanny. The young couple reminded James of Fanny and himself— genuinely in love. It would be a joyous wedding, theirs, almost as magical as his and Fanny's snow-swept ceremony. James was thrilled he'd finally convinced Fanny to marry. They'd forged a beautiful life together, despite her fears, and despite the constant hovering of the press.

They had resided for a few months in Fanny's apartments at Delancy House and started a slew of happy traditions. James especially liked their morning newspaper and coffee time. They'd sit with a stack of the day's periodicals and a pot of coffee between them and would read snippets aloud to each other, sometimes in giggles, oftentimes aghast. Look at this, they would say, pointing to some article of injustice or another. How can this be true? Why doesn't anyone do something? And it was usually at this point that Fanny would get that lovely determined look on her face, set her jaw, and dash away to write a column in response. "Speak the truth, my love," James would call to her as she rummaged for paper or sharpened her tip, "and shame the devil."

"I shall, indeed," Fanny'd reply, sometimes over her shoulder, sometimes under her breath, depending on how upset she was.

In early spring, after James had introduced his new acquaintance, Walt Whitman, to Fanny, she bought a house in Brooklyn and, once they finally settled in, were all very happy there—he, Fanny, Grace, Ellen, and their seemingly constant visitor, Walt. James had his biography work, which was getting more and more acclaim. His career success was modest and steady, nothing like Fanny's, but few were. He tried to explain that to Walt the other day, that there was no point in *trying* to reach Fanny's star, as Walt sometimes seemed so determined to do. *Trying* undermines the whole thing. It was like trying to get over the flu, or trying to fall in love, or trying to digest your food more quickly. One had no control over some things. Fanny had lived her life—passionately, responsibly, intelligently—and the world bent an ear. Of course, James and Fanny would try to help Walt all they could. Heaven knew, neither were strangers to writerly wants. But Walt simply didn't understand that he would be more successful if he spent more time listening and writing from his heart instead of trying to capture and versify the latest in-vogue sentiments in hopes of catapulting himself to the forefront of progressive thinkers.

Fanny agreed with James on that point, but was in as equal a quandary about how to tactfully make the idea known to Walt, who seemed to thrive on procuring names of Fanny's connections, invitations to meet her editors and publishers, introductions to her mentors. But Walt had a secret, a secret he told nobody but James. Walt had connections of his own (or else he had made good with Fanny's) and his forthcoming literary work was to be touted and pushed as the next best-seller, as the next *Fern Leaves*. James knew Fanny would be more than thrilled for Walt. She didn't hoard success as her own private experience. Still, Walt wanted to surprise her with his latest and had sworn James to secrecy. The only trifling was that his advance hadn't come through and he needed a small sum, say two hundred, to hold him until the royalties could be collected.

James, a master of his own living, had put just that amount aside to travel to New Orleans to complete his research about Andrew Jackson. He'd loaned the sum to Walt a little over a month before and was sure it would be soon repaid, certainly in time for his spring travels. Every time James came upon Walt, he'd rub his hands expectantly, waiting for the moment Walt would deliver the news of his literary good fortune to their little crowd. But Walt would just as quickly thwart James' hope with his downcast eyes and a quick shake of his head, and James would know not to ask any painful questions.

Most likely, on such occasions, the attention would soon turn to the young people. Grace, Ellen, Louisa, Mort, and Nanny were the centers of James' and Fanny's lives. Fanny's daughters were young ladies now. Ellen was already twelve and fast outgrowing her childhood roundness, though was far from outgrowing her sharp social analyses and pointed interrogations of her elders. Most children ask unending rounds of questions as toddlers. But such questions usually abate as those children assimilate into society and understand the workings of it. In this point, Ellen seemed to have inherited her mother's mind. She was forever questioning the status of living, why *that* woman, there, isn't coming to the theater, why *that* man asks for money, why people walk around *that* little girl. Granted, Ellen was bright enough to understand the superficial answers people gave to one another, but what James thought most amazing was that she refused to accept such platitudes at face value and would continue her lines of questioning—why are there no theater showings for the poor? what can be done for orphans? how does one become dependent on alcohol?—that James and Fanny would revel in the opportunity for deep discussion.

They'd taken family trips to orphanages and prisons, alms houses and factories. Afterward, Fanny would be grave for hours, sometimes days, until she could write about the injustices. James, Ellen, and Grace would talk about the specifics—the dirty sad man in the corner cell or the mill worker with that horrible cough—and their musings, too, would make their way out of Fanny, through her pen. James admired Fanny's ability to write to the core of the issue, to view the chaotic mesh of social problems and to gracefully pluck out the heart of the beast and display it on the page.

And then there was Grace, who, at fifteen, was still too thin, from nervous energy, both James and Fanny thought, though she was fast becoming more at home with herself. She walked with more ease, ate with less angst, and slept more soundly than she ever had. She was still easily frightened and, in new circumstances, would hang back, figuratively, and sometimes literally, behind Fanny's skirts, until she was comfortable with her surroundings and the people occupying them. Thank goodness Grace had Louisa now. James was as happy as Fanny was to welcome Louisa Jacobs to their home. Hatty had been such a steady friend to Fanny, even in those Boston years, even when Fanny's family was cruelest to her. James would always be grateful that Hatty, alone, it seemed, had stuck by Fanny, even when Nat wouldn't, especially when Nat wouldn't. The thought of Nat still made James bristle. They hadn't spoken a word to each other, nor had Nat and Fanny, for years. It was sad, but true, how family ties sometimes rotted like wet rope. Immersed too long in the moldy damp of self-centeredness, and before you know it, it has all turned to mush.

Fanny's losses sometimes still weighed too heavily upon her. There were days that she'd sink into a stupor of melancholy, complete with sick headache, and only a day or two spent mounded beneath her coverlet, a damp, lavender-scented cloth over her eyes, would eventually revive her. Conversely, there'd be midnight panics when she'd wake moaning and shivering. James would rush to her side to find her wild-eyed, still dreaming and utterly withdrawn. He'd whisper and pet her hair until she regained her sensibilities and realized that the imagined danger had passed, that she was safe and whole and healthy in her husband's arms. She was a woman with too enormous a heart. That was what James loved about her most. It was also what he'd like most to see changed. Fanny opened up, like a sunflower, whenever she thought she spotted the sun. She was loathe to spy opportunism in others, preferring instead to always always always place herself in their shoes, to wonder what *she'd* be like, how *she'd* manage through the gruesome life of another. Oh, to suffer slavery like Hatty or social indignities like young Louisa or literary rejection like Walt. Fanny empathized with everyone, and not just waifs on street corners that enlightened her columns and ravaged her spirit, but with those in her closest circle—with her family and friends. Too often, James knew, the most generous minded ignored the sufferings of their closest allies. Too often, people acted as Nat had toward Fanny.

Those days under the coverlet, those nights quaking in fear—once over, were never spoken of. That, in itself, conveyed Fanny's strength. She never counted up her pains, never displayed them or languished in them. Yet, they gnawed at her. She felt every injustice, every death, every slander, every blow, James knew, still and always, keenly and hot. Fanny felt them all and chronicled them in her words so that others could recognize suffering, so that others might not block their own knowledge, might extend compassion.

Oh, Fanny, Fanny, Fanny. James sighed. He was so very blessed and happy with his life. He'd gladly shoulder all of his wife's suffering, in an instant. If he only could.

Chapter Forty-Six

Fanny Fern, Brooklyn, Saturday, October 4th, 1856

"The hand that can make a pie is a continual feast to the husband that marries its owner."

Well, it is a humiliating reflection, that the straightest road to a man's heart is through his palate. He is never so amiable as when he has discussed a roast turkey. Then's your time, "Esther," for "half his kingdom," in the shape of a new bonnet, cap, shawl, or dress. He's too complacent to dispute the matter. Strike while the iron is hot; . . . There's nothing on earth so savage—except a bear robbed of her cubs—as a hungry husband. . . . After the first six mouthfuls you may venture to say your soul is your own; his eyes will lose their ferocity, his brow its furrows, and he will very likely recollect to help you to a cold potato! Never mind—eat it. You might have to swallow a worse pill—for instance, should he offer to kiss you, for of course you couldn't love such a carnivorous animal! Well, learn a lesson from it—keep him well fed and languid—live yourself on a low diet, and cultivate your thinking powers; and you'll be as spry as a cricket, and hop over all the objections and remonstrances that his dead-and-alive energies can muster. . . . If he was my husband, wouldn't I make heaps of pison things! Bless me! I've made a mistake in the spelling; it should have been pies-and-things!

—Fanny Fern, *True Flag*, April 23rd, 1853

Fanny burst through the front door. "James!" she called. But there was no answer. "He's gone for his walk," Molly called up from the kitchen.

Fanny slammed the door behind her and pounded up the stairs to her room. Once there, she paced, clumping over the carpet with her damp boots, struggling to untie the bonnet with her still-gloved hands. Of all the things!

She'd quarreled with Walt. Really quarreled this time. About Louisa and James and money and equality. Fanny was blistering. Just who did he think he was? A *man*. Yes, of course, it always came down to that. Walt Whitman was a man, a self-serving man, an opportunistic man, yet definitely, and in his words, *thankfully*, a man. He was man first, friend second. Man first, visionary second. Man first, of course, always, because he could be.

Fanny stopped pacing and stood before her looking glass, still struggling with the bonnet ties, her chin quivering. She thought *he* was different. She thought he was like James. Really believing the words he tossed around in the air and on paper. Really believing in equality and possibility and freedom. But from his comments about Louisa living with them, equality apparently ended with whites. And from his comments about women's sexuality, equality absolutely ended with men.

Fanny couldn't untie the bonnet with her gloves still on. She unbuttoned her gloves and yanked them off, then worked the knot in her bonnet loose. It'd started innocently enough, in mutual conversation with Robert Bonner. Walt had been dying to meet him, sure he could be one of Bonner's well-paid celebrities, like Fanny and Charles Dickens. Naturally, Fanny'd arranged the luncheon meeting, at a lovely new Broadway café, and did everything possible to promote Walt and his writing and his ideas. She'd already written, specifically, about him, twice, despite numerous suggestions from Walt to mention him, by name, associated with this idea or that one. Even last week, when Fanny had breathed notice to him about the column she was writing about masquerading the streets in men's clothes, he thought she could write a line, *just a line, Fanny*, how she dressed just like Walt Whitman, or how Walt Whitman would approve, or how she'd met her friend, Walt Whitman, while thus attired.

The column came up again, at luncheon. The point is, she told Walt, and Robert, that she, Grace, Ellen, and Louisa wanted to taste the freedom men take for granted, the freedom to stomp through puddles without worrying about soiling a hem, the freedom to walk with a God-given stride, to breathe all the way down to their stomachs, and to be ignored physically and respected intellectually in every exchange between doormen and waiter and shopkeeper.

Walt eyed Robert, sitting poker-faced. Walt cleared his throat. His voice boomed. What could Fanny be thinking? Exposing her daughters to danger and scrutiny? What if they'd been found out? What of their reputations?

Fanny had been shocked silent. What was this talk? From her Walt? Writer of:

The wife—and she is not one jot less than the husband.
The daughter—and she is just as good as the son.
The mother—and she is every bit as much as the father.

Fanny pulled the bonnet ties apart and yanked the bonnet off, flinging it onto her dresser top. Her stomach twisted thinking of how she'd promoted him, even wrote a glowing review (the only one) of *his Leaves*, never mind that he copied her title, binding and form, never mind that he suggested she write other, grander reviews for other papers, despite her sworn allegiance to write only for Robert.

But Walt didn't know Robert. That point was made crystal clear. As Robert sat, silently chewing his bread and butter, quietly eating his ham and peas, sipping coffee, dabbing his lips, Walt trenched himself deeper and deeper into what Fanny considered the pit of common ignorance, the pit of social typecasting and logical inaccuracies meant to *sound* progressive, all while polishing the status quo.

Of course Fanny had argued. Why should a woman's reputation be ruined because of a pair of trousers? They'd received such delicious treatment, free of wandering eyes and more respectful of their actual words and actions than ever before. Men are respected simply because of their sex! And women don't know what they're missing.

Walt lowered his voice then, replied that if Fanny didn't rein her daughters in, and soon, they would be missing the chance for a good match, despite her positioning them opposite Louisa.

Fanny was outraged. Positioning them opposite Louisa? What could that mean?

That although she was extremely *attractive*, Louisa was, well, *older*.

She was twenty-one. How was that old?

Well, maybe it wasn't just age.

Fanny's mouth dropped. He was talking about skin color. He was insinuating that Fanny housed Hatty's daughter to enhance her daughters' potential courtships, to provide a standard to measure against. Her dear friend's daughter. Her dear friend's *colored* daughter.

Fanny raged about how Hatty, *only* Hatty, had stood by her during those bleak Boston times, had provided her with, quite possibly, the best and only true female friendship she'd ever witnessed. If she could ease Hatty's brow by taking in Louisa, now, when Hatty so badly needed writing time, well, then Fanny would do it. It was because Fanny understood how it was when a woman had a story to tell, had a mission, a message. It was because Hatty and Louisa were family, more like family to Fanny than her own had proved to be. Black or white. Rich or poor. Male or female. Hatty and Louisa were the most decent of people, of *people*, Walt.

Of course, Walt quickly agreed, but I'm thinking only of your daughters' futures.

And what did Walt think would harm their futures more, Fanny asked, dressing up in men's clothes, or dressing up in men's clothes with a colored friend?

Walt turned a little pale, then, and Fanny almost regretted her harsh tone. But then he motioned to Robert, in that little manner, that implied all men thought alike, even progressive thinking men, like *he and Robert*, and Walt lowered his voice in such a condescending way and spoke to Fanny as if she were a simpleton. You don't really believe there are no differences between the sexes, do you, my dear?

My dear?! *My dear?!* Fanny was nobody's anything, thank you very much. And, aside from biological equipment, she saw no difference between the sexes.

Walt grinned. Biology indeed. But, it's more than equipment. It's everything that goes along with the equipment.

Robert choked a little, on his soup, Fanny noticed, as she turned her blazing eyes to Walt for explanation.

You've forced me to be blunt, Walt said. I'm sorry, but men and women are designed differently, ingeniously, I might add. Men are driven, day and night, by desire. Walt looked meaningfully at Robert then, but Robert kept his head down over his food. And, women, he added, haven't the foggiest idea what desire is.

I beg your pardon, Fanny blasted.

You misunderstand me. I realize you have a desire to write and to love and to raise your wonderful daughters. But, I'm talking about physical desire. Desire for the flesh.

Fanny raised her eyebrows. Was he saying women had no physical desire?

Well, *some* might, at times, but depending on their, and here Walt Whitman gave a little cough, *profession*, such women usually grow rather quickly out of those desires.

Grow out of? Profession?

Men's desire was the basis of women's survival. Without men's desire for women, women would have long ago been swept away as useless. Women's power rests in men's desire for them.

Fanny's cheeks glowed. And what of women who are deemed undesirable?

Exactly the point he'd been making about her daughters. Undesirable women had a harder go of it. She, herself, was tribute to that way of thinking.

"Me, undesirable?" Fanny sputtered.

Not to James. James must love you dearly to allow himself to be in your shadow.

But to any other *real* man? To one bright enough to understand about money and power and equality and how women must only rise to man's armpits? And I best learn this so as not to endanger my daughters' success in the husband-catching department?

Now, Fanny. Be reasonable.

Fanny rose, snatched her bonnet and gloves from the empty chair beside her and, rummaging in her pocketbook, tossed a five-dollar note onto the table. "There. Because you don't have money enough to pay for your own lunch, despite being the first sex, and despite the fact that women's only contribution to this world is in regard to men's physical satisfaction."

Robert clucked his tongue and grinned and Fanny saw the look of chagrin on Walt's face then. He'd played to win Robert over at the expense of their friendship, never conceiving that Fanny and Robert's friendship, forged these past several years, was unshakable. Fanny remembered Robert's earlier warnings about Walt and realized he'd been right. She was a fool not to have seen his opportunism, his self-promotion. She'd thought they were kindred spirits. She'd thought they shared a vision of life and people and society that few others understood. She'd thought he was a friend.

Chapter Forty-Seven

Walt Whitman, Brooklyn,
Saturday, October 4th, 1856

"A man will own that he is in the wrong—a woman, never; she is only *mistaken.*"*—Punch.*

Mr. Punch, did you ever see an enraged American female? She is the expressed essence of wild-cats. Perhaps you didn't know it, when you penned that incendiary paragraph; or perhaps you thought that in crossing the "big pond," salt water might neutralize it; or, perhaps you flattered yourself we should not see it over here; but here it is, in my clutches, in good strong English; I am not even "mistaken." Now, if you will bring me a live specimen of the genus homo, who was ever "to own that he was in the wrong," I will draw in my horns and claws, and sneak ingloriously back into my American shell. But you can't do it, Mr. Punch! . . . A man own he was in the wrong! I guess so! You might tear him in pieces with red-hot pincers, and he would keep on singing out "I didn't do it; I didn't do it."

—Fanny Fern, *Musical World and Times,* May 7th, 1853

Walt Whitman lay on the narrow bed in his room on the third floor at the end of the hall. He was curled on his right side, facing the window, and stared at the brown brick of the boardinghouse next door. His feet were cold but he didn't cover them and he jumped every time someone slammed a door or dropped a pot downstairs—he was that shaken. He held a scrap of paper between his hands, hands that were clasped together as if in prayer.

But Walt wasn't praying. He didn't believe in that. In moments of struggle you had to pull yourself along with your own thoughts and your own plans. Fools waited for some divine intercession, or worse, allowed life's feet to trample them, because of some twisted reasoning that suffering made one better. And Walt was no fool. He'd been in tougher tangles than this one and had always floated free. This little misunderstanding with Fanny and her editor would be just that—a misunderstanding. A little one. Small, especially when one thought of the expanse of friendship and the resiliency of it. The forgiveness for misspoken words. The allowance for human foibles. Walt could picture himself saying these very things to Fanny. He could picture those flashing eyes softening, once more, enveloping him in the generosity he'd apparently pushed a bit too far.

Maybe he'd flatter Louisa some, the next time he called, enough to show Fanny he thought her a fine young woman, but, *dear Lord*, not enough to give any false idea of his intentions. And he'd comment about how solidly Grace and Ellen were growing up, how strong-minded they were becoming and about how more men should know the joys of conversation with intelligent women. Just like he'd known the joys of conversing with their mother. Just like he'd known such a wonderful friendship with Fanny Fern.

Walt pressed his lips together in regret. Could it be he would miss her? He had never before felt anything even close to regret about any woman. Men, certainly. Always and endlessly. Walt sighed. But a woman? He examined his physical reaction—tight stomach, hollow chest, clenched jaw and hands and groin. It was physical, yet, it wasn't physical. Not *that* way. He had tried to explain it to her, a man's desire, a desire he assumed would be as encompassing even if directed at women. And that was the unalterable truth of it—men's desire was directed at women, not exchanged with women or reciprocated by women. Walt shuddered. This was biological common sense. It was Fanny who had gone too far, who had stretched the cover of the egalitarian drum she incessantly beat. She'd ruined it between them. Stimulating as she was, she couldn't see past her own nose to give him the little push with Bonner he'd needed. If she just could have tipped Bonner's ear his way, just would have engaged him in Walt's accomplishments as she was always so good at doing.

But Bonner had sat like a pig at the trough, steadily slurping and chomping his way through every course, oblivious to the conversation, oblivious to Walt. Walt moaned on his bed and drew his knees up closer to his chest. He let out a surprisingly rattling sigh. Oh, this remorse. Even now, with wonderful Fanny, it definitely wasn't physical regret and loss. It was emotional. The loss of a friend. The loss of an equal. She'd be so pleased.

And, there was, too, the issue of the money. Now that Bonner had turned him down flat, Walt would have to confide his bad news to James. There was no advance, no publishing contract. He'd been hoping, was all. He'd been sure, because of Fanny's and James' connections. And who could blame him? Any blind man could see he wasn't the first to have thought of it. Fanny's parlor was bursting with starving writers, eager to be her friend, eager to know her other friends. That Doesticks, for one. Mortimer Thomson. Walt winced. *Hilarious* writer of two-bit farce and not-quite amusing parodies. Why was he such a hit when Walt's brilliance had to be force fed to the public? Doesticks paraded his fiancée in nearly every evening, and while Nanny made it in close with Grace and Louisa, he, sly creature, spent every minute buttering up James and Fanny. Walt had to feign interest in the simpleton's newspaper articles, his little stories and poems, just to join the conversation. Interest, at least in Fanny's parlor, had moved on from his *Leaves*.

Walt relaxed his hands and uncrumpled the paper between them. He had almost burned it, with the other little notes of Fanny's, silly jokes and hastily scrawled invitations. This afternoon, after the debacle with Bonner, one by one, they'd all met the flame: "Come tonight for there is to be a fiddler!" "Jemmy is cooking again and you know that means there will be too much to eat. Please help!" "Smoking lessons start promptly at nine (preceded, of course, by dinner). Do come and learn this valuable social skill."

But he couldn't burn this one, not this one about his *Leaves*. She'd written right to his little book, addressed it as the immortal work it was destined to be, and in doing so, promised him the ripe review she'd later write for him in the *New York Ledger*. Oh, happy time! And just a few months before.

"Leaves of Grass"

> You are *delicious!* May my right hand wither if I don't tell the world before another week, what *one* woman thinks of you.
> "Walt"? "what *I* assume, *you* shall assume!" Some one evening this week you are to spend with Jemmy & me—Wednesday?—say.
>
> *Yours truly,*
> Fanny Fern

She'd even used his words right back at him, proving she had understood his work, predicting the glowing report she'd give of his tiny book a few weeks later. It was, of course, precisely because she'd used his words that he couldn't destroy this little note. Fanny Fern had quoted him. Fanny Fern had called him delicious. Well, she had called his work as much. Funny how when Walt covered up the salutation, this little missive could almost be read as a love note. If he could somehow transpose the direct addresses, then *he* could be delicious and his work could be more properly quoted. In fact, maybe he'd write just such a translation in a letter to some friend or two. Maybe he'd do it soon enough, too. He'd have to have his own story about their falling away, his and Fanny Fern's, because if Walt knew anything about Fanny, he knew from the way her eyes blazed at lunch that, truthfully, he would never be able to talk himself into her good graces again. He had betrayed her, just as so many others had. And if she couldn't forgive husbands and fathers and brothers, there was little hope for him, just another struggling writer.

Walt stroked his beard. He'd seen it in more than a few pairs of eyes—the assumption that there might be more between them than friendship. But he'd never felt any jealousy from James, and had never felt anything but maternal care from Fanny. Not that she wasn't a passionate woman. That she sat upon James's knee in full view of everyone and regularly kissed him on the mouth was proof enough for that. Oh, curses, what he'd said about desire. He had talked himself into circles. How was he to know female desire? How was he to know desire for a female? He knew himself, and he knew his observations, and that had to be good enough for any poet.

Yet, most people didn't have poetic sensibilities, and most people assumed a universal trajectory of desire, and most people equated desire with all things masculine. This was a fact Walt could bank on, even when he hadn't a single royalty check to his name and had only the occasional tiny sum to cash for local articles. He could cock his head a certain way, smile, lift his eyebrows, and whatever woman he was talking with would melt just a little around the edges and her male companion, if she had one, would dry crisp and brittle, like bacon left too long in the pan. It was for most people, these people, that Walt needed to protect his reputation. Protect it from whatever the likes of Fanny Fern might write. He was a poet for them, all of them. He would be remembered and celebrated by the masses. His good name would flit across the common mind and be branded upon the average heart. The average man would understand perfectly and the average woman could be made to understand by her husband. The problem with some women was that a little too much education ruined their natural sweetness, addled their brains. It was a matter of balance. Women needed enough education to be tolerable in conversation and to be progressive mothers and cheerful wives. But too much knowledge cultivated a diseased anger and perpetual dissatisfaction—such was the case with Fanny. Walt snorted. Truth told, the likes of Fanny and James were a liability to Walt and to the future of his work. They read too much into his words, took too literally what he was just supposing, expected some sort of uniform methodology and philosophy from him—a poet.

Walt took a deep breath and let it out. He uncurled his legs and shook them hard to warm them. He *was* a poet. He was a *man*. He could be anything. He could be everything. He was who he was when he was it. He was Walt Whitman and his name would go on. Longer than the likes of Fanny Fern. Longer than anybody. He'd pave the way. He'd sow the seeds. He'd rake the soil and he'd pour out the water. If it was the sweat of his brows or others' didn't matter so much as that the liquid nourished his work. His work was more important than his life. More important than any life. It was a life of its own.

Chapter Forty-Eight

Ellen Eldredge, New York, Thursday, May 26th, 1859

Here I have been sitting twiddling the morning paper between my fingers this half hour, reflecting upon the following paragraph in it: "Emma Wilson was arrested yesterday for wearing man's apparel." Now, why this should be an actionable offense is past my finding out, or where's the harm in it, I am as much at a loss to see. . . . Think of the married women who stay at home after their day's toil is done, waiting wearily for their thoughtless, truant husbands, when they might be taking the much needed independent walk in trousers, which custom forbids to petticoats. And this, I fancy, may be the secret to this famous law—who knows? . . . One evening, after a long rainy day of scribbling, when my nerves were in double-twisted knots, and I felt as if myriads of little ants were leisurely traveling over me, and all for want of the walk which is my daily salvation, I stood at the window, looking at the slanting, persistent rain and took my resolve: "I'll do it," said I, audibly, planting my slipper upon the carpet. "Do what?" asked Mr. Fern, looking up from a big book. "Put on a suit of your clothes and take a tramp with you," was the answer. . . . But oh, the delicious freedom of that walk; after we were well started! No skirts to hold up, or to draggle their wet folds against my ankles; no stifling vail flapping in my face, and blinding my eyes; no umbrella to turn inside out, but instead, the cool rain driving slap into my face, and resurrectionized blood coursing through my veins, and tingling in my cheeks. . . . Now, if any male or female Miss Nancy who reads this feels shocked, let 'em! Any woman who likes, may stay at home during a three weeks' rain, till her skin looks like parchment, and her eyes like those of a dead fish, or she may go out and get a consumption dragging round wet petticoats; I

won't—and I positively declare I won't. . . . they who choose may crook
their backs at home for fashion, and then send for the doctor to straighten
them; I prefer to patronize my shoe-maker and tailor. I've as good a right
to preserve the healthy body God gave me, as if I were not a woman.

—Fanny Fern, *New York Ledger*, July 10th, 1858

Ellen Eldredge was growing into a woman, too, although nobody noticed. She
was fourteen and a half, had been bleeding every month for six months, but
still had what mother called baby fat. Chubby little cheeks, squishy arms, jiggly
belly. Ellen woke up each morning expecting that grand metamorphosis she'd
witnessed in nearly every one of her schoolmates—the sudden appearance of
breasts, the whittled waist, the swan-long neck. But it hadn't happened, not
yet. And so everyone assumed Ellen was still a child, because she still looked
like a child, despite her regular bleeding, which proved she was turning into a
woman, at least on the inside.

Ellen missed Louisa, who'd gone back to live with Hatty—really missed
her. Ellen didn't tell anyone, but she often walked around with a stomachache
these days because she missed *too much*. Hatty was finally writing her book,
was finally living her dream, but she needed Louisa's help with all the chores
at Uncle Nat's in order to find enough time to work with Maria Child. Louisa,
alone, seemed to understand Ellen, seemed to sense that she, too, was joining the
ranks of womanhood. Louisa was halfway between sister and mother to Ellen.
She was much older than Grace and never fussed at Ellen over the last lemon
drop or the nearest seat to the fire. Louisa seemed to already have formed a
mother's instinct, even though she wasn't even married yet and certainly didn't
have any babies. She was patient and understanding and smiled sweetly without
comment as Ellen either turned somersaults or sat properly at the tea table.
Everyone assumed that only *Grace* might possibly miss their extra sister, only
Grace might be affected by two solid years of bonding with Louisa, only *Grace*
had a gentle-enough heart, or nervous-enough sentiments, to warrant anyone
worrying about her tender feelings. But nobody understood how Ellen missed
Louisa. Nobody even noticed.

Ellen missed more than Louisa. She missed Louisa, and, of course, she
missed their old house on Oxford Street, with its wonderful bedroom view of
the street and the comfort of the mother and father silhouettes on the fireplace
screen. But most of all, she missed Nanny. Yes, Nanny. *Grace's friend.* Nanny
had been Ellen's friend, too. Ellen had watched with pride as their dear, beautiful Nanny became Mrs. Thomson, wife of Mort, the dashing "Doesticks."
Oh, Ellen was jealous, to be sure, as were Grace and Louisa. You'd have to
be a fool not to notice Mort's lush dark waves, his thick curly eyelashes, and

honey-colored eyes. He'd burst into a room just radiating fun, and had saved many a dull evening with his natural buoyancy and spark. Nanny had been just right for him, though. She was fun, too, and so pretty, and just the right age—between Grace and Louisa. It all was perfectly right and beautiful, yet Ellen knew she shared secret fantasies with Louisa and Grace of *being* Nanny, of having gorgeous Mort's thrilling attention, just for one day or one night. Ellen wasn't too young for that.

Nanny had cut her hair short! They'd all played at dressing up in men's clothes and had had frequent outings together, and with Mother, to understand what Mother called male freedom and female enslavement. It was true that corsets, multiple skirts, tight shoes, bonnets, gloves, bags, collars, and shawls kept women forever occupied and fretsome. Not to mention restricted. Ellen loved feeling real rain on her cheeks, instead of some misty damp that might have gotten through both parasol and veil. Ellen loved feeling wind through her hair, instead of the hint of breeze through hat and ribbon and hairpins. Ellen loved stomping, flat-footed, through puddles and dirt without worrying about delicate hemlines, silk stockings, or paper-thin gator tops. But the day Nanny cut her hair was the day she'd become Ellen's idol. Nanny alone had had true courage. The courage to make a statement, to assert her own freedom.

Mort loved her all the more for her short hair. It was soon after her close brush with the shears that she found out she was expecting. What happy times for all of them, though Mother's jaw sometimes seemed clamped with worry when she'd spy Nanny's round belly through the layers of her dress and cloak and shawl. Mother insisted Nanny call her when the baby was coming. She wanted to be there herself to help Nanny through it.

Ellen knew Mother was worried because Aunt Jessie had just died in childbirth. Uncle Richard was heartbroken, and so was Mother. "So many women," Mother wailed through the closed double doors of the parlor. "So many good, good women."

James said hush now, you'll frighten the girls, but Ellen was already frightened. She had never expected Nanny to die. Not Nanny! Strong, incorrigible, effervescent nineteen-year-old Nanny! Mother had come back the next day, the day after she was called to the young couple's house, and said dear Nanny'd bled for twelve hours after little Mark was born. She had bled and she'd bled and she'd died. Mort was crushed, so depressed he'd sent the baby to stay with relatives in Minnesota. So were they all—crushed. Mort, though, lost weight, didn't bathe, wore the same stained cravat for weeks. We need to offer him our strength, Mother said, with droplets of tears hanging from her lashes. Ellen didn't feel as if she had any strength to give him.

Mother and James encouraged dear Mort to visit, and often. They doted on him, reading to him, wrapping him in wool blankets, and turning his face toward the fire. They pushed bread and butter on him at every hour and kept his glass full of wine. They were all in mourning. Dear dear Nanny. And suddenly, after several weeks of this, Ellen's stomachaches clenched extra hard with women's knowledge—if it could happen to Nanny, it could happen to anyone.

With Louisa and Nanny both gone, Grace and Ellen were the only young women left to try to cheer up Mort. At first Mother smiled approvingly when the girls would perform skits and sing for him, evenings. The day he came to supper in the yellow vest, celery cravat, and smelling of "jockey club," Mother's demeanor changed. She still adored Mort—who couldn't? But she said she suddenly felt that he'd outgrown his mourning and didn't require the constant ministrations of an entire family anymore. Maybe it was because Mr. Whitman had so recently disappointed her, too, or maybe, as James explained, Jessie's and Nanny's deaths reminded her of her mother's and sister's. But in any case, Mother allowed Mort's visits, but didn't entirely encourage them. And more often than not, she'd place her chair between his and Grace's when they'd sit for tea.

Mother hadn't noticed Ellen's diminished appetite for tea, nor her pensive stares into the fire while Grace and Mort worked puzzles together. Ellen was growing into a woman. Ellen missed Louisa and Nanny and Brooklyn. But nobody noticed. Not James, although he sometimes pushed her to work a puzzle with *him*. Not Mother, although she often added a dash of peppermint to Ellen's tea or brushed her fingers through Ellen's curls as she relaxed by the fire. Leastwise *Grace*.

Chapter Forty-Nine

James Parton, New York, Thursday, May 26th, 1859

Now if there is a proverb that needs re-vamping, it is "The patience of Job." In the first place, Job wasn't patient. Like all the rest of his sex, from that day to the present, he could be heroic only for a little while at a time. He began bravely; but ended, as most of them do under annoyance, by cursing and swearing. Patient as Job! Did Job ever try, when he was hungry, to eat shad with a frisky baby in his lap? Did Job ever, after nursing one all night, and upon taking his seat at the breakfast-table the morning after, pour coffee for six people, and second cups after that, before he had a chance to take a mouthful himself? Pshaw! I've no patience with "Job's patience." It is of no use to multiply instances; but there's not a faithful house-mother in the land who does not out-distance him in the sight of men and angels, every hour in the twenty-four.

—Fanny Fern, *New York Ledger*, August 8th, 1863

James pulled the door of 303 East Eighteenth Street, *hard*, to *slam it*, but at the last minute he let the door bounce off the heel of his boot. Fanny was probably working upstairs and he didn't want his burst of temper to interrupt her. He closed the door behind him, then shook himself irritably. What was wrong with him? As angry as he was, he still forever worried about bothering people. He clumped up the two stairs to the street and stood for a moment under the scanty shade of the sapling the city had just planted. The tree was still too young for James to discern its species from branch growth. The buds were there, but were seemingly slow to mature. The overgrown stick held all sorts of promise but it would take years to actually enjoy the benefits of this tree. Just like me and Fanny, James ruefully thought, an unfamiliar tightness striating his chest. All sorts of promise. And although most days, the promise of their love and the promise of their egalitarian commitment kept James' head floating well above his shoulders in contentment and pride, there were sometimes days like this one. Days when James didn't understand what he was doing with such a strong-minded woman, days when the snow-swept promises they'd made to each other over three years before seemed just short of coming true. They were equal, yet he sometimes felt like such an underling. They were equal, yet it was *her* income they'd used to purchase this glorious house. They were equal, yet he had to put on his top hat and play bill collector.

She was *making* him harangue Walt Whitman, *making* him beg for the paltry two hundred back. Anyone could see Walt didn't have it. It had probably kept him in sandwiches and ale for a dozen months, certainly hadn't been squandered betting or on wild nights. Asking Walt for two hundred was like asking Grace to stop stuttering when she was excited. The less attention paid the matter, the more likely favorable outcomes might result. But Fanny had been hurt and when Fanny was hurt, she masked it with rage. Walt Whitman would pay, one way or the other, for all the slights and digs and rubs he'd abused Fanny with these months. James had to admit that Walt was behaving abominably. Hinting at some sort of romantic crush. Postulating about the *natural* roles of women as mothers and wives, as bearers of strong, robust, free-thinking *men*, as better kept and less educated than men for their own good. He'd written, "One genuine woman is worth a dozen Fanny Ferns; and to make a woman a credit to her sex and an adornment to society, no further education is necessary." James winced. Fanny'd taken that one hard. To be fair, so had James. He'd underestimated Walt Whitman. They both had. Or maybe they had overestimated him. But whereas James just wanted to drop the connection, Fanny wanted to squeeze some kind of remorse or enlightenment or regret out of her lost friend. And she would do so by pressuring him *this* way, financially, the only way she guessed he'd feel it, since he hadn't seemed concerned to lose her friendship, her mentoring, her respect.

It was true that Walt seemed remorseless. James had often seen him, belly up to some rail or another, perfectly content to let anyone buy him his ale or oysters or tea. Walt had a funny sense about him that the world stood at his elbow, ready to serve, ready to promote him to the higher planes faster and more spectacularly than anyone else. And, yet, James' English upbringing shuddered at the task Fanny had forced upon him—to go to Walt Whitman in his hovel and to try to shake two hundred from the cuffs of his threadbare trousers. Thank Heaven Oliver Dyer had agreed to accompany James. James would never have been able to knock on the door alone.

James met Oliver a block from Walt's dwelling. Apparently Walt had moved back in with his mother, not being able to afford the rooming house on a sometime-journalist's wages. James and Oliver approached the house and were admitted by a woman in a headscarf who apologized, saying she was still wiping down the stairs, so they must be careful on their way up them. Was *this* Walt Whitman's mother? Scrubbing the stairs on her hands and knees while her son waited for visitors in his room?

James and Oliver gingerly stepped up the wet steps behind the mother, who knocked like a servant on her son's door. Walt admitted them, but not before inquiring of his mother when dinner would be ready and giving her instructions to keep the noise level down as he was conducting a business meeting. Yes, dear, the woman said, bowing at the visitors like they were royalty. She obviously had no idea James and Oliver had come to collect a past loan, more likely thought them important publishers or literary fans.

Walt closed his bedroom door then stretched out on his bed, leaving James and Oliver standing awkwardly near his washstand. Walt's beard had grown long and unkempt and he lounged on his bed clad only in his sleeping pants and a half-buttoned, very-wrinkled shirt. "Gentlemen, please sit," he said from the bed, flailing a loose arm in the direction of the chair by his desk.

Oliver took the chair and James perched on the desk's edge.

"I'm sure you know why we're here," Oliver said. "You've received the court's notices."

Walt snorted. "I'm sorry to say that I haven't got the two hundred, James." He turned his face so he could look at the men. "I haven't got anything. Just some chicken roasting downstairs, this comfortable mattress, and the light breaking through this window pane. Nothing of value to the likes of you, but all of value that I really need."

"It seems you made use of the two hundred when you had it," Oliver said.

"We must give to each other. We must care for our brothers."

James was suddenly very aware of the smell of roasting chicken wafting up the freshly scrubbed stairs to the bedroom where Walt Whitman lounged without any care of paying back the loan he'd lied to James in order to secure. He suddenly had a better understanding of Fanny's outrage and exasperation when it came to this man. "You told me the loan was temporary," James said. "That you'd pay it back before I'd need it for my trip to New Orleans."

"And what do you care for money?" Walt blasted. "Have *your wife* write you a check for your trip."

James felt the color rise to his cheeks.

Oliver rested his hand on James' arm. "This is between you and James, Walt," he said. "You know James and Fanny keep independent livings."

Walt leveled his eyes at Oliver. "It's between me and Fanny and you know it."

Oliver sucked a slow breath. "What have you got for the loan, Walt?"

Walt perused his sparsely furnished bedroom. "One roasting chicken, one comfortable mattress, rays of light falling through the glass."

"Walt," Oliver said.

Walt glanced at the opposite wall where a small bookcase held a few dozen books. "Some books, you see. And two pieces of art." Above the bookcase, held by a tack, was an engraving made from a daguerreotype of Walt himself, done by a friend for the first edition of his poetry book. Walt looked younger in the drawing, more robust. He had one hand in his pocket and the other on his hip, as if in challenge. His hat was tipped at a rakish angle and his shirt collar was open, exposing his throat like a workman. His beard was trimmed and significantly darker than it presently was, yet there was the same look about his eyes, the same fierce desire mixed with the sense of entitlement and perhaps some disdain. James caught Oliver's eyes. Fanny wouldn't want that. The other piece of art was a painting, probably done by some street artist—a nondescript snowy landscape, not horrible, but certainly nothing special.

James walked over to the bookcase. There were all of Fanny's books lined up on the top shelf. Under them was a smattering of novels—adventure tales and ghost stories. James felt ridiculous scanning a poor man's bookshelf for plunder.

"We'll take the landscape and a half dozen books," Oliver said.

Walt brightened. "To call it even?"

James winced, then nodded, his back still toward Walt and Oliver.

"Spectacular," Walt said.

James unclenched his hands to reach for some of the books on the shelf.

"Don't touch the top shelf," Walt called out. "If you please," he whispered.

Chapter Fifty

Fanny Fern, New York, Thursday, May 26th, 1859

Is my article for the *Ledger* ready? No sir, . . . it is NOT! Have I not been beset, since I left my bed this morning, with cook, chambermaid and sempstress? Have not butcher, baker, and grocer been tweaking that area-bell unceasingly, about matters which must be referred to my unpostponable decision? . . . Is not my head as woolly inside as out, with . . . the settling of the thousand and one little matters which take up, and must take up, the precious morning hours, which, alas! show for nothing, and yet which no housekeeper may dodge, even with her coffin or a prospective article for the *Ledger* in sight?

—Fanny Fern, *New York Ledger*, October 26th, 1861

"Molly!" Fanny yelled down the back stairs. "I really cannot wait any longer for that tonic. My head is splitting."

But Molly was already maneuvering around the turn in the narrow staircase holding a tray with a sloshing glass. "Can't you see I'm coming, ma'am?" Molly lilted, a smile playing along the creases near her eyes and mouth. "You might use the bell next time."

Molly had been with Fanny since Fanny had first moved to New York and wouldn't have it any other way. No namby-pambying with this mistress. If Fanny was happy, everyone knew it, and if she wasn't, the same was true. But Molly never took offense. Who could? It wasn't as if Fanny's irritation was directed at Molly. Fanny merely suffered from one of her headaches and Molly knew the whole household would probably see the sun rise at least once or twice before the blasted thing dissipated. That knowledge in itself, coupled with the debilitating pain, would make anyone a little cross. Truth be told, Molly felt sorry for her mistress sometimes—always juggling six times more than any living creature ought to, and ninety-nine days out of a hundred with a smile. Fanny lived her life with refreshing honesty and Molly, for one, appreciated that. In a world where women were encouraged to sit around parlors like wax dolls, sighing and mooning over missed stitches in their petticoats, Molly appreciated a mistress who, often as not, rolled up her sleeves and helped knead the bread, took a broom to the back steps if they needed it, and snitched as many cookies from Molly's cooling racks as the children.

Molly's skirts, brushing upon the railing, sounded like a hoard of buzzing insects to Fanny who hung over the top rail, as if her sharp gaze would make Molly, and the tonic, appear quicker. "The bell is too loud," Fanny said.

Molly reached the top of the staircase. "Of course it is," she said. "You holler if you want to."

"I don't mean to holler," Fanny said. "I just can't afford to feel ill today. I've got so much to do and I mean to do it all, headache or not."

"Ma'am, surely you could take an afternoon and rest? Let me bathe your temples with the camphor."

Fanny took the glass from the tray and swallowed the tonic. It was a natural remedy, recommended by the apothecary when she had refused to take the prescribed laudanum. Fanny'd seen too many people crippled by that particular treatment and she preferred letting the body heal itself whenever possible. This tonic was made with willow bark tincture, a remedy the apothecary said he had learned from a Mohegan friend. The tonic never completely relieved the headache—only time could remedy that—but it softened the pain to the point Fanny could function. She put the empty glass on the tray and squeezed Molly's forearm. "No time, Molly. My column's due."

Molly returned to the kitchen, muttering. She'd make a clear soup this evening and a hearty piece of roast beef with loads of vegetables. That would fortify Fanny.

Fanny returned to her room and yanked open the back of her dress. First thing, her corset must go. How she hated the thing. She would live all day long in her nightdress if she could. But not today—she had work to do. She pulled on a loose pair of James' trousers, a pair he'd recently given her since she wore them around the house more than he ever did, and one of his old shirts. Her hair was neatly coiffed, as it always was, and she removed a few combs to let it hang freely down her back. She dabbed some cotton soaked in camphor at her temples and took a deep breath. The headache slinked to some deep cavern of her skull, pulsing like the villain it was, but at least contained.

Fanny paced. She had a column to write by the end of the day and no firm ideas. She had Grace's blue silk to hem for tonight—Grace was going to the opera with Mort Thomson, the infamous "Doesticks," a match that was moving far too quickly to Fanny's way of thinking. She'd promised Ellen a turn in the park so they might happen upon some of Ellen's new schoolmates and maybe a social invitation. She still had boxes to unpack from the move last month, not to mention a thousand errands to attend to in setting up this new home of theirs. She'd promised some handpicked recipe to a magazine columnist who was doing a piece on the culinary habits of prominent New Yorkers. She had a stack of mail from her readers, deeper than her elbow, to attend to. She had this new set of problems Harriet Beecher Stowe had written about from England—that Harriet's book was selling like crazy but she wasn't receiving a penny of profit from the sales (Fanny had put a provision against just such treatment into her last contract, a provision James and his lawyer friends dubbed "copyright"). She had appointments to arrange—a tour of an uptown orphanage, a meeting with a group of women intent on increasing literacy among runaway slaves, her usual visit to the women's asylum in hopes that her regular presence might ward off abuse. And on top of all that, Walt had written another zinger about her in a small Brooklyn newspaper and James was angry that she insisted he collect Walt's loan and serve him up a heap of humble pie. It was all too much to think about, yet Fanny couldn't ignore any of it.

Fanny paced faster. So many injustices, great and small, public and private. "I could write flaming words," she blasted out loud to her newly painted ceiling and freshly papered walls, to the lovely Turkish carpet she pounded over and the old inkstand waiting patiently for her at her desk. It was no wonder she had a headache!

A fruit cart, with one shriekingly squeaky wheel, crawled past her open window. She looked down upon the bent frame of a weathered man calling hoarsely that he had apples, figs, and bananas. He walked with a mild limp, pushing the happily painted cart over the bumps of the cobblestones. Fanny's arms ached in empathy. Her head pounded, imagining herself clomping over the cobblestones, bent with age and affliction, calling for customers. It was so much like when she went begging to be published in Boston, so much like dragging little Ellen around town in all manner of weather and under wilting stares. The fruit man's voice floated down the street. Apples, figs, bananas, he called. Fanny sighed. Bananas! Now that would be a treat. And as if she'd read Fanny's mind, Molly was standing before the suddenly quiet cart arranging for bananas. Thank goodness for small blessings. Fanny would have a banana today. She would walk in search of friends with her sweet Ellen. She would devote at least an hour to writing letters of thanks to her grateful readers. She would give a recipe, her raisin nut pudding, to that young scribbling cohort when she called. She would arrange her appointments for next week, when this blasted headache would certainly be quelled. She would speak with James the moment he came in and make it right between them and forget about Walt Whitman forever. And she would hem Grace's dress, with love and trust, so her daughter might glow on her night out, and while she sewed, a column would come to her. It would. It always did.

Molly knocked on Fanny's door and delivered a banana, which Fanny instantly peeled and enjoyed. She wiped her fingers on her handkerchief and settled herself in the chair by the window with Grace's watercolor dress and her needle. To think of Grace possibly falling in love made Fanny hold her breath. She took a stitch, then a dozen more. Not Grace. No, never. She mustn't even try. More stitches. Grace was too frail. She could end up like Nanny, pale as an egg against her damp pillow, the bloody mess Fanny couldn't keep up with staining her bedclothes, the sheets, the mattress. It fairly pumped out of her in the end. Just like sister Ellen and Jessie and Mary Stace. Just like so many. And Mother. Stitch. Stitch. And Charly. And little Mary Stace. Fanny wiped her eyes on her handkerchief, careful not to spoil the lovely silk.

But Grace had been so *light* lately, as if she burned a hundred candles on the inside. The glow moved out of her very pores, oiling her speech, pinking her cheeks. She'd never looked better, not since before she'd had to go away. Lord, would her child ever outgrow that time? Would Grace ever be able to shake the cold fingers of Charly's parents from her neck? In that way, Mort was as good for her as she was for him. They were balm for each other, a healthy balm of affection and respect.

Fanny guessed she knew something of Mort and his way of thinking. He'd been crushed about Nanny's death and was too soon to turn to Grace. He meant to bury his grief in her, in Grace, Fanny's barely of age daughter. Grace had made enormous strides since rejoining the family, true, but was she ready to be a wife? Really ready? It wasn't all sugarplums and love pats. Fanny, with her three marriages, knew a thing or two about married life. There could be heady times, no doubt, especially in the beginning. But after a year or so of mooning over morning toast, plenty of couples lost reverence. They slid into a craggy place of stony silence and hurling words. Or worse. Fanny shuddered. Sometimes, she couldn't stop thinking about Samuel and their scant years of debilitating union. Even so many years later, as Fanny sat in her comfortable new home, married to wonderful James and stitching Grace's gown, her forehead broke out in tiny beads of sweat and her heart thumped against her breastbone thinking of some of those times, like that time in the kitchen.

Fanny bit her lip. Not all marriages were like that. She must remember. Always remember. Dear Charly. They'd been so young! So untested. Fanny hadn't given a thought to the dangers of childbirth, though she'd certainly seen and heard about the many women who didn't survive the ordeal. Still, those women weren't her. Those women hadn't her vitality and robust good health. Yet, after Ellen and Mother and little Mary Stace, Fanny had been terrified. What if her idyllic existence was finished? What if her time, too, was up? Charly had been a great comfort, the best, and, of course, here she still was and with Ellen to boot. Fanny sighed. She and James had hoped to be blessed and she'd shown all the signs last year. But the terrible cramping had turned those ideas around in a hurry. Fanny had been so sad, but not as sad as James. It was then that Fanny realized how much he *did* love Grace and Ellen, how natural his fathering skills were.

But Grace! Oh, no. She was the most delicate of them all. Despite her growing signs of courage and the quick wit and vivid tongue she more often displayed, Fanny knew her daughter. She *knew* her! Grace would be crushed by marriage. Fanny bit her lip. Grace would be crushed by marriage as most women are. Marriage was the hardest way to get a living. Oh, that more women could gain an education and use their skills and brains to earn their own keep. As she did. And that has really been the key to their success—hers and James'. Fanny's independence, funny as it sounded, was what made for their perfect companionship. Fanny didn't have to submit her wishes to another's, on any terms, whether in regard to where they'd live, how they'd travel, or—*Fanny shivered*—how many onions to put in the pot. Fanny's heart pounded fast again.

No, not all marriages ruined women, whether in body or spirit. She must remember. She must remember Charly and James. Yes, James was good.

Just then Ellen knocked, ready for their outing. Grace's gown was finished, but Fanny's heart was still unsettled. Fanny hung the dress on a peg, fanning out the skirt, and changed back into her own dress, then pulled on her bonnet. She and Ellen walked the few blocks to the iron-fenced green, Stuyvesant Square, then tramped round and round on the six-sided pavers. Ellen met quite a few acquaintances and traded engagements with several. Fanny's feet trudged forward, a smile on her face and bright comments abounding. Yet, her heart bent toward home, toward Grace, resting for her evening out, and all that might happen to her if this evening went as well as everyone guessed it would.

She must delay things. She must warn Grace of every possible danger. She must put Mort to the test, to see if he might be one to turn sour and cruel behind a closed front door. Perhaps a bit of gravy *on* his meat, instead of on the side, as he prefers, or maybe an accidentally crushed hat? They mightn't laugh so much when he tried to be funny, and, instead, could feign injury. How would he react? What was he capable of doing? And Grace must know his limits as well. She must flirt with another in his hearing. Drop lazily on the sofa instead of jumping up for a game of cards. She must bristle with a headache, moan with indigestion—in short, act herself. He must know who she is and she must know the same. They must really understand what will transpire if they go forward together.

She and James had begun perfectly. At least to Fanny's way of thinking. James always talked about how he loved her from the first, but Fanny preferred that their friendship preceded their love, *her* love, at least. *This* really *was* love.

A studied, growing, companionship, sparked, of course (and here Fanny smiled to herself) by passion. But it was the passion that grew out of a mutual respect and admiration, not the other way around. Fanny was more attracted to James every day. And more grateful for his gracious love.

Ellen decided they could go home, having filled her pocket with cards. She would be fine. It always took some adjustment to feel at home in a new home. Fanny smiled at her darling Ellen, who would make short work of this adjustment, as she had made of all the others. She wasn't like Grace, fragile as a bird, inside and out.

Fanny's heart beat fast again as they made their way home. Surely it was almost tea time. James would be back. Ellen and Fanny opened their front door and were assaulted with the smell of Molly's roast beef and vegetables. Strong vegetables. That's what Fanny smelled. Cabbage and rutabaga and loads and loads of onions. Her heart stuttered, then pounded desperately. She pulled at her bonnet ties. Everything was suddenly too confining. Beads of sweat rolled down her sides and dampened the curls around her face. Onions, onions, onions.

James was walking toward them. Walking toward them with an ugly look on his face. He was furious. Quietly, tightly furious. Ellen didn't notice, chattered away and ran off to count her cards, despite James' anger, despite the haunting odor of roasted vegetables. Ellen left and James was talking. Clipped, urgent words that cut through Fanny like a blade. He would never be forced to degrade himself so again. He would never feel so subservient in his life. He would never . . .

Fanny's head swam in a sea of onions and fear. She clamped her hands over her chest to quiet the pounding. She must escape. She must survive!

James would never go against his values and beliefs again. He would be her companion, but not her underling. He would . . .

Fanny gasped. The pain in her head beat behind her eyes, pushing pushing pushing. She must get away. She must not be trapped.

"I got a painting," James said. "One horrible painting and some neglected books. I felt like I was robbing him. I felt the criminal, seeking justice against a child." James pulled a badly executed painting from behind the foyer table. "Here it is," he said. "Is this what we needed so badly?"

James cracked the painting over his knee and the smell of onions rode that action straight into Fanny's bones. She gasped and stumbled back out the door, pulling at her bonnet ties, clutching her chest.

"Fanny! Wait!"

She ran out the door and down the block, in the opposite direction of the park, to the edges of the developed area. It wasn't far, maybe a quarter mile, but Fanny felt like she was again traveling the ten miles from Boston to Newton. Ellen on the train and Grace, a prisoner of the Eldredges. No money. No friends. With only cold and hunger and the threat of Samuel ahead of them. Fanny ran and ran. She ran until she came to the open fields and then she ran through them. Over rocks and dried wildflower stalks, through sticky mud and down small dirt mounds until she couldn't hear a single sound of the city, until she couldn't smell a single onion. Fanny collapsed, face down in the field, grief and pain and anger knotted like thread inside her. Oh Charly. Little Mary. Mother. Sister Ellen. Mary Stace. Sister Louisa. Jessie. Nanny. Nettie. Clare. Nat. And *Grace*!

Fanny sobbed. No, not Grace. Never Grace. She'd already ruined her. She'd already abandoned her and no amounts of money and care and attention and safety would ever change that. Grace's heart had been damaged as surely as if she'd survived rheumatic fever. And, *she*, the great Fanny Fern had done it to her. The magnanimous Fanny Fern. The wise and courageous Fanny Fern had *left* her daughter in the hands of turtle-hearted disciplinarians. And now she was watching Grace propel herself toward death! She was watching her chase the mirage of marriage.

Even *James* was not as he seemed. *Even James.*

Fanny wept onto her folded arms for what seemed like hours.

Slowly, she became aware of a sound. No, several sounds. Muffled breathing. Sparse, erratic chirps of meadow starlings and sparrows. Little coos of a mourning dove. The slow steady hum of bees. Just like at Fanny Miller's house. And the same smell of green all around, and flowers, and earth. A flower church. Fanny breathed in the green smells. Grass and trees and, yes, there it was, wild ferns. Eyes clamped tight, Fanny turned her face to the direction of the smell and her eyes leaked anew. Quiet. Resigned. Ah, Mother! A whisper touch against her forehead. Green green green on the breeze. Damp ground beneath her cheek. Then, another sound, and, suddenly, Fanny knew exactly where she was. She wasn't on the road to Newton or in the kitchen with Samuel or walking beneath the trees with Mother to Fanny Miller's house. She was lying in a field, a half mile from her spacious new home on East Eighteenth Street in New York, wrapped firmly in James' loving arms, listening to him weep softly on her shoulder.

Chapter Fifty-One

Grace Eldredge Thomson, New York, Tuesday, September 16th, 1862

Nothing like the old-fashioned long "engagements," say we. Then you have a chance to find out something about a young man before marriage. Now-a-days matrimony follows so close upon the heels of "an offer," that it is no wonder our young people have a deal of sad thinking to do afterward. There are a thousand little things in daily intercourse of any duration, which are constantly resolving themselves into tests of character; slight they may be, but very significant. Some forlorn old lady must have an escort home of a cold evening; she walks slow, and tells the same story many times: see how your lover comports himself under this. He is asked to read aloud to the home circle, some book which he has already perused in private, or some one in which he is not at all interested: watch him then. Notice, also, if he invariably takes the most comfortable chair in the room, "never thinking" to offer it to a person who may enter till he or she is already seated. Invite him to carve for you at table. Give him a letter to drop in the post-office, and find out if it ever leaves that grave—his pocket. Open and read his favorite newspaper before he gets a chance to do so. Mislay his cigar-case. Lose his cane. Sit accidentally on his new beaver. Praise another man's coat or cravat. Differ from him in a favorite opinion. Put a spoonful of gravy on his meat instead of his potatoes. Ah, you may laugh! But just try him in these ways, and see how he will wear; for it is not the great things of this life over which we mortals stumble. A rock we walk around; a mountain we cross: it is the unobserved, unexpected, unlooked-for little sticks and pebbles which cause us to halt on life's journey.

—Fanny Fern, *New York Ledger*, July 30th, 1859

What a wonderful, terrible time to be alive! Lately, Grace Thomson's emotions shifted more often than New England weather. She was married to the handsomest writer in the world! She was writing, like her mother, for the incredible *New York Ledger*! She was pregnant with her first child . . . but during this horrible war!

Grace lifted her skirts to climb the four steps to her home—*her* home, for she was now mistress of her own happy crowd. She shifted the parcels in her arms—her writing notebook, a peck of apples from the square, precious yellow yarn she would knit into booties—and fit her key into the keyhole.

Little Mark ran to her at once. "Mother, Mother, Aunt Ellen's here!"

Grace snatched up her darling three-year-old—she never thought of him as Nanny's anymore—and hugged him close. "I told you she'd come stay while Father was away."

Mort had left that morning to write another correspondence story, a newspaper account of life at the front lines that would be printed and reprinted in every respectable Northern publication. This war made for strange occupations. This war forced introspection. On a more practical level, this war was stealing the men. Mort's younger brother Clifford, when he wasn't begging Ellen for her hand, was off, like hundreds of others, on military missions to save the Union. Thank Heaven Mort worked as a war correspondent. *Only* a war correspondent. His duties brought out a curious mixture of judgment, envy, and respect in others. Yes, he was often in the thick of peril, but he almost never was near what Clifford called the real fighting. Yet, Mort was, of course, still in danger. Each time he left to do more research might be the last time Grace would see him. But Grace mustn't dwell on negative visions. She felt better when she told herself that Mort sometimes left to write a story and always came back to deliver it to his editors.

Besides the comings and goings of Clifford and Mort, Ellen's frequent visits, and the constant whirl of little Mark, Mort's father, Old Mr. Thomson, stayed with them, too. Despite his advanced age, Grace was grateful for his steady company. Old Mr. Thomson provided the starved-for male presence they all needed.

Ellen came out from the kitchen and took Mark from Grace. "You shouldn't be lifting such a big boy! Did you get apples? Maureen said you would try."

"Good day to you, too," Grace said, kissing her sister, then holding up the peck. "Glad to see I'm good for something."

"Bah," Ellen said. "Come see your article in the paper! It's just a little below Mother's this time."

"Did she write about the war, again?"

"Of course. She's crazier than ever over this. I swear she'd marry President Lincoln if anything happened to James."

"Hush your mouth," Grace said. "You know Mother and James adore each other. And knock on wood, now! Nothing will happen to James."

"I'm just saying I'm glad to have a little vacation here with you until Mort gets back. Mother and James have guests every evening and the war talk never ceases."

"It *is* important, Ellen. There's so much at stake. Think of Hatty! And Louisa!"

"Of course it is!" Ellen said as she led Grace into the kitchen, where she and Maureen already had the pie crusts rolled out. "But I want to talk more about you and Mort and the baby!"

Mark pulled on Grace's skirt. "Am I the baby?" he asked.

"You are for now," Grace said. "Until your little brother or sister comes."

He thought this idea over for a moment then said, "Let's make pie!"

Grace smiled. "Just let Mother change out of her nice dress, hmmm? You get started with Aunt Ellen and Maureen."

Maureen took Mark to the pump to let him wash the apples and Grace gave Ellen a hug. "We'll talk about the baby all night, then! I'm so excited."

Ellen smiled. "You look it. I've never seen you happier."

"Oh, Ellen! Married life! It *is* delightful. I have no idea what Mother was so nervous about. You really should give more thought to Clifford."

Ellen rolled her eyes. "Not this again."

"He's crazy about you."

"And what of me?" Ellen asked. "Mother always warns against one-way affection."

Grace smiled, suddenly more fatigued than she thought she was. "We'll talk more. All night if you want. About Clifford and Mort and the baby and everyone. But, would you mind starting the pies without me? I'm suddenly strangely tired."

Ellen instantly agreed, and once she surmised that there wasn't anything alarmingly wrong with Grace that a nice rest with a cool cloth over her brow wouldn't fix, she happily fit the first apple on the peeler and showed Mark how to turn the handle.

Upstairs, Grace unbuttoned her shoes and slipped her dress over her head. She'd stopped wearing full corsets several months before, but unhooked the mother's version she felt obligated to wear on days she went out. It was fairly loose and supportive and, especially with her new empire-waist gowns, hid her growing belly. Still, the number of eyes that quickly ran over her body and assessed her condition was increasing by the day. Mother said she didn't *have* to stay in, didn't have to hide. She could do what she liked as long as she felt strong enough. Grace, herself, wholeheartedly accepted this view of motherhood, but what sometimes bothered her was that not everybody else did.

Walking home from her errands that afternoon, feeling the growing number of appraising stares, Grace understood, *really understood*, the social scrutiny her mother had battled for years. It was one thing to have progressive beliefs and to expound upon them in like-minded company over plum cake and wine, but it was another thing altogether to hold onto one's beliefs walking among the neighborhood ninnies with their barbed tongues.

Grace poured water from the pitcher into the bowl, splashed her face and dried it. Lavender would be better, after all, than a cool cloth. It was more nerves than a coming headache. Grace dabbed lavender oil on a handkerchief and patted her temples, then stretched out on her bed holding the scented linen to her nose. She took a steady rush of deep breaths, the tiny bird-like quiverings in her chest quieting to something close to sleep. Social scrutiny was the least of her worries. Grace wanted this baby and she wanted it alive and healthy. She wanted this war to end so Mort could write from a position of safety. And she wanted to hold tight to the glorious feeling of almost-calm she had embraced since the very beginning of her courtship with her wonderful Mort. There had always been Mother and Ellen in her mind, in her life, had always been the idea of a safe haven in them. But although Grace basked in their comfort and love, she never quite trusted it, was so sure it would be snatched from her should she let her guard down for an instant. Things were different with Mort. She felt she could move mountains with him by her side. She could speak, she could write, she could mother a houseful of needy souls. And she could do so without the bird in her chest protesting, with the bird happily resting most of the time. *That* was the difference. Her sense of peace. As long as she had Mort.

She took another deep breath, inhaled the calming lavender, and tried to push away any thoughts that might agitate the bird in her chest. Her baby would be fine. The country would be fine. She would be fine. As long as she had her Mort.

Chapter Fifty-Two

Fanny Fern and Grace Thomson, New York, Tuesday, December 23rd, 1862

"Little Benny" so the simple head-stone said. Why did my eyes fill? I never saw the little creature. I never looked in his laughing eye, or heard his merry shout, or listened for his tripping tread; I never pillowed his little head, or bore his little form, or smoothed his silky locks, or laved his dimpled limbs, or fed his cherry lips with dainty bits, or kissed his rosy cheek as he lay sleeping. I did not see his eye grow dim; or his little hand droop powerless; or the dew of agony gather on his pale forehead: I stood not with clasped hands and suspended breath, and watched the look that comes but once, flit over his cherub face. And yet, "little Benny," my tears are falling, for somewhere, I know there's an empty crib, a vacant chair, useless robes and toys, a desolate hearth-stone and a weeping mother. "Little Benny." It was all her full heart could utter; and it was enough. It tells the whole story.

—Fanny Fern, *Musical World and Times*, May 14th, 1853

It was sometime after midnight. Everyone else—Mort, James, Ellen, little Mark—had succumbed to the ache for sleep, after whispering precautionary goodbyes, of course, leaving Fanny watching alone by Grace's bedside. The room glowed with a steady fire and candles enough for Fanny to have a clear view of Grace's flushed face. Fanny's stomach had worked itself hard as a cannonball.

She couldn't chastise herself enough. How could she have been fool enough to leave Grace for an instant, knowing she'd just had her baby and knowing, too, as she'd always known, deep in her blood, how fragile Grace was. If only Fanny hadn't been selfish, if only she hadn't struck home after that first paltry post-birth week for a leisurely bath and a fireside dinner with Jem. If she had stayed by Grace's side beyond when everyone told her it was safe to go, beyond when even Grace told her to refresh herself because Mother can't you see I'm fine and I'm stronger than you give me credit for and you are not always the rock you think you are.

Would Fanny never learn? Over and over again, she let people die. She watched them fall ill, and watched them worsen, then submit, under her miserable care. She couldn't save anyone, not a one! Sister Ellen grew paler by the second under Fanny's ministrations. Mother's mind flew from her fevered body, Little Mary whimpered to the very end, and even Charly, oh God, her beloved Charly—Fanny couldn't even save her loving husband. She'd missed even the first signs of his fever, hadn't seen his growing exhaustion, missed the small chance to keep him strong and vital, hadn't seen through his smiles and words to know how terribly sick he so quickly was. She should have sent for a doctor that first night, when his cheeks were flushed, that first day, when Ellen's red sheets needed constant changing, that first afternoon, when Mother refused her tea, that first minute when cheerful Mary grew sour. And now, she'd done it again. Fanny hadn't seen the signs of trouble, hadn't protected her loved ones from every possible danger.

It was Grace who'd convinced Fanny in the end, convinced her to leave the nurse room to *rest*, as Grace called it. Fanny had left for one evening, a fortnight ago, the same evening Grace had jovially called Little Mark to her bedside for company because he'd been begging for nothing else since Baby Effie had been born the week before. Mort hadn't arrived back from the battlefields yet and Maureen had thought Mark's peevishness was the usual sibling jealousy so sent him right up as soon as Grace called for him. It was but an hour after Fanny herself had left. Would she have noticed the change in Mark? Would she have spied the red speckles that marked the onset of scarlet fever? Maybe on his neck? Or behind his ears? Could she have prevented Grace—weak, fragile Grace—from contracting the blazing disease?

Fanny knew she would have seen the signs. This time she would have! If only she had stayed by Grace's side. She would have touched Mark's brow and noticed that it was slightly damp. She would have seen through his tractability to the first signs of illness, as only experienced mothers can, as she, *Grace's* mother, should have. But Fanny had been having her bath and her dinner and hadn't been thinking to safeguard Grace from her little son, hadn't been thinking, *again*, of Grace's ultimate good, and now Grace was dying *after all*, only three weeks a mother and dying of scarlet fever.

"Do you hear that?" Grace muttered through her cracked lips.

Fanny dipped the cloth, again, into the vinegar water, and bathed Grace's burning face. "I think it is distant church bells, love. There's advent services tonight."

Grace's eyelids fluttered. "No, it's . . . it's birds."

Birds! Fanny shuddered. Her daughter was delirious. She felt her throat close, knowing all too well what that meant. The doctor had told her that morning that he didn't expect Grace to pull through. She'd always been weak, to be sure, but would have had a respectable chance at recovery if she hadn't just given birth, if she hadn't already lost blood and energy. "I don't think it's birds, darling," Fanny said gently. "It's winter and dark out."

Grace wrinkled her brow. "Mine's got out," she breathed. "It's *my* bird. My blue one. Oh, Mother, it feels wonderful. The room. The space to breathe."

Fanny's breath caught in her chest. This was just like Mother and Charly. They'd both hallucinated in the last hours. Oh, to see Mother's wild eyes and Charly's vacant ones! Not to mention Sister Ellen's chalky face and Little Mary's frightened one. Fanny shook her head. She would not give into those thoughts. She would not and she must not. She had fought such memories her whole life, racing ahead faster than a steam engine in thought and deed whenever such a memory threatened to flood her again. She'd nearly drowned experiencing those deaths, not to mention Mary Stace, and Jessie and Nanny and all the others. She simply must keep her head above this river of pain and focus on her daughter, her still-living daughter, focus on dear Grace. Fanny tucked a wisp of hair behind Grace's ear. Her voice quivered. "You don't have a bird, love."

Grace's eyes cracked open. "Oh, but I do," she said. "I just never told you about it. I never told anyone, not even Mort."

Fanny gasped. "Oh, *Grace!*"

Grace sighed. "I got it when I went to live with Nana and Papa. And it lived here," she said, covering her chest with her hand, "right with me."

Fanny bit her lip. "Dear," she said. "I'm so terribly sorry I had to leave you there. If I could do it over again, I would have found another way. I would have made it work out."

Grace smiled. "I had my bird. It told me when I was safe."

"I would have written *more* articles, *earlier*. I would have kept you with me. Oh, darling." Fanny choked on a sob. "I would have been a better mother."

Grace blinked, as if she were looking at her mother in a new way, or maybe was not seeing her at all. "You are a wonderful mother. You gave me my bird, that day when you left me with Nana and Papa."

"*Left* you. Oh, Grace. Don't you see? I never *should* have left you. How can you ever forgive me? Can you possibly . . . possibly?"

"It fluttered when I should be worried. It really was the very best present."

Fanny lowered her head and covered her face with her hand. She'd never forgive *herself*. That was certain. How she could have walked as she did, down that frozen path, with Nelly clinging to her skirts and peeping back, with Grace screeching for her, *Mother, Mother,* with the killing thud of that door being closed, closing off the life force in Grace, ultimately destroying her own precious daughter. And, *too,* how she could have left, a fortnight ago, for the selfish delights of hot bubbles and roast beef?

"And when it was quiet, I knew I was fine. I knew I was happy and safe and loved. With Mort. With you."

"Dear Grace, I *do* love you. I always have. I know you can never know that, really know it, deep in your heart, after what I did, after how I placed such a load on your small shoulders . . ."

Grace's lips cracked into a broader smile. "And now there are so many, Mother! So many birds singing just for me. But they're not in me—they're out—and so I am not at all worried. My blue one is the leader. It's a girl bird after all. I knew it. She gets to pick the melody and the others follow her."

Fanny wiped her eyes with the back of her hand. Charly, Charly, Charly. Could he ever forgive her? Could he ever forgive that she was losing another of their precious girls?

Grace inhaled sharply, her eyes sweeping the room.

"What is it? Grace?"

"A red one," Grace said.

"A red bird?"

"Not a cardinal though. Something else. Something *so* beautiful, Mother. An important one."

Fanny's hair prickled at the base of her neck. She glanced behind her at the motionless washstand, at Grace's dressing gown on the wall hook, at the flickering shadows on the lilac-patterned paper. "Important? How so, darling?"

Grace breathed deeply in and out, once, twice. "I'm not sure yet."

Fanny glanced over her shoulder again in the direction of Grace's now-staring eyes.

Grace's breathing quickened.

"Grace?"

"It's a man, Mother. He wants me."

Fanny's breath caught in her throat. "A man? Tell him to go away. Tell him you don't want to come."

"I know him," Grace said. "It's safe."

Fanny blinked hard. Charly? "Is it Father?"

"It's Papa Eldredge."

"Hezekiah?"

"The red bird is in his hand and the blue one now, too."

Fanny's heart pounded. *Hezekiah!* What could he want with Grace? Something was wrong. Very very wrong. Fanny didn't know what she believed about the afterlife or the eternal soul or any of that but the one thing she knew for certain was that Hezekiah Eldredge had never had an ounce of real love for her daughters. Hadn't he let little Mary die? Hadn't he fought with Fanny over his need to control Grace and Ellen, over his need to stop her from treating them so softly, as he put it? "Grace, you mustn't go. You mustn't go to Papa," Fanny said urgently.

Just then Fanny thought she felt a draft. A shiver flew down her spine followed quickly by the quietest silence she'd ever heard. A silence too quiet for comfort. A silent silence. "Grace?" she whispered.

Grace continued to stare, just over Fanny's left shoulder, a tiny smile at the corner of her lips, her hand resting quietly over her heart.

"Grace," Fanny whispered again. "Grace, no!" she said louder, as if she could scold her daughter away from death as if from a hot stove. Fanny glanced over her shoulder once more, then bent her head over her daughter's body. *Grace.* The tears slid slowly at first. Soon, though, Fanny wept as she never had before. She wept for Grace, of course, and Little Mary, for Charly and Sister Ellen, for Mother and Sister Louisa and Jessie and Nanny and Mary Stace and all the babies and all the others. Even Hezekiah, horrible man that he was. Fanny even wept for him and for some reason, after racking herself inside out for all of her sorely-missed loved ones and for the father-in-law who tripped her up at every opportunity, Fanny eventually grew quiet, her head on her arm, and thought, for the smallest of moments, as her breaths came in softer and softer pulls, as her chest expanded, as her stomach unwound, that, far away, she heard birds chirping.

Chapter Fifty-Three

Fanny Fern and Effie Thomson, Wednesday, March 20th, 1867

I hope to live to see the time when it will be considered a disgrace to be sick. When people with flat chests and stooping shoulders, will creep round the back way, like other violators of known laws. Those who inherit sickly constitutions have my sincerest pity. . . . But a woman who laces so tightly that she breathes only by rare accident; who vibrates constantly between the confectioner's shop and the dentist's office; who has ball-robes and jewels in plenty, but who owns neither an umbrella, nor a water-proof cloak, nor a pair of thick boots; who lies in bed till noon, never exercises, and complains of "total want of appetite," save for pastry and pickles, is simply a disgusting nuisance. Sentiment is all very nice; but, were I a man, I would beware of a woman who "couldn't eat." Why don't she take care of herself? Why don't she take a nice little bit of beefsteak with her breakfast, and a nice walk—not ride—after it? Why don't she stop munching sweet stuff between meals? Why don't she go to bed at a decent time, and lead a clean, healthy life? The doctors and confectioners have ridden in their carriages long enough; let the butchers and shoemakers take a turn at it. A man or a woman who "can't eat" is never sound on any question. It is a waste of breath to converse with them.

—Fanny Fern, *New York Ledger*, July 27th, 1867

From the chair by the window in her bedroom, Fanny could see James striding down the street toward Stuyvesant Square where he had a meeting with one or another of his lawyer friends. He was determined to help pass a copyright law in this country. The day was cool and drizzly, yet James had that sway in his walk that told Fanny he was whistling. They'd just had one of their wonderful mornings together—they'd shared Fanny's bed, Molly's breakfast tray, the morning mail, a pot of coffee, and three newspapers. James had left the house happy, as was Fanny's intention. It was only later, when she could sit near the gloomy window alone, that Fanny allowed herself gloomy thoughts.

Her fingers roamed to their usual resting spot under her right armpit, to the pea-sized lump just under her skin. The doctor said it was a good thing it was mobile. Things were worse if the lump adhered to something else, say rib or spine. She'd just written about it to brother Richard (still heartsick about losing Jessie), and to sister Julia, traveling in Egypt. Fanny knew neither of them would tell another soul, which is what she wanted. She intended to live these last years—*only two or three at most!*—as if she were still alive and not any closer to dying, or to knowing she was dying, than someone who would step before a train tomorrow or fall flat from a choking spell next week. Two or three years! She had so much to do.

"Nanny, I'm coming!" Little Effie sang from somewhere outside Fanny's door.

Fanny shook her head of miserable thoughts and rushed to open her bedroom door. Four-year-old Effie was lugging the crate of building blocks up the stairs. She climbed the last step, a look of great concentration on her face, then carried the rattling case down the hall. "There you are, Lightening Bug," Fanny said. "Did you carry that crate all by yourself?"

Effie nodded, still concentrating on carting her load.

Fanny gently pulled the crate from Effie's arms. "Let me help. You can play in Nanny's room."

"*We* play, Nanny," Effie said, her blue eyes big with expectation.

Fanny leaned down and brushed a dark blonde curl from Effie's forehead. She had hair just like Grace had at that age. Gorgeous. Perfect. Fanny smiled. "Yes, *we* can play, if you like. Come, let's sit on Nanny's nice rug."

Effie unceremoniously dumped the entire container on the floor and began to sort the blocks by size, the large rectangles near Fanny's writing desk, the square blocks by the bed, the odd triangles and small rectangles mixed together near the door.

Sweet Effie. Who would mother her now? How is it that a child could be left motherless *twice*? And what would become of Mort? What a tale of tragedy he had, they all had. First, lovely Nanny died delivering Mark (who was now living, again, with Mort's relatives in Minnesota), then almost four years to the day, Grace died just a few weeks after birthing Effie. Mort never recovered. After Grace's death, it became shockingly clear that, with the drinking, he'd sailed through almost her entire inheritance from the Eldredges. To think they never would have entrusted Grace's money to *Fanny's* management, daughter-in-law that she was, nor even to *Grace's own* management, *woman* that she was, and preferred, as was the custom, to entrust a lifetime of savings to any young man who might become a husband. Any man at all would do, would be more competent than any woman.

Fanny handled her own finances, thank you. Between Oliver Dyer and Robert Bonner, she'd learned all she needed to know about negotiation, and never signed an unscrutinized contract, never took an offered deal as the final word. She set up a trust for Ellen, naturally, but now she needed to provide an income for Effie, too. She'd need to be cared for and educated, assuming she eventually had the desire and ability to meet her own financial needs. Fanny's mind turned. She'd get busy with another collection, and soon. And she'd set all the proceeds aside for Effie, weak compensation for having to leave her.

Effie made a square base of the large rectangle blocks and was building a structure on top of the base. "Here, Nanny," she said, handing Fanny a block. "You help."

"What are we building?"

"A tower, of course."

"Ah! And will we get to knock it down?"

Effie grinned. "Of course!"

Fanny smiled, while Effie proceeded to build, then she pressed a finger to the bridge of her nose and squeezed her eyes. Was she dizzy with apprehension over Effie's future or were these more symptoms of the disease? Fanny tried taking a few deep breaths. Last week she'd had a similar dizzy spell, walking down Broadway. She'd stopped in front of a confectionery and leaned on the display window to catch her breath and balance. She soon realized she wasn't the only woman leaning, sick, against the side of a building. Just in front of her, two young women, obviously laced much too tightly, were half-stooped, half-sitting on the bench against the confectionery's facade. "I should have known not to drink a full cup of tea," the woman with the sky-blue bonnet said.

Her companion, a brunette with emerald eyes replied, "It's not the tea. It's the three lumps you used."

"I need something to keep my energy up. Heaven knows I can't eat a thing."

"Next time, do as I do," the brunette said. "Eat a little of something rich every few hours. You won't need to spoil your digestion with meals nor loosen your stays, either."

"Do you have any camphor?" The blue-bonnet woman asked. "I don't know if I can walk the block to the carriage."

The brunette glanced over her shoulder, then lowered her voice. "Have a little of my tonic. It'll help. I couldn't live without it."

Fanny recognized the bottle the brunette withdrew from her pocket—laudanum. "Don't!" she warned the blue-bonnet woman.

The women looked, incredulously, at Fanny.

Fanny attempted a smile. "It's a habit you'll wish you never tasted." Fanny had seen countless women given this same tonic by apothecaries. It was meant to cure headaches, chase away the doldrums, lighten one's appetite, and calm one's nerves—all at once. Many times, it did provide the relief so many women sought, but only for a while. Soon, it took more and larger doses of the tonic just to maintain even moderate levels of mental coherence and sociability. Fanny was squarely against it.

The brunette eyed Fanny, leaning as she was, against the building, her hand splayed on her chest. "Looks as if you know a thing or two, indeed." She held the bottle out to Fanny. "Want some?"

Fanny caught her breath. "Not at all. I don't use it."

The brunette smiled. "You just need a nip, right?"

"No," Fanny said. She turned her attention to the blue-bonnet woman. "And neither would I, if I were you."

The blue-bonnet woman nodded, sneaking her eyes to the face of her companion.

Fanny, still breathless, continued. "What bothers me presently is a medical condition, not the effects of trying to live on sweets and tea. Women need food—beefsteaks and ale—for good health. We need the same things that keep men's constitutions strong—exercise, air, and uncumbersome clothing."

The blue-bonnet woman and the brunette locked eyes, then suppressed smiles. "Of course," the blue bonnet woman said. "Which is why you, presumed eater of red meat and drinker of pints, are laced so tight you're heaving against the side of the confectionery shop."

The brunette patted Fanny's arm. "If I ever tried to eat a steak or drink a pint with these stays, I'd feel very sorry for the help who'd have to wash the table linens." She patted the bottle she still held. "This is the secret to a woman's well-being. Go see the apothecary on Seventh and Twelfth—he'll charge a fair price."

Fanny's jaw tightened and her dizzy spell worsened, but not so bad that she didn't see the blue-bonnet woman take a sip of laudanum. The women uncurled their fans and waved them at their faces as they righted themselves and made their way slowly down the road, nodding to Fanny, sister-like, as they left. How provoking to have the same symptoms as the twittering members of her sex. How enraging to have one's habits inspected or one's values assumed. Fanny *never* laced so tightly she couldn't breathe or eat, no matter how fashionable her dress might be. And she *did* enjoy beefsteak and ale—frequently! Moreover, in addition to her still-regular forays into the streets dressed as James Parton's gentlemanly acquaintance, Fanny spent many a day writing or playing with Effie in a loose shift or a night dress. How ironic that she'd finally succumbed to the very symptoms that plagued "fashionable" women every day, and that despite her healthful precautions, she had been reduced to the same invalidism that so many women pursued, all because of this temporary weakness, all because of this . . . cancer.

Effie pressed a triangle block into Fanny's hand. "*You* put the top on our tower."

Fanny smiled thinly and placed the block, just so, on the carefully constructed two-foot tower.

"Ready?" Effie said, her arm lifted back, ready to swing, her tiny teeth set into a beaming smile.

"Ready!" Fanny said and no sooner had Fanny spoken than Effie hit the block tower with her outstretched arm, toppling the blocks all over Fanny's bedroom.

Effie clapped her hands and squealed with delight. The blocks had been flung all the way to the window and some had even slid under the bed. Effie giggled, looking at the mess, then looked worriedly at the grandmother. She leaned over and clasped her pudgy hands to Fanny's somber cheeks. "Why don't *you* laugh?" Effie asked.

Fanny bit her lip. So much to do. So much to take care of before she (Fanny swallowed a sob) *left* Effie. Oh, *God*. She'd be *leaving* Effie. There was no doubt about it. She'd be leaving Ellen, too. And Jem. Just as she had left Grace so many years before. Just as she had left sister Ellen and Mother and Charly and little Mary at death's door.

Effie leaned closer still to Fanny and kissed her grandmother on the lips. "Effie make it better, Nanny," she said soberly.

Fanny burst out laughing, tears of gratitude and sorrow at the corners of her eyes. Dear child. Yes, Fanny would be leaving her. But not yet. She still had time—at least two or three years. She'd take good care of herself and would stretch that remaining time like so much saltwater taffy. "Yes, my love," she said, scooping Effie into her arms and rock rock rocking her in her lap. She kissed the top of her granddaughter's head. "Effie does make it better."

Chapter Fifty-Four

James Parton, New York, Saturday, April 11th, 1868

"No person should be delicate about asking for what is properly his due. If he neglects doing so, he is deficient in that spirit of independence which he should observe in all his actions. Rights are rights, and, if not granted, should be demanded."

A little "Bunker Hill" atmosphere about that! It suits my republicanism; but I hope no female sister will be such a novice as to suppose it refers to any but masculine rights. In the first place, my dear woman, "female rights" is debatable ground; what you may call a "vexed question." In the next place (just put your ear down, a little nearer), granted we had "rights," the more we "demand," the more we shan't get 'em. I've been converted to that faith this some time. No sort of use to waste lungs and leather trotting to Sigh-racuse about it. The instant the subject is mentioned, the lords of creation are up and dressed; guns and bayonets the order of the day; no surrender on every flag that floats! The only way left is to pursue the "Uriah Heep" policy; look 'umble, and be almighty cunning. Bait 'em with submission, and then throw the noose over the will. Appear not to have any choice, and as true as gospel you'll get it. Ask their advice, and they'll be sure to follow yours. Look one way, and pull another! Make your reins of silk, keep out of sight, and drive where you like!

—Fanny Fern, *Olive Branch*, December 18th, 1852

Charles Dickens was visiting the United States and James Parton got to shake his hand. He, Fanny, and about two hundred others had crowded into Henry

Ward Beecher's church, first listening to a lulling organ concert by Fanny's brother, Richard, then feasting on the presence and words of the famous Charles Dickens. Robert Bonner had recently contracted with Dickens to write a new series for the *Ledger*, which was another feather in Robert's hat (somehow he got all the big names), but nobody knew their correspondence would result in Dickens actually appearing on their shores, gracing them all with his wisdom and marvelous verbal fluency.

They'd watched, with the others, as the stagehands positioned Dickens' fancy birch podium directly in the center of a gold and red Indian rug. The podium was custom-designed to accommodate Dickens' lanky height and speaking style. There was a slanting arm and book rest on one side of the podium and a little shelf that held a crystal water pitcher and glass on the other side. The podium was decorated with red fabric, trimmed with gold fringe, and when Dickens himself slashed through the heavy red velvet curtains and rested his arm on the arm rest and sipped from the glass of water, the audience quieted to a hush.

Dickens was dressed impeccably in a long striped gray coat, a silver satin vest, snowy collar, embroidered handkerchief, and shiny black shoes. He wore a red carnation in his buttonhole and a gray patterned cravat stuck with a gleaming pin. Once the audience swallowed its collective awe, Dickens smiled and played quite the actor, interspersing dramatic readings of his most beloved works with poignant introspections of his sometimes difficult life—his times as a small, sickly boy being read to by his mother or chased into employment at a blacking factory at the tender age of eleven by his father's rakish debt; his times struggling to survive the poverty that infected him, his family, and everyone he knew; his first awkward attempts at writing. When Dickens said, "Everyone has just enough religion to make them hate but not enough to make them love one another," James clapped his hands until he thought they might blister, then turned to Fanny. "How do you like him?"

Fanny just stared, marble-faced, at the orator. "I hate him," she said.

James ducked his head to her ear. She couldn't be serious! Why, he was magnificent, cultured, *British*! How could she *hate* him? *Why*?

"Because despite his lilting verbiage, I've come to understand that that woman over there," and Fanny pointed to a handsome, raven-haired beauty, "the one we thought was a servant or secretary, is, in fact, his mistress."

James, still clapping, let out a breath of exasperation. "What of it? We're not his moral judges."

Fanny clenched James' elbow. "He threw his wife out, when she had a breakdown in the face of his ambition. Signed her into at least a few institutions and abuses her, I'm told, *emotionally*, like . . . ," and here Fanny whispered through gritted teeth, "Samuel."

James let his hands drop and leaned toward her again. "*You*? Listening to gossip?"

"I've had it on good account, but didn't believe it until I assessed the man myself. Look at him! He's the picture of hypocrisy! A man of the people who carts his own furniture along. A social crusader who insists on the finest hotels and meals. I guess he walks right past urchins and beggars, both, to deliver speeches about charitable duty."

"Fanny."

"I've seen enough of the great Charles Dickens. What I'd really like is an audience with his poor wife!"

Fanny had pushed out of their row, even as the church swelled in standing ovation, and James let her. Instead of following her, he faced forward, clapping wildly in hail of this social and literary great, and *that's* when it happened, when Charles Dickens first pulled the red carnation from his buttonhole and flung it to the crowd, then walked among the pews, reaching for and shaking hands right and left. James thrust his hand forward with everyone else's and felt a jolt when his fellow Brit, his fellow British author, clasped James' paw in his own, squeezed and shook. Their eyes met. They were kindred souls.

When James finally made his way through the crowds to the gathering hall across the street, he saw two separate groups forming, one around the estimable Dickens and the other, of course, around Fanny.

Fanny saw him walk in and smiled in a way that told James he could go where he pleased, she was sure he'd be leaving, though, with her. There was a dinner, later, only for the literary among the group, so James was sure they'd get a closer audience with Dickens then. Maybe Fanny would change her mind about the man after speaking directly with him?

Among the crowd circling Dickens, James saw a familiar figure—long graying beard and rough-and-ready manner—it was none other than Walt Whitman trying for a place near the star. James made his way to Fanny. Their eyes met, then simultaneously flicked toward the other group. Yes, she'd seen Walt, too. Fanny had gathered her usual contingent of women writing friends—Lydia Maria Child, Jennie June, and others.

"Jem, I want you to meet some people," Fanny said. "Here is Louisa May Alcott—we've just read her in the *Ledger*."

James well remembered the thoughtful essay from the New England writer. He gladly shook her hand as well as those of her companions—Waldo Emerson, Nathaniel Hawthorne, and Hawthorne's wife, Sophia.

"We're thrilled to finally meet the wonderful Fanny Fern," Sophia said to James. "Nath and I have followed her work for years."

James smiled. He was used to hearing Fanny's praises sung. He returned the compliment, telling Sophia how much he and Fanny adored Hawthorne's stories and novels. Mr. Hawthorne welcomed a younger man into the group and introduced him as Henry Thoreau, Miss Alcott's friend. Thoreau soon settled into conversation with Emerson and Hawthorne. James listened in and came to the conclusion that these three enjoyed nature expeditions together. "Are you a country man?" Thoreau asked James.

"Probably at heart, though I've never lived long beyond the city limits to test the theory."

Suddenly, the crowd seemed to be moving toward the double doors that led to the dining hall. Dickens had somehow disappeared and an employee, presumably the dining director, stood on a chair by the door and announced that diners should present their invitations to him before taking their seats. James leaned toward Fanny. "I'd like us to get an audience with Dickens sometime this evening, so we can make a fair assessment."

Fanny nodded. "I might have reacted too hastily. Forgive me, darling. His work *is* good. Look at this crowd. Surely his character can't be all bad."

James smiled back. That was more like it. They worked their way to the double doors of the dining hall with their contingent of friends and new acquaintances. James was at the head of the group, with Fanny, and presented the invitation to the director.

"Mr. Parton is certainly welcomed. Ladies may take a place in the balcony, if they choose, but no dinner will be served there."

Fanny smiled. "Since I intend to have my dinner, I'll sit with Mr. Parton."

The director cleared his throat. "I'm afraid you don't understand. Ladies are not allowed to the dinner, ma'am."

"Ma'am?" James said. "Do you know who this is? This is not just a *lady*. This is Fanny Fern. The *writer*. Coming to the literary dinner."

The director blushed. "Oh, *Fanny Fern*, did you say? Let me check to be sure."

He disappeared into the hall while the group made eyes at one another. Imagine, not letting *Fanny Fern* into a literary event! James Bonner wouldn't hear of it. *They* wouldn't hear of it. Not to mention the other fine women among them, whether writers or wives of writers. Surely they deserved to dine with Dickens? They were all in the literary circle.

The director came back from his errand. "I'm sorry, but Mr. Dickens explicitly insists that this dinner is for men only."

"Mr. Dickens!" Hawthorne said. "He's the one who's making this rule? Did you tell him who's out here? Fanny Fern. Jennie June."

The director lowered his voice. "I made it perfectly clear, sir. Mr. Dickens wants to see to the comfort of his male guests—so they may smoke and drink and talk freely."

Fanny rolled her eyes. "Tell him I'll have a drink with him if it'll put him at ease." She looked around her. "Honestly, are we women going to shrivel up at a curse or two?"

The director shrugged his shoulders, but still told them no.

Some of the women discussed ordering their own suppers and taking them up to the balcony.

Hawthorne put an arm around Sophia. "If that's how it is to be, I'll dine elsewhere with Sophia. I guess I won't need to speak personally with Mr. Dickens after all."

"But Mr. Dickens specifically wants you at his table," the director said.

"It'll make room for someone less squeamish to insults against his wife," Hawthorne replied just as Walt Whitman pushed forward toward the director.

The director took Walt's newly penned invitation. "Very well, then," he said to Walt. "Mr. Dickens' table is the one in the center with the spray of flowers adorning it."

Walt beamed. "Excuse me, gentlemen," he said. "Ladies," and here he looked straight at Fanny. "I'll not be kept another instant from one of the literary greats."

"I guess not!" Fanny sputtered into James' ear.

Nathaniel and Sophia Hawthorne were already making their ways toward the hall's perimeter, heads huddled together in conversation. The rest of the crowd soon divided itself, with the invitation-holding men standing in line for admittance into the dining hall and the dozen or so women gathered to one side of it.

"I'll leave with you if you want," James said to Fanny.

"Nonsense. Just because I can't go, doesn't mean you shouldn't."

"But it's not right."

"Of course not. But, little really is!"

James held his forefinger under Fanny's chin and looked into her eyes. Her chin quivered and her flushed cheeks had given way to an ashen pallor. "How are you? Really?"

"Furious!" Fanny said, then whispered. "And tired."

"All the more reason you should have a healthy meal. Let's stop and have our dinner on the way home. I don't need to—"

"You go and dine with Dickens," Fanny said with a smile as she tucked a curl behind her ear. "And then, come home and tell me all about it."

"Fanny."

She patted his chest. "We women will get our suppers and I'll meet you at home."

"Yes," Jennie June said. "We'll make our own literary society and Fanny Fern will be our president."

The other women nodded in agreement.

James locked eyes with Fanny. You'll do no such thing, he seemed to be telling her. Your health depends on as much rest as you can manage. She nodded her agreement. She wanted to spend as much time as possible with Ellen and Effie before the cancer took her. James watched the group move to depart and heard Fanny begin her plea to sidestep the presidency. She'd find a way to be a part of the group without running it, to support women without taxing her condition. She was remarkable that way, in every way, really. James felt a pang in his chest and pressed his lips together. He would so sorely miss her.

But he wouldn't think of that now. He had a dinner to get through. James gave his invitation to the director and was told he could take his place at Dickens' center table. "He's excited to meet you," the director breathed. James suddenly was less excited himself.

James walked into the dining hall, already filling with smoke and the splayed-legged, belly-laughing rumble of any gathering of men. At a side table, holding a pipe, was a bright figure. White pants, yellow Marseilles vest, salmon necktie, dark blue body coat weighted down with dozens of brass buttons. When the gentleman turned to present a profile, James immediately recognized the bulging stomach, the neatly trimmed beard. It was Nat. Nat turned toward James just as James recognized him and upon seeing James, placed his hand over his heart and bowed. James nodded his head in sad reply. To think they hadn't spoken in so many years, and with Fanny not long for this world. The upstairs balcony was empty as was the place of honor. Dickens, presumably, would make an entrance after everyone had been seated. Walt Whitman beckoned to James and when James got close, Walt, who had seated himself to the right of the guest of honor, pointed to the chair that would be on Dickens' left. "I've saved that for you," Walt said with a smile. "After all we've been through . . . it's the least I could do."

James smiled his thanks and put his hand on the back of the chair. He surveyed the room, once again, and noticed the plethora of up-and-coming male writers mixed with the handful of solid literary names and a great many unknowns. *This* is the group that would exclude Fanny? James suddenly felt his stomach spasm and took a deep breath.

"I'm terribly sorry," he said to the near-dozen gentleman in loose conversation around the table. "But I've suddenly lost my appetite."

Without waiting to hear a word and without looking for Walt's reaction, James straightened his shoulders and walked briskly out of the dining hall.

Chapter Fifty-Five

Fanny Fern and James Parton,
Newport, Monday, August 26th, 1872

As for me, whether I go early or late, whether my eyes are open or shut, memory will always make pictures for me of dear blessed Newport, full of sparkle and sunrise . . . which makes me say with Festus, "Oh, God, I thank thee that I live."

—Fanny Fern, *New York Ledger*, October 12th, 1872

Fanny Fern's breast still hurt. Terribly. *Phantom pain*, Dr. Sturgis had told her, for how could her breast still hurt when he'd sawed it off, along with significant amounts of her armpit, upper arm and shoulder, six months before? (*Deep draughts of chloroform, yet, still, the dizzying pierce and gnaw of the blade.*) Fanny knew better. This was no ghost pain. It was real and sharply new. Different. Fanny was startled by the ferocity it displayed; this pain was no tired-out ache like the sort she'd been living with the past half decade. It was hot and strong and coursed like acid deep within her systems, spreading some toxicity that seared then rose like bread dough. This pain would kill her.

The familiar guilt rose in her throat. How could she prevent this end? She simply mustn't give into it, couldn't, wouldn't leave Ellen and Effie. She thought of Grace, as she did every day, several times every day. Grace screaming *Mother Mother*, then the sickening thud of the door closing behind Fanny like a coffin. Fanny had scaled so many mountains these past sixty-one years, had conquered poverty and ostracism and ignorance. She'd become the writer, the woman, the *person*, she always knew she could be—independent, strong, and capable—but why couldn't she ever quite be the *mother* she envisioned? A perfect mother. Calm, wise, and always available. Fanny was anything but that. She had muddled so much with her daughters, and now Ellen was overburdened and Mary Stace and Grace were dead and Grace's little Effie—Effie, who she'd sworn to protect and raise—would learn the lesson of loss much too early for *her* health. Fanny dabbed at the corners of her eyes with her left hand, the one she could still somewhat-skillfully maneuver. Across the room, sitting on the indigo horsehair settee, Jem noticed her movement. He noticed everything, dear man, which made this process of dying a little too public for Fanny.

Fanny blinked hard. No need to break down. She'd get through this. She had survived three years longer than every doctor predicted. She would figure out this new symptom and would do what it took to contain it, and she'd live some more. She simply wouldn't leave Ellen and Effie. She would not.

Fanny took an authoritative breath. She had a column to write. Everything started and ended around this routine. As long as she wrote, she lived. As long as she lived, she could take care of the girls. *And* she had her *New York Ledger* readership to answer to. Not to mention Robert Bonner. She simply *would* go on. Much longer than anyone could suppose. She hadn't shirked her weekly duty in well over seventeen years, and she wasn't about to start now.

Fanny stared at the tip of her pencil, still strangely impressed with how much easier it was to write with than the old-styled ink pens with which she'd started her writing career. Scritch, scritch, scritch. And her awful stained fingers. She'd looked like a laborer—which, she *was*. No shame in that. She focused her blue eyes on the charcoal pencil tip. It truly was amazing she could be impressed with anything anymore, and with that realization—the realization that she could still feel anything other than pain, and recently, fear—Fanny was grateful. She was grateful to feel this pencil respect, so grateful to feel anything at all not in the least connected with the humiliating way her body was rotting before everyone.

The pain had started that morning as the usual ever-present throbbing—in her legs, in her back, down her arms—before transforming to this burrowing sensation that was rooting itself into her core and mushrooming. Over the past few weeks, of course, she had noticed the new pain approaching, but hadn't officially greeted it until just the day before, when it made its home in her and began to demand all of her attention. Now, the alarming tightness bloomed warm in her chest, a growing pressure under her ribs, fed by the poisonous current, tight as a thick-rooted flower sucking rain from every bit of the pot. It was a flower grown too large. A shiver raced down Fanny's spine as she thought of her mother—walking through a rolling field with a little fern leaf tucked into her bodice. How Fanny could use a calming stroll. How she could use her mother.

Childish thoughts for a woman who was a grandmother herself. Never mind that she'd come to despise her body and the way it had betrayed her these last few years, both in form and function—Fanny still clung to it. And she had to admit, even though she was as ready to die as anyone who'd been living with the idea so long, sometimes she was a little nervous about it, and other times—Fanny swallowed hard—other times she was cold-sweat, choke-throated frightened, in spite of her many blessings, and even with the steady presence of James. This morning, with the sun shining sweet and white and the windows thrown open and the warm breeze stirring the lace curtains and the half dozen flies buzzing lazily from table to lamp fringe to wallpaper, was turning out to be one of those frightening times, and Fanny was determined not to succumb to her terror, and so she took slow, deep breaths and concentrated, first on the pencil tip, and eventually, on what she knew.

Just as she knew the sun, so bright it threatened to fade her eyes like it did carpets, was the real warmth of this world, she knew the blooming warmth inside of her was false, like a tight-lipped acquaintance delivering a compliment (and there'd been plenty of those in her life). Moreover, she knew the presence of James, her Jemmy, was like the sun, genuine. She was glad for him, glad they'd married and thrived. She mustn't tell him about the strange bloom. He had enough on his mind.

Fanny looked up at James, who was watching her intently, as was his habit these days. He still had those lively dark eyes, that endearing lopsided smile, which he couldn't help, even when he was concerned. "I'm starting right now," she said to him.

"I thought you said that at quarter past. Do you need help?"

Fanny snorted. "Help. I should think not. I can still work."

James nodded once. "Of course you can." He knew better than to argue that point. Excess conversation would only further fatigue her. Better to let her have her run with her writing, no matter how it drained her, than to postpone the ordeal with useless remonstrations.

"Just gathering the wool."

James smiled, then went back to reading the manuscript he was editing, or to pretending he was reading it. Fanny could see him rereading the same page over and over again. In his own way, he was frantic. She wished she could appease him. But she couldn't, and she knew it. People had keep over themselves.

Fanny flipped back the cover of the small notebook she'd come to favor these past few months. Pocket-sized, and, thankfully, light enough for her to manage without too much trouble. The ache under her arms sometimes made it difficult to hold even a calling card. It pulsed all the way down to her fingers, making them want to go limp like some languid jellyfish. Such a side effect. She'd complained about it to Dr. Sturgis, but he'd just given her one of his baleful looks, and she knew enough not to pursue *that* line of conversation.

It couldn't be helped, and she must learn to manage another way. Fanny supposed it was no worse than when she'd had to write with frozen fingers, way back when, that also had the bad habit of not wanting to work properly. She'd finally come full circle, from writing with fingers stiff with cold to writing with fingers floppy with disease. And she, like a general, forever ordering herself, and her fingers, to perform despite conditions. Just the picture of her life, come to think, and Fanny suddenly had an image of her fingers pushing out, warm and pliant, like stamens toward the sun, the stamens of her chest flower. It was comforting and frightening at the same time. Oh, to write about that. Now that would be something to present to Robert. Fanny snorted.

"Sounds like you've found your point," James said from behind the manuscript.

"I'm circling in."

James looked at Fanny over the top of the sheaf of papers, his dark eyes glinting with a little extra dampness. He sighed.

"*Jem*," Fanny said.

He continued looking at her with those generous eyes, as if waiting, hanging for another word.

"You are something," she finally said.

He blessed her with one of his smiles, a quick version of the kind that could melt nails, and pretended, once again, to return to his work.

Fanny accessed her hands. She could tell her right hand would be useless again that day, so she casually shifted the pencil to her left. It was harder to control the shape of the letters with her left hand, but at least she could press down more firmly. She noticed James' eyes following her movements from their watch over the top of the manuscript. She suddenly wished she'd stayed in her office instead of joining him in the parlor.

" '*Bridal of earth and sky*,'" she wrote. She wanted to capture something of the flower pot idea. That and maybe a word about joy. There must always be hope. She must find her point and put it down just right but without conveying fear. To write of the spirit without leaning on the ho hum of religion, which she was still suspicious of, even as she sometimes welcomed its restfulness. A tricky balance, but nothing she hadn't faced before. She'd meld emotion within the confines of the appropriate, whatever *that* was these days. Yes, it'd be one of those columns. And why not? She couldn't push the world uphill every day. She would write about observing services from the carriage yesterday, about the lively music and the fashionable dress of the worshipers, some obviously more concerned with seeing and being seen. Blasphemous? Hardly. Though more than a few might believe it to be. Church was a social gathering as well as a spiritual one. People got out of it what they would, or could. And because some saw Sundays as a way to parade their new clothes, or as a place to compare horses, was no matter to Fanny, though her eyes crinkled at the irony. She saw God's benevolent hands spread over them all. *Her* God. *Her* idea of a loving God, a motherly God, doting on even the most feather-brained of his creations with a bemused smile.

And just like that, the column idea crystallized, as it usually did, *en masse*, and Fanny strove to capture it. She scribbled the title *"Fashionable Worship at Newport"* at the top of the page, then moved the pencil painstakingly across the paper with her quivering left hand. *"Only these words fitly express that glorious Sunday morning. Being on the invalid list, and unable to join the worshippers inside the church, I sat in my open carriage, in the shade of a large tree nearby to catch . . ."*

"Fanny!" James said as both pencil and notebook fell to the floor. He rushed to her, scouring her face for signs of worsening health.

Fanny raised her eyebrows. "I can't seem to keep a grip."

"Let me help you," James said, picking up the notebook and pencil and perching on a cricket he pulled near her chair.

Fanny clenched her jaw.

"*Please*," James said. "Just tell me what words you want to write."

Only one word came to mind. Cancer. Fanny didn't like to think of that word, so cold, so plotting. It'd been six years, and precious few knew. Cancer. You'd think a word as fearsome as that would swoop and swallow her whole, not lap around her edges dainty as a kitten. Still, she'd had that new symptom yesterday, when she'd first felt the sizzle turn into the swelling bloom. Something novel was happening. Something different from anything she'd felt before. Maybe it was true. Maybe.

And just like that, Fanny understood. She sat quiet with her tight realization. She would have to prepare Ellen and Effie. They must be as ready as she could make them. Then she must face the next task, as she'd faced many a task—alone. She wouldn't burden anyone. Nobody would feel a speck of guilt with her passing. Nobody.

She nodded once to James, sitting dedicated as always near her, and rapidly dictated what she could about the pot and the bloom, about color and sound, about spirit and the church in what seemed like one giant breath. Her erratic scrawl had already occupied two pages of the small notebook. James's neat hand quickly added eleven more.

"Will you call Johnny and send it on?" Fanny said of the column when it was as finished as she could hope. "I think I'd better have a rest."

"Of course. Just now," James said.

"And Jemmy," Fanny added, her graying tendrils stirring in the breeze, "I think I'm ready to return to New York."

James blanched. "So soon? Why not stay here in Newport? Finish the season? The weather's fine and Ellen and Effie are enjoying themselves."

A fly buzzed around and around and landed on the notebook. James shooed it away.

"I want to go home," Fanny said.

"But you're not strong enough," James said.

Fanny smiled gently. "All the more reason, don't you think?"

James blinked twice.

As Fanny positioned herself on the chaise for a nap, James first covered her with her shawl, then went to his desk in the study where he copied her column onto a clean page, sealed it, and rang for Johnny to have it immediately sent to Bonner. James knew the weekly column was already a bit overdue, but he also knew Robert wasn't counting on it at all. He was one of the few who knew the state of Fanny's health. Of course Ellen knew, too, but not little Effie. James swallowed a moan. He would *always* take care of them.

None of their friends were positive, but James had exchanged knowing glances with a growing circle within the last six months. Only Robert was certain. He knew everything about Fanny since they'd started their professional relationship and friendship almost two decades before. Robert had turned out to be Fanny's father substitute, brother substitute, a substitute she had sorely needed. But Fanny's readers surely didn't know. And they're who James suddenly thought of now—the hundreds of thousands of loyal patrons who'd read their Fanny's words weekly for as long as they could remember. Fanny had certainly been pontificating for some time. James smiled remembering some of their excursions—to prisons, work houses, literary fetes. There was really no place and no topic Fanny hadn't addressed. She was the national conscience. A mirror that reflected glaring truths but pointed those truths out with tact and humor. James shook his head. Well, not always tact. But passion was part of Fanny, and he loved every bit of her. Every bit he'd been able to see. Not that he was complaining. Not at all.

"Sir?" Johnny said from the doorway. James sprung from his chair and gave Johnny the letter and the dispatching directions, then watched the vibrant young man bounce out the door and down the road, despite the heat, despite Fanny's dying. After Johnny was out of sight, James continued to stare at the empty road and down it, through the hazy heat and his growing grief. After a while, he realized he was still clutching the small notebook. He held it to his chest for a moment more before he moved back to his desk, opened the top drawer, slid the notebook under a small pile of papers, and quietly closed all inside. He'd get Fanny to soak her hands in hot Epsom's after dinner. That sometimes seemed to help. That and a good rest. He was glad she'd made no fuss about a nap, but her traveling request *did* bother him. He knew what it implied. He lowered his forehead to the desktop, felt the smooth black walnut flat beneath him, spreading out his thoughts, lining them up to articulate the inarguable truth. It wouldn't be long.

Chapter Fifty-Six

Ellen Eldredge, Cambridge, Tuesday, October 13th, 1872

I thank the gods, too, that [she] has had the courage to assert herself—to be what nature intended her to be—a genius—even at the risk of being called unfeminine, eccentric, and unwomanly. "Unwomanly?" because crotchet-stitching and worsted foolery could not satisfy her soul! . . . Well, let her be unwomanly, then, I say; I wish there were more women bitten with the same complaint; let her be "eccentric," if nature made her so, so long as she outrages only the feelings of those conservative old ladies of both sexes, who would destroy individuality by running all our sex in the same mold of artificial nonentity—who are shocked if a woman calls things by their right names. . . . I am glad that a new order of women is arising . . . , who are evidently sufficient unto themselves, both as it regards love and bread and butter; in the meantime, there are plenty of monosyllabic dolls left for those men who, being of small mental stature themselves, are desirous of finding a wife who will "look up to them."

—Fanny Fern, *New York Ledger*, December 19th, 1857

Ellen was twenty-eight and Effie was almost ten and James looked old as the moon. It was mid-morning and strangely sunny on this, the saddest day of Ellen's life. Ellen stood wooden next to the open grave, James swaying to her left, Effie clasping her right hand like a vise, and Mother, directly opposite in the gleaming walnut coffin.

Ellen had made all the arrangements. She'd had to. James was useless. She'd picked the white satin liner and the bouquet of red roses and fern leaves her mother would hold to her chest. She'd helped Robert design the marble headstone (which wouldn't be ready until spring) of the giant cross entwined with fern leaves. Fanny Fern, it would read because everyone knew that Ellen's mother *was* Fanny Fern. She was *the* Fanny Fern. The only. The original. Robert insisted on paying for the headstone, the least he could do, he tearily told Ellen. Mother's admirers would want nothing less.

So far, the world didn't know Fanny Fern had left them. Ellen and James wanted it that way. They wanted to spend these last moments quietly, without fanfare. Ellen had set up the luncheon arrangements for the modest number of invited guests—chicken, ham and roast beef; sweet potatoes, squash and pole beans; brown bread and rye; date pudding and apple pie; tea and ale; little dishes of nuts and raisins; a punchbowl for the children. Ellen liked to think her mother would approve. No Charlotte Russe or salmon mousse, no sugared almonds or white cake. Ellen wanted the luncheon to be as hearty and earthy, as real and nutritious, as her mother.

Mother! There'd be no substitute, ever, ever. For Ellen. For everyone. Ellen remembered so many times shared with her—weaving dandelion crowns sitting in the damp grass of the Boston square (while both pined hard and constantly for Grace); ordering her first lamb chop at Delmonico's (Mother, what's *mint jelly*? I can't possibly *explain*, Nelly. Why don't you try it?). Ellen's chest tightened. She took shallow breaths. Henry Ward Beecher was finishing his blessing. Blessings on the famous Fanny Fern, who had touched the lives of so many with her writing. Blessings on his *friend*, Sara Payson Willis Eldredge (he left out Farrington) Parton, the purveyor of shenanigans and human connection. She had always understood what was important—people. Blessings on her family and friends, those who'd have to figure out how to live without her. Blessings on *Mother*, Ellen thought, who'd always given her as much as she could. The larger share of bread and milk. A sorry piece of Christmas peppermint. Constant care and attention.

Henry finished and took a place beside his sisters, Harriet, Katy, Mary, and Isabelle. Harriet looked, ashen-faced, at a spot near her feet. Everyone knew Harriet hated death, hated funerals. Mother said it was because they reminded her of her son's death, a death Mother said she had never gotten over. How had Mother managed so well, then? She'd had so *many* deaths to get over, though she didn't like to talk about them much, Grace being the exception because Effie, naturally, needed to know all about her mother. And, now, Ellen supposed she'd have to follow in her mother's footsteps that way. But Ellen was not her mother. She was no Fanny Fern. But she'd have to cope, nevertheless.

Ellen really couldn't remember Father or little Mary very well, but then there were Nanny and Grace. Oh, God, *Grace*. Ellen should have taken Mark back to their house, as James had so often suggested. She should have thought of it herself, instead of saddling Maureen with most of his care while Mother watched over Grace, and Ellen managed their house on East Eighteenth. *She'd* sent for mother. *She* had. Ellen had wanted to show off her domestic skills—how she could order and help prepare one of Mother's favorite meals, how she could care for others, too.

Katy Beecher stood near Harriet and suppressed sobs, her fist covering her quivering mouth. Ellen loved Katy—she reminded her of Grace, a woman with a strong spirit and a fragile body. Mary Beecher was also there, along with her son-in-law, Frederic Perkins. Frederic was one of the many writers Ellen had watched Mother mentor through the years. Before his marriage, he was a constant companion of theirs when they'd go to the theater or to a concert. He and Mort got along famously. Something happened to Frederic, after his marriage, though, something Ellen couldn't figure out. He'd had two children with his wife, but spent as much time away from them as Ellen had ever witnessed. Little Charlotte, especially, seemed forever to be visiting her great-aunts. Considering that Charlotte and Effie were nearly the same age, and got along happily, Ellen wasn't complaining, especially these past few days, when she'd gratefully accepted as much help with Effie as possible. Ellen adored Effie, of course, almost as much as Mother had, certainly as much as James did. But since Saturday, since the day Mother closed her lovely eyes for good, Ellen's Effie-smile was hard to find. And she hadn't her usual patience with Effie's never-ending stream of questions.

Twelve-year-old Charlotte Perkins held her Aunt Isabelle's hand—another Beecher sister—and kept eyeing Effie to see how she was managing. Neither girl had a sister and Ellen wondered if they'd play the role for each other. Sisters. Mother leaned on Aunt Julia. Ellen marked her life by her times with and without Grace. Now, who did she have? Effie was more like her daughter than her sister. And James wasn't even her legal parent.

Uncle Nat and Uncle Richard were the only members of Mother's family that could attend the funeral, though Ellen knew, if there was a way of reaching Julia, that Julia would have dropped everything to sail home from India. Richard stood next to Henry and smiled when Henry finished the blessing. He had a songbook with him and turned to a page he'd marked, then began a haunting melody in German, which hung in the sunshiny air like fog.

Nat stood next to the Beechers. Ellen was so happy the day he and mother buried the hatchet, as Mother called it. Nat had come over, hat in hand, and ate enough crow that Mother couldn't be angry at him another minute. Nat stayed for supper and pretended to like Maureen's meatloaf and boiled potatoes, the misshapen oatmeal cookies Ellen and Effie had made that afternoon and the dishes of vanilla ice cream sprinkled with cinnamon. It was clear he was used to fancier fare, but they were all impressed at his humbling.

He and Mother reminisced about their childhood and caught each other up on family news. After Nat left that first night—for he'd come back a half dozen other times—Mother told Ellen and James that she would forgive, of course, of course, but she didn't think she would ever be able to forget. Ellen wouldn't be able to forget either, especially once she clearly understood how little help Mother's family offered them during those lean years, how they were effectively to blame not only for those cruel days of cold and hunger, but strangely, also, for the bountiful ones that followed. She, too, though, could forgive. Maybe it was because of the bounty. She hoped it was because of more than that.

Mort stood next to Effie. They didn't hold hands. His eyes kept swaying just beyond Fanny's casket, laid out in the warm sunshine, to the place where Grace lay, next to sister Mary Stace and Father. A gentle breeze stirred the fallen leaves and they made crackling sounds as they bounced off of Fanny's casket. Mort jumped with each sound, seemed strung tighter than a newly tuned harpsichord. Ellen remembered when she and Grace and Louisa found Mort irresistible. Who knew that a man's substance could so easily be broken?

Louisa Jacobs stood behind Ellen, next to her mother, Hatty. Hatty's book *Incidents in the Life of a Slave Girl*, written under the pseudonym Linda Brent, had been a good-seller for more than a decade, and both she and Louisa were living in comfort and safety for the first time in their lives. Hatty no longer worked for Nat, though he begged and begged her to come back and be his cook. Nobody makes better biscuits than Hatty, he'd tell anyone who would listen. Mother would reply that Hatty has more baking in her life now than biscuits and that Nat might consider learning to make them himself.

Oliver Dyer and Robert Bonner stood next to James. They both looked grim and serious, more like the way most people probably picture editors to be than how Ellen really knew them to be. Oliver and Robert were Mother's closest friends. She trusted Oliver's advice over anyone else's, save James', and never let a fortnight go by without some sort of acquaintance with him. Ellen thought of Oliver as one of her several father-substitutes, the other two being Robert and James. And, of course, Robert had been responsible for bringing Mother's writing, weekly, into the homes of so many. There still weren't any copyright laws, as James liked to call his legal project, which meant that Mother's work was pirated left and right. But everyone *knew* where her columns originated. Everyone knew Mother wrote only for Robert.

Richard finished the hymn and Henry Beecher handed twin spades to James and Ellen. There were ropes attached to Mother's casket and several of the men—Robert, Oliver, Nat, and Richard—pulled the ropes taut and lowered Mother in her swaying case to the bottom of the grave.

Effie's hand, in Ellen's right, and the shovel handle, in her left, were equally cold. To her left, James' breathing rattled the still air.

He pressed his fingers to his eyes, sucked an erratic breath, then scooped a shovelful of dirt and let it scatter dryly on top of the wood.

All eyes turned to Ellen.

Oh, she just couldn't.

It was then that she broke down for the first time in these three days, wrung her face and let the tears fly forth. Ellen let go of Effie's hand and leaned all of her weight on the shovel. Effie clutched Ellen's dress and James had an arm around her heaving shoulders. "You don't have to," he whispered in her ear. "Everyone will understand."

But then Ellen was ashamed. Hadn't she talked this very moment over with Mother? Hadn't Mother told her that she'd just be burying her body, that her essence would always be available to Ellen—she just had to look around for it? Ellen looked wildly around. There was no essence anywhere, just bare-branched trees and a carpet of crackly leaves and a chilling breeze and a weak sun and a crowd of dourly dressed mourners and a broken man to her left and a frightened child to her right. There was no comfort for *Ellen*, not in this scene. There was no mother. No motherly essence.

Ellen sobbed anew.

James gently took the shovel from her hands and Effie slipped a small arm around her aunt's waist. They were going to Newburyport, Effie and Ellen, to live together. It wasn't considered proper for them to stay with James, even though he'd played the part of their stepfather ever since Effie was born and Ellen could remember. It just wasn't proper, a young woman and a girl, Ellen had heard people say. So, James had rented them a beautiful place in one of their favorite cities and they would be able to buy it soon enough and set up their home there, together, as sisters, or mother and daughter, or aunt and niece, however they preferred. And Ellen could educate Effie or send her to school. She could work at a career or just manage the domicile. It was all her choice and choice was exactly what Mother would have wanted.

Others took turns with the shovels, solemnly approaching the grave and scooping then dropping piles of dirt down down down. Both of Effie's arms tightened around Ellen's waist and Ellen smoothed the straw-colored curls spilling out from under Effie's bonnet.

A pair of yellow finches flitted past and landed, swaying on stalk tops, in a patch of wildflowers. They pecked the dry seed heads until the food loosened and flew up in bounty around them. They ate all they could of the freed seed, then sat, satisfied, rocking the flower heads in the autumn sun.

Beyond the grave and the passel of mourners, beyond the finches and the wildflowers, a man with a long, gray beard and a tattered hat leaned, arms crossed over his broad chest, against a great oak, under the expanse of sun-quieted stars, and watched Ellen and Effie and the others. He willed himself to join spirits with them, to commune, to become a part of this great cycle of life and death, joy and sorrow. He was grass and breeze, bird and flower, daughter and mother, friend and lover. He felt the earth's heart pumping through his boots, the tree's love warming his back. A sparkly tingle went through him as distant Ellen unclasped the arms of the child wrapped around her and finally took her turn with the shovel. Scoop, pause, frizzle. And the finches flew twittering to the sky.

Epilogue

With her dying breath, Fanny Fern made known her wishes for James, Ellen, and Effie—that they'd "always live together." After Fanny's death, James helped Ellen and Effie move to the house in Newburyport. They all missed each other immensely, and wrote frequently. Although he visited Ellen and Effie often, James continued to live in New York for at least a year, where he completed *Fanny Fern: A Memorial Volume*. Sometime after that, James bought a house in Newburyport, and lived there with Ellen and Effie. Ellen and James, brought together in their care of Effie, married on February 4, 1876. Because they were stepfather and stepdaughter, Massachusetts law declared the marriage invalid, but New York sanctioned the union. Upon marriage, Ellen received her inheritance from Hezekiah Eldredge's will. James and Ellen Parton had a daughter, Mabel, born in 1877, and a son, Hugo, born in 1878.